GUILTY
OF LOVE

GUILTY OF LOVE

PAT SIMMONS

URBAN CHRISTIAN

www.urbanchristianonline.net

URBAN BOOKS, LLC
78 East Industry Court
Deer Park, NY 11729

ISBN 13: 978-1-60162-850-3
ISBN 10: 1-60162-850-1

First Trade Paperback Printing September 2007
First Mass Paperback Printing March 2010
Printed in the United States of America

10 9 8 7 6 5 4 3 2

This is a work of fiction. Any references or similarities to actual events, real people, living, or dead, or to real locales are intended to give the novel a sense of reality. Any similarity in other names, characters, places, and incidents is entirely coincidental.

Distributed by Kensington Corp.
Submit Wholesale Orders to:
Kensington Publishing Corp.
C/O Penguin Group (USA) Inc.
Attention: Order Processing
405 Murray Hill Parkway
East Rutherford, NJ 07073-2316
Phone: 1-800-526-0275
Fax: 1-800-227-9604

Acknowledgments

I have to say this novel was inspired as a word from God. The pages ahead are from the books of our lives that He reads daily. I thank God for helping me page by page. Enjoy and be set free.

I thank God for the following blessings in my life: New York magazine publisher, Carol Stacy, a true soul sister. Philly-born, but internationally published author Leslie Esdaile, aka L.A. Banks—our connection is sure. Brooklyn author, friend, and mentor, Loure' Bussey, who made me believe writing is easy . . . girl wait until I see you! St. Louis author, Bobbi Smith, who knows how to hold a friend's hand, speak encouragement, and show love. Floridian and website guru, Mary Griffin—thanks for feeling my testimony. My very best friend who is always available when I need a "friend-fix," a prayer partner, proofreader, and a sister from another life, Angella "AJ" Jones . . . God's going to bless ya . . . you'll see. You can not be replaced! God truly knew what He was doing when He created friends. Author extraordinaire, critique and business partner, Lisa Watson—The next up and coming bestseller . . . two minds thinking alike could be dangerous. Pam Bonds, broker.

I appreciate Joylynn as well for her sound advice.

To my husband, Kerry, who thinks I'm beautiful and shows me that with his special love. Thanks for the laptop so that I could "get her done." He has unselfishly put my happiness before his. Love always. Ruth 1:16. To my son and daughter, Jared and Simi, who I've taught how to pray and from whom I'm expecting great things.

To my Sunday School Relationship class teachers, Ron and Dorretta Stephens, and my pastor, Bishop James Johnson, for giving me the inspiration and knowledge behind the words I write. To Alicia Brown, the hairstylist who is not only my friend, but a trendsetter in the hair industry. Thanks for keeping me dolled up and most of all, thanks for all your love over the years. To Louis Smith for taking my computer skills to the next level or millennium, and for answering my how-do-I-fix-this questions even after you checked the caller ID. The Simmons family will always be grateful to his wife, Chrystal, and our God-baby, Leah.

I praise God for Family: Coles, Wades, Simmons, Sinkfields, Thompsons, Scotts, Carters, Thomases, Browns, and others I've yet to meet.

PROLOGUE

Durham, North Carolina

"Larry," a trembling voice whispered into the phone, "I'm pregnant."

Gripping the receiver, Cheney Reynolds sniffed back tears. She waited and waited for soothing words of comfort, shouts of jubilation, or any response from her boyfriend. Instead, silence ensued. Second dragged into minutes.

A boom of laughter exploded in the hall outside her dorm, startling Cheney. High-pitched voices consumed with gaiety seemed to belittle her predicament. Fellow Duke University students were making plans for a night of partying. Cheney had to think beyond tonight. Somehow, she had lost focus and allowed her promising, a secure future to fall in the hands of one man.

Larry Thimes exhaled a restless breath through the phone before speaking, as if his teeth were glued together. His words were measured and his tone was stiff, like the ugly all-season brown curtains hanging in her dorm window.

"Then you know what you have to do," he responded in a clipped tone.

"No. What?"

"Get rid of it."

"Just like that? No discussion?" Cheney shut her eyes as darkness invaded her mind. "But—" She tasted the bile racing up her throat. "Oh, my God, no. You can't mean that." The room began to spin. She closed her eyes, but the dizziness was already set in motion. This wasn't supposed to happen. She and Larry had practiced safe sex. Now she wondered if the phrase was a misnomer.

"Sweetheart," Larry said as if talking to a child, "you're scheduled to graduate next semester, remember?"

"I know, but—"

"You're enrolling in Duke's Global Executive MBA program. Plus, I'm completing my J.D. and will be busy studying for the bar."

"Maybe—"

"I can't even support myself. Sorry, a baby isn't an option for us right now."

Stress deepened the lines in Cheney's forehead. What Larry said was true. Besides, Cheney did want to be married before she had a baby. At least that's what society deemed acceptable. Cheney didn't think about etiquette when she was with Larry. What would her parents say about her pregnancy? Her mother would faint from the thought of embarrassment. Her philosophical father would gather his thoughts before advising her of his disappointment. Her older sister, Janae, would be shocked, and her twin brother—he would be ecstatic. Rainey always loved children.

Sifting through her situation for the third time that day, Cheney had to concur with Larry. A baby wasn't in their plans. After all, she had won a four-year scholarship. *I can't just throw it all away*. She was an educated, up-and-coming professional, but her heart pounded against her chest, refusing to comply. "Larry, maybe we should think about this. There has to be another way."

"No, Love. There isn't."

She gnawed on her fist, crying. Larry was the calm, reasonable decision-maker in their relationship. He was the strong black man every sistah craved and every woman would endure drastic measures to keep. His charm opened doors for him as if he were royalty. He had shown her how to love and would be the father of her child. Larry mocked her when he didn't hesitate to say, "kill it." No, it was like a slap in the face from her lover.

A collage of their romantic moments played in Cheney's mind. She sighed, visualizing Larry's long, dark-chocolate fingers outlining her lips when she smiled or right before he smothered them with kisses. Cheney remembered the night they shared their first slow dance at a campus fraternity party at the end of her freshmen year. At that magical moment, she wanted to be with Larry for the rest of her life. By the end of her sophomore year, she had shared her entire being with the self-confident, look-twice-handsome and sensitive Larry Thimes.

I could use some sensitivity right now, she pleaded silently. Didn't Larry realize how much she was in love with him? Their souls had connected in passionate lovemaking that had produced a little miracle. A baby; their baby. Cheney shook her head in disbelief—she wanted to wake up from this nightmare.

"Larry—"

"Cheney. There's no point in discussing this anymore."

"There is no discussion. You're dictating to me what I should do."

"We'll have another child later," he consoled before snapping, "How could you've been so stupid and allowed this to happen anyway?"

"Me?"

Did he just blame me? Larry's harshness caused Cheney's head to pound. Her heart ached as her stomach contracted. Suddenly, her prenatal, PMS, post-menopause, and any other hormones that scientists had yet to identify kicked in. *I am not one to mess with*, she shouted inwardly. She couldn't talk anymore, much less breathe. Without a good-bye, she slammed the phone down.

It had taken Cheney seven days to accept the fact that she was a pregnant, unmarried college student. Larry only needed five seconds to give a resounding, "no." At least *she* had juggled the idea of motherhood versus a career, and the sacrifice they would have to make.

"Why couldn't he say, 'A baby? Honey, that's wonderful,' or 'What do you want to do?' or 'We can get married now or later'," she fussed to no one. Instead, Larry had failed the ultimate test. Sitting still on her narrow twin bed, Cheney listened as water dripped from a corner sink and voices shouted in her head.

The boisterous women had moved inside to the adjoining suite connected by a small bathroom. Mentally tormented, Cheney collapsed against the wall, rubbing her belly. The phone rang, but it was her prerogative to ignore it.

She couldn't stand Larry's name at the moment. "I sure don't want to hear your voice," Cheney said, needing time to think and pray. She sobbed instead.

As an hour ticked by, Cheney's swollen eyes half-registered the room's blackness. To wake up from the bad dream she was having, she forced her body to the sink and patted cold water on her numbed, red face. She sighed at her tousled reflection. "I'm pregnant." Cheney yanked her long, black hair as if she was about to yank weeds from a manicured lawn. "Career or motherhood, what am I going to do? God, if I ever needed you, it's now."

CHAPTER 1

Five years later
Ferguson, Missouri

*F*our-year-old Cheyenne Reynolds slammed the screened door, limping into the house. Tears trickled down her plump cheeks. Faint traces of blood and grass marks stained her pink and watermelon-green short set. Dirt played tag with her once clean ruffled socks and new Keds.

"Mommy, I fell off my bike. I'm bleedin'. Am I goin' die?" Her bottom lip trembled.

Kneeling, Cheney examined the scraped skin below Cheyenne's knee, and relaxed—nothing required stitches. She was still amazed how her daughter's temperament was so much like hers when she was younger, especially the over-dramatization about the smallest mishap.

"No, sweetie, you'll live to be an old woman with a house full of your own munchkins," Cheney smiled.

The child giggled, forgetting her accident.

Cheney laughed and opened her arms wide to comfort her daughter whose eye lashes were saturated with tears. Meticulously, Cheney picked leaf fragments from her daughter's hair, smoothing back wild black strands that had escaped from two braids. Cheyenne laid her head

*against Cheney's chest, casting an angelic upward look.
"Ooh, Mommy, it hurts. It hurts," she whimpered. "I
can't walk."*

*"I bet a Bugs Bunny Band-Aid will make it feel better,
and then you'll be able to ride your bike again. Okay,
sweetie?"*

*Liking the sound of that, Cheyenne nodded and
squeezed her mother with all the strength her tiny arms
could muster. "You're the best." She smacked a hard, wet
kiss against Cheney's cheek. "I wuv you, Mommy." Sa-
voring the moment, Cheney closed her eyes, rocking the
preschooler she had created with Larry—no doubt an established attorney by now, but a non-existent father who
had fought her daily to terminate the pregnancy.*

*"Just do it! It'll be over before you realize it, and we
can get back to the way we were," Larry had said in a
frustrated whisper, waiting outside her dorm room. She
hadn't returned his calls for days and had avoided him in
the dining hall.*

*Tired of being disregarded, Larry had come to see her
after a morning exam. Presenting a long-stemmed rose,
he displayed an expression laden with guilt. Without
much coaxing, he guided her to a secluded bench on the
other side of campus. Neither hinted at the turmoil rag-
ing between them as they walked unhurried.*

*Once they were seated, Larry intertwined his fingers
through hers. He inhaled, held his breath, and exhaled as
he stared at a passing car. Cheney didn't rush him. Her
heart was heavy too. She turned and looked at his dark
skin, high cheekbones, and large lips. She wondered who
their baby would look like.*

*Larry allowed Cheney the scrutiny before loosening his
fingers. He snuggled closer, cherishing her like she meant
everything to him.*

"You know I love you," Larry whispered.

Cheney's eyes welled with tears. She needed to hear that. "Larry, I love you so very, very much, but I'm scared, confused, and excited."

Larry grabbed her around the waist, recoiling when he touched her stomach. "Baby, our love is strong and endless. We can't let anything—I mean anything—come between us, including this mistake. That's all this is, a mistake, not a baby. We'll get through this. I'm here for you like always. Just do it."

Within days, their tranquility shattered. Tempers flared and disagreements became commonplace. Larry accused her of not thinking rationally about their future. To the contrary, that's all she had been contemplating, and she was starting to accept the idea of becoming a mother. But the stress and despair overtook Cheney in her weakest state. She submitted to Larry's demand, beguiled by a romantic dinner, a seductive body massage, and a dozen roses.

Honking horns jolted Cheney back to the present and the green traffic light in front of her. Fanning her sweaty face, she swallowed back tears. A trembling hand gripped the steering wheel. She cleared her throat, and mumbled, "It's water under the bridge."

Yeah, right, but the recollections caused Cheney's nostrils to flare. Anger rose within her. She felt as if she had enough hostility to beat down an army, agreeing to something that had succeeded in pulling her into hell.

She didn't ask for them, but the memories had faded in and out during the past five years. Sometimes Cheney could still taste the fear and feel the uncertainty of being an unwed pregnant college student.

Their loving relationship disintegrated after she allowed Larry to take her to Crist Clinic in Jacksonville, North Carolina. She cried all the way; he concentrated on driving. Once inside, Larry didn't hold her hand or glance into her grief-stricken eyes as they waited. To add further insult to injury, he had refused to go into the counseling room with her. "It's nothing more than woman talk. I know you can handle it."

Cheney found herself begging God for some guidance. When He didn't answer, Cheney knew she was on her own. The nurse's words of wisdom seemed to reinforce what Larry had suggested, "You made the right decision because your man doesn't look like he wants to be tied down with a *small fry*."

The final nail in her coffin was his nonchalant attitude after their child was ripped from her womb. No whispers of I love you, or warm hugs. Basically, *get over it*. Larry wasn't even cordial enough to ask if she was okay. "I should've recognized the signs," she told herself. God didn't give her any signs so the decision was hers.

Four days later, Cheney laid in Duke University Medical Center as blood drained from her body. The doctor who had performed the abortion had perforated her uterus. She endured fitful nights of excruciating pain—alone.

The physical loss was small, but her mind lashed out. Ashamed, she couldn't tell her family. Only a close friend knew about her stupidity. Leaving the hospital, Cheney had experienced post-abortion stress syndrome.

The child's spirit lingered, haunting Cheney when she least expected. If only God had spoken to Cheney, directing her. The beautiful child that God seemed bent on tormenting her with would have been with Cheney now, strapped in a booster seat and singing a nursery rhyme. Thousands of women aborted their babies every year so what's the big deal? *They got over it, didn't they? Sure.*

She had read about other women's grief on an internet website and learned even after ten or twenty years, some still regretted their decision. "I am not one of them, God," she taunted as if God was a passenger in her vehicle. "The dreams are not funny, either. You gave me free will, and I used it!"

The move from Durham back home to Missouri was a big step. Remaining in North Carolina would only serve to remind her of the guilt from what went wrong in her life. For the past five years she had been too ashamed to come home and tell her family the good, bad, and the extremely ugly decisions she had made so she did what she thought was best—shut them out.

Cheney didn't want to admit it, but God helped her make that decision. A month before she had hesitantly asked for a job transfer, put her condo up for sale, and gave most of her belongings away.

The decision came after she sped past a little storefront church and refused to give it a sideways glance. That didn't stop the sensation that God was peeping out from the building watching her. God seemed to pluck her out of the car and thrust her into a tarnished Garden of Eden. Like Adam and Eve, God was letting Cheney know she couldn't cover the shame of her nakedness. She audibly heard a scripture whispered into her ear, but to this day, Cheney refused to read Revelation 3:17-18. Besides, she didn't own a Bible.

CHAPTER 2

"Well?" Imani Segall, Cheney's best friend since childhood, asked from her hotel room in Amsterdam. As an American Airlines flight attendant, Imani had the opportunity to stop-and-shop in at least three cities a day.

"Well what?"

"Cheney, it's me. Did going back home bring the peace you expected?" Imani paused then continued without giving Cheney time to answer. "You know I'm probably one of the biggest hypocrites God created, but when things aren't going my way, I'm the first one to ride on someone else's coattails to get a prayer through. It can't hurt, girl."

"It won't help either." As far as Cheney was concerned, God didn't appear on the scene until after the baby was gone. She despised Him because of the nightmares. What could God and she possibly have to talk about? *Absolutely nothing!*

Imani sighed. "Okay, okay. Bore me with details about your palace," she joked.

Cheney's mood did a turn around. "Technically, it's still a shack, but it's coming along. I love fixing up this place," Cheney said, laughing as she scanned the kitchen's worn tiled floor. "It's good therapy," she added. For two months, she had labored on her house after work. Sanding and staining hardwood floors, wallpapering rooms, and stripping pink paint from her brick fireplace. *Ugh!*

Cheney's pride and joy were the two front bedrooms. Although she believed in using proper speech, Cheney could get downright ghetto and curse out the devil himself if he tried to stop her from putting children in those rooms one day. And a husband wasn't required. The six-windowed sun porch over the garage would make an excellent playroom. She could imagine pastel balloon curtains filtering in the morning sun.

"I can't wait for your housewarming to see it, Cheney. So, how's the neighborhood? Is it quiet, any kids, or any handsome bachelors nearby?"

"I've got drama living next door by the name of Mrs. Beacon. We haven't formally met and that's okay with me. From a distance, she could be dangerous."

"In what way?"

"From the rumors I've heard, in every way. Beatrice Tilly Beacon is an annoying eighty-something widow, known for monitoring the comings and goings of her neighbors," Cheney explained, groaning.

"Lucky you."

"Yeah. Residents call her 'the neighborhood watch unit' unofficially, because no one will fess up to appointing her, but the police show up every time she calls. She has a rep of taking matters into her own hands. The cops are afraid she'll hurt someone."

"She's scary."

"That's what I heard. I figured Mrs. Beacon is a menace." Cheney glanced out the pillow-size window above her kitchen sink, and did a double take. Sure enough, Mrs. Beacon was trying to peep through her window with a magnifying glass. Cheney was about to hang up the phone and go outside to confront her neighbor, but didn't know when she would talk to Imani again. Cheney decided to deal with Mrs. Beacon later.

Imani's hardy laugh echoed through the phone and drew Cheney back into their conversation. "Well, if it isn't for the drama in your life, it's comedy."

"I can do without overkill from both."

"Then life would be boring. How's the job?"

"Challenging."

"Aren't they all? Okay, I've held off long enough, your family. Are they excited about your move back home?"

"I guess so," Cheney stuttered with a shrug. "Most of the time we play phone tag."

"And I guess you don't know your way home?"

"Imani, it isn't that easy. *I* damaged our relationship when I was away in North Carolina, even with Rainey, and you know how close I use to be with my brother. Anyway, I thought I was ready to mend the pieces, but I need a little more time."

"Well, I'll pray for ya."

Cheney ignored Imani's offer. One thing Cheney knew from experience was not to depend on God when she really needed Him. That way He couldn't disappoint her. Then there was getting cozy with a family she had rejected. "Well, if you're asking if they've seen the house—no, if we've gone shopping—no, if we have long phone chats—no," she answered, trying to hide her disappointment.

"Mmm," Imani murmured. "Okay, now that the preliminaries are out of the way, I'm coming back to, how are you *really* doing?"

"Trying to be strong and get on with my life. I've wasted five years pining over Larry, and the choices I made."

"That's what I'm talking about," Imani shouted, causing Cheney to chuckle. "I just don't want to see my friend bitter."

"Me, bitter? Nah, but my sabbatical from men continues."

"Oh."

The phone line was quiet. Cheney sighed. "I'm just taking charge of my life. I won't allow another man, or woman for that matter, to cause me anymore grief."

"Good for you. So I guess that means you haven't had anymore of those dreams."

"I wish. I had one last week. It was the first in months."

"I'm sorry, Cheney. I know how they freak you out. Hopefully, with your new house, job, and surroundings, those apparitions will stop."

"They will. I'll be okay."

After another hour, they ended their conversation when Imani had to get dressed for her next trip. Inseparable growing up, they parted ways when

Imani started a career as a flight attendant and Cheney enrolled at Duke. They knew things about each other that had sworn them to secrecy.

Imani cried with Cheney when Cheney called and lamented about her pregnancy. Imani made frequent flights to Durham as Cheney recovered from her surgery. She cheered when Cheney broke up with Larry, they celebrated with a trip to Brazil. Opposites may attract, but they were attached at the hip. Physically, Imani was known for her good-looking legs while Cheney was nothing, but legs. Mentally, Cheney was strong when Imani was weak, and now Imani was the strong one.

Later in the day, Cheney experienced first-hand the buzz circulating about Mrs. Beacon. Peering over a pair of dark octagon-shaped sunglasses, the woman tapped her black bamboo cane to get Cheney's attention.

"Yoo-hoo, missy. Over here, chile. You should try Year-Round Green Lawn Care Service. That's what I use, and my yard is the best-looking on the block," Mrs. Beacon bragged.

Resembling a midget from the *Wizard of Oz*, Mrs. Beacon hobbled down the steps of an enclosed side porch. Cheney could see yellow and purple floral cushions on white wicker furniture inside. The setup was cozy for lounging around and sipping tea.

The woman's red-brick bungalow was commanding as the block's poster house. It was larger than Cheney's with an enclosed area connecting the main house and the garage. Three large dormers made the half story appear like a full second floor.

Cheney thought about revving up the motor on her weed whacker to drown out her neighbor who was still talking, but her conscience and upbringing dictated she be cordial. She guided the dormant lawn tool toward the old woman.

"You know what you doin' with that thing, missy?"

"I do." *Or at least, I think I do*, Cheney thought. Up close, she was surprised to see Mrs. Beacon's wrinkle-free mocha skin. Snowy white strands mingled with silver hair to form a tight bun anchored off-center on top of her head. Cheney examined the small-framed woman who couldn't be five feet in heels. *There's no way this little woman could be a terror.*

Her neighbor's attire was a bright coral crocheted sweater over a dull plaid housedress. Earlobes sparkled with tiny diamonds. Everything about Mrs. Beacon's appearance suggested she was in her right mind . . . until Cheney scanned her feet. They were swallowed up in men's shoes—army-polished Stacy Adams.

Extending her hand, Cheney gripped soft slender fingers. "I'm Cheney Reynolds."

The woman lifted her eyebrows. "Cheney? Like the vice president?"

Cheney nodded.

"Humph! Thought you were a WNBA player."

"No, madam, I wasn't offered the opportunity. I guess I could've been since Tamara Moore is five-ten and Lindsay Taylor is six-eight. The only basketball I've played was in college on a scholarship, not in the Women's National Basketball Association."

"You didn't steal those clothes from a homeless

shelter, did you? This is a conservative neighborhood, young lady. We don't take too kindly to the likes of hippies living among us."

Cheney wondered what prompted that question. Mrs. Beacon was living up to her bold reputation. Evidently the woman didn't look in her own mirror. Cheney had awakened Saturday morning with a busy day planned. Okay, she'll admit that she hadn't combed her hair with care. Her jet-black, shoulder-length mane was thick and itchy, demanding a warm shampoo and a cool conditioner. Why primp? Plus, Cheney hadn't washed clothes in days.

"Sorry, I grabbed the first thing I saw," Cheney said, looking down at her clothes, knowing she didn't owe an explanation. "I didn't know there was a dress code to work in the yard." Cheney hadn't thought her mismatched socks, gray sweatpants, and over-sized red shirt were offensive.

Mrs. Beacon tapped her cane. "You should. White folks might say, 'there goes the neighborhood.' Didn't your parents teach you anything? You should know better. Anyway, I'm Mrs. Beatrice Tilley Beacon. My close friends call me Grandma BB. Don't *you* even think about it," she warned, squinting while she jabbed her cane in the air at Cheney. "I'll let you know if you will have that privilege. I'm going to keep an eye on you."

How do I respond to that? Cheney rolled her eyes, but kept silent. Weren't neighbors suppose to be friendly, kind, and bearing gifts or making small talk over a fence? If Cheney could move, she would, but she had sunk a lot of money into the house. Years ago,

Cheney would've prayed for patience. Since the abortion, she stopped praying. Without God informing her, Cheney was sure He had cursed her life.

Mrs. Beacon grabbed Cheney's attention again when the woman shrugged and twisted her lips. "Humph, uppity thang, ain't you? Well, those weeds better not spread my way," she scolded, drawing an imaginary property line.

Okaaayy. Let me tiptoe back to my property and leave old Mrs. Grouchy to herself. "Nice to meet you," Cheney lied, restarting her weed whacker. The motor reaped power. She scurried away. *Watch it, Grandma.* "Why couldn't I have neighbors like the Huxtables?"

Hours later, Mrs. Beacon returned, clunking in her oversized men's shoes, leaning on her cane, and carrying a tall drink. "You've done enough work for one day, although more sun would do your color good." She thrust the glass in Cheney's hand. "Here, quench your thirst with my homemade lemonade squeezed with secret ingredients—a little of this, a touch of that."

Cheney eyed the glass with suspicion. First impressions were lasting. The senior citizen had the nerve to mix compassion and insult in the same day. A little of this or that could be cherry-flavored arsenic. The smart thing to do would be to decline. "You shouldn't be so kind."

"I'm not."

Cheney hesitated.

"Go on, chile. I used genetically enhanced lemons and limes mixed with fresh pineapple juice and a slice of mandarin orange."

Accepting the drink, Cheney sampled a baby sip and licked her lips. "Mmmm, it's good."

"I know." Mrs. Beacon nodded with pride before turning and pointing her cane. "Now, Heney, when you get through cutting, I was thinking you need to plant some hydrangea shrubs. The ones that bloom pink flowers during the summer, and if you plant some sage between our properties, you can smell it as you walk in your front door."

Sucking in her lips, Cheney tapped her foot to keep time with her neighbor's rambling dictates. "Mrs. Beacon," she spoke in mocked sweetness, "I'm planting more than a hundred bulbs, shrubs, and plants this Saturday. Perhaps you'd like to come off your porch and help me dig?"

"Oh no, Heney, ain't got time for that. My summer salsa classes are beginning. I'll be gone most of the day."

Figures.

The radio's alarm blared, shocking Cheney from her sleep. She frowned at the time. "Am I an idiot for waking up at five on a Saturday morning to do yard work?" she mumbled as one eye refused to open.

Cheney dragged her comatose body to the bathroom where she haphazardly dressed in a white St. Louis Cardinals T-shirt and black sweats, swept her hair into a ponytail and slapped a baseball cap on her head. She marched down the stairs mimicking a soldier reporting for duty.

The previous day, the nursery had delivered a mountain of dirt that resided on one side of her driveway. She had purchased burning bushes for the sole purpose of separating her property from Mrs. Beacon's. She wondered if any bush would be tall enough.

Moisture lingered in the pre-dawn air, a sure sign of a hot, humid day to come. Birds dancing in flight and swaying tree branches provided the only movement on the block until a cool breeze caressed her cheeks.

"I wish I had company. I'll even take Mrs. Beacon," she paused, "maybe not." Flexing her muscles, she started wheeling dirt.

Hours passed as Cheney dug a three-inch ditch to separate her lawn from her kidney-shaped flowerbed. Halfway through the dirt pile, Mrs. Beacon made her irksome appearance. Standing regal on her porch in a multicolored orange and red wrap skirt, a red ruffled blouse, and red sling-back heels, Mrs. Beacon cleared her throat. When Cheney didn't acknowledge her, Mrs. Beacon went on her way.

"What? No Stacy Adams?" Cheney mocked under her breath. She rubbed her eyes, leaned her head forward, and checked the house address. "Maybe it was her medication the other day."

Mrs. Beacon backed out from her garage, gunning a new white Lincoln Continental. She rolled down her window and waved. "I do hope you'll have a professional supervise the job. There's nothing more tacky to a neighborhood than an amateur landscaper," she yelled as she sped off, blasting a Boys II Men tune.

Cheney shook her head. *Why couldn't I have a neighbor like Mr. Rogers?*

At noon, the sun was beaming high in the summer

sky and Cheney had planted most of her purchases. Resting on her porch steps, she wiped perspiration from her brow, smearing dirt across her forehead. She snatched the cap off her head and used it as a fan.

"Should've had the mulch delivered too," she scolded herself.

Running into the house, Cheney retrieved her keys for a drive to *Home Depot*. She returned from the hardware store with her trunk over-stuffed with bags.

"And the nursery workers said I needed a truck. Hah!" When she lifted the trunk, Cheney realized she would need Houdini or the Hulk to get the bags out. "Cramming was a bad idea. Where's a man when you need one?"

Flexing her muscles again, she began to pull. "Give," she pleaded. "C'mon. If I can get just one out, the rest will be eas—"

Two bags torpedoed from the stack with a force that had Cheney running backwards. She knew she was going to hit her concrete driveway, and the scene wasn't going to be pretty, but she was already in motion and couldn't stop. *God, I know you haven't always been there for me, but I would really appreciate it if you can keep me from breaking any of my bones,* she thought absentmindedly. *Someone call an ambulance if I don't move.*

"Whoa!" she yelled as her hands flew up in the air, and she didn't have time to manipulate her fall. When she looked up, the bag she had released was heading back to Earth. Destination—her face.

Suddenly, a muscular arm wrapped around her

stomach. With force and quickness, a solid body collided with Cheney, cushioning her fall. Dazed, Cheney lay still, trying to figure out what just happened. Who rescued her with a seat belt-like grip and smelled like a men's cologne counter?

"You can let me go now."

Parke K. Jamieson VI released his new neighbor. "Hey, you all right?" he asked.

The woman seemed to gasp as she patted her head, rubbed a knee, and squeezed an ankle. "It all depends if I have any broken bones."

Holding in his laugh, he examined her. She was covered with more grime than a slugger sliding to home plate. He stood and extended his hand. "Here, let me help you."

Accepting, she pulled herself up. She was tall—very tall, at least six feet. *Were her parents the descendants of the Alton Giant?* he wondered facetiously, referring to Robert Wadlow who is listed in the *Guinness Book of World Records* as the tallest man in the world. He had once lived across the Mississippi River in Alton, Illinois. The man had grown to eight feet eleven inches and died at twenty-two.

"Where did you come from?" she asked, still dazed.

"From across the street. I was jogging when I saw an accident in the making." Personally, he was glad someone bought this eyesore. Vacant buildings attracted the wrong kind of tenants—drug addicts and the homeless.

There was nothing appealing about an Amazon

woman. Parke considered them too long to be shapely, and they always walked stooped instead of showing off their full height. And their clothes, ugh! The sleeves were too short and the skirts too short, although he didn't have a complaint about the skirts. She was a perfect poster child to back up his argument. She had so much dirt and grass in her hair that she looked like she was wearing a hat. Contestants on *Survivor* fared better.

"I'm so clumsy. Sorry to bother you," she apologized. "I'm okay. Did I hurt you? I'm not exactly petite."

She was right about that. My muscles are still screaming, a thought he kept to himself. Her soft, melodic voice grabbed his attention. It didn't match her body. Parke chuckled. This new neighbor was intriguing. Turning, he walked to the trunk of her car. "Let me get those for you. Where do you want them?"

The neighbor waved her well-worn, dirty glove in the air. "Oh, don't bother. I couldn't ask you to help. I don't even know you."

"You didn't ask. I'm offering."

Her politeness, rather than being flirtatious, got his attention. Somehow he thought it was attractive. Aggressive females wore down his nerves and worked his good manners.

A descendent of kings, Parke was a connoisseur of women—short, shapely, cuddly females. He was also a man driven by the history and profiles of people, places, and things. Taking his early morning jog through the historic Ferguson neighborhood, sometimes called Old Ferguson, he wanted to see the new owner not necessarily meet her. Accosting her to the ground was not a good introduction. Since he wasn't trying to impress, he felt downright silly.

"Then, let me introduce myself." He grinned and bowed. "Parke Jamieson VI."

Amused, she gave him a mock curtsy. "I'm Cheney Denise Reynolds, the first and last."

Parke unknowingly found himself enchanted with their childish exchange. Most women who eventually became his dates, manipulated their smiles, laughs, and orchestrated struts into an art of seduction. "Hey, where you want your stuff? I'll stack them for you." Cheney pointed to the front of the house and the expert-crafted landscaping in progress. *Who helped her do this?* he wondered.

Carrying two, sometimes three bags at a time, Parke didn't stop until he was finished unloading. He moseyed over to Cheney who was at the other end of the lawn inserting more flowers. Kneeling, he unconsciously picked up a garden tool and began poking in the dirt.

"This is nice, very nice. I didn't notice it at first. You didn't do all this yourself, did you?"

She didn't look up or stop her rhythm. "Yes. I've been at it since five this morning."

"You're kiddin'?" Parke stared, unbelieving. "Didn't your husband help?" When she didn't answer, he cleared his throat. "Oops. Sorry, I didn't mean to pry. Uh, how many of those things are you planting anyway?"

"About two hundred and no husband and glad about it," she said unfazed.

"Why?"

"Why what?"

Parke had no business asking or wanting to know about Cheney personally. It was best to play it safe. "Why so many bulbs since they multiply? What kind are they?"

"Caladiums, peonies, three different colors of begonias, and my favorite, gladioli. To answer your first question, so I'll have enough to cut and put inside."

Parke continued to dig as he tried indiscreetly to snoop for more information, but Cheney Reynolds answered sporadically as she planted at a steady pace.

"That's a beautiful and unique name. Is there a story behind it?"

"Nope."

After an hour, Parke realized he wasn't going to get the full scoop, so he stood and brushed off his sweats. "Well, I better head home. Welcome to our neighborhood."

Cheney surprised Parke when she stopped and glanced up. At that moment, the sun shone on her face. He had never seen brown eyes as dark as hers with long lashes. *Nice.*

"I appreciate your help today. Eventually, I'd have gotten all the bags out, without killing myself. Thanks again."

A genuine smile and the sweet tone of her voice did something to Parke's heart. It skipped, stopped, or sucked in an extra dose of oxygen. He shrugged to hide his sudden flare of emotion.

If his recently-saved, good friend, Annette, was with him, she'd call him a dog and probably haul him to church. Annette wasn't there, so Parke could be as carnal-minded as he wanted. The problem with Annette's church. He was the pastor. He expected more than what God did and that was to live sanctified.

"No problem, any time," Parke said, shrugging as he backed away. Doing an about-face, he jogged on down the street. His mind was boggled. Cheney Denise Reynolds' sincerity tugged at him.

Meeting Cheney appeased his appetite as a nosy neighbor, but prompted other curiosities. The following week, Parke guided his SUV onto Benton Street at various times. Instead of house-watching, he found himself watching Cheney. Parke wasn't disappointed when Cheney's male visitors were non-existent. "I still can't believe what she did to the front lawn," he thought out loud, driving off. None of the women he dated would've lifted a finger to toil in dirt.

One Monday evening, as the blazing sun was retiring, Parke cruised pass her house as he chatted on the phone through his Onstar car speakers. *Bingo*. Cheney was toying with accent lights that dotted the path from the sidewalk to her front door. He parked, locked his vehicle and rudely trampled across her yard. "Good evening."

Startled, Cheney jumped, dropped her screwdriver, and twirled around. Frowning, she planted a hand on her hip. "Do you always sneak up on your neighbors, Parkay?"

Throwing his head back, Parke laughed. "You almost had it right." The first day, she was adorably quiet; now she had her attack wings on, ready for battle. He did scare her. "I'm sorry." He gripped his stomach. "I've been called many names before, but never butter. It's Parke, like Parker, without the 'r.'"

"Right, sorry," she apologized as she bent to retrieve her tool.

Dressed in clean white sweats, Cheney's face was the color of a lemon. It was flawless, dirt-free, and without makeup. Parke eyed the shape of her black eyebrows. He imagined a painter's finger dipped in ink tracing a smooth line, arching it to perfection. They were natural. Her hair, pulled again in a ponytail, was neater.

What was he doing here? Parke had no reason for his visit. Call him nosy. Wearing his shirt, tie, and brown slacks, Parke thought about the appointment he just left. His clients had been a distraught young married couple who hadn't taken his advice to diversify their stocks before the company filed for bankruptcy. He had another client in a few hours. He needed to prepare their portfolio.

Common sense told Parke he should go home, but he, like any other man, didn't take rejection well. This woman was brushing him off again. She didn't fit his profile, but Cheney fascinated him. If he kept her talking, maybe he would learn more about her. "You didn't install the lights, did you?"

Cheney stooped and adjusted a spotlight. "Yeah, I know it made more sense to do it while I was planting, but I couldn't take the electrical class until last night."

This woman was a jackie-of-all trades. Parke's mouth dropped opened as she walked to an electrical box in the garage and flipped a switch. The strategically placed lights illuminated, transforming the former old shack to the likes of a new display model.

"Lady, what can't you do?"

"You'd be surprised," Cheney said as she walked inside, never looking back.

CHAPTER 3

The old wives' tale, *If you take one step, then God will take two*, nagged Cheney from her sleep as it revolved around in her head. Irritated, she sat up and threw back her woven chenille jacquard comforter. Spoiling herself, she had dared to indulge in the expensive super-soft sateen sheets that coordinated with the earth tone colors of stone, topaz and terracotta in the comforter. Matching curtains and an off white recliner transformed her bedroom into a sanctuary. She padded across the cool wood floor, repeating the adage. Once inside her bathroom, she faced her reflection. "I'll concede to one step. Don't think I'll make two," she spoke aloud to herself, but hoped God had eavesdropped.

Less than an hour later she stood in her living room staring out the window. Sipping her coffee, she stalled for time. When the last drop dried in the bottom of her cup, she realized she couldn't put the task off any longer.

She lifted her cordless phone from its holder.

With her other hand, she pulled the tiny yellow post-it note out of her pocket. The scribbling was so small another person would need a magnifying glass to read it, but Cheney had not only written it, she had memorized her sister's phone number as the pen stroked the paper. Non-published, Cheney risked her job to retrieve it from the company's internal phone database system. There were strict guidelines in place to protect customer's privacy.

"Allen Residence," her young niece answered.

"Hi, is your Mommy home?" Cheney wanted to say more, at least introduced herself as Aunt Cheney. Besides knowing the child's name was Natalie, Cheney knew nothing else, not even who she looked like. Choking back a flood of tears, she gulped a deep breath. It would be okay. Someday a child would call her mommy.

"Hello?" Janae's clear voice came on the line.

"Hey, Sis." Cheney picked at her sweater until she formed lint-shaped knots on the front.

"Cheney Reynolds. Did Mother give you my number?" Janae asked annoyed.

"I, well, I," Cheney paused and grimaced.

"Never mind, you have it now. What can I do for you?"

The wound was open and the nerve severed. Was this the seed she sowed five years ago? She was now reaping the remains of what locusts left behind from the harvest. Cheney cleared her throat. "How about getting together for lunch?"

"Can't. We've got a family picnic. Maybe next time."

"I could tag . . ."

Click.

The tone amplified the disconnection. Shrugging, Cheney sniffed and lifted her chin in defiance. Bouncing back from stumbling off step one, she decided to take another step. Luckily Rainey's number was listed and hadn't changed. She punched it in, and relaxed like the call was her normal daily routine.

"Yeah," Rainey snapped on the first ring.

"Hey, it's me."

Silence.

Rainey recovered before Cheney could say anything. "How are you?"

"I'm fine," Cheney answered, pausing to bite her lip. *Where do I begin?* she asked the invisible connection that binds twins. She opened her mouth, but another woman beat her to the punch.

"Girl, can you believe her nerve? Calling my man while I was right there with him—"

Frowning, Cheney listened and realized the lines were crossed on a party line. "Rainey? You hear that?"

He said nothing, but the woman said plenty, "Who is this? Get off my line."

"Hello? Sorry, but we were on this line first," Cheney informed them, wondering why Rainey didn't jump in.

A loud burst of gum popping preceded the voice of a teenage girl. "Listen . . ." and she began throwing out profanity Cheney had never heard. Then without a click, the two were gone.

"Don't sweat it, happens all the time," Rainey said then added sarcastically, "That's our new millennium phone system working, and just think I pay for that great service every month. Usually after a heavy storm, I use my cell phone. The landlines are so unpredictable."

Cheney tried to read between the lines. Was the remark cast at her personally, or the company that employed her? She made a note to look into the problem on Monday. Someone must be tapping into Rainey's phone line, have access to his outside phone box regardless of the company's lock; or heavy downpours were to blame for deteriorating his phone lines.

"So, what do I owe this call?"

She heard him sigh, but ignored it. "You feel like hanging out?"

"Can't. I'm going to the Juneteeth celebration this evening."

"Yeah, that's right. Are you still with…" Cheney paused, racking her brain to remember the girl he was in love with before she moved to Durham, "Shanice!" She grinned, pleased with herself, considering she was more than out of touch.

"Shanice and I split years ago."

"Oh, well, I'd love to go with you."

"Sorry. I've got a date. You wouldn't want to be a third wheel."

Cheney scratched at the dandruff that she forgot was washed out yesterday. Strike two. She didn't need a third strike to be out. "No, no I wouldn't. Well have fun."

"I will. Thanks," Rainey said, hanging up.

She considered going to the festival, but somehow a crowd would only make her feel lonely. As Cheney set the phone back in its holder, she took a look around her house. It wouldn't be hard for her to find something to do, but she had to start getting out. If not, her palace would become her prison.

Parke was dreaming about the house on Benton Street when a buzzer startled him, but before he was fully awake he had dreamt he heard his mother say, "Don't dismiss your thoughts while sleeping. Your dreams could be telling you something about the future."

He chuckled at the absurdity of the statement. There was nothing on Benton Street that could be part of his future. When his doorbell buzzed again, he got up. He went into the bathroom and quickly washed his face and brushed his hair at the same time a trick he learned as a kid when he got up late for school. After stepping into sweatpants and putting on a T-shirt, he ran downstairs to the front door.

He wasn't surprised to see his younger brother leaning on his doorbell without any regard. "Knock it off, Malcolm. I'm not deaf. What's up?" he warned after opening the door.

"Thought you might be up for a whippin'. Name your poison—slam dunks or one-on-one," Malcolm Jamieson challenged, wearing a cocky grin and workout clothes. He thrust the ball into Parke's chest.

"You're trying to kill me, ain't ya?"

"Yep."

"Where's your better half?"

"Thanks for asking. Hallison's at the beauty shop." Parke smirked. "And you're like a lost puppy without your woman. Judging from your bulging biceps, you've probably already been on the court for hours."

Identical facial features, including long noses and dimpled smiles, mirrored the brothers. Each sported short, wavy jet-black hair and thick silky eyebrows. Whereas Parke wore a long, thin mustache, Malcolm preferred a well-groomed beard. Ladies often mistook them for Rick Fox of the L.A. Lakers. The youngest brother, Cameron, was away at college.

"What can I say? Hali and I have a standing gym date every other Saturday."

"And a non stop romantic dating experience the other days of the week."

At twenty-six, Malcolm was three years younger than Parke, but stood an inch taller at six-foot-five. His honey skin was a shade darker than Parke's cocoa-butter complexion. Malcolm's weightlifting regimen made his body appear thicker and heavier than his sibling's.

The Jamiesons were confident black men in their professional goals and beliefs. Their similarities ended when it came to the opposite sex. Malcolm preferred consistency in a relationship, dating one woman at one time. Parke lost all his common sense when it came to women, playing them like a deck of cards. The search wasn't a game he played as he looked for the Mrs. Jamieson to bear Parke K. Jamieson VII.

"You and your Miss Dinkins," Parke teased, swooping up his keys from a nearby hall table. Locking the door, he nudged his brother forward. "I've got a better idea. How 'bout instead of playing ball, we take a short run around the hood? C'mon. You can keep up, can't ya?"

Parke leaped off three steps, landing on the brick walkway of his turn-of-the-nineteenth-century house. He dashed down the sidewalk for a jumpstart. Malcolm sped by him. Their jog increased to a marathon race as they passed chemically-treated green lawns, luscious flowers beds, and elegant homes. Some houses were too massive to hide behind the aging oaks and spruces lining Darst Avenue.

Parke knew Malcolm wouldn't figure out his zigzag route. Two blocks north, then two streets east, a shortcut through a pathway, and then one long block south to "the street." For weeks, out of a nagging habit, he had cruised down Benton, which was five blocks in the opposite direction of his house. He was obsessed and enjoyed putting Malcolm through a maze for the fun of it.

Malcolm stopped and bent down, panting. "PJ, wait. What's with the obstacle course? Why are we going this way? Wabash Park is on the other side."

"Yeah, I know," Parke said, jogging in place. "There's a house I want to check out."

As they stood stretching, a cherry-red Chrysler convertible slowed down. Two Halle Berry look-alikes honked the horn, blew kisses, and sped away.

"Women, you gotta love 'em," the brothers said in unison as their hands met in a high five.

"The market isn't performing to your expectations? You're contemplating forsaking your stocks and bonds for investment property? Smart move."

"Malcolm, you know all my moves are deliberate. My interest has nothing to do with financial investments. For awhile, I've been watching the progress of a neighborhood eyesore. Man, death almost kissed me as I drove past that property."

"Death?"

"I'm serious. I nearly broke my neck trying to see if the for sale sign was plucked and lights were burning. When I turned around, I was face-to-face with oncoming traffic."

Malcolm burst out laughing. "It must've been a sight to see. You ruin your Envoy?"

Parke shivered at the thought of that ramshackle house causing his demise and sending his pride and joy to a body shop. "You know it! Plus—" Parke veered to another side street and emerged into a slow trot. "I wanted a glimpse at the losers who would buy anything to boast an Old Ferguson zip code."

"Now you're a nosy neighbor, huh? I'm glad I'm not worthy of your visits or you'd snoop on me."

As they rounded the corner, Parke slowed and rested against a tree. Crossing his arms, he stared across Benton Street. The house in his dream was Cheney's. Parke stopped breathing.

"What's so fascinating, or did I wear you out, old man?"

"You wish. Impressive, isn't it?" Parke made the statement, pointing.

"Who ya talkin' about? The house or the babe inside?"

Parke squinted to verify a rag was tied around Cheney's head like Aunt Jemima as she wiped inside a bay window. "Toss up." He had seen her the previous night rolling blue paint on a bedroom wall.

Bored, Malcolm shoved his brother before heading back toward Parke's house. "C'mon, man. Haven't you seen enough? Who are you bringing to Juneteeth later?"

Shrugging, Parke answered, "I thought about Kelsi."

Malcolm's eyes bucked. "Kelsi, again? That's two dates in a row, but who's counting?"

"You, and probably her. So far, she's fitting the profile."

"Run your profile by me again."

Annoyed at his brother's forgetfulness, Parke rattled off, "Intelligent, sexy—meaning short, compact, good-looking legs, and a warm personality. So far, Kelsi's got the sexy part right."

"This is where you lose me, PJ. Why bother?"

"Because I enjoy her other assets." Parke winked. Kelsi and Parke had one thing in common. They played each other for what they could get.

"Okay, keep it up and you'll have a houseguest in your castle."

"That's why I dumped Vanessa last month." Parke sucked in his lips. "It hurt to cut her loose. That woman had the most gorgeous, milkchocolate legs I've ever seen. But I needed a honey who's makin' her own money so I could throw my hands up at her," Parke said, paraphrasing lyrics to "Independent Woman" an old song penned by the defunct group Destiny's Child.

"Slow down, playboy, that profile of yours might lead you astray. We control our destiny, not the gods of the kings and princes of our ancestral tribes."

"Malcolm, I won't ignore the past. It holds the direction of our future."

"Maybe. I just don't believe that rule applies to our soul mate. Now back to Vanessa. Wasn't she the elementary school teacher who invited you to a career day?"

"Yeah, and I was up against a firefighter, a black race car driver, and a television news anchor."

"Stiff competition."

Parke loved these philosophical exchanges with his brother so he wasn't ready to change subjects. "I can't turn off or on our ancestral connection. The warrior in my blood tells me the right woman will be from a line of African queens."

"God help the poor woman. Let's not digress, PJ. I'm talking about the career day event. You know, the firefighter, news—"

"Yeah, right. Not one kid had questions for me. A little white boy raised his hand once he learned I was an investment broker. He couldn't have been more than eight-years-old. He announced he had stock in McDonald's, Microsoft, and Walgreens."

Malcolm snickered. "Watch out, the next Bill Gates. We need to reach out to our youths about saving and investing. Okay, refresh my memory on Kelsi?"

"A loan officer I met a few weeks ago after one of my investment seminars. She's about five-five with short hair. Man, her skin is like bronze. She's a hottie who drives a yellow BMW convertible, and likes her men to lavish her before . . ."

"Okay, okay, we're having a G-rated conversation here. That's too much information. So, Kelsi is coming with you to the Juneteeth celebration?"

Parke grinned. "I said I was thinking about it. I think I'll give that honor to Monica"

Malcolm slapped Parke on the back. "Work it, my brother. Work it."

"I am."

A half hour later, Parke punched his security code

on the keypad after he closed his exquisitely carved black front door. The previous owners had the mouse-gray house custom-built. The structure greeted, invited, and sheltered its homeowners while beckoning curious visitors inside.

His footsteps echoed as he crossed the polished mahogany floor. Detouring to the family room with four double theater seats and a forty-two inch plasma screen television as the focal point, Parke snatched up the sports page from the newspaper he had left littered across the floor. Turning to run upstairs to shower, the flashing green light on his phone tempted him to check his missed calls.

Eying the name, he smirked when former girlfriend Annette Barber's number appeared on the caller ID. It had been a while since they had spoken. Annette was a knockout with her gorgeous, tiny and mature body, but it was her gregarious personality that opened many hearts and doors. Despite all her assets, Parke didn't feel she was 'the one.'

Annette had refused to indulge in intimacy with Parke without a commitment. So it was his appetite for other women that resulted in the dissolution of their romantic relationship. Incredulous as it seemed, she liked Parke enough to maintain a friendship. Now the bombshell left Parke baffled. Annette was getting too excited about going to church. He couldn't believe his party partner and close friend was trading in the 'good times' for pew-warming.

"I'm happy for you," he had lied.

Her conversion was twenty-four-seven. Not the usual "do whatever I want through the week, and repent on Sunday." Since her recent salvation, An-

nette, in one breath, classified Parke as her best
whoremonger, woman-chasing friend who God was
counting the days before Parke's salvation.

It was Annette who changed the course of Parke's
life without knowing it when she introduced him to
her great-grandmother. Mrs. Beard was a fascinating
and determined woman who started investing in the
early 1960s with one hundred dollars. Parke couldn't
believe a black woman had engaged in the stock
market in the middle of the civil rights era. She had
been able to put five daughters through college because of her discipline and determination. The pay-
off was opening her hat and dress shop. Mrs. Ada
Mae Beard now lived comfortably in an upscale
assisted-living apartment complex.

Three years ago, Parke's purpose in life had
changed when Annette invited him to attend an investment seminar. That meeting resulted in Stiles,
Davis, and Crowley Brokerage recruiting Parke as
an investment rep in its minority training program.
They enticed him with a six-figure earning potential. *Only fools turn down an opportunity*, he thought
so Parke began a personal mission to help every
black family become financially secured.

One day his boss, Mr. Crowley, pulled Parke
aside. "You're wasting your time. There's no money
in black communities," he had warned Parke. "They
spend it as soon as they get it. Focus on the white
middle and upper-class families. They're bred to invest in the market, to succeed, and pass their wealth
on to the next generation."

At the mention of 'generation,' Parke believed
his role in life was to positively change the way of

life for future generations. He realized that brief en-counter with Mr. Crowley was already set in motion from his ancestors. Parke didn't fully understand why he felt that, but he just felt it in his heart. He never did determine if the older white partner was insulting his race or advising him, so he expanded his prospects, concentrating on whoever would give him thirty minutes—blacks, whites, Hispanics, or Asians—and Parke didn't regret his decision as his clientele and bank account flourished.

His true love was uncovering African-American history—slave bills of sale, probate court records, or post-slavery marriage certificates. His weekend trips to black cemeteries were commonplace. However, Parke's dates never seemed to share his passion. *Passion.* Their passion was to get him down the aisle.

Parke had yet to meet a woman who knew her heritage. He couldn't fault them entirely. Blacks and whites read the same history books in school, and black folks didn't always appear in them. Yes, Parke couldn't think of success without thinking of An-nette and her great-grandmother. He owed her.

He pushed play on the recorder and waited.

"Hey, Parke, call me when you get in. I want to share some exciting news with you. Love you. Bye"

Annette sounded like she was about to fly. Smil-ing, he checked the time. She had called about an hour ago. *I might be able to catch her*, he thought be-fore dialing her number.

"Okay, my girl, what's got you so upbeat?" he said when she answered the phone. Often they chatted over lunch, attended parties together, and shared wonderful news about what was going on in their lives.

"I've been waiting forever for you to call me back!"

"Sorry, babe. So, what's all the excitement about?"

"You know I've been attending this Holy Ghost-filled church."

Parke nodded as if she could see, and slumped down into one of the chairs so he could listen attentively.

"Did you know that the Bible is an eye opener?" Annette paused, "Well, I've met this guy who seems to have the same hunger and thirst for righteousness. And you know what God says about that, don't you?

"No, but I'm sure you're going to tell me."

"Of course. God says He will fill us to the brim. It's in that Bible I brought you. You know, the one you probably stuffed in a box and packed away in the basement, but if you decide that you're hungry, check out Matthew chapter five or Luke chapter six."

Parke didn't want to engage in a sermon with Annette so he reined in his teasing. With her new salvation thing, he'd learned ribbing Annette would only cause her to pull out her Bible, Sunday School notes, and find marked pages from the current Christian living book she bought. Nope, he was keeping quiet and letting Annette have her way.

"I feel in my soul that I can grow with him. He could be the one God has for me, Parke."

All Parke heard was "he could be the one," and his big brother and protector role kicked in. "I need to check him out, Nettie."

"Why do you think I called, dude?"

"Name the time, place, and day. I'm there."

"Next week, revival service, seven o'clock," she recited.

"You played me."

Annette didn't try to conceal the triumphant laugh. "Did it work?"

"Nope." Parke grinned. He could imagine Annette was pouting and stomping her feet.

"Okay, let me come through a side door since the front entrance isn't working."

"Talk in plain English, Nettie."

"PJ, you're a historian slash broker. You're a magnet for information. Aren't you a little curious about my conversion and fascination with a Book that has sustained wars, copies burnt, yet the words live on? People all over the world, regardless of their language and culture, know who Jesus is. The Bible will change you."

"Since I like the way I look, love my life, enjoy the company I keep, even the way I smell, I'm as content as a baby with a warm bottle and a dry diaper. I'm cool. I see I'm going to have to meet your guy on my territory, not yours. Listen, I've got to go."

After a few more exchanges about what he wasn't going to do, they ended their phone call, agreeing to eventually disagree. Parke disconnected, debating if now was the time he and Annette should go their separate ways. No, he shook the absurd thought from his mind. God wasn't big enough to break up their friendship. Sex was.

Hours later with excitement buzzing around him, Parke was determined to dismiss Annette's evangelistic phone call. He was at the Juneteeth Heritage and Jazz Festival to have a good time, not feel guilty about the pursuit of his happiness. Keiner Plaza, in downtown St. Louis, was a hot spot for any public celebration from sport championship rallies to holiday parades.

Tim Cunningham and his ensemble serenaded thousands with his signature saxophone melodies. Vendors lined Market Street, selling everything from authentic ethnic dishes to apparel sewn from the finest African fabrics not generally available.

Parke linked his fingers with his date's manicured ones. They had been strolling through the maze of people sampling food and chatting with acquaintances either one of them ran into.

Spying Malcolm's arm around Hallison, he waved them over. For some reason he couldn't comprehend why Malcolm liked all his women tall and medium-brown. Parke preferred petite honeys in all shades. He considered them daintier, more feminine, and full of surprises.

Hallison was at least five-foot-ten. Golden highlights streaked the dark brown hair that swayed past her shoulders. A long sleeveless multicolored dress flowed inches above her ankles. Seductive long side splits offered peeks at her tanned legs as she and Malcolm glided toward him. They looked ridiculously content and happy.

Releasing Hallison, Malcolm nodded, gripping Parke in a handshake and hug. Standing back, Malcolm smiled at Parke's date. "Monica."

Without making eye contact with the woman standing beside him, Parke cleared his throat before making introductions, "Ah, Monica couldn't make it, bro."

His date's eyes glared at him. Hallison and Malcolm's eyes bucked from embarrassment. Parke ignored their expressions.

"Change of plans. This is Nyla. Nyla, meet my younger brother, Malcolm, and his lady, Hallison." He then whispered an apology in Nyla's ear, "I asked you to be with me because I wanted you here."

Forcing a smile, Nyla did a terrible job of recovering from the humiliation. She took a deep breath and tilted her head. "It's nice to meet you both."

"Hey, Malcolm, ah, good turnout," Parke commented, searching for a diversion. "Was it like this last year, man?" A business conference had taken him out of town, so he attended festivities in Texas.

Malcolm shrugged. "It was bigger."

"Well, you've got to get down to Galveston. I'm talking serious. They go all the way out for their celebration."

Parke chanced a glance at Nyla. She looked bored, struggling with residual effects from the identification mix-up. He felt bad. He'd never purposely do anything to degrade a woman. It was an honest mistake. He may be a 'dog,' as Annette called him, but he was a pedigree. Parke was well-mannered and respectful. He squeezed her hand.

Nyla squeezed back. Still, Parke felt the woman had to work through her own insecurities. He had told her up front he wasn't committed to any one woman. She had boldly retorted, "I don't recall asking for one."

Back on track, Parke continued to discuss the different exhibits with Malcolm and Hallison until Nyla's whining voice interrupted them.

"Juneteeth is a made-up holiday like Kwanzaa, isn't it?" When no one responded, she rephrased her question, "I mean, like Kwanzaa was created by Nelson Mandela when he was released from prison, right?"

For some unexplained reason, a scripture that Annette had forced on him came to mind. Hosea 4:6, *"My people are destroyed for lack of knowledge: because thou hast rejected knowledge . . ."* the rest of the words didn't matter to Parke. He had plenty of knowledge about plenty of things. Parke wanted to impart some ancestral knowledge to Nyla.

"Nope, it's the oldest known African-American celebration, dating back to June 1865. It symbolizes the end of slavery," Parke explained. "Dr. Maulana Karenga introduced Kwanzaa in this county in 1966. The name means celebration of first fruits, and some say the celebrations are recorded as far back as ancient Egypt."

Nyla frowned and listened without interrupting.

"Now, back to Juneteeth, in some states, people of all races, nationalities, and religious backgrounds acknowledge that dark period in our history and commemorate slaves' freedom for a day or week. In some places, celebrations last a month," Malcolm added.

Fascinated, Nyla's eyes widened. "Wow. I thought Lincoln signed the Emancipation Proclamation in 1863."

"He did, but millions of blacks throughout the deep south didn't get the word," Malcolm advised as he unconsciously stroked Hallison's arm. "Many masters kept blacks enslaved for two-and-a-half years longer."

"Let me tell my favorite part of the festivities," Hallison interjected excitedly.

"Tell us, baby, like Parke and I don't already know."

"Imagine more than eighteen hundred union army soldiers—no doubt the strongest, finest, and most determined black men—marching into Galveston, Texas. I can just see them parading in grand style with authority, proclaiming the slaves' freedom. Whew, rescue me." Hallison fanned herself.

"God sent me to rescue you," Malcolm cooed.

"He had nothing to do with it," Hallison stated, her expression blank.

CHAPTER 4

A week later . . .

"You change your dates more than a woman shops," Malcolm teased Parke over the phone.

"There is a reason behind my madness as you call it. Not that I'm an extremely religious person, but I feel God is leading me to somebody."

"I doubt it, PJ. Your recent choices are causing you to lose your mind. If it's contagious, then stay away from me."

"Okay, I agree with you, Malcolm. Nyla was a mistake on my part. It's partially your fault, too. I'll never tell you another one of my date's names."

"I'll never ask again." Malcolm laughed.

"I admit I strayed away from my protocol with that one."

"With that one? PJ, you're looking in the wrong places. You need a woman like Hali. Say the word. I can ask when I surprise my baby for lunch later."

"I don't need any help."

"Oh, you need help, all right."

"That's your problem. Is Hallison so much a

woman that she's got you in a headlock? I can't see a woman putting me in that position. I'm not ready to be tangled up like that."

"Suit yourself. Have a crummy day, big brother," Malcolm barked, laughing. He pushed the off button, and picked up the company file scheduled for an audit. He was happy he didn't build barriers like Parke did. Setting a personal goal, Malcolm hoped he could crunch the numbers on three companies' records before noon so he could surprise Hallison. Amazingly, they worked about ten blocks away, but met for lunch when they could, or talked over the phone when either could get away.

Hours later Malcolm walked out the automatic doors from his office in the Metropolitan Square Building downtown. Malcolm didn't have a care in the world. All was good, and according to the three sistahs in the elevator he had stepped out from moments ago, he looked delicious. One cooed, another whispered, but one boldly proclaimed how intoxicating his cologne smelled. Malcolm appreciated the kudos, but ignored their overtures. Like his brother, he enjoyed the attention of beautiful women, but only one lady set his soul on fire, Hallison.

At one minute after one in the afternoon, Malcolm entered the revolving doors to the Bank of America lobby. He scanned the wall for the building directory. With his finger he line-read the names until he found personnel.

On the same floor to his right, Malcolm smoothed his gray and-mint-green paisley tie against his shirt as he walked down a short hall and opened a glass door. Matching suspenders complimented his smoke-gray pleated pants. His worn, but polished shoes squeaked on the tiled floor.

One side of the office had a row of computers. A few applicants looked up from their cubbyholes that lined a back wall. Some nodded. When Malcolm removed his dark sunglasses, a few women ogled him. Hallison said his glasses made him look sexy, rugged, and dangerously appealing.

He approached a large executive-style desk that seemed to separate the common area from the secluded private offices. It was neat and housed every functional item from a computer to calendar, but a name plate was missing. A dark-skinned woman with fashionable glasses and a head full of twisted curls glanced up. She dropped her pen. Staring, she caught her breath.

To keep from disturbing job applicants, Malcolm leaned down and whispered, "Is Hallison Dinkins in?"

The receptionist gave Malcolm a milk-white smile. "Your name, please, sir?" She scanned an appointment book with a pink manicured fingernail.

Stuffing both hands in his pockets, he cocked his head to the left. "Malcolm Jamieson, Miss Dinkins' personal certified public accountant."

An odd expression masked her face. She pushed back from her desk and stood. Taking a cautionary glance around the room, she locked her desk. Without a word, she turned and her shoes began a two-tap rhythm across the room. She didn't instruct Malcolm to wait, so he followed.

Unlike the common area, a maroon thick carpet arrested her noisy heels. Complementing brown and maroon wallpaper escorted them past two opened doors. The woman stopped at a closed dark wood door with the title Director of Human Resources centered on a distorted portrait-sized glass window.

Malcolm was impressed. At least he knew his baby worked in a nice environment. He hoped she liked surprises. Knocking, the receptionist stuck her head in the office and then waved Malcolm forward as if knowing he followed. She left.

Entering her office, Malcolm's eyes were transfixed on Hallison's mouth as her smile blossomed. Without closing the door, he headed straight to her mahogany desk. He inhaled and waited as if a doctor would tell him to breathe out. When her big brown eyes sparkled, Malcolm exhaled.

"Roomy place," slipped from his mouth, but he would get a good look around later. "I was hoping I would get this reaction." Without a word, he leaned over and took her lips in a slow kiss before whispering, "Hi."

"Hi, back. What are you doing here?"

Aware of his seduction, Malcolm pecked soft kisses on her lips. "Oh, convincing my lady to have lunch with me."

"Hmm," Hallison moaned, lifting an eyebrow. "I don't know."

"Uh-huh, we have to celebrate," he teased, meeting Hallison's questioning eyes, "our four incredible months together. The future looks pretty good to me right now."

Hallison blushed and rubbed her nose against his. "And, I've enjoyed every moment. About lunch, I may need more convin—"

Malcolm's response was an urgent, demanding

kiss before helping her to stand. He massaged her fingers. "You never have to tease me to get what you want, woman. My kisses have your name written all over them." Hallison opened her mouth to reply, but stopped. "Baby, is Calico's okay, or would you rather eat at the Bread Company?"

Coming around the desk, Hallison snaked her arms around his neck in a hug. "I'll eat White Castle gas burgers just to share lunch with you. I like Calico's."

"I had a taste for some Hallison Dinkins, and the sight of you satisfies my craving for now. C'mon, let's eat."

Surveying Hallison's red silk suit, Malcolm whistled when she walked to a wall mirror to finger-comb her hair and check her makeup.

The long-sleeve double-breasted jacket fell below her hips. The matching skirt stopped inches above her knees with teasing splits on both sides. Her sheer nylons and three-inch red pumps had Malcolm's heart pumping faster than running on a treadmill.

"You need a bodyguard, Miss Dinkins, and I'm here to offer my services." He reached for her. "I like being with you."

Hallison linked her fingers through his. "And, I like you being with me."

Hand in hand, Malcolm escorted her to the downtown Italian restaurant. It was already packed with the lunchtime crowd. As the waitress led them to a cozy window seat, he teased Hallison's ear with his breath. "You look breathtaking."

Looking into his dark brown eyes, Hallison mouthed her thank you.

They ordered sodas and decided to share a house salad and a maximum meat topping pizza. While waiting, Malcolm reached over and played with Hallison's fingers. A woman sitting behind Hallison distracted Malcolm. She tried to seduce him in a stare. Malcolm had he was being checked out and the woman was interested.

Hallison glanced over her shoulder. Her gaze challenged a hazel-eyed beauty. With constraint and grace, Hallison lifted her chin in a silent challenge before turning back to Malcolm. Only her eyes wouldn't meet his.

"She's not a treat or a threat," Malcolm assured her and he stretched across the table, closing the distance between them.

Nodding, Hallison looked away unconvinced. Her beautiful lips were twisted in contemplation. To recapture her attention, Malcolm squeezed her fingers. "Hali, forget her. This lunch, this moment is about you and me. Anyway, Wabash Park is kicking off its weekly summer concerts tomorrow night. I'd love to have my lady wrapped in my arms while listening to live music under the stars."

Malcolm watched as Hallison struggled to answer. He wondered if the woman's boldness had upset her. Maybe now was the perfect time for them to plan a romantic getaway. He brought her hand to his lips and placed soft kisses inside her palm. "I want to be with you. No other woman, but you. You don't have competition."

"There's always competition, always."

"Not against you, Hali. I want just you."

"I want to be with you, too."

"Good." He inched his mouth closer to her lips. "They can look, but only you can touch."

"That's what I wanted to hear." She kissed him.

For the past week, Cheney had struggled to avoid Mrs. Beacon at all costs. So far the woman was proving to be a pest addicted to pesticide. Lately, Cheney was starting to have nightmares. It had nothing to do with her past. It was the present, and it lived right next door. She had the strangest sensation that at night Mrs. Beacon's neck stretched like a crane and peeped inside her bedroom with eyes like E.T.

Tuesday evening, Cheney's nightmare became reality. Before one of Cheney's heels could hit the driveway, Mrs. Beacon was frantically beckoning for her.

Cheney slumped her shoulders. "Now what?" she whispered.

Mrs. Beacon's hair was parted down the middle and pulled in two doughnut-shaped buns above her ears. A red housedress with two large front pockets draped her small frame and Stacy Adams engulfed her feet.

"Heney, lace sheer curtains would be my choice in your front windows. They make a statement that speaks of elegance and class." She turned up her nose. "Anything, but those cheap vinyl blinds."

Shocked into silence, Cheney's mouth dropped. Her elderly neighbor had a lot of nerve. *The gossip about the woman was kind*, Cheney thought. If Imani was present, Cheney knew she wouldn't take the insults quietly and would probably pluck every strand of the woman's gray hair. *The old bat knew her name. What was her problem, anyway?* Cheney took a deep breath to calm down.

The day before, Cheney's work week started off terribly. A major pipe had burst over the computer room, damaging several computers used for dispatching 911 calls and medical emergency alerts. She was able to have service routed to another building while the repairs were made, so customers wouldn't experience any phone interruption. The day had been long and exhausting.

That morning, she confronted Clint Kim, a middle-aged employee with more than twenty years of service. Rumors surfaced that he'd been cheating the company for years, charging excessive overtime for everything from changing a light bulb, reprogramming a door code to restarting a fan after a power outage. Cheney could still hear Clint's stuttering excuses.

"W-well, Cheney, it's a technical thing. It may s-sound s-simple, but it takes years of training to troubleshoot a problem and correct it."

What Clint didn't know was the phone company had enrolled her in property and facility management classes. Without question, Cheney was certified to fully maintain her office buildings. She knew restarting a fan took sixty seconds.

"Hmm, I see. Clint, I've checked your hours against your coworkers. They seem to do the job in less time, so maybe I'll save the company money and free up your time by removing you from the call-out list." The look on Clint's face was priceless. Cheney wanted to laugh.

Clint took a deep breath as his face turned red.

"Look, you just can't come in here and think you know how to run this department. You and I both know they hired you because they needed somebody black."

No he didn't go there. Closing the distance, Cheney had braced herself for a professional battle. "Clint, first, I was hired to manage this building from top to bottom, so I run the show. Second, if you ever imply, whisper, or gossip that I'm not capable of doing this job because of the color of my skin, I'll take disciplinary action for discriminatory remarks. Don't give me two reasons to fire you. You've only got one left."

Cheney left Clint standing outside her office with clenched fists. Thank God all the men in her crew didn't share his viewpoint. Now, Mrs. Beacon was like a loaded gun with plenty of ammunition ready to finish off the headache Clint had started. She was once somebody's fool, but not anymore. Not for a man, work, or a neighbor.

"Considering I live at 947 Benton and pay the house note to prove it, I'll choose what to put in my bay windows. Oak wood shutters will be installed before my upcoming housewarming party. Now, if you'll excuse me, I'm running late." *Whew, did I say that?* Although Imani would be proud, Cheney knew she didn't need this stress. She rubbed her temples.

Cheney was convinced everything and everybody was out to get her. *You can run, but you can't hide,* thinking she heard a mockery voice she couldn't identify. Cheney thought she was imagining things about a child who never lived, now she was hearing things when no one was around. "I am not going crazy, so what am I going?" she mumbled. Lifting her mail from the box, Cheney unlocked her front door, walked inside, and locked it without looking back to see if Mrs. Beacon was still there.

Moving back home was suppose to be easy. Reconnect with family, make new friends, and live her life to the fullest. So far, she was questioning the move. Her world consisted of no close relationships—family, friends, and definitely not men. Her sister, Janae, was busy with a family. Her dad, Roland, was always at work.

Cheney alternated between sorting through her bills and turning on lamps. Her mind didn't stray far from her family. She still couldn't confide in her older brother, Rainey. She wanted to but could never form the words to describe what she'd done and what she had gone through because of it. He knew she had returned home, but she guessed he was waiting for her to make the first move. After all, when she lived in Durham and had the surgery, he called and called until he finally took a flight to see her.

Only she wouldn't see him. She couldn't—the abortion had left her too weak. So now here she was, at home and still no warm family ties because of her own doing. Cheney had made ten phone calls to her mother, Gayle, in recent weeks. Only two were returned. The olive tree was dried up before Cheney could extend it. Gayle had even declined Cheney's offer to visit.

"Why don't you and Janae stop by?" Cheney had asked during phone call number seven. It was a Saturday afternoon, and working around the house was starting to loose its luster.

"Don't have time. Your sister and I are going shopping," her mother had replied.

"Oh."

"We'll wait for your housewarming. Surprise us," she had told Cheney.

Cheney wanted to shout, "I'd like to go. I'm back home now, invite me," but she didn't. Her mother did have a point, she supposed. Cheney didn't want anyone to see her masterpiece until it was presentable.

Her house, she smiled. It would become her work of art. Cheney glided up the hardwood stairs, passing the first bedroom that she had recently painted blue. She back-tracked and stared before touching the light switch that activated the ceiling fan. Folding her arms, Cheney leaned against the doorframe and admired the denim bedspreads on the bunk beds. Thin chambray stripes contrasted with the large stripes on the bed skirt. A blue-plaid rectangular rug covered most of the room's hardwood floor. She hoped one day children would be tucked inside them.

Cheney backed out of the room and stepped into the adjacent one—her favorite. She had stenciled white daisies around the wall about fives inches below the ceiling. Twin lilac comforters scattered with large white daisies complemented the white juvenile furniture. Colorful toss pillows were stacked against a corner wall. The room's focal point was an adorable pink dollhouse-shaped bookshelf artistically displaying dolls from various countries.

Settling into a rocker, Cheney squeezed a teddy bear dressed in a pink ballerina skirt. "I wish I had made another choice. Since I didn't, I'll have to redeem myself." Closing her eyes, Cheney imagined a teenager stretched across the bed, dressed in faded jean shorts with a red shirt with the latest designer shoes crisscrossed at the ankles.

Cheyenne chattered non-stop on a three-way call with her girlfriends, twisting a long, thick, black ponytail. On the wall were posters of teenage idols mixed with expensive children's oil paintings.

Soon Cheyenne's skinny, shapeless body would blossom into a beautiful young woman. Then her daughter would exchange her sweet girlfriends for pimpled-faced, hormone-driven boys.

"Mom says if I keep up my grades, I can have a birthday party when I turn thirteen next month or go on a shopping spree." Her head bobbed up and down. "Yeah, I know. I've got the best mom."

Moisture spilled as Cheney opened her eyes. "If only I'd been a good mother and given you a chance from the beginning. I was afraid and weak. I never gave you a chance, my beautiful daughter. I vow to right my wrong with or without God."

Wiping away the lone tear, Cheney glanced down at her watch. "Oh no, I'm going to be late." She sprang to her feet. Her pity party was over. She couldn't change the past. What's done is done. *"If My people, which are called by My name, shall humble themselves, and pray, and seek my face, and turn from their wicked ways, then I will hear from heaven, and will forgive their sin, and will heal their land. II Chronicle, verse 7:14."* Indignation filled Cheney. "I'm not your people, God," Cheney shouted as she raced down the hall, jumping three stairs at a time to hit the landing and out the door to her home improvement class. She was behind the wheel and turning the key before she shut her car door. Besides, she didn't own a Bible.

Cheney arrived minutes before the start of a ceramic tile installation class at *Home Depot*. She and five other women had fun intimidating two men who stopped boasting as know-it-alls once they saw the ladies' skills. Cheney eyed an elderly woman, dressed in white overalls and a white cap, who was eager to get home and try the techniques. Cheney snapped numerous how-to pictures, asked plenty of what-if questions, and scribbled several pages of notes. The following week, she would install a Himalayan Rock ceramic floor tile in her kitchen.

She had enrolled in home improvement classes the day she signed the title on the house. As a single homeowner, she knew home repair was essential. Two hours later, Cheney was exhausted, but her mental activity was full of energy. The recurring child phantoms almost caused Cheney to be late for the class. She dragged her body to her Nissan and deactivated the alarm. The classes and preparations were for one thing—her housewarming.

She craved the togetherness she once had enjoyed with her family prior to attending Duke. God knows she had pushed them away. So much was riding on her housewarming.

"Why aren't you coming home?" Gayle Reynolds had asked concerned.

"Can't get away from my job," Cheney had lied as she recuperated at her apartment from the surgical procedure gone wrong.

"What do you have to hide?" Janae had asked in a separate phone call weeks later.

"Nothing," she told her sister.

"What's going on up there? That boyfriend of yours isn't abusing you, is he?" Roland demanded.

Despite her family's concerns, she told them nothing. She had stayed in Durham for five years living undercover as a professional who had her life together. In her darkest hour, Cheney had rejected her family's love. "Talk to us, Cheney. We love you. We're your family," her sister had consoled while Cheney was in the hospital unbeknownst to them.

Angry and hormonal, Cheney had pushed them to the point of no return. She was unable to deal with them or life. The shame, the guilt, and the loss continued to overpower her to the present day. The housewarming will determine if she can ever mend the communication she had cut off with her family. If not, Cheney was doomed to live alone like Mrs. Beacon. *Maybe, she'll break a leg at her salsa class,* Cheney thought.

Silly fears nagged at her every now and then. "I've got to stay away from bad thoughts," giving herself a pep talk as her cell phone chimed. "This is Cheney."

"How are ya, girl. Please tell me you're on a hot date, and I'm interrupting."

Cheney laughed at Imani. "Better. I'm leaving a home improvement workshop for installing a ceramic floor. The housewarming is in two short weeks."

"I wouldn't miss it. I'm in Atlanta tonight, but I'm flying out to London in the morning. You settling in?"

Tightening her lips in frustration, Cheney drummed her fingers on the steering wheel as she waited at the light. Throngs of people carrying lawn chairs, blankets, and sleepy kids were leaving a neighborhood park. The traffic was exceptionally heavy on a Tuesday night. "Work and the house are keeping me busy, but I'm hyped about the party."

"Me, too. Well, hon, I've got to go. I'm working with Captain Rodgers tomorrow, and I must look my best."

"Is this someone special?"

"Temporarily," Imani purred.

Cheney chuckled as they disconnected. Imani was a survivor. It amazed Cheney how Imani could pick up her life after living with an abusive husband for three years. Imani made peace with her mistakes after the divorce and was living life to the fullest.

She pulled up in her driveway. With no sign of Mrs. Beacon, Cheney turned off the ignition and wiggled her aching muscles out. After activating the car alarm, she staggered to her porch and unlocked her front door. Cheney wondered what her own future would hold.

Malcolm arrived at Hallison's Hazelwood Apartment Complex dressed in khaki pants, a short-sleeve olive green shirt opened at the collar, and Italian black leather sandals displaying well-groomed feet. He could eat, breathe, and sleep Hallison Dinkins and never grow tired of her wit, honesty, and seductive lips. Malcolm wished she had a sister for Parke. He shrugged. His big brother was on his own. Knocking on her door, he waited for his vision to appear.

Sucking in the night air, Malcolm patted his chest when Hallison opened the door. She stepped outside in a long beige crochet tank-dress molded to her figure. A scooped neckline teased his senses. She was stunning.

Reaching down, Malcolm pulled her chin to his lips, murmuring, "Maybe, we should skip the concert and spend some time alone."

Hallison batted her long lashes. "Oh no, you don't. You promised me a night filled with music under the stars."

Malcolm grabbed her around the waist, causing her to gasp as he pulled her closer. "Hali, what we can create is more romantic than a concert. I'll show you stars."

Detangling from each other, Hallison peered at him with half-closed eyes before planting a fist on her hip. "Listen, Malcolm, we both decided to just let things happen between us. You're making it hard for me to fight—"

"Whoa, baby. I didn't mean to charge your battery. We're both attracted to each other, and it's natural for that attraction to lead to affection." Grinning, Malcolm held up both hands in surrender. "Okay, okay. No more pressure. I was just making a suggestion. C'mon. Let me show off my beautiful woman."

They looped their arms together and walked the pathway to his silver Chevy Monte Carlo. Malcolm had to cool it. Hallison confided that she hadn't slept with a man because of her church upbringing. She also said that he was different from any other man, and she needed to be sure there wouldn't be any guilt when she slept with the man she loved. Malcolm knew he was the man. Now he had to give Hallison time to realize that. *Let God in heaven give him strength to hold out.*

"Any idea which woman Parke is bringing to-night?"

Throwing his head back, Malcolm released a deep chuckle. He opened the passenger door. "I have no idea, and I've stopped asking. I don't assume names anymore or ask how she's been since the last time we met."

"I'm keeping my mouth shut, that's for sure. There's got to be a woman out there to light Parke's fire. I have a few coworkers and girlfriends who would love to have a Malcolm look-alike."

"We're nothing alike when it comes to women. I know a good thing when I see her. Parke is one of a kind. He wouldn't know a good woman if she knocked him to the ground."

Twenty minutes later, Malcolm parked four blocks away from the park. After briefly speaking with Parke on the cell phone, Malcolm knew where to meet him. Hand in hand, he and Hallison strolled down the crowded sidewalk with other concertgoers. It was crowded, but still enough room to walk at a normal pace without running into the back of someone.

They spotted Parke in the distance hugging a dark-skinned woman who sported long micro braids, adorned with eye-stopping beads. She wore what appeared to be four-inch heels.

"Wow, her halter top is barely holding her boobs, and those hoochie-mama shorts would make some hoochies blush," Malcolm mumbled.

"Your brother's dates are getting stranger and stranger, babe."

"Tell me about it. The mosquitoes are going to have a munch-feast on sistah-girl tonight with all her back and legs out. Hali, some of his choices are mind boggling."

"Some?"

"Okay, most."

"Try all of them."

Malcolm snickered and kissed the top of her hair. "It's his quest to find the perfect woman. His business and world history acumen are well noted, but his personal picks remain a mystery."

Leaning into Malcolm, Hallison met his stare. "You mentioned your family tree before. I think it's so fascinating to know your history like that. You've uncovered some invaluable information.

"Yeah, unfortunately, I think it's that information that drives Parke to craziness," Malcolm voiced his thoughts.

"If you were Parke Jamieson VI, would you change your woman every day like you change your und—"

Malcolm's finger to her lips silenced her. "I would've stopped searching the day I saw you at that job fair. Does that answer your question?"

She reached up and fingered the silky hairs of his beard before standing on her toes and brushing her lips against his. "Yes."

They joined Parke and his date at a stoplight. The brothers exchanged hugs like they hadn't seen each other in years. Malcolm and Hallison offered Parke's companion a cordial smile. The woman had a pretty face.

"This is Wanda," Parke said, positioning his hand around the woman's waist. "C'mon, let's find a spot before it gets packed."

"Wanda," Malcolm mouthed the new name to

Hallison with mischief dancing in his eyes. "Not only does my brother pick women with his eyes closed, but he must have a mental rolodex to keep the names straight."

Hallison giggled.

The foursome wormed their way between folks who were sitting, standing, and stretched out on a large hill. They all faced a makeshift stage that had been erected in front of the swimming pool. Local band, Summer Magic, entertained the audience with an array of pop, rock, and love ballads.

Malcolm sat with his legs drawn, bopping his head to the band's beat until they played a rendition of Earth, Wind, and Fire's "Reasons." He relaxed his legs and coached Hallison to sit in front of him, offering his chest for support.

Closing her eyes, Hallison rested and hummed along as music floated throughout the night air. Malcolm tightened his arms around her stomach while massaging his beard against her cheek. "Hmm, sounds like you're having a good time."

She answered by rocking her head back and forth. "You know I am. This is so mellow and hypnotic. The best part is that I'm here with you. I wish I could wrap up this moment and take it home."

"Hali, you'll experience that same feeling when I make love to you. I can cast some serious spells on you, baby."

Grabbing his hand, she turned it inside and kissed his palm. "You already make love to me when you spend time with me, kiss me, hold my hand, and surprise me for lunch."

"Yeah," Malcolm said dryly, "and you seduce me

with those form-fitting clothes you wear, the way your body moves when you walk, and that scent you wear behind your ears. You're killing me, sweetheart."

Parke didn't know how Annette was doing it, but he was sure she was sending some sort of subliminal biblical messages to keep him from enjoying his evening. Parke spent the night spying on Malcolm and Hallison as they absorbed each other's touches, eye contact, and air kisses. They easily forgot about everyone else around them. What was the secret of them connecting so well?

Wanda began fingering the muscles hidden under Parke's brown Adidas T-shirt, reminding him he was too busy being a spectator instead of a participant. When he sighed, she winked, thinking she was doing something, but she wasn't. He liked opened relationships like any man, but this woman was too eager to please after the second date. *Who am I to complain if a woman wanted my body?*

He eyeballed Malcolm again. His brother was acting like a man in love and didn't have a burden to carry on the family name. Parke's heritage consumed him, searching high and low in an effort not to miss his princess, his black Cinderella. *I'm doing something wrong*, Parke surmised. Women always seemed to come on to him. It was time for him to begin the hunt for his soul mate.

Parke both dreamt and dreaded the day he would fall for a woman. His ideal woman would be intellectually and spiritually in tune with herself as a black woman, physically exquisite, and definitely petite. He turned and looked at Wanda. She was strictly a night partner, not a life partner. He had to stop picking up women who were CEOs by day and desperate women after dark.

"This night with you has been a better investment than the stock tip you gave me earlier," Wanda said, closing her eyes and leaning in for a kiss.

Parke felt obliged to kiss her neck, hum along with the band, and pray the date would end very soon. *God, I'm convinced you're trying to tell me something, but I need You to speak clearer or write it down.*

CHAPTER 5

Parke's speakers in his SUV rung, interrupting his music and thoughts. He touched the button to answer his Onstar phone. "Hello."

"It's Annette."

"What's going on with my favorite little church mouse?" Parke teased as he steered his vehicle pass Cheney's house.

"Well, I'm at your house."

He scanned his memory and didn't remember if they were supposed to get together.

Before he could ask a question, she answered, "Actually, I'm on your block. I'm with a few evangelists who are passing out gospel tracts in your neighborhood."

"Then let me keep going."

"Parke, if you don't come home, I will hunt you down and pray that the Holy Ghost will . . . I just expect better from you. Even though you act like a dog that needs to be neutered, I still love and respect you."

"Ouch," Parke said, cringing. "Okay, I'll be there in a sec.

Annette and her team of three church goers didn't stay long. As a matter of fact, they didn't say much except to ask how he was doing and to complimented his house. One chubby teenager Annette called Eric who seemed to be the leader said, "The best witness we can give you is the way we live our life in sanctification. The best knowledge *you* can obtain is in *your* Bible. Read it sometime."

Odd. Parke was expecting more of a beat-over-the-head event, then being taken hostage and dragged to church. He was relieved when the group, including Annette, stood to leave. At his front door, Annette nudged Eric.

"Do you mind if we pray for you?" Eric asked.

Parke should've expected something. When he nodded, Eric opened his Bible and flipped through the pages. Parke started to lift his hands and let them know he agreed to prayer only, but he decided against it. After all, he did have a relationship with God, despite what Annette thought.

" '*Seek ye the Lord while He may be found, call ye upon Him while He is near. Let the wicked forsake his way, and the unrighteous man his thoughts, and let him return unto the Lord, and He will have mercy upon him, and to our God, for He will abundantly pardon. For My thoughts are not your thoughts, neither are your ways My ways, saith the Lord.*' That's in Isaiah, 55:6-8."

Although Parke respected the scriptures he didn't believe they pertained to him. Church for him and his family was a social affair. Annette was the first person he knew who had been changed as a result of a church. Otherwise, it was a meeting hall on Sundays.

"Do you mind if we annoint your head with Holy Oil before we pray?" Eric asked already unscrewing the top off a small bottle that looked like a sample-size of cologne. Eric turned it upside down for the contents to touch his finger and dabbed everyone's forehead with it, including Parke.

When the group bowed their heads, so did Parke as Eric prayed, "Father, in the name of Jesus, we thank you for the opportunity to be in your presence. We thank You for the opportunity to warn others about the devices of the devil, and we further pray that you will draw Parke into your fold when the time is right. We ask that you save and sanctify not only his mind, but his body, in Jesus' name, amen."

Without another word, Parke opened his eyes to see them leaving. At first, Parke thought they resembled Jehovah's Witnesses, but they weren't ringing bells or knocking on doors when he pulled up. They were merely laying small comic strip-looking books inside storm doors. Was it because of Annette they prayed for him? Shrugging, he dismissed their visit as he closed his front door. He decided to call and check up on his mother.

"Hi, Mama."

"PJ, my long lost oldest man-child. How you doin', son?" Charlotte Jamieson's soft singsong voice greeted Parke over the phone.

Chuckling, Parke loosened his tie and unbuttoned his shirt. He peeked inside his stainless steel refrigerator, grabbed a pint-sized juice carton, and bumped the door closed with his hip. They chatted about what the family was up to.

"Now, when are you comin' for dinner? We haven't had an old-fashioned family night in a while. We'll play your favorite game. I miss my boys. Cameron decided to stay in Boston to take summer classes and work that internship, your crazy schedule makes you a stranger, and Malcolm is spending more time with Hallison. She's such a cute little thing."

"Ma, you see how tall she is? Ain't nothing little on her."

"Stop it, PJ. She's good for Malcolm. So, when are you visiting?"

"Cook my favorites and you'll see me soon."

Parke returned to the refrigerator, scanning for leftovers. He thought about his family's Friday night tradition of bonding through games. "Yeah, I'm craving some Black Heritage Trivia and The Underground Railroad board games."

His mother's sigh came through loud and clear. "Anything, but Life As A Blackman."

"Hey, you just said we could play my favorite."

"Hmm, I was hoping you didn't hear that," she teased. "That game lasts longer than Monopoly, especially when you all start arguing."

"Humph! It's called debating, Mama."

"Debating to you, but arguing to me. Just the same, you Jamieson men are loud."

Grinning, Parke leaned against the counter. "Can I help it if I'm usually the only one smart enough to survive Glamourwood Districts, The Ghetto, Corporate America, and Prison before advancing to Freedom and winning?"

"Then you set off Cameron arguing about the social and racial injustices, roadblocks, and the driving-while-black patrol," Charlotte reminded her son. "You forget Churches are positioned at every corner to help guide each player toward the ultimate goal."

"You're stirring the pot now, Mama. Set the date." They laughed. She agreed to let him know before Parke disconnected.

More than a simple pastime, the ethnic games influenced Parke to major first in African-American studies at Lincoln University in Jefferson City, Missouri, the state's first historically black college. It was founded by former slave James Milton Turner. On campus, Parke thrived in the black history classes, participated in African cultural events, and committed himself to black history preservation, but Parke's choice of a college major had infuriated his parents.

"It's good to know who you are and where you came from, but white folks only want to hear so much about *Roots*, the slave ship, and breeding slave women as cattle, son. Take some business courses and focus on economic empowerment," his father had strongly advised with an underlying threat.

Of course his parents had been right. Six years earlier, Parke had graduated cum laude with a B.S. in Business and a minor in History. He wanted to teach in a college setting, if nothing but a weekly night class, but local universities didn't see the need for an African-American history curriculum. So he became a traveling one-room school house. All he needed was a place and one person, and the stage would be set to bring the past to life.

Otherwise, hundreds of thousands of slave narratives wouldn't be heard. Parke couldn't allow that to happen. He took a position in the business world to feed his stomach while his passion for history fed his starving soul. He believed his ancestors spoke to him through his dreams, and guided him through his financial transactions.

The spirits also spoke of his future mate—a strong woman disguised by her outer appearance. Malcolm and others thought his choice of dates were crazy, but he was searching. Parke knew his bride was living "undercover," but her grand entrance was nigh.

A detour pass Cheney's house became Parke's new route. Her nonchalant attitude bugged him. She was one of thousands of women who didn't respond to the Jamieson charm. Parke cringed just thinking about her 'heaven-kissing' height. Normally it was a turnoff, but Cheney's saucy attitude was entertaining.

Yet, Parke could sniff out a cover-up. Cheney had something buried, either physical or mental, and he sensed she dared anyone to find the key. Why the facade? Parke tapped his brakes at the same time realization hit. *Wait a minute, Cheney Reynolds? Nah.* What Parke saw was what he wasn't getting. He didn't want. *It must've been the spicy hot links I gobbled down at lunch because my imagination is running wild,* he consoled himself.

CHAPTER 6

A week later . . .

Cheney's arms refused to move. Her knees couldn't. Finally, her body obeyed her command and stood. It demanded a break from applying grout to her kitchen floor. Massaging her back while rolling her head, Cheney admitted that the task was taking longer than she expected.

Entering her living room, she admired the newly installed oak shutters in one of the twin bay windows. *Her home.*

"They're beautiful," Cheney said, complimenting a man who looked like he had skipped too many breakfasts, lunches, and dinners.

The owner of Harrison's Custom Windows stood back and viewed his handiwork. "Yeah, I think so, too, Miss Reynolds. They'll give your room a relaxed look. They will allow the sunrise to wake you and filter the sunset."

"I like the sound of that." Cheney arched her back then touched her toes. As she tilted from side to side like window-shield blades, she could feel the blood circulating through every area of her body. When she noticed the man staring at her with amused curiosity, Cheney stopped and stood at attention. "Sorry, now let me get a better look." She walked closer and danced her finger on the smooth wood grain. She turned back and faced the owner. "They're adding character to my room already. I can't wait to get furniture. So far, I haven't seen anything that has caught my eye."

Mr. Harrison moved to the other bare bay window and began prepping it. "You might want to stop by Ferguson Sofa Store on South Florissant. My wife finds something unique every time she remodels, which seems like practically every year."

"I'll do that. I'm having a housewarming Saturday, and I need furniture fast."

"Housewarming? You're new to the neighborhood?" he asked.

"Yes, I am. I've lived here almost three months."

"Well, well. I'll take ten percent off my job as a welcome-to-the-neighborhood gift."

Just as Cheney was about to thank him, a large spotlight crossed her yard. Its aim was a brown Envoy parked not far from her house.

"Did you see that flash?" Mr. Harrison's panicked expression looked like he was about to duck.

"My neighbor no doubt is up to something."

By accident or intentional, the bright light found its mark. The driver sped off. For the next few minutes, the spotlight did formations against houses like a circus act. Then the block returned to a semi-dark state.

"What was that all about?"

"Who knows," Cheney answered, adding, "I'm sure it was Mrs. Beacon."

"Grandma BB?"

"You know her?"

Mr. Harrison grinned. "Her reputation is legendary."

It was almost midnight on Wednesday when Cheney came home from work, tuckered out. She grabbed her mail out the mailbox, opened her door, and locked it after closing it. She briefly thought about a light snack before bed, but she was too tired to fantasize about food.

At work, she had tackled one building problem after another. Menopausal women complained their offices were too hot, iron-deficient workers griped about freezing to death. They threatened to plug in space heaters in every available outlet throughout the building. Plus, Cheney had scheduled the annual fire detection system testing, a job that couldn't start until after the last shift had worked. The three-day process checked alarm horns, emergency lights, and the smoke detectors.

She was not only responsible for the employees' safety, but for protecting expensive telephone equipment. A small fire could reap more damage than a severe storm and disrupt phone service to thousands of customers in North St. Louis County.

Walking through the house, Cheney stared wearily at her bare living and dining rooms and admitted time was running out. Her brain was falling asleep.

Before she climbed the stairs for bed, Cheney sorted her mail. As she separated bills from junk, she scrutinized two pocket-size comic books in the mix. When she opened one book, she blinked at the name of God mentioned several times then she realized she was reading a gospel tract. Cheney immediately pitched them along with the other solicitations and went to bed.

On Thursday morning, Cheney woke with hope that the day would be uneventful and she could leave work early. Six hours later, Cheney rushed home from work. She whipped off her business suit so fast she almost tripped over her slip as it shimmied down her legs. She landed on her hands like she was a participant in a game of twister.

Laughing at her own clumsiness, she finally dressed in a green sleeveless T-shirt, green loose cotton pants, and white tennis shoes. Cramming her wallet into her back pocket, Cheney grabbed her house keys, and decided to walk the one mile to downtown Old Ferguson. Shielding her eyes from the evening sun with dark glasses, she donned a white baseball cap and was on her way.

Once Cheney reached Chambers Road's steep hill, her walk increased to a jog. She admired vintage three-story houses as they stood dignified. Large address tags identified them as historic. Their unusual colors, sloped roofs, and huge wrap-around porches seemed out of place with the smaller bungalows in the same neighborhood. As she passed Walgreens, a horn made Cheney glance over her right shoulder at the offending driver.

"Parke? How ghetto," she said, twisting her mouth in disgust.

"Hey," he yelled from a shiny brown SUV, stopping in busy traffic. "Need a lift?"

Shaking her head, Cheney increased her speed. *Ghetto.*

He blew his horn again. "You sure?"

His vehicle looked similar to the one Mrs. Beacon ran off the block the other night. Nodding again, she jogged past a quaint outdoor café called The Corner Coffee House.

She admired the old town charm that she never noticed in the months she lived in Ferguson. Out of the corner of her eye, she watched as four-lane traffic converged into two lanes under a railroad trestle, forcing Parke to merge right. She laughed, and didn't stop until she blinked away a tear. Her neighborhood was comprised of some colorful characters.

"What an idiot," she said, shaking her head.

A tall street clock encased with wildflowers greeted her, announcing Ferguson's downtown shopping and business district.

"Hmm, one day my garden will be just as beautiful," she proclaimed as another horn honked. *What is it with people honking their horns today?* Turning around, Cheney rolled her eyes, annoyed.

"You sure I can't give you a ride? I'm going your way." Parke grinned like a flirty teenager. His brilliant white smile matched his white polo shirt.

"Yep." She pointed to the furniture store. "I'm already here." Clenching her teeth, Cheney opened the front door and removed her sunglasses. "Good riddance, Mr. Jamieson."

An older man sauntered toward Cheney. Patting her wallet containing credit and debit cards, Cheney was ready to shop until her money dropped out of her accounts.

"May I help you look for anything in particular?" his question lacked pressure.

Cheney scanned the crowded showroom. "Yes, living room furniture. I want something unique, but contemporary that will look just as fashionable years later, and dining room furniture, depending on the price."

"Of course, follow me," the salesman instructed.

Despite the cluttered appearance, the selection was endless. Cheney purchased a sofa, two high-back chairs, a marble coffee table, and other accessories. *There goes the last of my savings*, she thought. It would be months before she could afford another spree. She limited herself to purchasing three African-American pictures. She had never seen such an extensive selection. It was only after she paid for everything, Cheney realized the pictures portrayed scenes with a small church faded in the background. *Nope, just a coincidence*. She had handpicked the pictures because of their brilliant colors.

"Now, Jim," Cheney addressed the salesman who now seemed like an old friend. "You're sure you'll be able to deliver my order tomorrow evening after four? I'm having a party on Saturday."

He scratched his thinning hairline. "You have my word on it, Miss Reynolds."

"Thank you. Good night."

Streetlights flickered on as Cheney closed the doors to the showroom. She wondered how long she had been in the store. In the parking lot, Parke sat behind the wheel of his Envoy, lazily bobbing his head to music. Watching her, his stare wasn't scary or uncomfortable, but more of a "you're here so I'm here" look like he was part of security.

"Hey, Parke," Jim yelled with a wave of his hands.

"How's it going, Jim? Thanks for the client referral," Parke called back before Jim locked the showroom door.

"This guy is worst than Mrs. Beacon," she mumbled, thinking Parke was some kind of salesman which explained why he was a professional nuisance.

Speaking of which, Cheney hadn't seen the mean old bat of late. Maybe she had broken a leg. Why did seeing Parke trigger thoughts of Mrs. Beacon? *Both are pests* she thought. Still concerned, Cheney decided she would check on her.

"Need a ride home?" Parke hurried out of his vehicle to her. His demeanor was still non-threatening, his voice was gentle, and his appearance was casual and very nice. He was handsome without trying, she admitted. *Wait a minute. Did I just appraise a man?*

"You expect me to say yes and climb in?" Cheney rammed a fist in her side and glared up about five inches at him. "Think again. Are you crazy? I don't really know you well enough to get inside a vehicle with someone who hangs out of a window yelling like a fool. Go away. I know how to get home."

"Never said you didn't," he said coolly, ignoring her insults. As an enticement, Parke jingled his keys. "You know, women have called me softer, more intimate names. I'm only being neighborly." He wiggled his thick brows.

"Ha! You're one step away from stalking me."

Forming a devious smile, Parke mixed it with an innocent expression. Maybe his charm worked on

most women, but she wasn't like most women anymore. Male charm, deceit, and fake love had almost
destroyed her five years ago. *What little she was able
to salvage had made her immune to the opposite sex*, she
thought.

"C'mon, Cheney, surely we can be neighbors and
friends."

"We can, but not tonight. I'm not getting into
that SUV. Bye." Tipping her cap, she dismissed
him. As she began her trek back to Benton Street,
Parke followed at a snail's pace. When two red
lights restricted him, Cheney laughed with glee, but
missed his company even if it was at a distance.

Like a bloodhound, he was back on her trail, until
she entered her house and turned on the lights. Cheney didn't wave her thanks. She didn't want to acknowledge or encourage a man who needed to get a
life. Secretly, his gesture made her feel secure—an
emotion she thought had packed up and moved
away with Larry.

Friday morning, Cheney anxiously awoke as she
dressed for work. The furniture and floor samples
she had purchased would transform her house into a
home, but the anticipation of seeing her family the
next day left her feeling akin to a prisoner granted a
visitor's pass. She hadn't seen them in years, and
after the last series of phone call debacles, she
spared herself further humiliation and mailed invi-
tations instead.

She had to remember that five years ago her family tried to embrace her, but she broke the family
circle. The truth was Cheney wasn't ready to relive

her abortion through explaining why she had needed the distance. At least Imani would be in town and present. *Let the good times roll.*

Unlocking her front door, Cheney thought about Mrs. Beacon, briefly. She glanced at her watch. Unfortunately there *was* time to check on her neighbor before work. Cheney inhaled a fortifying breath and crossed over the imaginary property line. "Why do I even feel obligated to check on the neighborhood terror?" she drilled herself.

Cheney's knuckles froze in mid-air. She was inches away from tapping on Mrs. Beacon's front door when it flung open and bass-pounding music of Janet Jackson filtered outside. Stunned, Cheney stared. *So she is alive and kickin'.*

Mrs. Beacon didn't miss a beat as she bounced from one foot to the other lifting a gray dumbbell weight in one hand.

"Well, what do you want, Heney? You're interrupting my morning workout. I sure hope you won't become a worrisome neighbor."

Taken aback, Cheney threw up her hands. How could a person be so rude? If Cheney was meanspirited, she could knock out Mrs. Beacon's false teeth—if she wore them. Instead, she turned and stormed away. *There goes my good intention.*

CHAPTER 7

"Hey, baby," Malcolm whispered as his soft, wet kisses seduced Hallison into submission.

"You're torturing me," Hallison mumbled, collapsing in his arms.

"No, I'm going to love you."

She had waited long enough. Hallison didn't stop Malcolm as he fumbled with the buttons on her blouse. This moment is what she wanted to experience with him. His touch felt scandalous. Moaning, Hallison didn't want to think anymore.

She was ready. No more holding back. *Eat your heart out, God!*, she shouted as she was . . . she was . . . What was that annoying buzzing in her ear? Her arm disengaged from Malcolm's neck to swat at the pesky insect, but it returned closer and louder. Frustrated, Hallison snatched the first thing closest to her. The noise changed to a familiar voice. Hallison frowned at the interruption. She realized she was dreaming and had picked up the phone. "Mom?" she asked breathless.

"Hali? Is that you? Are you alone?"

She gripped the receiver. "Ah, oh, yeah, I think so. Hi, Mama. I guess I was dreaming."

"I guess I know what about. Remember first Corinthians 6:18: *'He that committeth fornication sinneth against his own body.'* Don't ever forget, sweetie."

Hallison blushed. She was twenty-four years old, gainfully employed, living alone, and busted by her mama. Typical Addison Dinkins—chastened her with a scripture and then sweetened the blow with an endearment. God aside, they sometimes acted like girlfriends.

She heard her mother softly sipping, no doubt drinking her first cup of coffee. Her mother would always begin her day with an hour of prayer, an hour of Bible reading and mediation, and then an hour of making phone calls. Addison's mission was reminding Hallison and the world that Jesus was coming back. She only wished her mother would spare her.

The more Hallison tried to push away, the more Addison pulled her back. She sighed. Breaking the child-parent string meant Hallison finding her own church with her own pastor and friends. She could get preaching from any church. If the man of the cloth didn't preach the Word, Hallison would know it. She knew the difference between right and wrong, and God loved her no matter what. *Do your dirt, girl, and repent. It's that simple.* Hallison grinned. She knew how to get around going to hell.

The members of Addison's prayer group, Saving Souls For Jesus, ranged in age from eight to ninety-seven. Rain or shine, they made daily calls, delivering inspirational messages and reciting scriptures. Without requesting, Hallison was on more than one list.

She wanted to tell her mother she wasn't a baby living under her roof and set of rules, but Hallison knew if she even hinted of insulting and hurting her mother's feelings, Addison Dinkins would hunt her down with a switch and wouldn't care who knew it.

"Hali, what's going on with you?" the voice was compassionate.

She could picture her mother frowning, marring a face resembling a younger Della Reese. Addison was a petite woman standing five-two. Hallison inherited her five-foot-ten height from her dad who stood over six feet.

"Huh?" Hallison knew she couldn't fool her mother, but that wasn't going to stop her from trying. The only child of middle-aged parents, Addison and Harold Dinkins, Hallison attended Sunday school and worship, Monday prayer meeting, Wednesday Bible class, Thursday youth activities, Friday evangelistic services, and anything else when the church doors were opened. When her dad passed away ten years ago, her mother seemed to increase her prayer time with God. Against her will, Hallison found herself on her knees, too.

"What man has you moaning? Thank God you were dreaming." Her mother's voice always was gentle, her interest, genuine.

Sighing, Hallison heard her mother shuffling pages. Odds were Addison was hunting down a scripture to throw at her. Hallison didn't have to wait long.

"Hali, we have to be careful even in our sleep. Satan can plant his seeds at any time and then wait for us to act upon them. St. James chapter 1:15 says, *'When lust hath conceived, it bringth forth sin'*."

"Mother, you're condemning me—"

"No, I'm not, sweetheart. Only God can condemn. I'm just reminding you. I'll never stop being Mama. Now tell me about this captivating young man."

Smiling, Hallison flipped her hair back off her face. Their conversations always began the same way, scriptures before girl talk. "Malcolm Jamieson is a wonderful man. He's a CPA, very handsome, intelligent, and he worships me."

"So, you're his god, huh?"

"Mama!"

"Okay. I'm listening."

"He makes me feel so beautiful, like I'm an Egyptian or African queen. I really like spending time with him, Mama."

"Hmm." Addison wasn't impressed. "Please tell me you didn't meet him at some nightclub."

Hallison and her mother had enjoyed open communication, but this time Hallison needed privacy. Addison would call what Hallison was feeling for Malcolm scandalous. She wouldn't allow herself to be held captive by words interpreted by every person who could read. Hallison would never forget the day she and Malcolm connected. He was the best thing that had ever happened to her.

"No. We met at a minority job fair. I was representing my bank. He and another good-looking black guy were recruiting for their accounting firm. There were about fifty black-owned companies or firms recruiting blacks that were in attendance. I'm surprised he even noticed me. It was packed."

"You're a beautiful daughter who has become a woman. What man wouldn't notice you?" Addison chimed in.

"I'm just glad it was Malcolm. I remember how striking he looked, dressed in a show-stopping, deep-brown pinstripe suit. Mmmm, he made the suit, not the other way around. He watched me throughout the fair."

"He looked that good, and I've never met him?" her mother teased. "Well, that's a safe way to happen upon someone, a professional setting. Church would've been better."

"I never would've found a man like him in the church."

"So, I guess you were watching him, too. I hope you were dressed to the nines."

Starry eyed, Hallison chuckled at her mother's expression. "Mama, it wasn't as if I was watching him so much as I could feel him watching me. His stare held me hostage."

"How long ago was this?"

"Four months."

Addison gasped. "And I'm just now hearing about him? Hali, I thought we were closer than that."

"We are, Ma," she whined. "This is different. I cherish this relationship. Our feelings took me by surprise. Now, Malcolm's the only man I want in my life."

"I see. Four months, and I've never met him."

Checking her alarm clock, Hallison noted the time. Later that evening, she and Malcolm would attend the St. Louis Black Journalists' silent photo auction. She was excited about bidding on black-and-white memorabilia and unusual prints for her apartment.

"Just remember, I trust you, but not the devil. Four months is a long time to hide a special man from your mother."

Closing her eyes, Hallison imagined breathing in Malcolm's Michael Jordan cologne. She loved to watch his thick, black eyebrow lift when he was contemplating a decision.

During the past few months, Malcolm had invited her to his apartment for dinner. Hallison had declined, knowing the heat between them alone would cook more than a meal. She was determined to sleep with Malcolm, just not yet. When Hallison did, she wouldn't feel guilty about it.

Addison must have known where her thoughts were leading because she broke out with a Bible verse. "Baby, just this morning I was meditating on Saint Matthew 16:26 *'For what is a man profited, if he shall gain the whole world, and lose his own soul? Or what shall a man give in exchange for his soul?'* "

"Mama, I'm not selling my so—"

"No man, job, or desire is worth you losing your soul. Why don't you come to church with me tomorrow and bring your exciting young man?"

Irritated, Hallison began picking her teeth with her fingernail. "Mother, God gave me a choice. You can't save me. I have to save myself."

Addison was deadly silent as she digested this information. Her voice softened, sprinkled with sweetness. "Hallison, *'Be not deceived; God is not mocked: for whatsoever a man soweth, that shall he also reap.'* When you get time, read Galatians, the sixth chapter. Be careful what you're sowing out there, baby. Are you ready for the harvest? Remember I love you."

Hallison was long past her churchgoing days. The things she wore, the way she acted, how she talked, and other indulgences would probably make her mother begin a forty-day fast. She even started smoking, because she was big and bad enough. Pastors didn't know everything and Hallison didn't want them trying to dictate her life. That's what happened to her friends, Tavia and David, who fell in love and despite everybody in their business, married and were happy.

Unfortunately guilty tears streamed down Hallison's cheeks. Sometimes she wished she didn't know the scriptures and the consequences of her actions.

"I love you, too, Mama. Just pray for me, okay?"

"I always do."

Hallison hung up, too scared to recapture the erotic dream that previously had her enthralled. "No offense, Lord, but I want Malcolm. You'll just have to understand."

CHAPTER 8

Saturday morning Cheney prayed. If a person counted, *Blessed are the peacemakers* as a prayer. She couldn't remember the rest, but it would have to do because she needed to pull the party off, and act like nothing had separated them five years ago, but this was her family she was trying to fool. Grudge was their middle name, and Payback could be their last.

After dressing in a sleeveless black shirt and multicolored capris, she walked outside to the curb. Standing behind a large tree, she fumbled with ribbons tied to balloons when Parke, clothed in a jogging suit, zoomed by.

"Keep going, keep going, keep going," she chanted as she concentrated on the task in front of her, pretending not to notice him.

Parke glanced over his right shoulder and stopped abruptly. "Cheney? Is that you?"

Ignoring him, Cheney finished looping the ribbons in knots. "Yes, Parke," she answered dryly.

"Wow." He strutted back toward her with his head cocked, doing a slow inspection. "Woman, you clean up real good. I hardly recognized you without the sweats. And you're wearing makeup, too?" He slapped the hands on his hips and stepped back, whispering, "Nice."

A compliment. Cheney hid the unexpected pleasure one word had caused. "Thanks. Funny, my radar picked you up, and I'm getting warning signals to run for my life."

"Smooth, Miss Reynolds, I'm sure there's flattery hidden somewhere in there. Hey, are you going to work or something, and what's with the balloons?"

"I don't have time for Twenty Questions. I'm having a housewarming, so good-bye."

Parke didn't move, frowning, he looked her up and down. "You know, red lipstick brings out your full lips, and you look kinda cute in civilian clothes."

She laughed. "I can't come out and play right now. Go away. I'm already nervous."

"Unbelievable."

"What?"

"When you just laughed, your face glowed. It's not your lipstick. It's definitely your lips."

"Parkay, I've already been romanced by the world's finest, most charming and the biggest lying brotha God ever made, so you can put your sweet words under your shoe and stomp on them." She turned and sped back to her porch just as Mrs. Beacon peeked out her window.

"Cheney!"

She looked over her shoulder.

"A hostile attitude is unbecoming. I'm not your enemy," Parke yelled after her.

She slammed her front door in response.

He was right, Cheney could hear Imani scolding her. Every man was not Cheney's adversary. She would apologize next time she saw Parke. At the moment she was gearing for a reunion in the making. She missed her family.

At noon, Cheney's doorbell chimed. Her heart played volleyball between anticipation and caution. She did one last inspection. Everything was perfect. Cheney raced to the door as she smoothed her hair back into a ponytail. She sniffed to control happy tears. She didn't realize how much she ached to see them.

Cheney opened the door and came face-to-face with a picture-perfect family. Her mind flashed back to when Larry said they would have a family later. She cursed Larry a hundred times for taking away her happy ending, but she'd have a happy ending. *I control my destiny*.

Janae Reynolds Allen was a shorter and a butterscotch version of Cheney. Cradling her one-year-old son, Alex, Janae's lips moved. It might have been a smile. Her husband, Bryce, enfolded their three-year-old daughter Natalie's small hand.

Bryce appeared uncomfortable as he shifted his eyes from his wife to Cheney's shoes to an antique porch light. For some reason, he didn't meet her eyes. *What's his problem?* Cheney wondered. Refocusing, Cheney smiled at her cute little niece and nephew, forcing back anymore flashbacks that would cause her to shut the door and run upstairs sobbing for the child she chose not to have.

"Janae, they're beautiful. Natalie looks just like

me, and Alex favors Rainey," Cheney said, hoping for an olive branch.

"That's what I told her. She didn't even need me," Bryce tried to joke.

" 'Bout time you came home and saw them. Too bad you refused to be here when they were born. I still don't understand what your problem was anyway," Janae snapped in a neutral tone.

"Not now, Jay," Bryce admonished his wife.

Any reply would be weak. Cheney felt guilty she had chosen not to be a mother, and guiltier she wasn't around to witness her sister become one. Stepping back, Cheney allowed her guests carrying wrapped gifts to enter.

Her mother, Gayle Francine Reynolds, who was casually coordinated, tapped her beaded-strapped sandal impatiently, craning her neck over Janae's shoulder to look inside her daughter's home. "Your father couldn't make it. He sends his regards and a very nice gift."

Shoulders slumped, Cheney bowed her head to hide her disappointment. This was not the reception she had expected. *How could he not be here?* She was daddy's little girl. At one time she would talk to him about all the men in her life. That stopped with Larry. Of all the family members who might have knowledge about her abortion, Dr. Roland Jerome Reynolds was the likely candidate.

Gayle air-kissed Cheney's cheeks as she sauntered pass the others into the house, leading the small procession. *I needed physical contact.* Disappointed, Cheney looked away. *I could begin to heal with a hug.*

"Roland is speaking at a medical conference on hormone replacement therapy," her mother added.

That was unusual since her father usually skipped medical conferences, joking he could achieve boredom from reading the journals, so why listen to the verbiage.

Rainey, Cheney's fraternal twin brother, hovered over her by four inches. He was strikingly handsome, muscular, and several shades darker than Cheney. His jet-black curly hair and thick mustache gave him a Hispanic look. Rainey brushed a kiss against her cheek as he stepped into the house. "Hey, Twin."

A touch. Warmth spread throughout her body. Ahhh, she hadn't heard that expression in years; since they were kids. "Hey, Twin." She knew she could count on her brother.

Without turning around, Cheney could feel everyone's eyes staring at her back, even little Natalie's.

Her brother broke the ice. Everything would be all right now. "Welcome to *mi casa*. Feel free to look around and make yourselves at home."

Rainey rubbed his hands together. "All right, you don't have to tell me twice. Where's the food?"

Janae flopped down on Cheney's new teal sofa, cuddling and rocking Alex. She fingered the purple, plum, and yellow accent pillows. "Hmm, flashy colors, I'm surprised since you've always preferred earth-tones." Janae observed, scanning the rooms, then added, "but nice."

Bryce cleared his throat and shook his head, his eyes scolding his wife. That was a clear indication that Cheney had been discussed beforehand, and some type of instructions were given.

She suggested a tour when her doorbell rung. Cheney half-hoped her father had changed his mind. Her heart plummeted as the 'ready-made migraine' stood on her porch, not waiting to be invited inside. Dressed in a long violet linen skirt, a beige short-sleeved knit top, and bone Naturalizer shoes, Mrs. Beacon leaned on her bamboo cane, grinning. Cheney lifted a brow. *Her Stacy Adams must be at the repair shop.*

A black hair net held Mrs. Beacon's silver curls in place. *Please, not the dear, old sweet senior citizen act.* Cheney, with her own two eyes, had seen the woman move like one of Janet Jackson's backup dancers.

Mrs. Beacon tapped Cheney on the leg. "I saw the balloons. Thanks for the invitation. Step aside, Heney, and let an old woman through. Was I suppose to bring a gift?"

The headache started while Cheney held her tongue. As she was about to close the door, Imani made a production of gliding onto Cheney's porch. Her headache vanished. In tote was another girlfriend from high school. The three screamed their greetings, hugging, and grinning. Cheney relaxed. A good time was now guaranteed. She knew Imani was responsible for coercing the woman there. Cheney wouldn't be surprised if Imani paid bribe money because Imani and Cheney only had one class with the woman. It didn't matter. Cheney could use a rent-a-friend at the moment. Imani continued to prove her friendship throughout the years.

"You guys came," Cheney spoke through happy tears at Imani.

"Nothing would've stopped me and when I saw Deb at the mall, she insisted on coming, too."

Deb nodded, and Imani grinned. *Yep, Imani paid her big money.*

"Deb Davidson, I haven't seen you since—"

"Graduation," the threesome said.

"I'm a Matthews now with two adorable boys," Deb corrected Cheney.

Imani grabbed Cheney's hand for support as Cheney blinked. "Well, Mrs. Matthews, you look wonderful with your short self.

The former Debra Davidson stood five-one without the three-inch heels she had on. Her brown eyes and skin tone resembled caramel candy. She struggled with some type of plant that was wrapped in gold-foiled paper.

Mrs. Beacon tapped her cane. "Heney, you going to let those girls in, or is the party moving outside?"

"Who's that?" Imani whispered, lifting a brow.

"Mrs. Beacon," Cheney mouthed back.

Imani snickered. "This oughta be good. This is going to be worth the flight from Australia."

"Who's she?" Deb wanted to know.

"I'm her neighbor," Mrs. Beacon answered.

Cheney rolled her eyes. "C'mon in."

"Be nice," Deb offered.

"She doesn't have to. This is her house," Imani tossed back loud enough for the crazy neighbor to hear. Once inside, Imani's eyes sparkled as she glanced around. "Cheney, this is nice. Your flair for decorating is commendable. The hardwood looks wet and the shutters' stain is a perfect match. Girl, I have to hand it to you, this is your palace."

Setting aside their gifts, Deb greeted Cheney's family, and Imani hugged them. An hour later after touring every room, the gaiety began to dissipate as guests nibbled on sandwiches, fruit, and vegetables. Her friends sighed from Cheney's elaborate renovations, her mother and sister moaned their displeasure, and Natalie didn't want to leave the little girl's bedroom upstairs.

Her mother smacked her lips as she bit into a strawberry cheese cup dessert. "Che, I love the hardwood floors, but why would you pick such loud colors for the furniture? You'll grow tired of that teal sofa. A neutral color would've been better." Her mother lifted her chin in a show of superiority.

Before Cheney could comment, Mrs. Beacon's voice boomed across the room. She had been quietly observing until that moment. "Leading decorators suggest using bright colors liberally as accents when home remodeling because it symbolizes life and emits cheerful energy."

Gayle brushed imaginary dirt from her spotless pants. "Hmm, I see." She glared at Cheney as if she had made the statement.

Imani grinned. Cheney was also amused although she did a double-take at the woman posing as Mrs. Beacon. The woman defended her. *Maybe she's the wicked sister's twin.*

Natalie clapped her hands as Bryce bounced her on his knee. "Ant Che wooks wike my box of crayos."

Everybody chuckled.

Rainey's deep voice broke through the laughter. "Mom, I think the colors blend well." He shrugged. "Personally, I would've built a house from the ground up in one of the newer subdivisions in West County rather than repairing a shack way out here in North County." He crossed his ankle on his knee exposing his wheat nylon socks, which matched his pants.

What is going on? Rainey prided himself for taking up for me since he's the older twin. Maybe he hadn't mel-

lowed out after her phone call. "I was attracted to Old Ferguson's mature trees, well-maintained neighborhoods, and established neighbors." *Minus Mrs. Beacon, of course.* "Plus, I'm close to work."

Janae wrinkled her nose as she lovingly passed her sleeping son to her mother. "The couch is okay. It's the dust from the wood shutters that would drive my allergies crazy. I would've chosen custom-made window treatments."

Imani stood from the couch and walked to the window, fingering the shutters before she peeked outside. "Woo-wee, if this drop-dead gorgeous man is part of the neighborhood, girl, you've got a roommate," Imani purred, lifting them as she twirled around.

"Huh? I haven't met one good-looking guy since I moved here." Cheney gave her friend an odd look as her doorbell sounded.

Cheney's eyes almost popped out of her head when she answered the door. Parke Jamieson, the first, second, or third, stood there wearing a cream collarless shirt, cream pleated cuffed pants with dark brown snakeskin shoes and a matching belt. The soft colors highlighted his summer tan, showing off his well-maintained body, like she cared.

Parke's subtle cologne drifted past Cheney's nose. She stared at him like she'd never seen him before. Handsome minus the arrogance and he could be charming.

"Look, Parke if it's about the comment I made earlier, You're right. You aren't my enemy. I'm sorry," Cheney apologized.

Methodically, he removed his dark shades, grinning like a model on a photo shoot with a dash of innocence brushed on. His teeth were beautiful. *What's up his sleeve?* Cheney wondered.

"You gonna invite the young man inside to join us, or cool the outside with the door standing open?" Mrs. Beacon shouted, scooting across the floor with her cane on her way to Cheney's kitchen as if the woman was at home.

Losing her patience, Cheney groaned as an old movie came to mind. If Danny Devito could *Throw Mama from the Train*, surely she could get rid of Mrs. Beacon. She looked back at Parke. "I said, I was sorry," she repeated through clenched teeth.

Parke stood erect with his legs spread as if he was assessing a situation. He was taking his own sweet time to answer. "Accepted. May I come in?"

"Parke, this is not a good time. I'm having a party," she whispered, annoyed. "If you're coming to crash the party, you're too late. It's already been crashed."

Parke's smile and scent must have put Imani and Deb under hypnosis as they breezed by her, itching to welcome the stranger into her house. Cheney was seconds away from informing him this was a private party, but it was too late, Imani had him inside and was shutting the door behind him. *Did Deb forget she was Mrs. Matthews?* Cheney rolled her eyes.

Eyes followed Parke as he looked around, nodding appreciatively at Cheney's furnishings. "The place looks great."

Deb and Imani watched him, smiling ridiculously and flirting outrageously. What would Mr. Matthews say?

"Everybody, this is Parke. He lives somewhere in the neighborhood. Parke, this is my family. My sister Janae and her husband Bryce. These are their children Alex and Natalie. Finally, this is my mother, Mrs. Reynolds and my twin brother, Rainey."

"Twin?" Parke asked.

"Twin," Cheney repeated.

Nodding, Parke smiled. Imani and Deb cleared their throats. *Help yourself to him.* What good-looking men like Parke subjected women to wasn't any of Cheney's business. "These are my friends, Mrs. Deb Matthews and Imani, and my neighbor Mrs. Beacon."

Skipping up to Cheney, Natalie patted her leg. "Ant Che, can I play with your dollies upstairs?"

Cheney bent down and smoothed back Natalie's thick curly bangs. "No, sweetie. Those aren't for you."

Natalie started building into a fit of tears, pouting. Janae moved quickly to console her daughter and confront her sister. "Why can't she play with them? Who are you saving them for? You don't even have kids."

Gayle stopped sipping her raspberry smoothie and stood. "Yes, Cheney, why are those rooms decorated like that?" She folded her arms in a challenge. "Is there anything you want to tell us?"

Was her mother purposely baiting her? Did she know? Conversations ceased. Why did she feel like battle lines were being drawn? What did her family want from her, a confession? She looked around the room.

Imani frowned, letting Cheney know, *just say the word.* No one else knew about the abortion except Imani. Knowing Imani, she was not only the mistress of sealed lips, but the master of causing a major diversion. Deb, ignorant to the undercurrent, started to fidget, looking ready to bolt any minute, but only Parke's presence kept her there.

Mrs. Beacon's expression remained unreadable, but knowing her neighbor, she was cooking up something, too. Cheney could sense it.

"Cheney," Imani called out as she crossed her long legs in a slow, over-dramatized manner, glancing in Parke's direction. "This is a good time to open your gifts, girlfriend."

A diversion, Imani, not flirtation. Could her girl think of something else? Cheney guessed not.

Parke seemed oblivious until his deep voice sliced through the air from across the room. With ease, he answered in a gentle, non-threatening way, "I'm sure your rooms are displayed like many of ours around here as if they're livable for the upcoming block house tour."

What house tour? Cheney nodded, and played along like she knew what the man was talking about. Did Parke just come to her rescue and did his voice drop an octave and sound huskier than normal? Who was flirting with whom?

"We don't—" Mrs. Beacon began.

Parke and Cheney cut her a look.

The older woman wiggled in her seat. "Well, ain't nobody comin' up in my house."

Cheney collapsed in one of six chairs at her dining table, hoping for the cease-fire reprieve.

"Back to the gifts. I hope you like this peace lily. The plant would look nice beside the couch or really thrive in one of your bay windows," Deb suggested.

Standing, Cheney hugged her friend with all her

might. "Thank you, short-stuff. I'll try and remember to water it."

"She'll kill it," her mother stated.

"That's my line," Mrs. Beacon snarled at Gayle Reynolds.

Everyone except Cheney gave Mrs. Beacon a puzzled look.

Imani went near the front door and lifted a large silver wicker basket from the floor. Cheney barely noticed it when Imani had set it aside when she first came. In typical Imani fashion, she made a big production of standing. Swaying her hips, she walked passed Parke to Cheney. "Indulge yourself in calming lavender aromatherapy. It should help relieve everyday stress." Imani tilted her head toward Cheney's sister and mother.

Cheney fingered bottles of lavender, Hawaiian musk, peach, jasmine, and pear body oils and sprays. She sniffed the oatmeal and almond, strawberry shortcake, and rose petal body washes. She hadn't pampered herself in years.

"It's perfect," Cheney said as they air kissed each other.

Flaunting a smile a little too sexy, Imani waved manicured nails. "Girl, it's nothing. Just make sure you use every drop of it." She winked then kept on winking.

"I will," Cheney assured her.

Reaching for a plum gift-wrapped box, Imani handed it to Cheney. "This looks pretty. Open it."

After reading her mother's signature on the card, Cheney ripped off the paper. "Wow, a music box that plays lullabies. It's beautiful. Thank you, Mom."

Cheney masked the shock of the musical selection. Why lullabies and not musicals or soundtracks?

Gayle smiled. "Roland and I chose it together."

Daddy. Cheney swallowed to wash down the hurt from her father's absence. Imani passed a gift bearing more tape than wrapping paper. She recognized her brother's handiwork. Cheney carefully unwrapped it.

"It's beautiful, Rainey. Thank you."

"Yeah, it's a genuine *Lladro*. I know you don't have any kids, but the woman looked so much like you, I had to get it. Maybe one day. "

Maybe. The piece was a young mother cradling a baby with a toddler sitting at her feet. First her mother's gift, now Rainey's. Were they taunting her? Did they know? Choking back tears, Cheney stood on her toes and embraced her linebacker-sized brother. "Thank you, Twin."

"Welcome, Twin."

Janae clapped her hands, interrupting the tranquil moment. "Okay, open my gift," she demanded, urging Imani to pass Cheney a long silver box. Janae waited as Cheney uncovered four bright white monogrammed hand towels. "When, or if you marry, you can add his first name."

"Thanks, Sis," Cheney said, slightly leaning in towards her sister, but Janae folded her arms, preventing a hug.

The rejection sparked a major headache for Cheney that began moving like a nonstop locomotive. She had pushed them away, now they were shunning her big time. Parke distracted her when he handed Imani an envelope, and Mrs. Beacon did the same.

Recovering from the shock of her uninvited guests at her front door, Cheney hadn't noticed anything in their hands.

"Here are two more," Imani advised, passing them on.

Cheney pulled the Mahogany card from the envelope Imani gave her. "Welcome to the neighborhood. I hope you find peace of mind and plenty of people who are kind. Then it's a sign you're among the best neighbors. Mrs. Beatrice T. Beacon."

Cheney had taunted the woman by mentioning a housewarming party, but her neighbor had no prior notice it was this day. Waiting for something to crawl out of the card and bite her, Cheney eyed her next door neighbor. When a slip of paper fell out, she laughed. Mrs. Beacon always managed to get the upper hand.

The joke was truly on Cheney as she stared at the paper. Finally she found her voice again, "Thank you for the one hundred dollar gift certificate to Friscilla's Nursery."

When she stood to give a hug, Mrs. Beacon held up her cane to ward Cheney off. Everyone laughed, including Cheney.

"This is from that handsome gentleman in the corner," Imani advised.

Cheney squinted at Parke. What could he have gotten her? Parke also chose a Mahogany card. The African-American woman portrayed on the cover had extremely long lashes like Cheney and wore bright red lipstick. Cheney smiled as she opened the card and read, "You are truly unique, Miss Reynolds. Parke Kokumuo Jamieson VI."

Deb chuckled. "What a mouthful."

Janae thumped on Rainey's back as he gagged on his iced tea. "*Cu cu moe?*"

The first genuine sounds of laughter filled the house, including Natalie, who mimicked the adults. Even Parke looked amused. "It's pronounced *Ko-ku-mu-o.*"

Imani scooped up the two tickets that fell on Cheney's lap. "What's this? Ooh, tickets to see *Bubbling Brown Sugar!*"

Janae smacked her lips together. "That show is sold out."

Gayle waved her hand. "Bryce has been trying to get tickets for months. If you can't find anyone to go with you, why not give your tickets to your sister. They'd enjoy an evening without the children."

Clearing his throat, Parke butted in, "Correction, it's a matinee, and Cheney has a date."

Parke's beeper interrupted the growing argument as Cheney's family shot him an annoyed look. Cheney's mouth dropped open. She didn't know if she was more stunned with her family—their behavior was bordering on hostile—or Parke, who had lied for her again. First Mrs. Beacon, now Parke. The day was turning into an unsolved mystery.

"I do?"

"She does?" Imani questioned.

Reading the message on his pager, Parke stood. "I'll take Cheney," he said with finality. "Excuse me, I have another appointment. It was nice meeting everyone." He stood, strolled to the door, opened it, and left without glancing back.

Fanning her face, Deb sucked in her lips. "Girl, if

you don't go out with him, I'll go." She pointed out the window. "That brother is some kind of fine."

"What about your husband and two kids?" Cheney teased.

"What husband? What crumb snatchers?" Deb played dumb.

Imani positioned her hands on her narrow hips. "Don't waste the tickets, girlfriend."

Gayle gathered her purse and sleepy grandson. "Well, I wouldn't advise going anywhere with him. He seems like trouble. You know, the kind who would love you and leave you. I think you've had enough trouble with men."

She gave Cheney a knowing look and walked to the door. Janae followed, dragging Natalie and Bryce. For the slightest second, Cheney felt her heart stop beating. That wasn't an innuendo Gayle tossed out. It was an affirmation that Cheney's family knew. *How?*

At the moment, it didn't seem to matter. With mixed emotions, Cheney didn't know who made her feel guiltier, God or her family. She didn't yearn for God, so he didn't count, but she hungered and thirsted for her family's attention.

Stretching out on Cheney's brand-new sofa like he belonged there, Rainey made himself comfortable. He picked up a remote and pointed it toward her twenty-seven inch television that rested on a glass and silver stand, that complemented Cheney's center table. If her brother did know about her past, at least he understood it wasn't anybody else's business.

"Rainey, aren't you coming?"

Looking at his watch, he shook his head at Gayle.

"Nah, Mama, I'm going to hang out with Twin for a while."

"I'm sure your father will want to talk to you once he's home from the conference."

Janae interjected, "Remember, Rainey, you wanted to meet my girl, Leah. C'mon. We're all going out to dinner."

Cheney watched as her family spoke in a secret code. Yes, she served finger food, but it was enough, so that no one would leave hungry.

Rainey clicked off the TV, stood, and brushed a kiss against Cheney's cheek. "I'll be back, Twin, when I can leave the naggers at home." He grinned and winked.

Giving a weak smile, Cheney hugged her brother good-bye. When she turned back to her remaining guests, Imani and Deb were examining the theater tickets and Mrs. Beacon was inspecting Cheney's shutters.

Imani ran her fingers through her salon-set curls. "You sure you aren't a stepchild? At least they gave nice gifts before PMS kicked in. Remind me not to stop by the same time next month. Forget them, how about going clubbing with Deb and me later?"

"I'll pass. I'm drained."

Mrs. Beacon made her presence known. "I'm drained, and I'm not that old. Don't worry about them. You'll always have me." She grinned like she was showing off a new set of dentures.

Cheney didn't really know what to expect at her housewarming, but that drama wasn't it. Maybe moving back to her hometown wasn't a good idea. They acted as if they could barely tolerate her.

Imani and Deb collected their purses to leave. Both encouraged her to go see the sold-out play with the fine-looking brother to lift her spirits. "If not," Deb joked, "Give the tickets to Imani to make a love connection."

Imani kissed Cheney's cheek. "I wish. You know I don't pass up having a good time. Anyway, I have to fly out in the morning then I'm out of the country for the next three weeks, but we'll talk tonight and compare notes on today."

Cheney chuckled as they nodded to her neighbor. Imani had her hand on Cheney's door knob when she whirled around. "The hypocrite in me is coming out. Let's just say a quick prayer. Cheney shrugged okay. Deb nodded.

Mrs. Beacon remained rooted to her seat. "Don't look at me."

The trio bowed their heads.

"God, we know you have the solution. Please help my friend to find it," Imani said amen and the others followed, except Mrs. Beacon.

They left but, her next door neighbor looked as if she had no intention of leaving any time soon. As Cheney flopped down in the matching chair to her sofa, she braced herself for her neighbor's whiplash of words. Instead, Mrs. Beacon sprang to her feet, announcing she was going home. *What a strange person*, Cheney thought.

As the old woman wobbled to the door, she turned abruptly, almost scaring Cheney. She locked Cheney in a bear hug with the strength she must've gained from her morning workouts.

"You've done a good job, Cheney."

Cheney's eyes widened, registering her shock at the compliment. "What? No Heney?"

"Nah, not after meeting the weirdos you call a family. And call me Grandma BB. You're going to need me to watch your back."

CHAPTER 9

Malcolm tapped on Hallison's door, dressed in a black Christian Dior custom-tailored tuxedo for the night's silent auction. His heart pounded faster, not from his nerves, but from the anticipation of seeing Hallison's soft features again. She always stirred him up.

Hallison opened it, wearing a gold-metallic lace and sequin dress. Her hair was swept to the top with stray curls falling to her shoulders. That meant he would plant kisses on her irresistible neck throughout the night, causing her lids to flutter and moans to escape.

Shimmers dusted her face and neck. *She is really trying to give me a heart attack*, he thought. *She's gorgeous*. His eyes descended to the dress' fringed hem. Acrylic high heels showed off her shimmering gold pedicure.

"Can I touch you?"

Watching his assessment of her, Hallison tilted her head yes.

Under hooded lids, Malcolm brought the inside of her hand to his lips. He repeated the ritual on her other hand, her chin, and her neck. The worship was done methodically as he knelt and lifted her foot to kiss her ankle.

The submission unbearable, Hallison draped her matching fringed shawl around Malcolm's neck, drawing him to stand. "You're possessing me."

Her breathy admission forced Malcolm to smear her lipstick. Afterward, he held her chin. "And you possess my heart, my thoughts, all my days and nights."

Taking her key, Malcolm locked the door before leading her to his Monte Carlo. "C'mon, baby. I'm looking forward to spending every moment tonight smelling, looking at, and tasting you."

The seduction continued inside his car. Malcolm slipped in his CD with love ballads by Freddie Jackson, Brian McKnight, and Luther Vandross. Content, he played with her fingers, returning to the ring finger.

If Hallison was his cat, she would've meowed. Malcolm was sure of it as she snuggled into his leather seats, inhaling. Her face's blissful expression was evidence of her happiness.

When they arrived at their destination, Hallison was quiet. Shutting off the engine, Malcolm turned in his seat at the same time a valet from Tony's Restaurant approached Hallison's door. Malcolm couldn't keep from touching her. He twisted his finger around a curl. "Open your eyes."

Obeying his command, he edged closer to her lips. "I want your attention all night. I don't want you to focus on anything or anybody tonight except me, just me. I want us to get so wrapped up and tangled up together that it will be impossible to let go."

Reaching over, Hallison smoothed his beard. "Malcolm, I'm so wrapped up in you now that I can't help myself."

Malcolm escorted her to one of the restaurant's largest banquet rooms. The annual event not only showcased the best photographs taken by local black journalists, it also served as a fundraiser for several underprivileged children's programs. As the night progressed, Malcolm cherished Hallison with stares, touches, and soft kisses to her neck as promised.

"How can I concentrate when you're distracting me, Hali?"

She smiled. "You've got to be kiddin.' I'm bidding and you're kissing *me*." She jerked her head around when the auctioneer described a black-and-white print of three kids waving from an ascending hot air balloon. "Stop it, Malcolm. I want that picture."

The bidding war began with Hallison and others sitting at three different tables. In the end, the twenty-by-sixteen picture's price tag had climbed to five hundred dollars. Hallison shook her hand, sighing with disappointment.

Before the auctioneer could finish saying, going twice, Malcolm purchased it for seven hundred dollars. "The sky is the limit for you."

"Malcolm, you can't buy nor can I accept such an expensive gift from you."

He winked. "Watch me buy and you accept."

* * *

Parke thought he had it all figured out. He would trade in his BankOne shares if Chency was seeing anyone. Where was the guy? After the fiasco he witnessed earlier at her housewarming, he couldn't stop thinking about her. *Whew! What a circus.*

That would explain her do-it-yourself attitude. She tried too hard to give the appearance of independence. Today, he saw the telltale signs of a yearning. He contributed his interest in Cheney's house to neighborhood pride. As unattractive as she was to him, something about her had caught Parke's attention. It was weird because he couldn't shake the feeling. He figured it had to be her lipstick.

As was customary, when he first met a woman, he wondered about her ancestry and if her bloodline included a royal African tribe. Parke wouldn't be surprised if Cheney was a direct descendant of Amina, the queen of Zaria, Nigeria. In the sixteenth century, Amina began running the country when she was sixteen. She had learned military skills from warriors and fought battles to protect her people during the thirty-four years she reigned. Historians labeled her "a woman as capable as a man." Cheney was just as capable.

What made Parke think about the Nigerian queen? Dismissing any possible connection, he reflected on the housewarming again. It was anything but warm and cozy. He was saved by the bell—or beeper. Parke's family gatherings, on the other hand, sparked instant camaraderie. They were too busy matching wits in games and conversations to waste time with snobbish remarks.

And what was the deal with her girlfriends? he wondered, steering his Envoy toward the city. Imani—

or was it Deb who was the short, caramel delight who had popped her contact winking at him? "Nope, it was definitely Imani. She had the best looking pair of legs he had ever seen on a white woman." He chuckled. "A white woman with a black name." He wondered what the story behind that was.

He looked down at the text message again. *I need investment advice for my mother. Can we meet at my place, say in about an hour? Dinner and dessert will be served, Roslyn.*

Later, Parke sat in Roslyn's Central West End town house, witnessing another woman's attempt at seduction. His mind drifted back to Benton Street. Cheney was pretty enough, but her height almost matched his. *Did I just say she was pretty? I did utter that word. Have I lost my mind?* No, his mind must be slipping. He preferred petite women in tall heels, tight jeans, and long lashes. Cheney's lashes were incredible.

For the rest of the evening, Parke couldn't dismiss Cheney's image from his head. It was like he was playing a game of spades and her face was on every card. He had a nagging urge to see if she recovered from her house-chill party.

Parke went into Roslyn's bathroom and used his cell phone to call his pager. He flushed the toilet without using it, and washed his hands. When he opened the door, his beeper sounded as planned. Faking annoyance, he snatched it off his belt and glanced at the blank screen. "Ros, I'm sorry, but I need to go."

She pouted. "Parke, I was hoping we could relax,

take our time and get to know each other while you go over my portfolio."

"You said it was for your mother." Parke was getting tired of these same old games that even he played.

"Yes, I mean my mom's."

"I'll take the portfolio with me and get back to you." With that statement, he picked up the folder, grabbed his keys, and left.

Thirty minutes later after driving from the Central West End to North County, Parke parked his SUV. He almost jogged to Cheney's front door and pressed the bell. He turned to leave when her door cracked open. Without trying, she looked a wreck. Worse than the first day he had cushioned her from a nasty fall. *What had happened after I left?* he wondered.

"Parke? What are you doing here? My party was over hours ago."

The sadness in Cheney's voice tugged at his heart. The puffiness under her eyes did not become her—she had been crying. Oh man, he hated when a woman cried.

Squeezing his lips, Parke looked away to gather his thoughts then met her stare. "I thought I'd come back and check on you."

"Why?"

Why? Wasn't it obvious? Yet, Parke was at a loss for words. "Well, well, uh," he stuttered, never having to give any woman a reason to visit.

Sniffing, Cheney seemed to gather her strength to give him the black woman's attitude thing—the hands on her hips, neck rolling, and nostrils flaring.

"Look, I appreciate the tickets to the play, but I can't go. I'll give them back so you can enjoy them with someone else."

Beautiful eyebrows, lashes, and her feisty spirit enchanted Parke. He wanted Cheney to like him. Parke folded his arms. "Are you returning the other gifts?"

"No."

"Then, why insult me and return mine?"

"Look, I don't know what you're after, but I'm not interested."

Didn't she know black men didn't handle rejection well? Before he could stop himself, the words slipped out. "I'm not after you. I was just trying to be friendly. I've got so many women chasing me, I could print a phone book." Parke could've slapped himself for taunting her.

Cocking her head to the side, the resilient Cheney Reynolds bounced back. *Ah, let the battles begin.* Cheney was two seconds from going off on him, so why was he smiling?

"Let me introduce myself. I'm the new millennium woman." Fiery darts flashed from her eyes. "I'm realistic enough to know not every woman will marry." Cheney pointed to herself. "I'm one of them because I'm too intelligent, confident, and independent—"

"And you're kinda pretty."

"Parke, we're in the middle of a disagreement. You aren't suppose to contradict the situation." Cheney puffed out her cheeks like she was about to blow up a balloon then clenched her teeth. "Look, men like you see beauty in women of other races before you'll appreciate the richness of brown beauties.

"I don't understand that, but I accepted that fact a long time ago, and sometimes it's best to be without a man than have a husband who is cheating on you with other men. In the past, we only had to worry about other women. Today, sisters are also competing with other men. Black women are the fastest growing group infected with HIV/AIDS because often our men fall short."

Parke held up his hands in confusion. "Whoa, how did we get from going to see *Bubbling Brown Sugar* to sisters with AIDS?"

Taking a deep breath, Cheney ran out of her steam. "The bottom line is—" Cheney shook her head, chuckling. "I can't remember my argument."

"You wouldn't make a good lawyer." Tickled, Parke laughed so loud, Mrs. Beacon's porch light flickered off and on.

"It's been a long day, and I had to vent, and you did knock on my door."

Annette had once told him that women were emotional beings, and when they were upset, to get ready. Women could reach way back into their memory from decades ago. True to Annette's words, Cheney seemed to be yanking stuff from across the world. He better walk softly around Cheney.

"That's the second time I've been in the line of your cross-firing, Miss Reynolds."

"I'm sorry, for the second time today, Mr. Jamieson."

Getting comfortable, Parke leaned against the

door jam. "I'm curious, and you have the right not to answer, but I'll ask it anyway. Who is he?"

"Who?"

"The man who hurt you, Cheney? Was it your dad? It can't be your brother. You two seemed to get along. Maybe an old boyfriend or an ex-husband?" he pried.

"All of the above except there never was a husband."

"Let me make a difference." *What was he saying?* Roslyn must have spiked his drink.

"I don't need a hero, Parke."

"Too bad, because I'm a warrior. I'll make a great friend."

"Or pest."

"Feisty and headstrong women have never been a problem for me. Accept the play next weekend as a peace offering."

Wearily, Cheney spoke slower and calmer this time. "Question."

Parke tilted his head. He liked sparring with her. "Answer."

"Were you lying about the block house tour? I didn't know anything about it."

"Yes. I believe in diffusing potential volatile situations and the bomb was ticking during your party earlier."

"How embarrassing. How can I say thank you?"

"Next Saturday at two."

Cheney folded her arms and grunted. "I should've seen it coming, Parkay."

"So do we have a date?"

"No, I'm not going on a date with you." Her eyes took on a far-away look before she bowed her head.

"This is not a date. I just want to have a good time without a woman wanting my body."

A whooping laugh split the air. They turned to see Mrs. Beacon on her porch holding her stomach, chuckling. "Cheney, go out with the man so I can stop eavesdropping and go to bed."

"I have a better idea, Mrs. Beacon. Why don't you go with him?" Cheney stated.

"Chile, don't think I won't. I'm not too old to want his body."

"I must be dreaming, and you two have invaded my sleep. Good night." Cheney shut the door and turned her deadbolt lock.

Amused and not offended, Parke remained rooted in the same spot, fingering the contents in his pants pocket, thinking that Cheney was as complex as she was tall.

"Psst."

Jerking his head around, Parke tried to follow the faint sound.

"Psst." The sound grew louder and more forceful. "Look, Parkie, I know your hearing is better than mine, so step over here."

His long legs reached her porch in seconds. Parke grinned as he looked down at the petite older woman. He imagined she was something else in her day. "Yes. Mrs. Beacon?"

She gripped his arm, and forced him down closer to her face. "Yeah, you can call me that for now. Look, I'll get to the point. I'm glad you checked on her. Poor thing, her family came lookin' to pick a fight."

Shivering, he admitted, "I felt it too."

Mrs. Beacon patted his hand. "Ah, don't get too comfortable. I like Heney—my pet name for her, and I've got her back. I pack more than what you see, and I know how to use it."

CHAPTER 10

Cheney woke Sunday morning, surprisingly re-
freshed. Parke's return visit the previous night
probably kept her from crying herself to sleep, and
she didn't know what to think about her next door
neighbor. "There must be two women who live next
door—Grandma BB and Mrs. Beacon," she spoke
out loud.

Only Imani understood Cheney's disappointment
at the party the previous day, and their chat late last
night only proved the extent of her friend's uncon-
ditional love. It was the one thing she hadn't felt
from her family or God. Cheney had waited so long
for some type of closure and had such high hopes
for reconciliation, but the party was a debacle. Cheney realized she had prayed a useless prayer.

*"Take the gifts away and my family might as well hate
me."*

"Give it time, Cheney. You've been away five years,"
Imani tried to comfort her friend over the phone.

"I think they know." Cheney sniffed.

"Doesn't matter, it's over. That's your body and your business."

"I know, but I've worked so hard on the house. I wanted everything to be perfect . . ."

"You need to stop working on that house, and work on you. Honey, if you don't stop crying, you'll make me quit the best job I've ever had, and babysit you."

"It's the only job you've ever had, my privileged white friend." They laughed.

"You were privileged, too, a doctor's daughter. It took me years to realize your family was black. I always thought you were white with a tan."

Cheney smiled, thinking about their phone call last night until Imani threatened to send Cheney one of those Gideon Bibles planted in the drawers of the hotel rooms where she stayed. Cheney laughed because Imani would curse someone out then say her prayers at night. Yes, Imani was a certified hypocrite.

Cheney didn't want to stay home and mope after yesterday's housewarming disaster. She remembered grabbing a brochure about a Ferguson walking tour. After putting on a short-sleeve bright mango wrap shirt, printed cotton pants, and white tennis shoes, Cheney slapped on a white baseball cap to shield her head from the sun. In her kitchen, she poured a cup of orange juice, dropped a frozen waffle in the toaster, and munched on a few grapes. After eating, she straightened the kitchen and walked out her door.

"A stroll would be nice," she said to anyone who could hear within a yard of her.

Ringing church bells echoed throughout the neighborhood, announcing Sunday service. It beckoned for neighbors to come pray, worship, and praise God. *Enter expectantly, depart triumphantly*, she mused. The beckoning was for folks who followed Christ. Cheney ignored the summons. She had followed Larry instead of her heart.

Church was a building she hadn't stepped inside since recovering from her surgery five years ago. How could she? Cheney Reynolds was guilty of destroying a life God had created—she made a stupid choice fooling around with a stupid man. Church wasn't an option. Shuddering at her own condemnation, Cheney preceded to the corner of Elizabeth Avenue.

The young money-hungry doctor who performed her abortion had perforated her uterus and damaged her bowel. At least, that's what a doctor at Duke University Hospital had told her in recovery.

Cheney clutched her fist as she walked, seeing nothing, but painful memories. *I lost so much blood.* She would never forget that pulsating pain the doctor associated with hemorrhagic shock. The chills, the steady vomiting, and the tubes were the most frightening experience. *Why couldn't I have died in that hospital bed?*

Because you have a purpose, a voice answered, but when she turned around nobody was there.

Despite the warm sun, Cheney trembled. Tears streamed down her cheeks as she remembered. The walking tour was briefly forgotten as she edged along down the street, dazed. After a while, Cheney realized she had no idea if she was still on the tour path or how long she had been walking.

Cheney read the street sign on the corner—Darst and North Clay. She pulled out the folded brochure from her pocket to see if any historic houses were on the block. As she crossed the street, she heard a voice again this time yelling, "Cheney. Cheney, over here."

Cheney whirled around and through blurred vision saw a tall, muscular guy wearing a raggedy muscle man T-shirt and shorts that barely hid what God had given him. She squinted, trying to recognize the half-naked man, her mind too jumbled to focus. She didn't know if she should stand there and wait, or take off running.

The latter made more sense. Cheney broke into a marathon run. She could hear her attacker gaining speed. If she looked back, it would only slow her down.

"Cheney," the man shouted, "if you run any faster, you just might kill me and win the race."

The voice was familiar. Cheney stopped, turned around, and put a hand on her hip, ignoring her racing heart. "What is wrong with you? Why were you chasing me like a crazy man?"

Winded, Parke collapsed against a large tree, bracing his hands on his knees. "Me? Why were you running like a crazy woman?"

She pointed her finger. "I didn't know who you were, running up to me half dressed!"

"Did I not call your name? It's not like you've never seen me before. What are you doing on my street anyway? Taking the Old Ferguson walking tour?"

Cheney gave him an incredulous look. "Your street? You mean you do actually live in the neighborhood? Right now, I have no idea where I am."

Wiggling his brows, Parke gave a sly grin. "I can guide you on the tour of the east and west part of the neighborhood. I know it like the back of my hand."

Scrunching up her nose, she eyed him from head to toe. "I'm not walking anywhere with you dressed like that."

"What's the problem? You're wearing orange, I'm wearing orange. I think we match."

Her previous melancholy forgotten, Cheney lifted her shoulder and folded her arms. She was about to open her mouth just as a lime-colored Volkswagen Beetle honked its horn and the driver waved at Parke. He flexed his muscle at the pretty female driver like he was a contestant in a national body builder competition. Cheney shook her head in disgust.

"Ah, hello? Parkay, correction, I'm wearing clothes. You're showcasing body parts." Cheney gave him a salute and did an about-face. "Good-bye."

"Hold on." Parke grasped Cheney's arm and held it firmly in place. "I'll change. C'mon, I'm a better tour guide than that brochure anyway," Parke stated, mischief sparkling in his eyes.

Fighting back a smile, Cheney conceded. "Okay, but I bore easily, and if you become a drag, I may not know the neighborhood like you, but I'll leave you and walk home."

"Deal."

After strolling down a long block, Parke stopped her. "Here we are," Parke said, sweeping his arm in the air like he was announcing "The Greatest Show in the World."

Shocked, Cheney looked up at the three-story dark gray house, almost the color of a mouse. "Wow, Parke. This is very nice. I'm impressed."

"Thanks. What you've done to your house is pretty impressive too. I like it. C'mon inside."

"I'm not coming inside with you. How do I know you're not like Maury Travis?"

"Who?"

Cheney cocked her head to the side. "C'mon, don't tell me you haven't read the paper or watched television. The scavenger lived somewhere in Ferguson, leading a double life. He was normal by day—a good neighbor, boyfriend, and worker. But at night, he tortured, raped, and murdered prostitutes right in his own home."

His mouth twisted as he contemplated what Cheney said. Evidently Parke saw her point of view then he scratched his curly black hair. "Yeah, you can't be too careful these days. No telling what you may try to do to my body. Give me fifteen minutes to shower and change."

Cheney cackled despite her mood. "Make it fourteen, or I'm out of here."

Racing up the stairs into his house, Parke left a trail of his haughty laugh. "Only a black woman would give a black man an ultimatum."

"Humph! Only a black man would give black women heartache," Cheney mumbled, knowing her statement wasn't true, but many sistahs believed it.

While Parke showered, Cheney inspected his lawn. His simple, well-maintained feminine colors of pink geraniums and red petunias mixed nicely with the awe of the home's grandeur. She studied the unique style of the three dormers. "One man, and this entire house," she muttered.

Coming from around the back of the house,

Parke snuck up behind her. "Ah, but not any man, I'm an African prince, and this is my small palace."

Rolling her eyes, Cheney examined Parke up and down. He was dressed in tan khakis and a beige short-sleeved T-shirt. He was always fashionably dressed, casual or business, except for the baby clothes he had been wearing earlier. "Yeah, right, Parkay. C'mon, I'll let you walk with me."

Without thinking, she allowed Parke to loop her arm through his, guiding her to the corner. She ignored Parke's blossoming smile as if he had won a prize or game. Since the first time she met him, Parke always seemed to push her buttons and then acted as her parachute back to normalcy.

Sweeping his arm in the air again, Parke was in his element. He deepened his voice, "The Atwoods were kin to the town's second mayor. They built this fourteen-room mansion in 1910, using walnut lumber from a previous steamboat to construct this Gothic-style house. "

"It looks way bigger than fourteen rooms."

Parke nodded in agreement.

Four doors down, a large three-story white house stood with huge columns at least two stories high. A tall pine tree partially hid a screened-in sun porch on the second level.

"That's different," Cheney pointed.

"Yep, the columns of the portico are remnants of the 1904 St. Louis World's Fair."

The couple finished the block, doubled back, and turned right on Adams Avenue. Parke stopped at the first home on a hilly corner.

"It's amazing how each house is different."

"Yeah, the norm of custom-designed buildings is pretty much gone. Today we have to pay big time to have a house that doesn't look like every other one on the block. That's what drew me to the neighborhood and my house," Parke said, staring.

"I didn't realize third-floor dormers were so popular back then."

"Ah, there's more. See the extra-wide front door? Charles Ferguson had it built in the 1870s to accommodate caskets for family funerals. It's commonly known as the Wake House."

Lifting her eyebrow, Cheney smacked him on the arm. "Get out of here. Are you serious?"

"Impressed, huh?" he teased with a suggestive tone.

"Yeah, with the house, not you."

For the next two hours, Parke steered Cheney up and down streets, giving her more information than she could ever remember.

"This would be a better tour if we could peep inside," Cheney admitted.

"I don't think the present homeowners would appreciate it."

She shrugged. "I would. I'd get some decorating tips."

"I wouldn't change a thing about what you've done to your house, single-handedly mind you."

Cheney's chest swelled from his compliment. Aside from Parke being a typical male, she enjoyed being around him. That thought shocked her.

Staring at a large Queen Anne-style three-story house, Parke rattled off the details. "Note the house's wrap-around veranda and the large corner square bay window with a bay-shaped covered porch on the second floor."

Keyed up, Parke almost left Cheney, rushing ahead, pointing to another dwelling. "Generations of the Crabb family lived here on Hereford for almost eighty years."

After two hours, Cheney was famished, and had enough history. "I'm becoming crabby. It's almost noon, and I'm starving. Thanks for the tour, but I'm heading home."

Shoving both hands into his pockets, Parke twisted his lips. "You're no fun. You've only seen half the tour." His face brightened. "How about we grab something to eat at the Whistle Stop? It's a former train depot that was converted into an ice cream parlor.

"Ah, c'mon, there're almost fifty houses west of there on the tour, including local prominent doctor, George Case. He built his house on Wesley in 1894, for his daughter. A year later, the famous inventor of the barbecue sauce, Louis Maull, bought it."

Fifty more houses. When Cheney looked as if she was going to protest, Parke put his arm around her shoulder like they were old buddies. "My treat."

Cheney stiffened. Parke was becoming a little too comfortable. No man had hugged her shoulders since Larry. *She knew she'd said the day before she needed contact, but she wasn't desperate.* "If you don't get your arm off me, I'll show you everything I've learned in my kickboxing class and then some."

Backing away, Parke held his hands up in surrender. "Whoa, a woman with attitude and skills. That's a deadly combination. C'mon, the Whistle Stop has the best frozen custard and ice cream concretes."

Licking her lips, Cheney gave in. "Okay, you're forcing me, but no more house tours today."

"I doubt if anyone could force you to do anything."

"Hmm," Cheney mumbled. *He just doesn't know.* At one time she thought the same thing too. "I wasn't always strong when it counted, Parke."

"But you're strong now. Whatever circumstances you've faced made you a survivor."

"How do you know that?" She had never met Parke before. How could this man, who didn't know her, believe in her when she was still trying to believe in herself?

"Let's just say our spirits are in tune."

Fifteen minutes later, Cheney and Parke strolled under the Wabash train trestle to Carson Road.

"This is charming, Parke. It looks like a miniature park." And it did. Cheney remembered passing it when she was furniture shopping.

"It's also a historic landmark."

"Figures. What isn't historic or a landmark?"

Parke held her elbow as they headed up the ramp. "Oh, there're plenty of newer businesses and houses. The original Ferguson Station was built during the slave era in 1855." Parke opened the door. "The Whistle Stop bought the building years ago."

"How do you know so much?"

Eyes twinkling, Parke smirked. "I'm a history buff—African, African-American, American, world, local history. You name it, and I probably know something about it. I guess you could say it's part of who I am."

"Well, you can talk all you want as long as I can rest my feet. I can't guarantee I'll listen." She looked around at the one-room eatery. It did resemble an ice cream parlor. Dozens of black square tables, with four chairs posted at each, were scattered about in no particular order. Cheney pointed. "I guess that's the original window where people purchased their tickets. Clever, I like the nostalgia the booth and metal bars bring to the order counter."

Parke motioned with the nod of his head. "See the Western Union Telegraph and Cable office sign?"

"And just think, I moved to Ferguson with no idea it had historic significance."

"You sure you don't want to finish the walking tour?"

"Positive." Cheney used to exercise regularly, but it had been a while since she did that much walking "Now, what do you recommend?"

"They make a mean Italian meatball sandwich."

"Okay, how about you order for me since this is your place."

"I'll share. Let's make it our place," Parke suggested before smiling at the young female attendant. "We'll take two Brakemen, one Tolono, and one Coal Car," he said to the cashier.

"Our Coal Car is the best toasted ravioli I ever tasted. You'll like that," she replied, referring to a St. Louis favorite Italian appetizer of meat and other ingredients wrapped in square pasta.

"Mmm-hmm, I know. Better give us one Grinder, chips, two brownies, and one slice of frozen custard pie," he added.

"Who is going to eat all that?" Cheney gave Parke an incredulous look.

Patting his chest, Parke admitted with little embarrassment, "I am, and if you're nice, I might give you a nibble."

Bumping Parke out of the way, Cheney faced the young girl. "I'd like to order—"

Rubbing his hip, Parke mumbled, "Okay, Miss Brickhouse. I ordered you a Brakeman. It's the Italian meatball with mozzarella cheese baked inside an Italian roll."

Satisfied, Cheney grinned. Waiting for their orders, Parke gave her another tour inside the small parlor. Moving from wall to wall, they viewed photos of the city in its early days. Blacks weren't in them even as porters, as if the race didn't exist.

"Let's eat outside on the train's former deck," Cheney suggested. Within minutes of sitting down, Cheney stared at Parke who was consuming his food as if it was his last meal. "You know, three balanced meals a day would eliminate overkill."

Feigning embarrassment, Parke paused and wiped his mouth. "Oh, sorry, I guess we should pray."

Cheney nodded, although she always said a silent quick prayer before eating. When Parke reached across the table, she assumed, to touch her hand, he surprised her instead. His large hands cupped her wrist. His hold was gentle, almost endearing. She watched him close his eyes. When he did, a content mask seemed to drape his face. Even as he prayed, she continued to watch him.

"God, you know I love you, and I know you love Cheney. Bless us today and bless our food. Amen," he finished. Opening his eyes, he met her stare.

"Why did you pray that way?" Cheney experienced an eerie feeling she couldn't explain.

"I have no idea," he said, shrugging. "But hey, it

couldn't hurt." He laughed and continued where he left off before he caught her staring. "I have always had a hearty appetite. Did anybody ever say there's never a dull moment around you?"

"Believe me, there is nothing exciting about me," she mumbled, still trying to detach herself from the prayer. She took a deep breath and released the sensation.

"I disagree. You are an unusual woman, Cheney Reynolds."

She could tell their conversation was about to change, but she wasn't in the mood for a heart-to-heart, not with a man about another man, and definitely not with Parke. Cheney crunched on a chip. "Yeah, I'm a new millennium woman—" she glanced at her watch, "who has a checkers match in a few hours."

Folding his arms, Parke leaned back in his chair. "Hmm, I never figured you for a checkers girl. Do you play with your neighbor, or are you in some type of new millennium women checkers club?"

Purposely distracted, Cheney watched customers exit the parlor with sundaes, frozen custards, and concretes an ice cream so thick it was like cement. "Neither. Brian and I play twice a week."

"Can't your boyfriend find anything more stimulating than checkers?"

Men. Gutter mind. "Brian is an eight-year-old, and if we did anything more stimulating over the Internet, I'd be arrested as a pedophile."

He almost choked on his soda. The scene was hilarious. Parke always had a way of making Cheney laugh. It was like he provided doses of healing medicine.

"I know." Cheney chuckled as she tapped the table with her fingernails. "I was surfing the Net one night and found a site for interactive games. After playing three tic-tac-toe games against the computer and losing, I opted for a human player. I chose checkers—an intermediate level, of course."

Totally absorbed, Parke listened with fascination.

"Anyway, my partner and I matched wits for a few hours, brainstorming each move. At the end of the game, we agreed to play again at a set time every week. Soon after that, my partner started asking me personal questions like my name, if I had any kids, was I married," Cheney sipped her Coke. "That scared me a little."

"You, scared, Queen Amina? I don't believe it."

Cheney ignored his reference to her as a queen. She wasn't foolish enough to think of herself as extraordinary anymore. *Cheney, you're so special to me. When we plan for a baby, I want everything to be just as special as you are.* For once, the flashback of Larry's words didn't pierce her heart, so she continued explaining, "I didn't know what kind of sick person I was possibly dealing with—a stalker or a rapist. I never inquired about anything personal nor did my partner ever offer."

"How did you find out you were playing against a kid?"

"Well," Cheney started, but dissolved into a fit of giggles. "During the middle of one game, which I was winning mind you, he told me his mother was making him get off to go to bed.

"Dumbfounded, I stared at the computer screen. Before Brian signed off, I asked him just how old was he. I'm thinking teenager or a pre-teen at the least. When he replied back that he had just turned eight years-old the previous week, I almost fell out the chair."

Laughing in earnest, Parke joined Cheney, ignoring the tears that escaped. Waving her hand, Cheney unsuccessfully tried to make him stop, but the moment was contagious. She joined him, laughing harder than before. Incredibly, she felt like she was releasing suppressed anger, depression, and pity. "I don't know if I was more relieved or disappointed that I couldn't beat an eight-year-old."

"No one would believe that story, you know."

"It's true. That's why I better head back."

"The new millennium woman plays checkers with an eight-year-old." Parke shook his head. "Who would've guessed? Hey, how about a pineapple concrete to keep us cool while we walk back?"

Standing, Cheney gathered her trash. "Sure. That sounds good. I've been eyeing everybody else's."

"I still can't get over it. Your best friend is an eight year-old."

"Believe it. Friends are hard to come by. Beggars can't be choosey although I'm not desperate. One good friend like Imani is worth more than a bunch of fakes."

After making the purchase, Parke relayed stories about his family nights and the types of games they played. Cheney was going in the opposite direction from her house before she realized Parke had slyly walked her into another house tour.

CHAPTER 11

A few evenings later, Cheney drove from work thinking about her family. The housewarming proved her relationship with her mother and sister was beyond repair, but she felt hope with her brother. She made up her mind to call him when she got home, hoping that the work order she requested on his phone was complete. She couldn't deal with another party line conversation.

Cheney arrived home to find a note taped to her front door from Mrs. Beacon: *Stop by as soon as you get home, Grandma BB.* "Who will I see today, the crazy Mrs. Stacy Adams or the sweet old lady?" she said out loud. Against better judgment, Cheney strolled across her property line and stepped onto her neighbor's long, spacious porch. She barely touched the doorbell, secretly hoping the woman wouldn't hear it. *Oh well, at least I tried.*

As Cheney turned to leave, Mrs. Beacon cracked the door. *Busted!* A strong fragrance permeated the air. Cheney sniffed; her stomach growled. "Mrs. Beacon—"

"Ah, ah, remember, call me Grandma BB." She wagged a finger from left to right.

"Okay, Grandma BB. Is anything wrong? I got your note."

The woman looped her arm through Cheney's and tugged her into a large marble floor foyer closer to the smell. "Chile, I've been watching out for you since four o'clock to offer you dinner. Now, it's after eight. You must be starvin'. I made homemade beef stew with vegetables from my garden and my special lemonade."

Mistrusting, Cheney froze in her tracks, causing Mrs. Beacon to slightly bounce off her like a rubber band. "Mrs . . . ah, Grandma BB, why would you care if I ate dinner?"

Releasing Cheney's arm, Mrs. Beacon clunked in her oversized shoes to the kitchen, turning off the fire to a boiling pot. Cheney followed and jumped when Mrs. Beacon spun around.

"Because, Cheney, I admire your determination, strength, and humble quietness."

That's the second person to see strength that I didn't know I had. Maybe everything will be okay, Cheney thought as Mrs. Beacon kept talking.

"It's no fault of your own you're genetically linked to those stuck-up people called family, so I adopted you as kin. You'll be grateful later."

Cheney's eyes could've popped out of their sockets. *From one crazy family to another*. She was horrified. Maybe her hearing had faded for a minute because she knew she hadn't heard right. Cheney tapped her chest with her thumb. "Me?"

Dragging her feet to the refrigerator, Mrs. Beacon grabbed a large glass pitcher. "You remind me of myself."

Should I seek professional help now? Cheney's keys slipped to the floor. "Then, I'm in trouble."

The phone rung and Mrs. Beacon glanced at her sunflower wall clock.

Frowning, the woman squeezed her lips together. She seemed to revert back to her Mrs. Beatrice Tilly Beacon mode before picking up the phone as if she knew who was calling. "Hello?" She rolled her eyes before slamming the receiver back on the wall. "You would think she has homework or watching cartoons," she mumbled.

There are strange shenanigans going on in this house, Cheney thought as Mrs. Beacon recovered from the mysterious call, pulling two floral china bowls from the cabinet and began setting the table. She picked up the conversation like she was never interrupted.

"You could learn a lot from me. What you've seen so far is just a farce. Senior citizens have to protect themselves, you know. The toughness is an act to play on people's emotions. Over the age of sixty, we're very vulnerable. I'm not a young woman anymore."

That explains everything, maybe. Cheney plopped down in a bone-colored leather chair at a small glass-top wrought-iron table. She didn't know what to think. Scanning her surroundings, the updated kitchen was decorated in off-white with splashes of bright colors.

"I see we both like pretty colors."

"Darn straight. Your mother didn't know what she was talking about."

Cheney's stomach growled again as if it sensed a feast was minutes away, but she was still curious about Mrs. Beacon's comparison. "I've witnessed you dancing like Janet Jackson. You're in better shape than some twenty-year-olds."

Mrs. Beacon's eyes sparkled at the compliment. "Why, thank you, Cheney. That's our secret. If thugs try to prey on this defenseless old woman, then they got another thing coming—like my fist in their stomach." She demonstrated her quick reflexes. "Or my shoe in their knee. Or—" Mrs. Beacon grinned, "a strong grip and yank down on his family jewels."

The woman was pure comedy. Cheney almost fell out of the chair laughing. "I might learn something from you indeed."

"No doubt about it," Mrs. Beacon said, scooping large chunks of beef tips, peas, carrots, and potatoes out of a pot into Cheney's bowl.

Cheney reached for a hot biscuit. She bowed her head to say a quick silent prayer, but decided to wait on Mrs. Beacon.

"Go on. I ain't got nothing to say." She waved Cheney on before turning her back.

"So, that's why you wear men's shoes, for protection?"

"Of course not, silly. They were Henry's."

Okay. She ain't normal. I hope she didn't drug this stew so she can cut me up in small pieces and eat me like Jeffery Dahmer.

Pouring lemonade into two tall glasses, Mrs. Beacon sat down across the table from Cheney. "Ah, Henry's." She sighed. "Henry and I fell hard for each other when we were young teenagers and married the day I turned eighteen. We were so in love and so happy and did everything together—fishing, cooking, gardening, you name it."

Curiously, Cheney listened, sipping the hot broth from her stew. She enjoy hearing old-time stories and she could tell Mrs. Beacon was itching to tell her one, but Cheney saw no similarities between her and Mrs. Beacon.

"Henry and I were married just shy of fifty years when God snatched him away from me." She closed her eyes, sniffing as if she would cry. "I felt like someone had ripped out my heart." She opened one eye to see if Cheney was watching and pumped up the drama. "That's why I ain't speakin' to God today," Mrs. Beacon confessed with a stern bitterness, sniffing.

"You have children and grandchildren, right?"

"Nope. Never could have any children, but I had Henry. He said we'd baby each other. The lack of children wasn't as important to us like it was for other couples. We had each other. How could a mighty God leave me alone like this? Henry was killed in a hit and run car accident. That was almost twenty years ago, and the driver was never caught. I'll never forget or forgive God for that. I'm determined to be bitter until the end. And when I get on the other side, I'll still be mad."

Cheney trembled at the fierceness in Mrs. Beacon's voice. Although she hated Larry, she didn't want to carry that bitterness her whole life. She changed the topic and asked, "So why does everybody call you Grandma BB if you don't have any kids?"

Staring in a far away place, Mrs. Beacon's eyes watered. Cheney recognized the look as genuine, probably resembling her own when she thought about how she had killed her baby, ripping it away. *"The timing isn't right. Think of this as a mistake, not a baby," Larry had consoled her.* Cheney reached across the table and patted the old woman's hand.

"Years ago, I used to babysit neighborhood children all the time. That's what the little ones would call me. I liked the name so much I insisted all my friends call me that." In a serene manner, Mrs. Beacon placed a soft, small hand on top of Cheney's, smiling. "I don't have anybody now, and with a family like yours, you don't either."

The connection was made. Cheney knew she had found a friend. This woman was a survivor and could teach her how to survive as well. During the rest of the meal, Mrs. Beacon filled Cheney's ears with special moments in the life she shared with Henry.

As the evening slipped into the night, Cheney stood and stretched. She patted her tight stomach. "That was delicious, but I'd better head next door and get ready for bed, Grandma BB."

Disappointment flashed and lingered across the older woman's face. "Okay, but take a look at some pictures of Henry and me first."

Cheney knew Mrs. Beacon was stalling. *Fifty years of marriage? She probably has a library full of pictures.* She would have to spend more time with her eccentric neighbor. "I'm just curious, you don't wear any of Henry's other clothes, do you?"

Chuckling, Mrs. Beacon's face lit up. "No, dear, but that's a thought. Henry was a tall, strong, and very handsome man. Light-skinned like you and wavy hair—he would've been called a mulatto in slavery times. The man had the longest feet I ever did see. I've been trying to fill his shoes ever since he died," Mrs. Beacon said, closing her eyes. "Whew! Chile, enough of that." Mrs. Beacon's nostalgia changed to anger. "God could've let me live out my life with my husband. Yep! God is on my do-not-talk-to list."

Mrs. Beacon won't forgive God and God probably won't forgive me. Cheney shook her head. "C'mon, Grandma BB, show me the pictures so I can go to bed."

Cheney fingered oval antique brass and square crystal frames housed on a massive dark wood mantel. Mrs. Beacon guided her to several large wall portraits, regaling stories about each pose as if they stood in an art gallery. Cheney didn't leave for another hour. It was too late to call Rainey.

CHAPTER 12

"Not another note," Cheney said, groaning. "Grandma BB, you're adding a new definition of becoming a pest." She snatched the yellow legal-size paper off the door.

Are we still on for Bubbling Brown Sugar *this Saturday? I looked up your phone number in the directory. You aren't listed. I called directory assistance and got it, but I won't call since you didn't give it to me personally. I've never had to ask a woman for her number before, so I don't know what to do here. I will accept your calls . . .*

"Ha," Cheney choked out as she balled up the note without looking at his phone number. She rolled her eyes instead. "Then you'll be waiting until Parke Jamieson the hundredth is born."

The rest of the week was uneventful at work and no more notes at home. Twice Cheney thought about Rainey. She didn't have an excuse not to call her brother, Cheney just didn't want to. Her resolve was to let her Friday evening, she knocked on her neighbor's door.

Mrs. Beacon's tired face brightened once she saw Cheney. "About time you came and checked on an old woman." She bowed her head shyly. "I didn't want to bug you. If you've got an appetite, I made meatloaf, mashed potatoes, corn bread, tossed salad, and lima beans."

Cheney chided herself for her earlier thoughts as she licked her lips. "Not only do I have an appetite, but I've got room. Why did you cook so much?"

"I was hoping you liked my beef stew enough to come back."

She engulfed Mrs. Beacon in an endearing hug. "How about I join you for dinner twice a week and I can bring something?"

"No need. Probably can't cook anyway," she teased. "Just come starving, Heney."

"Don't start, Grandma."

Both women laughed as they trekked to the kitchen and talked late into the night.

Saturday morning, Cheney woke and decided to do something nice for Mrs. Beacon just as her phone rang.

"Hello?"

"You weren't going to call me, were you?"

Parke? Cheney stifled a laugh, realizing she'd bested him. He sounded so disappointed and innocent—like a child. He had dropped his voice an octave, but it still was all man. She couldn't pass up the opportunity to take advantage of the situation. "Who's calling? I'm sorry, but I don't accept calls from strange men."

"Very funny, this is Parke. Do you mind if I call?"

She squeezed her lips shut to keep from bursting.

"Yes, I mind. What do you want?" Cheney erupted in laughter.

Sighing, Parke joined in. "Whoa. You had me going there for a moment. Are we still on for the three o'clock show of *Bubbling Brown Sugar*?"

"I never said yes."

"Your lips said no, but your eyes said yes. C'mon, woman. You know we're going to have a good time so dress up and get out."

My heart says yes, too. Maybe, I'm starting to live again.

Parke couldn't explain why he had tricked Cheney into completing the walking tour or suckered her in to attending the play. He had a list of "women in waiting," but he enjoyed Cheney's wit and humor. Parke kinda liked the mixed-up feelings she ignited in him. The more Cheney pushed him away, the harder he tried to pull her closer. She was straightforward and put great effort into offending him instead of impressing him.

"Doesn't she find me attractive and irresistible?" he asked his reflection in the bathroom mirror. What did it matter? Parke wasn't desperate to want more than friendship. He winked at his image before stroking his cheek with a razor. After shaving, he showered.

Leaving the bathroom, Parke stood barefoot in the middle of a room-sized walk-in closet, scanning through shirts and jackets. "Let's see, what do the ladies like? Hmm, black suggests sexy, devastating, and you want me, but Cheney's not my type." As soon as the words spilled from his mouth, he felt like he should've been slapped for lying. Shrugging, he confided to the clothes in his closet, "But she's like a jigsaw with thousands of pieces."

Parke lifted copper-colored linen pants off a hanger. "Yeah, this will make the grandmamas whistle." He selected a matching shirt and an off-white blazer. After dressing, he headed out the door a few minutes later. Parke knew it was a matter of time before he admitted that he was attracted to Cheney.

On time, Parke steered his SUV in front of Cheney's house. "Women always expect men to be on time while they make us wait. No doubt, they're the masters of waiting games." To his surprise, Cheney was dressed—not to flatter—and standing outside talking with her neighbor.

As he approached, Mrs. Beacon raced toward him and kept going, without speaking. She stopped in front of his vehicle and pulled a small notepad from her pocket.

"She's writing down my license plate number?" Parke asked Cheney. He would've laughed if he thought it was a joke. "Is she serious?"

"Yep," Cheney answered nonchalantly.

"What!" Perturbed, he gritted his teeth. *There went my good mood.* No one had ever questioned his integrity before. "Why?"

Mrs. Beacon walked up quietly behind him. "First of all, I own guns and well, every once in a while, I like to use them. Seeing your SUV is equipped with Onstar, I'll just call the police. The car's satellite global positioning system will track you immediately, especially once I report you've abducted my neighbor."

"What!" He couldn't believe the old woman. Cheney turned her head and tried to hide a beautiful smile, but Parke saw it. *Okay, maybe this is a practical joke.*

He decided to play along. "I'm surprised you don't want my finger and footprints."

Craning her neck, Mrs. Beacon challenged Parke's stare as he towered a couple of feet over her. "Don't be silly. Your feet are too big, but I did bring a pad for a thumb print. It'll just take a second."

Her composure slipping, Cheney laughed hysterically. Parke was in shock as Mrs. Beacon finished wiping the black dye off his thumb with a towelette. *She ain't jokin'.* He curled his lips downward in disbelief. "C'mon, before she asks about my dental records," he snidely remarked to Cheney.

Grabbing Cheney's arm, Parke almost dragged her to his Envoy. In the background, he heard Mrs. Beacon's voice fading.

"What's your dentist's name and phone number?"

Mrs. Beacon's mistrust put Parke in an uncommonly foul mood. The play was simply a housewarming gift, tickets he had originally purchased with someone else in mind. He could live without this much humor.

Wounded that Mrs. Beacon would think so little of his character, Parke was silent during the drive downtown. Cheney, however, seemed to be in an exceptionally good spirit as she listened to his Paul Rozmus jazz CD.

The closest available spot was a block away from the Black Repertory Theatre. After Parke parked, he helped Cheney out of his vehicle, still fuming and unforgiving. *At least she could've worn a dress or skirt so I could've seen her legs. She's got more clothes on than a nun. Ever heard of dress to impress?* He guessed not.

Cheney's three-piece pantsuit reminded him of sapphire. A matching embroidered top, nothing to brag about, lay underneath her jacket. As soon as the show was over, Parke would get a real date with a real woman who knew how to dress to entice a real man. *Did the woman not understand him when he told her to dress up?* he fussed inwardly. Forget an elegant dinner sit-down dinner.

Entering the theater's crowded lobby, Parke's eyes met other men's who gave Cheney appreciative stares and smiles. Even women watched her move as if Cheney was a runaway model—an unusual occurrence since he was used to garnishing their admiration. Parke admitted Cheney was pretty when she smiled, which she hardly did until he irritated her.

Bubbling Brown Sugar was entertaining, lively, but too long for Parke. He sat debating whether he should dump Cheney after the play. Once the music started, the songs and dances hypnotized Cheney. She hadn't said another word to him.

A man who boldly admired beautiful women, Parke felt like an idiot sneaking glances at her one-of-a-kind eyebrows. Cheney again wore very little makeup, but he could see where other men would find her lemon-colored skin attractive. Her eyebrows were the focal point on her face. They arched when an attitude was coming, knitted together when she was upset, but when she was at peace, like now, her brows were still, relaxing the look on her face. They were shiny, silky-looking, and naturally beautiful.

When the show ended, Parke latched on to Cheney's hand like she belonged to him. Chency tried to snatch her hand back, but Parke kept it in his strong grip.

"Parke, I know my way back. I'm not going to get lost in the crowd."

"I'm not worried about the crowd. I'm worried about Mrs. Beacon."

Causing a small scene, Cheney abruptly halted in the crowd. "If you don't let go of my hand, you're going to be worrying about me in a minute."

Complying, Parke's fingers opened like a mechanical gadget. He repositioned his hand on her back, guiding them through throngs of people. "How about grabbing a bite at our place, the Whistle Stop?"

"That's your place, Parkay, not mine."

Throwing his head back, laughing at her irritation, Parke wiggled his brows as he helped her into the car. Now he was having a good time. She was fired up.

A half hour later, Parke sat inside the Whistle Stop devouring his Sicilian Express—Italian focaccia bread with salami, roasted red peppers, and provolone cheese. Again, Parke realized he hadn't blessed his food. He looked at Cheney.

She shrugged. "I said a quick one for both of us. This time the blessing was only for the food."

Parke nodded, thinking about that prayer. To this day, he didn't know where those words came from. He cleared his throat. "How about checking out some more houses on the walking tour? It's only six o'clock."

Cheney bit into her Cannonball sundae—a chocolate frozen custard with hot fudge wrapped in a chocolate waffle cone. She closed her eyes, moaning her pleasure before licking her lips. "Give Grandma BB a heart attack because she can't track us? Never."

"Who's Grandma BB?"

"Mrs. Beacon."

"I didn't even know she had children and grandchildren."

"She doesn't." Cheney shook her head anticipating his question. "Don't start."

Parke chuckled. "Okay. Does BB stand for BB gun or real gun?"

"Do you want to find out?"

"Nope."

They ate in silence until Parke cleared his voice. "You're all right, you know that? I actually enjoyed myself with you today."

"Did you doubt that you would?"

"Yeah, I did after your neighbor put me through a criminal background check."

"Admit it. That was funny." Cheney grinned.

"Do you see me laughing?"

Before either could take another bite, an unannounced contest started. Parke was determined to maintain a straight face. Cheney refused to look his way, preferring to survey the floor and her food. When their eyes met, their laughs detonated, echoing throughout the parlor.

Parke composed himself as he stared at Cheney. When she smiled, she seemed to open the doors to his heart. She was something else. He grinned. "So, what are you doing next Thursday after work?"

"Not going on a walking tour, a musical, or anything else with Parke Jamieson, whatever your number."

Laying a hand over his heart, Parke pretended he was hurt. "Whoa, you wound me woman. Since the moment we met, you don't sugarcoat anything, do you? I like that, but if we're going to hang out, you've got to know my number." Parke watched as her beautiful eyebrows worked their magic on him.

"What are you talking about? I didn't ask for your phone number, remember?"

Wiping his mouth, Parke displayed an idiotic grin. "You're sitting with royalty and don't even know it."

Parke could see her challenge rising as Cheney sat straight up in her chair. "I'm sitting with a royal nut, and we both know it."

Their light banter fueled Parke and subconsciously excited him, regardless of Cheney's height and lack of skimpy clothes. He reached over and tapped Cheney's hand.

"No, seriously, it's a love story that was forbidden by law, but not by God," Parke paused, frowning. Something he couldn't explain was happening to him. Every time he was with Cheney, he seemed to mention God more and more. It started after Annette and her group prayed for him. Maybe there was power in prayer, but Parke still hadn't figured out what that had to do with him. He knew now wasn't the time to analyze it.

"Anyway, it not only existed, but flourished. My great-great-great-great-great-great-great-grand-father and great-great-great-great-great-great-great-grandmother fell in love in the late 1700s. It endured during almost a century of slavery through the end of the civil war. Wanna hear about it?"

Twisting her mouth, Cheney cocked her head to the side, and studied Parke's expression. She laid down her napkin. "Sure. You've got a couple of hours before Grandma BB puts out her all-points bulletin. I'm listening."

"Ah, a woman who's focused." Parke smiled mischievously, rubbing his hands together, leaned back in his chair, and recited the history that had been passed down to him. "Paki Kokumuo Jaja was born in December 1770 in Cote d'Ivoire, Africa," Parke said, rolling his tongue to authenticate an African dialect.

"You're supposed to tell me about your family tree, not some made-up fairy tale."

He continued as if she hadn't interrupted, "His name means a 'witness that this one will not die.' He was in the Mande tribe and should've never been captured the fretful day he and his warriors were attacked, severely beaten, and kidnapped. Tribe leaders thought their country was too far west, nestled relatively safe between kingdoms that would later become French or British colonies, known today as Liberia, Guinea, Mali, Burkina, and Ghana, and supposedly untouchable from slave traders." Parke took a deep breath. "FYI, America resettled freed slaves to Liberia from ships leaving New Bedford, Massachusetts about 1821."

"So, that's why former Liberian President, Charles Taylor, felt American troops were obligated to be peacekeepers during the uprising years ago? I didn't know America had any colonies, but I do remember hearing reports that connect him to al-Qaida. He disappeared before he was suppose to go on trial for maiming millions of Africans," Cheney stated in awe.

"Yeah." Parke's appreciation for Cheney's intelligence grew. Finally, he met a woman who was interested in history.

"Wait a minute. Let's go back to slavery exploitation. I didn't think any Africans were safe from the human hunters."

"Not really. Their skin color was the deciding factor, even though millions of Africans had already been captured on the coast off the Indian Ocean, and in the Midwestern countries. They were driven across the Sahara desert and northern Africa like herd."

"Boy, Parke, that's interesting. Too bad none of that stuff is printed in school history books."

"That's why I give lectures, do story time at local libraries, and participate in black cultural events."

"It means a lot to you."

Parke stared into her eyes. "Yes, it's my world."

"It's our world." She tapped her finger on Parke's hand.

His heart raced. He didn't know if it was what she said or did, but there goes his heart again. Parke fanned his face to regain his original concentration. "Paki's ship landed in Maryland, a state known for harsh slave laws. He was automatically separated from his bodyguards and warriors, and sold for a couple hundred dollars. Many slaves prayed they would die, including Paki."

With folded hands, Cheney leaned forward on the table, giving Parke her undivided attention. "How could anyone find love in so much misery?"

"It wasn't easy. Many male slaves refused to marry female slaves owned by the same master because they couldn't bear to see their wives whipped unmercifully when they didn't move fast enough for the overseer. It wasn't uncommon for wives and children to be sold to another plantation to punish the husbands. We know masters and overseers physically violated many women."

Closing her eyes, Cheney tried to re-create the picture Parke was painting.

"But Paki wouldn't have survived without love when he was sold to Jethro Turner, the largest slave owner in Maryland. He had more than one hundred slaves. My great-great-great . . . you know what I mean, was isolated from the other slaves because he refused to submit to orders. He was repeatedly tied to a tree and whipped with cowhide."

"The love story, Parke. Just tell me the love story. You're depressing me."

"Sorry. I'm so used to the story that the bitter details no longer anger me. They empower me. Well, the master had six sons and one daughter, Elaine. She was seventeen years-old and fascinated with the tall, dark-skinned warrior from a country called Africa."

Cheney chuckled. "Uh-oh, I bet she was."

"I understand she was very beautiful. Stop interrupting." Parke's eyes sparkled. "Here comes your love story. Elaine taught Paki how to communicate in English through symbols and signs. As time passed, Elaine became protective of Paki. When she witnessed him tied to a tree and beaten, she ordered him down, and after dark, applied salve to his wounds.

Later, Elaine snuck Paki clothes and food from her dinner table."

"Okay, so they fell in love."

"Yes. It was a love against all odds, risking punishment and death to be together." Parke smiled. "Paki became a fugitive slave when he escaped, taking Elaine with him as they journeyed toward Kansas, a free state, but they decided to settle in Illinois rather than chance crossing another slave territory—Missouri."

Reaching into his back pocket, Parke pulled out a business size laminated card from his wallet. "I actually have a copy of the ad from *The Baltimore Star*. 'FOUR HUNDRED AND FIFTY DOLLARS REWARD—Ran away from subscriber. *Negro man* kidnapped only daughter, Elaine Turner. The said Negro is nearly black, between twenty and twenty-five years old, very good-looking and tall, over six feet and muscular. I hereby forewarn all persons not to harbor or employ the said man or woman at the peril of the law. Reward is for his capture in the state or out, dead or alive. I want my daughter alive.' "

Cheney looked up, confused. "Why do you carry this in your wallet?"

Rubbing his chin, Parke stared in another direction. "Two reasons. First, they described my seventh great-grandfather as good-looking—see any resemblance?"

"Black man, please." She slapped his arm.

"Okay. Second, Paki and Elaine, or Alai as he affectionately called her, were never captured. Both lived to see the end of slavery."

"A hundred years, Parke?"

"Almost. Elaine and Paki were married eighty-two years." Parke twisted his mouth. "What can I say? I'm a descendant of a strong African tribe. Elaine, a white-skinned, green-eyed brunette was willing to live as a slave to be with my great-great-great, etc. You know what I mean."

"I'm sure the old master went ballistic, judging from that ad."

"I read that he did." Parke closed his eyes. "Bits and pieces of what happened have been passed down through the years in Elaine's journal."

"What did she say?"

"Basically, that she was in love with Paki Koku-muo Jaja, Chief Prince of the Diomande Tribe of Africa. She also wrote that Paki was a whole man and not the three-fifths as slavemen were considered under the Maryland Constitution.

"Her father, Jethro, argued that if any white woman marries a black man, she'd become a slave until her husband's death and his grandbabies would be mulattoes, basically born into slavery."

"What did Paki say about her decision?" Cheney asked.

"In his country, she would be his first concubine."

"Unbelievable. Even your ancestors were arrogant."

"Elaine set him straight. She wrote she'd be queen and he wouldn't have time for another woman."

"Good for her. Go girl." Cheney smirked, pounding a fist on the table. "Wow. It's amazing you know your family's history like this."

"Not really. Elaine was smart enough to keep a diary. When she overheard plans to sell Paki, they ran away."

Cheney stole one of Parke's chips and crunched, sending crumbs to the table. Parke grinned. Sometimes, peeks of her feminine charm melted his heart.

"Why do I have the strangest feeling there's more to their story than what you've told me?"

Parke tilted his head. "Ah, so you really are listening. Yes, there's more, Miss Reynolds."

Snapping her finger, Cheney encouraged him to finish. "Then continue Mr. Parke Jamieson, number what again?"

They laughed as they finished off the chips. Parke paused when a dimple winked in her right cheek. *Only one. How unique, like her.*

"I'm number six, but I really should be number ten."

"Finish your story and forget the mathematics."

Parke smirked, sharing more of the story, filling it with twists and turns.

"Humph. Love comes with too much drama."

Parke ogled Cheney's long lashes, silently moaning. *Her eyes are really beautiful.* Parke lifted his finger. "The Jamiesons thrive on drama. My great-great-great-great-great-great-great-grandparents secretly married. Soon Elaine gave birth to a son, thus, continuing Paki's legacy."

Teasingly, Cheney covered her mouth in a mock yawn. "Well, now I know how you got here."

Parke leaned closer. "What's your opinion on seeing a man crying?"

"Are they capable? It seems to me that men lack emotion."

For a quick second, Parke sensed that Cheney was about to open up to him, then she shut down again. The jigsaw puzzle was adding pieces. "Elaine wrote that Paki sobbed uncontrollably as he looked down at his firstborn son's bright yellow face. He lifted the child to his god, mumbling a native blessing, *Dankie, kind aansoek doen*—thank you, the child I hoped for.

"He was named Parker Kokumuo Jamieson and so was the first male born each generation thereafter. Paki cherished his wife and five sons until the day he died, so the Jamiesons keep the story about our heritage alive."

Parke watched strands of Cheney's hair that weren't tucked in her boring ponytail dance with the wind against her flawless face. "Then, in 1867, a few years after slavery was abolished, Paki altered the name. He removed the last 'r' to symbolize the first child removed from slavery. I guess that's why I carry the reward notice. Elaine and Paki were always a step ahead of their racist and hateful society, so I must use my intellect to overcome today's subtle discrimination ploys."

Cheney rested her chin in the palm of her hand. "What a family legacy. You're lucky. I'm surprised Paki and Elaine could trust each other in their environment, living so long under the dreadful codes of slavery without being separated."

Reflective, Parke bit his bottom lip. "Yeah, I know. My mom's side wasn't so lucky. I could only trace it back to 1860, and that's where my great-great-aunt Lettie was promised her freedom if she bore fifteen children."

"Oh my God!"

"It gets worse. She was one of many young *wenches*

advertised in Virginia as good breeding stock. For mere dollars, white men had a chance to impregnate Negro slave women. It added slaves and gave restless young white men something to do."

With sad eyes, Cheney sighed. Parke reached over and touched her hand.

"I have seven great-great-uncles who are brothers with different last names. Their fathers were different overseers, masters, or clients. I located them on the 1880 census because they happened to be living in one place, all unmarried."

"I'm glad I ate before story time. Whew, I've lost my appetite."

"Sorry. My heritage is very important to me. I'm committed to choosing a wife who is not only beautiful, but also not afraid to be strong like you. Plus, she has to appreciate my ancestry."

"Good luck. I'm not getting married."

"Nonsense, you'll meet someone special one day."

Cheney gave a mock laugh. "Already did. Now, let's just say, I'm a recycled lover. I won't be used again."

"Life's a journey with all kind of detours, but I believe our ancestors will lead us."

She looked away, but not before Parke watched her brows knit together and hurt flash across her face.

"Let me ask you a question. Why did you invite me to the Black Repertory Theatre? You could be using your time interviewing for Elaine's position."

"See, that's an easy answer. You're much more exciting than Tracey."

"Who's Tracey?"

"Someone I was going to take to the play."

Gathering her purse, Cheney stood to leave. "You better keep looking, Parke. I am not the one for you."

Boy, don't I know it, Parke thought.

CHAPTER 13

Cheney and Mrs. Beacon, Friday night, one week later . . .

At least three hundred couples, teenagers, and seniors had invaded the ritzy ballroom of the Chase Park Plaza for an annual dance event.

"Reverse," the live disc jockey commanded.

"Reverse."

"How low can you go? All the way to the floor," the dread-locks wearing man taunted the guests.

Some cheered, others bit down on their tongues as they painstakingly followed instructions for the Cha-Cha Slide.

"Let me see you Charlie Brown," the man hyped the crowd.

Cheney watched with amazement as a slightly overweight older Asian man to her right rocked back and forth. His lips puckered as he concentrated to stay in step with everyone else in the line. To his credit, he did a better job than Cheney.

She glanced over her shoulder and saw Mrs. Beacon's long silver ponytail anchored from the top right side of her head, bouncing back and forth as she moved with ease. Her neighbor's gold glittery sweater sparkled every time a strobe light spotted her. Mrs. Beacon's fitted faded jeans matched the denim two-inch sandals.

"Pump it up now, y'all," the deejay shouted.

Laughing, Cheney jumped to stay in step. She was enjoying herself. At first, she couldn't believe she had let Mrs. Beacon talk her into an all night dance-a-thon.

"It's a yearly fundraiser to benefit the Sickle Cell Foundation, Foster Kids of Greater St. Louis, and the Safe House for abused women and children," Mrs. Beacon convinced Cheney to go.

Kids? Since her abortion, Cheney didn't think twice about helping children. She'd do whatever she could to redeem herself. "But all night?" she had quizzed her neighbor. "How can you stay awake until six o'clock in the morning?"

"Geritol and a morning workout with Janet Jackson's "When I Think of You" Video will do the trick."

"All right, but please tell me I won't have to suffer through the fox trot, waltzes, and big band sounds all night."

Mrs. Beacon revealed a toothy grin as she pulled long hairpins out of her mass of curls. "Chile, please. Get ready to rumble," she shouted. "Usually we do a little moon walking, bumpin,' and the old folks have a contest to see who can do the Harlem Shake without fracturing a collarbone."

Cheney couldn't contain her laughter. "You're kiddin', right?"

"Nope, brush up on your dance moves, Heney, because you haven't seen anything until you see me salsa and mambo to the Latin beat." Mrs. Beacon demonstrated a quick spin, almost scaring Cheney with the sudden movement.

She hadn't missed Mrs. Beacon referring to her as Heney. It was no longer an irritation. The nickname had become an endearment. Cheney held up one hand like she was stopping traffic. "Okay, okay I see you're ready to go. I hope for your sake they play some slow jams so you won't hurt yourself and something familiar for me, so I can stay awake all night to carry you home."

Her adopted grandma had shooed Cheney off her porch. "Now go get dressed. I'll drive. I'm in a rush to get there."

"We've got all night," Cheney had reminded her as she rushed next door to get dressed.

Now, hours later, sipping punch, Cheney watched Mrs. Beacon mingle with other older women, fashionably dressed and just as youthful looking as Tina Turner and Cher. Cheney fanned herself, exhausted from three repeats of the Cha-Cha Slide—the long version.

Tapping her sandal, Cheney hummed along as the band wooed its guests with Motown favorites.

"R-E-S-P-E-C-T."

"Yeah, Retha, that's what I'm talking about," yelled a middle-aged white woman who blushed when some twenty-something sistahs walked up to her and raised their hands in high fives.

Pairing off to rumba, the band jammed until switching to a slow, romantic Latin beat. Men openly flirted with their women as they spun them around, turning them under their arms. The couples' touching was possessive, the stares seductive, and the movements natural. Like Cheney asked for it, Larry's dark face materialized.

Without an invitation, memories of them dancing the night away appeared. They were celebrating after acing their finals. The memory dissolved like an old black-and-white movie, replaced with something colorful, full of energy, and blossoming with love. For a moment Cheney imagined Parke's Paki and Elaine dressed in African garb, dancing together in sync, oozing with passion, hypnotized by love. A defying love that would accept challenges together, no matter what the cost. *Why Larry? Why couldn't you accept the challenge?*

Munching on hors d'oeuvres, Cheney continued to watch. "Because you were a loser. I'm a loser. Good luck, Parke, with finding your Elaine." Cheney shrugged. "The prince I found was an imposter—the dog, wolf, and mutt."

"Stop eating and talking to your self, girl, it's time to get some exercise. C'mon, it's salsa time, baby," Mrs. Beacon said in an Austin Powers drawl.

Groaning, Cheney complied. Mrs. Beacon dragged her to the center of the dance floor. Together they resembled Arnold Schwarzenegger and Danny Divito, but Cheney was having a ball despite the lateness of the hour. Funny how first impressions could be deceiving. The ruthless, tactless Mrs. Beacon was fast becoming one of her closest friends.

Cheney also didn't know what to think about Parke. After spending that day with him and listening to his family background, she'd have to rethink her opinion of him as annoying. He was as fascinating as he was fine, and she hated that she noticed. Parke also caused her to miss the dysfunctional family she was born into. Plus, she had yet to figure out what was the deal with his prayer over their food.

She stole a moment to fantasize about a genuine family. If she could have one wish, one hope, one blessing, or one prayer, it would be for her to start her own family. When her one moment was up, she gave back her dream. When Mrs. Beacon wasn't looking, Cheney sneaked off the dance floor.

CHAPTER 14

Looping a leather belt through the waist of his jeans, Parke hummed along with Brian McKnight's "Love of My Life." Closing his eyes, Parke stopped as the singer's pitch grasped at an incredible, and sometimes unimaginable love, causing Parke to crave it.

A long, carefree paintbrush appeared in Parke's imagination, stroking a canvas, building layers of what he proposed consisted of a relationship—admiration, deep attraction, and mutual respect. A woman sexy as a goddess wouldn't hurt either, but he couldn't live without a sense of humor.

Despite yearning for a son to continue the Jamieson name, Parke wanted a daughter, too. The beautiful little girl featured in one of Brian McKnight's video came to his mind. She was adorable. So far, none of his many dates had generated that desire. Something was always missing. Since he reminisced about his ancestors when he was with Cheney not long ago, his yearning to continue the Jamieson bloodline was taking over his mind.

The sound of the phone ended his daydream. Parke reached for his cordless and lowered the volume on his CD player. Checking the caller ID, he relaxed when he saw it wasn't a client, but he was still guarded.

"Hello, Nettie."

"Hey, did I disturb you or ya heading out for a wild, sinful date?"

"Ooh, Nettie, you know me so well," Parke baited her because for once she was wrong. "No, as a matter of fact, I'm on my way to Mom and Dad's for family night. Believe it or not, I'm going alone."

"Hallelujah. My prayers are being answered. Please keep working on him, *Lord.*"

"Nettie, Jesus and I are just fine. I believe in Him, and I accept Him. You don't have to request a work order for me."

Her tone became softer. "Parke, we all need Jesus to work on us. How's your prayer life?"

"It's good when I remember to do it." Parke racked his brain to actually pinpoint the last time. It had been with Cheney. Surely there were other times. He couldn't put his finger on it. "Look, just because I don't go around quoting scriptures, praying for people, living celibate, and bugging folks about Jesus, doesn't mean I'm going to hell. Jesus and I have an understanding. He accepts me as I am, and I'm cool with that."

"Parke, know that God always gives a warning before destruction. Pay attention, okay? I'm not going to keep you, but God told me to tell you '*Be-*

hold, now is the day of salvation.' When you get a chance read 2 Corinthians, sixth chapter and remember *'God so loved the world that He gave His only begotten son, that whosoever believeth in Him, won't perish.'* I love you, Parke, too much to see you perish."

"Annette, Annette, Annette, you've got too much church drama for me."

"That's okay. You can't insult me, because I'm praying for your soul. God revealed to me that somebody close to you really needs the Lord. Pay attention!"

Parke couldn't ignore the desperation behind Annette's words. He didn't ever recall her pleading with him before. He wanted to lighten the moment and say something witty like bribing her to back slide, but thought better of it.

"I love you, Parke," Annette whispered so soft, Parke barely heard her.

"I love you, Nettie."

"God gave me a job to do, and I plan to carry it out."

Parke smiled. Always the little soldier to fight for whatever she believed in. That's why he could honestly say he loved her, just not enough to be his wife. "Bye."

Disconnecting, Parke grabbed his keys and headed for his Envoy, dismissing Annette's so-called prophecy that someone in his family needed any more of God.

Things were about to change for Hallison Dinkins. After leaving 'the church' five years ago, she still felt the invisible hands holding her back from things others might have considered sinful. How long would Malcolm Jamieson deny his sexual needs before turning to another woman? She had made up her mind to move in that direction to make sure that didn't happen. If she felt guilty afterwards, she would repent. Didn't God say, "*If we confess our sins, He is faithful and just to forgive us our sins and to cleanse us from all unrighteousness?*" *Exactly*, she convinced herself. This was something she wanted to experience, presumptuous sin or not.

Hallison glanced at her bed clock. Malcolm would arrive in fifteen minutes to take her to his parents' house. Massaging ripe-raspberry cream into her pores, Hallison hoped the scent would seep into Malcolm's brain throughout the night and drive him crazy. She dressed in a brown short sleeve, off-the-shoulder crocheted top with an ankle-length, leopard-print crinkle skirt, with side splits that stopped at her upper thighs, which was sure to keep Malcolm's attention.

She slipped her feet into two-inch brown, wide-band leather thongs as the doorbell rang. Taking a deep breath, Hallison examined herself in the mirror, smiling. "Your temptress is coming." Swinging open the door, Hallison stood surprised, embarrassed, flabbergasted, and felt as naked as Eve. "Mama?" Suddenly, she needed a cigarette.

Addison Dinkins smiled, impeccably dressed in a two-piece periwinkle suit. The skirt was long and narrow, stopping inches above her ankle. Long, black wavy hair with strands of gray hung behind her shoulders in a tight curled flip.

Her fifty-nine-year-old face was naturally beautiful and youthful with no need for makeup. Confidence mixed with humility was her trademark. Her aura and modest appearance was unmistakably that of a Holy Ghost-filled saint. It wasn't in her hair, face, or clothes, but her spirit. She had the brightest smile and a soft-spoken voice that had comforted Hallison on many occasions. Her mother reached up and kissed her cheek.

"Hi, baby. I was leaving prayer meeting and the Lord sent me over to check on you."

Hallison's manicured nails tapped her chest. "Me? Mama, church is twenty-five minutes in the opposite direction. You could've just called. We've already spoken once this morning. See, I'm fine, but I got a date tonight."

Addison didn't budge as she waited patiently to be invited inside. "I won't hold you. Mind if I sit a few minutes before I travel all the way back home?"

Chuckling, Hallison tightly hugged her mother. "You mean until you've met Malcolm?"

Addison's eyes danced with merriment as she nodded, stepping over the threshold. "Well, since I'm here, that would be nice too." Sitting comfortably on a mustard-yellow suede sofa, Addison scanned her daughter's attire, but she didn't comment as Hallison walked past her to the kitchen.

"Is grape juice okay, Mama? I know you don't like soda."

The doorbell interrupted her mother's response. Hallison took a deep breath, mumbling, "Inspection time," before yelling, "I'll get it."

Her mother nodded as she sat with her hands and legs crossed, smiling.

Hallison had planned to crack the door and whisper a warning to Malcolm, but a large colorful bouquet caressed her face. Malcolm slowly moved the flowers to capture Hallison in an alluring kiss. She placed her fingers on his chest before he could deepen it. "Behave. My mother's here."

"Is she as beautiful as you?" he whispered as he handed her the flowers.

"You're a big flirt, Mr. Jamieson."

After pulling Malcolm inside, he kissed her hair. "Only with you, Miss Dinkins."

Meeting his stare, their communication was silent. Malcolm didn't have to utter what Hallison's heart craved. With inhibition, Hallison turned and walked to her mother who sat expectantly.

"Mama, this is Malcolm Jamieson. Malcolm, Mrs. Dinkins."

Instead of extending his right hand, he bent and kissed Addison on the cheek. Hallison smiled, crossing her fingers. *Brownie point.*

Addison patted the space beside her. "Hali, why don't you give Malcolm and me a few minutes to chat?"

Hallison groaned, offering Malcolm an apologetic smile. "I'm her baby."

He winked. "Mine, too." Facing her mother, Malcolm crossed one knee over the other, folding his hands. "I guess you want to know something about me."

"That would be nice."

"I'm twenty-six years old. I'm gainfully employed as a CPA at Winfield & Young Accounting Firm. I earned my business degree at the University of Missouri at Columbia. I'm Charlotte and Parke Jamieson V's middle son, I have two other brothers. I'm—"

"But are you saved, young man?"

"Saved from what, Mrs. Dinkins?"

Addison gave him a stern look with no forthcoming smile. "Your sins, son. Do you know who Jesus is?"

"Oh, ah, yes, I know who Jesus is."

"Good, then maybe you and Hali will come visit my church one Sunday."

This is not happening. Hallison quickly reappeared after eavesdropping. She handed Malcolm a glass of 7-Up and her mother a bottle of grape juice. "Mama, your church doesn't have anything to offer me anymore. I mean, I need fresh material, new ideas, youthful approaches, things like that."

Malcolm watched their exchange. Stretching out his hand to Hallison for support, she grabbed it. He squeezed gently.

For a few minutes, Addison didn't speak. Tilting her head, her eyes scanned Hallison's face then Addison nodded an understanding. "I see. A few weeks ago, I counted seven young ministers heading several youth ministries. You seemed to have forgotten my church, our church, has something for every member. Singles, divorcees, teenagers, children, new couples, new mothers—"

"Mama, that's not the only church in St. Louis. I'm asking God to lead me to a good church." *I haven't asked Him yet, but it's on a to-do list.* She didn't believe anything she heard from preachers, therefore she questioned everything.

Sipping her juice, Addison wore an unreadable expression. "Well, sweetheart, sooner or later, He'll answer. By the way, when is the last time you two have been to church?"

You don't have to answer, Hallison wanted to scream but it was too late.

Malcolm shrugged. "It's been a long time, Mrs. Dinkins, but I do pray before I eat my food."

Placing her bottle on a coaster on the end table, Addison stood. "I see. Then, you won't mind if I pray for you two right now?"

Malcolm also stood, grinning. "Of course not, do we, Hali?"

Fretting, Hallison bowed her head. *Malcolm, you just don't know what you agreed to.*

Reaching inside her lilac handbag, Addison withdrew an aspirin-sized bottle. She untwisted the cap and turned it upside down against her finger. "With this Holy Oil I'll anoint you for protection against the devil." She dabbed a spot on their foreheads. Bowing her head, Addison began her prayer.

"Father God, in the name of Jesus, we come boldly to your throne of grace, thanking you for your mercy and your goodness. Lord, I especially thank you for watching over and protecting my only daughter. Jesus, you said you're married to the backslider. Let her come back before it's too late."

The more Addison prayed, the tighter she gripped their hands. "And, Jesus, you know where Malcolm Jamieson's mind and thoughts are at this time. Your Word says, *'No man can come unto the Father, unless You draw him.'* Draw Malcolm tonight. Lord, show him your way."

Hallison watched as one of her mother's closed eyes popped opened. "Please lead him to read Colossians three, verses two and five. That's the book of Colossians, 3:25. '*Set your affection on the things above, not on things on the earth*' and '*Mortify therefore your members which are upon the earth; fornication, uncleanness, inordinate affection, evil concupiscence, and covetousness, which is idolatry.*' Again, the Book of Colossians, that's in the New Testament between Philippians and First Thessalonians, chapter three."

Despite being annoyed with her mother for taking advantage of an open door, Hallison couldn't help but smile at Addison's slick way of witnessing to Malcolm. It sounded almost as if her mother was ready to preach.

Then Addison's strong voice dropped to a whisper, "Thank you, Jesus. Thank you, Jesus. Thank you, Jesus for what's already done."

It's almost over, Hallison thought as she relaxed. She readied herself for the conclusion. Then, suddenly her mother came back with renewed strength.

"God, we know the wages of sin is death, but the gift of God is eternal life through Jesus Christ our Lord."

Without a doubt, Hallison knew that wasn't an idle hint. It was for Malcolm. Her message was probably next.

"Lord, you told the saints in Romans, 12:1: '*I beseech you, therefore, brethren, by the mercies of God, that ye present your bodies a living sacrifice, holy, acceptable unto God, which is your reasonable service*'."

Okay, Mama. I got the message from you and the Lord. Can we close the prayer now? Hallison wanted to ask.

"Verse two says," Addison continued, " '*And be*

*not conformed to this world but be ye transformed by the
renewing of your mind, that ye may prove what is that
good, and acceptable, and perfect, will of God.'* In Jesus's
name. Amen."

Amen, it was over. Hallison was afraid to look at
Malcolm as they released hands. Her mother, however, seemed exceptionally happy as she reached to
retrieve her purse off the sofa, but Malcolm beat her
to it.

"Well, I came and did what the Lord had me to
do, pray. You two have a blessed night in the Lord.
Malcolm, it was a pleasure meeting you. Take care
of my daughter."

Hugging Hallison, Addison whispered in her ear.
"I love you, and Jesus loves you too. By the way,
Malcolm is handsome and unsaved. Be careful."

Releasing her mother, Hallison sniffed, hoping
Malcolm wouldn't see the tears in her eyes. Walking
to the door, both women hugged again. "I love you,
Mama. I'll find my way." But Hallison wasn't looking. She'd seen with her own eyes church folks
stealing and sleeping around, and they got blessed
anyway with cars, jobs, and homes. She'd heard with
her own ears, women gossip and men curse. Lightning didn't strike them dead. They were in excellent
health.

What she was feeling for Malcolm and what she
planned to do about it was her business. No pastor
was going to tell her what not to do with her man
like the advice given to Tavia, an old friend. God
wasn't in control. Sinners got blessed while children
suffered and died. When she was ready to fool herself again, she would return to church.

With tenderness, Addison brushed a kiss against her cheek. "Jesus is the only way, the truth, and the light. I know He will lead you if you allow Him."

As Hallison opened the door, Malcolm strolled behind her. "Mrs. Dinkins, let me walk you to your car," he said, facing Hallison, giving her a loving look. "I'll be right back."

Hallison paced the wheat-colored carpet in her living room, waiting. Finally, Malcolm came through the door, smiling.

"I'm sorry. I'm so embarrassed." Hallison's hands covered her face.

"Why, baby?"

"My mother's beliefs aren't mine anymore."

Pushing her hands away, Malcolm guided her chin to his face. "Hali, I like your mother. She's beautiful, sweet, and a strong person, just like the woman I'm crazy about who promised to spend some time with me and my family tonight." Malcolm gathered Hallison in a secure embrace. "You're the woman who has had my attention for the past six months, two weeks, and one day. I haven't counted the hours and minutes yet."

"Can I share something out loud?" When he nodded, she continued, "I chose not to have God in my life. I detest dictatorship or censorship of my decisions. I don't even want Him in a box to pull out when I get ready."

"Baby, don't upset yourself. I can take or leave God. We've got each other. That's what's important."

Hallison encircled his neck with her arms. Through blurred vision, she met him in a soft kiss. "Malcolm, you are too much of what I want and need. Thank you for understanding." She blew out a sigh of relief. Thank God Malcolm had not been swayed.

"C'mon, Miss Dinkins, my parents, Parke, plus his woman of the hour are waiting."

As Hallison locked her apartment door, Malcolm chuckled. "You know, sweetheart, if I ever get deathly sick, please have your mom pray for me."

"I couldn't stop her."

Parke walked through the front door of his parents' Paddock Estates ranch home in North St. Louis County yelling, "Hello."

Charlotte Jamieson, dressed in a colorful two-piece pants set, greeted him with opened arms. "PJ, welcome home, it's been lonely without you and your brothers."

Closing his eyes, Parke welcomed his mother's hug. "Hi, Mama."

Releasing him, she stepped back, giving him a curious look.

"What?" he asked.

"Where's your date? You didn't bring anybody?"

A strong baritone voice approached the foyer. "What's that, Charlotte? PJ's alone?"

Father and son, shoulder to shoulder, embraced.

"Ah, I just didn't feel like being bothered," Parke replied, shrugging his shoulders as if it was no big deal.

His parents froze. Charlotte looked bewildered and reached up several inches to touch his forehead. "Is something wrong, son? You aren't sick or dying, are you?"

"I'm sure if anything were wrong, PJ would let us

know." His father nodded to encourage the right response from his son.

Parke received his father's message, which meant there were no secrets within the Jamieson family. Parke rubbed his clean-shaven chin as he and his parents moved to the back of the house toward the great room.

Collapsing in an oversized recliner, Parke elevated the foot rest. "Mom, Dad, I'm losing my mind."

"Actually, son, your dad and I felt you lost part of it years ago," Charlotte said in all seriousness.

"Huh? You're not joking, are you?"

"She's not, PJ, and she's right," his father answered. "We've always thought your mental facilities needed adjusting when you'd walk in here with some of your choices of women. What's going on?"

"Physically, nothing, mentally, I've been thinking."

"We don't need to have an intellectual conversation," his dad advised.

"I can't figure this out, but I'm getting a kick out of irritating this woman I'm not attracted to, but I can't stop thinking about or comparing others to her. She represents so much of what I don't want, yet she seems to connect with spiritual needs, if that makes sense," Parke confessed. "The only thing I like about her is her eyebrows."

"For me, it was your mother's hazel eyes."

"He was annoying at first, but he got my attention." Giggling, Charlotte left the men alone and walked into the kitchen. Parke didn't miss his dad's wink to his mother.

Charlotte returned a few minutes later with a platter laden with sliced deli meats.

Mr. Jamieson stood and quickly retrieved the tray. "Sweetheart, I told you I'd carry those. You relax." He bent down and smacked a kiss on her lips.

"I take that back. Her lips are enticing enough, especially when she smiles. Her face lightens up," Parke said more to himself about Cheney than he did to his parents.

Smiling, Charlotte faced her son. "A man only irritates a woman he's attracted to, so stop lying to yourself. Do I detect some seriousness in your selection? My only requirement for a daughter-in-law is that she has her own hair and teeth."

"I'll store that information, but there is no one, Mama."

"Hmm. Sure there is. You're not telling, yet. It'll either slip, or I'll get it out of you."

"Dad, help me out here," Parke pleaded with false irritation. There was never anything too private that he couldn't discuss with his family. He never felt the need to withhold anything from them until now. He had to first figure out what importance did Cheney have in his life. Was it for him to rescue her emotionally, or for her to rescue him, and then from what?

His father held up his hands in surrender. "When it comes to our sons, your mother has eminent domain."

Door chimes echoed throughout the house seconds before Malcolm strolled in with Hallison.

The elder Parke stood and hugged his second eldest son, then kissed Hallison on the cheek. "It's good seeing you, again. I trust you've been keeping Mal out of trouble?"

"Of course, she has, Dad. Hallison's my angel," Malcolm answered.

Stepping around her husband, Charlotte kissed Malcolm and looped her arms with his date. "Hali, you're looking lovely as usual." She leaned in closer and whispered, "And, I'm sure Malcolm can't keep his eyes off those sexy splits."

"I heard that, Mama," Malcolm said.

Blinking, Hallison froze. "Oh, you don't think they're too much, Mrs. Jamieson, do you?"

Eyes sparkling and smiling mischievously at Hallison, Charlotte's hand waved off her son. "Child no, you're young and beautiful. I say show what you got while you still got it."

Both women laughed.

Standing from the recliner, Parke greeted his brother in a bear hug.

Walking toward Parke, Hallison scanned the room. He knew who she was looking for before she asked, "Where's your date?"

"No date," his father said, grinning suspiciously.

"What!" Hallison and Malcolm said in unison.

"You're not still stalking your neighbor, are you?" Malcolm asked amusingly.

Everybody's neck whipped around and mouthed, "Stalking?"

Uncomfortable, Parke laughed off their concerned looks. "Women stalk me, Malcolm. I don't stalk the ladies."

"Is she beautiful?" his father asked with merriment dancing in his eyes.

"More importantly, does she have her own hair and teeth?" Charlotte chuckled, adding, "Because that one woman floored me when she removed her teeth to eat."

"Tell me she's taller than five feet," Hallison teased. "That way you don't have to bend your knees to hold her hand."

Amused, a captive audience followed Parke into the dining room as he flopped down in a chair. Resting his elbow on the oak table, he began massaging his thin mustache. "Funny you should ask, Hallison. She's six feet."

Malcolm leaned forward, his hand cupping his left ear. "Say what?"

"I said Cheney stands about six feet tall," Parke answered not amused by his brother's teasing.

"Ooh, is she a model?" quizzed his mother while Malcolm doubled over, laughing hysterically.

Finger-combing his hair, Parke glared at his brother. "I doubt it. As a matter of fact, I'm not sure what she does, but when we went to see *Bubbling Brown Sugar* a while back, everyone stared at her like she was on a runway. They must've been mistaken. She wasn't all that."

"I bet," Charlotte murmured, smiling.

"I have to give her this though. I've never seen a woman with her height move with such alluring grace. She does this thing with her hips I've never seen and I don't even think she knows it," Parke reminisced.

Interested and fascinated, Charlotte put both fists on her hips. "Why didn't you invite Cheney—is that her name?"

Parke nodded. "She probably wouldn't have come. I think she's too tall to notice me," he joked.

"Do you care?" his mother probed.

"Nope."

Malcolm and his father shouted in unison, "Liar," and fell into more fits of laughter.

"Okay, okay, okay. Are we playing any games tonight or what?" Charlotte asked.

"How about Journey to the Motherland or Black Heritage Trivia?" Malcolm suggested, pulling a chair out for Hallison before walking to the hall closet for the games.

Charlotte and her husband sat on the other side of the table across from Malcolm and Hallison while Parke sat at the end.

Loaded with several board games, Malcolm fumbled with an overstuffed shoebox, causing some items to spill on the table. He laid the games on the table, and picked up one of the colorful booklets. "What's this?"

"Oh, silly tracts some customers sent to the gas company along with their bill payments." Charlotte dismissed the items with a wave of her hand. "Most of the time I pitch them. I've been reading those. They're religious comic books. Some stories are scary, others are pretty good."

The elder Parke drummed his fingers against the table. "Charlotte, why are you wasting your time keeping things? Folks who send that stuff assume people don't know the difference between right and wrong. Good grief. I'd rather go to church and hear a bad sermon."

Hallison squirmed. All of a sudden she seemed uncomfortable. Malcolm immediately scooted next to his lady and whispered something in her ear before planting a kiss on it. The couple stared at each other until Hallison smiled. Parke squinted. *Now what was that all about?*

Mr. Jamieson clapped his hands to get everybody's attention. "Okay, PJ, brief me on the latest stock tip while we set up the Motherland game."

"Dad, your portfolio is still diversified, isn't it?"

"Yeah, but I thought trouble on Wall Street spelled buy low and sell high." The elder Parke gave his son a puzzled look.

Straightening to a professional pose, Parke slipped into his business mode. "True, but you need to invest very selectively in bonds and real estate investment trusts. They're doing real good."

"PJ, you know I like the tech funds."

"That was in the nineties when technology was booming."

Nodding, his father turned to Malcolm. "How's your job holding up, son? No one is cooking the books at Winfield & Young, I hope."

"After the Arthur Andersen fiasco, firms are doing more checks and balances," Malcolm assured him.

The women exchanged bored looks and deep sighs. Charlotte nodded to the platters she had brought in from the kitchen. Hallison helped herself as she fixed plates for her and Malcolm. Charlotte piled meats, salad, and breads on saucers, passing one to her husband and the other to Parke, commenting, "If you would've brought Cheney, then we could've picked her brain instead of all this shop talk."

Bowing her head, Hallison said a record-setting silent prayer over her food while Malcolm shoved a spoonful of pasta salad into his mouth, chewed, and barely swallowed before pointing. "I volunteer Parke's house for next month's family night, so we can meet this mystery lady."

Charlotte smiled. "I second the motion."

The elder Parke slammed his fist on the table like a judge calling a court into session. "It's a done deal."

"Ooh, I can't wait to meet the diva," Hallison joshed giddily.

CHAPTER 15

The following week, the heat was on

"Cheney, I need a favor," Parke said, short of begging as he talked through Onstar as he steered his SUV.

"Just ran out," she replied.

Not to be deterred, he pressed on. "How about an evening of fun with my family?"

"Do fish fly?"

"Actually, there are some." Parke paused, realizing he had to stop aggravating Cheney.

That was how Parke's Monday began. His schedule was booked for the next couple of days after work, so short breaks were all he had to convince Cheney to come to the next family night. It was so tempting. She seemed to come alive whenever he pushed her.

Thursday evening, Parke slowed his SUV after noticing Cheney's Altima in the driveway. As he parked, he imagined objections spilling from Cheney's mouth as to why she wouldn't go with him to a family night. Too bad he was looking forward to a face-to-face confrontation. For him, their spats were akin to over-dosing on an energy drink.

When Cheney didn't answer the doorbell after three tries, he knocked impatiently. "Where is she?" He knocked harder. "I hope she's okay."

"Of course she's okay, you woodpecker," Mrs. Beacon fussed from across the lawn. "Don't make sense, can't even enjoy a quiet dinner without someone banging next door. The mayor needs to enforce that noise ordinance."

Cheney's tall, slender body appeared in the doorway towering over her neighbor, making Mrs. Beacon appear as a midget. Folding her arms, Cheney quietly assessed him. As a matter of fact, Cheney seemed to quietly laugh at him.

"I wasn't that loud, was I?" Parke questioned.

"Yep," the women answered in unison.

Squinting, Mrs. Beacon eyed him up and down. "What's wrong? You've got to use the bathroom or something?"

Parke frowned at the absurdity of the idea. "No, ma'am, I'm on my way to the Ferguson library for story hour and was hoping Cheney would join me."

Mrs. Beacon twisted her mouth like she was chewing tobacco. "Ya kinda old for that stuff, ain't you?"

Groaning, he explained, sweeping his arm in the air with a slight bow. "It's my turn to spin African tales, slave adventures, and mystical folklores."

"What about Tracey?" Cheney baited him.

"I want you."

They stared at each other again in a showdown. Nothing intimidated him, especially a woman. Discreetly, Parke scanned Cheney's copper-colored attire. The sheen shining from it highlighted her soft dark facial features. She *was* pretty. Funny he didn't notice them when they first met. Well, dirt can hide beauty.

Parke won the staring contest when Cheney looked away before meeting his eyes again. She asked, "Not that depressing stuff again?"

"I'm a master storyteller with skills." He grinned. "I guarantee every child will laugh at least once. Plus, my good looks will make women beg for my unlisted phone number."

"Sounds like you've already started story hour with tales about an okay-looking man whose head is bigger than his body. You may know the character," Cheney teased.

"Look at the time. C'mon. We're going to be late. You're both invited," Parke offered.

"You young folks go on. I'm going to play bingo at that big Catholic church around the corner. I heard they draw a big crowd, plus, the only way I'll step foot in a chapel is to get my blessing in fives, tens, and twenties."

Parke folded his hands in a praying gesture. It was a mock plead for Cheney to come.

Tapping her finger on her lips, Cheney debated before shrugging. "Sure, why not?"

Fifteen minutes later, Parke's heart swelled with pride, pleased at the number of people present to hear African-American stories—blacks, whites, Latinos, and even a few Bosnian kids attended.

"My name is Parke Jamieson VI. Let's start with a question. What color am I?"

A young teenage boy, sporting a large Afro, frowned before raising his hand with a smirk. "That's easy. You're black, man."

"Oh?" Parke lifted his brow. "What year did I become black or an African- American?"

"Huh?" The child's face was puzzled.

"We've always been African-American," shouted a fair-skinned girl about eight years old with long corn rows.

Parke rallied in their perplexed expressions. "Actually, depending on what year I was born, I could be a mulatto, Melungeon, black, or colored." Looking around the room, Parke nodded, pleased he had everybody's attention. "Fascinating question, isn't it? How could one group of people be called so many different names?"

An Asian father, not sitting far from his son raised his hand. "Frankly, I'm confused. Since Jesse Jackson demanded blacks be called African-Americans, I don't know how to refer to your race anymore."

"Honest concern. It wasn't black or white during slavery." Parke leaned forward and lowered his voice to a hush, lifting one finger. "If a person had white, Negro, Native American, or another ethnic heritage, he was called a Melungeon. A mulatto is one-half Negro and one-half white. In Spanish and Portuguese, mulatto means a young mule."

"Sounds like a recipe for a cake," an elderly Bosnian woman holding her grandson commented.

A conservatively dressed middle-aged white man leaning against a bookcase raised his hand. Parke acknowledged him. "My understanding is one drop of Negro blood automatically makes the person black."

Parke's eyes sparkled. His lips curled into a smile.

"Not always. During the nineteenth century, a person with one-eighth Negro and seven-eights white was considered an Octoroon. A quarter Negro and three-quarters white was a Quadroon."

The man shook his head in disbelief. "People actually went to those extremes? It does sound like baking instructions."

Kids giggled. The adults chuckled.

"Yep. Okay, ready for a story?" Parke asked as more people joined the group.

"Yeah," the children shouted.

"Okay. Paris, a high-yalla, mostly white, or a light-skinned black teenager was born in the 1820s."

Parke knew he had erased the tension when a few white parents relaxed their skeptical expressions and bunkered down on the floor with their children. So he continued, "Sometimes it was easy for slaves to make the decision to run away. If they were caught, it would be terrible. If they were slick, like Paris, slaves would out trick the catchers and never be returned to their old masters."

"Why did he run away?" a young girl asked.

"Because he wanted to be free," Parke replied simply before exciting the kids with a belly laugh. He knew how to turn the gory details of slavery into comical adventures. "But it wasn't always easy. They never did catch Paris. You know why?"

"Why?" the children screamed.

"Because Paris had lots of disguises, including wigs. He wore preacher's, women's, even patroller's clothes—the bad guys. He made dummy slaves from scarecrows to trick catchers."

"What did he eat?" one boy shouted.

"Fruit from the trees."

"What did he drink?" another boy asked.

"Milk from cows."

"Where did he sleep?" the first young girl demanded.

"High in the trees or deep in the caves," Parke whispered, searching the crowd, winking when he met Cheney's eyes. She blushed. Parke became bewitched, speechless that he could get that reaction from her. Clearing his voice, Parke continued, "Paris traveled near back roads and made animal sounds to scare away his enemies."

"Did patrollers ever catch him?" Cheney quizzed.

"Yeah," the children pressed.

"Nope. Although he wasn't born free, he died free seventy years later. My research shows he had five sons." He bowed. "The end."

Cheney wasn't surprised that Parke received a hardy applause. With more patience than Santa Claus, Parke listened and answered each child's questions. He didn't miss a beat as he followed her movements. Captivated, she absorbed every word of Parke's animated story. Her imagination painted a heroic scene of Paki and Elaine escaping into the night.

Without trying, Cheney realized she had always enjoyed Parke's company. At first his sense of humor was exasperating. Lately though, it was entertaining, even when they argued about anything and nothing. The man had so many different sides to him that Cheney was beginning to look forward to his visits.

She focused on Parke's curly eyelashes and mustache. *He's nice looking and intelligent. He really resembles* Rick Fox. Cheney sighed, toying with her right earlobe. *He deserves a woman who personifies an Elaine.* Old memories surfaced, piercing Cheney's heart. Larry's face popped up like an unwanted weed.

Why is Parke staring at me? She ignored him as she turned and fingered some of the books on a shelf.

Appearing interested, Cheney pulled a book and scanned the pages. She had the weirdest feeling that Parke was behind her. Turning around, Parke was less than a foot away, smiling. There was no smirk, cockiness, or boasting, just a friendly, gentle, and inviting, "Hi."

"That was wonderful. You held the children spellbound with Paris' antics," Cheney praised.

"Yeah, I'm told that often." Parke's lips formed a crooked, mischievous smile.

She felt like knocking that silly grin off his face. "Too many compliments definitely go straight to your head. Not you, the stories, Parkay." The man was incorrigible, and Cheney admitted to herself, she liked his multi-personalities.

Later that night, hold up in her house, Cheney reflected on how things were changing in her life, not drastically but subtly enough for her to notice. Mrs. Beacon had become a surrogate mother, Parke an ally, and she had gained greater respect from the employees she supervised.

Although Cheney's family was missing from the picture, she would no longer beat herself up about it. She accepted that some mistakes couldn't be changed. When she mailed thank you notes for the gifts she received at her housewarming, she wasn't surprised when no one made an effort to call her.

The saving grace was Rainey. Although, they hadn't hung out together, she called him from time to time and they spoke briefly. Her bitterness was fading, yet she wanted more. During one of her lunches with Parke, in addition to blessing their food, he asked God to bless her. Maybe God was starting to. What was that scripture she thought of when she first moved back home? With urgency, she wanted to read it. Maybe for once, Imani wasn't joking about sending her a Bible. Cheney didn't own one and didn't know how to go about choosing one. She thought about Mrs. Beacon. She was almost certain her neighbor wouldn't look at one if it were dropped at her doorsteps like a Yellow Pages book.

Going to her computer, Cheney signed on, and googled Revelation 3:17-18.

CHAPTER 16

On a lazy Sunday afternoon, Parke coerced Cheney to walk with him to the Whistle Stop for her favorite weakness—a frozen custard.

"I can't believe how everything is turning out for us." Parke kicked at a small pile of pebbles on the sidewalk.

Cheney frowned. "What do you mean us? Parke, the earth revolves in space, not around you. The only *us* is us walking to get this dessert."

"I see you're in denial."

Cheney had shrugged and kept walking.

Brick walls could be knocked down, but Parke could only chip away at Cheney's cement exterior one piece at a time. Sensing her withdrawal, Parke teased her about her hair.

"I like your hair down. It suits you. Have I ever told you how beautiful you are?"

Cheney burst into laughter, elbowing him in the side. "Am I suppose to return the compliment, or can I keep it?"

That wasn't the reaction Parke was hoping for. He stopped short as she continued walking. Noticing his absence, Cheney glanced over her shoulder with a puzzled look.

"You can have my car, house, family, and stocks if we can call a truce." Extending his hand, he reached out to her. "Friends."

"Friends." She conceded without an argument. Parke stared to make sure it was really Cheney. That was it! Crickets chirping, the sun setting, and Cheney smiling, with her hair flowing for a change, caused Parke to caress Cheney's soft, long fingers. Her smiling was his undoing. "I need a hug, woman."

On a busy Ferguson Street, Parke touched Cheney, physically and maybe emotionally. She let him. Memories of that moment stayed with Parke. The next day when he arrived home, Malcolm was just pulling up.

"Hey, PJ, where you been, man?"

"With my neighbor."

"Is this the neighbor you are trying to get for our family night?" When Parke nodded, Malcolm grinned. "Newsflash. Man, a neighbor lives next door. Cheney is at least ten blocks away."

"Five."

Malcolm smirked. "I stand corrected."

"And I've got a problem."

"What?"

"It's a 'who.' Cheney doesn't fit my profile."

"Then I suggest you either alter your profile or destroy it."

* * *

Meeting for lunch at a café within the St. Louis airport terminal, Cheney waited for Imani to take her first sip of cappuccino.

"I'm scared," Cheney said out of nowhere.

Imani didn't swallow. "Why?"

"Parke held my hand, gave me a hug, and told me I was beautiful—"

Her friend leaned forward. "And the problem with that is?" Imani waited for an explanation that didn't come.

"And I bought a Bible."

Imani rested her chin in the palm of her hand anchored by her left elbow. "Am I suppose to be shocked? Every house should have one."

"Maybe," Cheney said, smiling. Although very little shocked Imani.

"It's nice to have someone to hold your hand, but what prompted you to go into a bookstore, number one?" Imani counted on her finger. "And two, what made you buy a Bible of all things?" Imani tapped a second finger.

Frowning, Cheney tried to pinpoint a lightening strike moment. She shrugged. "I don't know. I was with Parke—"

"Parke, again," Imani moaned his name. "Okay, continue."

"We were at this neighborhood eatery, and Parke was scoffing down on his sandwich when he remembered to bless his food. Parke asked God to bless me in addition to his meal."

"So?" Imani picked the lettuce off her chicken sandwich.

"Well, when I asked him why he prayed that, his response was 'I have no idea'."

"Is he a Christian?"

Cheney poured extra Ranch dressing on her salad, thinking. "I don't think he's not a Christian."

"Good point. Sometimes you can't tell the difference. Look at me, I can hang with the best of them when it comes to praying. Ask me about a scripture, and I'm googling it. I guess it's a good thing I didn't take that Gideon Bible from my hotel room."

They must be related, Cheney thought because that's exactly what she did without a Bible. Maybe Cheney would know when God was talking to her.

Straightening her shoulders, Imani squinted and braced for the news. "Back to Prince Parke."

"He reminds me of Larry."

"Girl, I thought you had something to tell." Imani stood and checked her watch. "My layover is about up. Stop fighting whatever is happening in your life, and start praying."

"How could you give out advice that you don't follow?"

Imani stood and brushed a kiss against Cheney cheek. "That's easy. I haven't been tortured for the past five years."

After Cheney watched her walk through airport security at Lambert Airport, Imani's words were still ringing in Cheney's head even an hour later when she returned home. Another gospel tract had appeared near her front door. This time she was reading it when her doorbell rang.

"What's going on? Why are you lugging that basket to my house?"

"It's not just any basket, Cheney. It's filled with goodies from Schnucks' deli—fruits, cheeses, and finger sandwiches," Parke relied. Schnucks was a locally-owned supermarket. When she didn't object, he busied himself, transforming her small porch into a picnic area complete with a portable radio. Grinning wickedly, Parke teased, "Suspicious, Miss Reynolds?"

"Shouldn't I be?" Cheney folded her arms and leaned against her doorframe. "Are you buttering me up for a big investment pitch? Funny, you hardly mention stocks or bonds."

"When I'm with you, shop talk doesn't come to mind. I'm more interested in our relaxed atmosphere. We have easy conversation and unforgettable moments."

"Parke, we argue."

"Funny, I see it as we discuss and you respond and I disagree with whatever you say. It's unrehearsed. Should I say more? Because there is more. Like the fact I'm drawn to you. You're still pushing me away, but not as hard."

Cheney didn't offer a rebuttal. She watched as Parke fiddled with the radio, stopping on a gospel music station. He waited for Cheney to sit down before reaching for her hand to pray. They bowed their heads. Since Parke was quiet, Cheney assumed he was praying silently.

"I'm still not sure what to say, God, except bless Cheney, bless me, and bless our food."

She looked up. "Why do you keep asking God to bless me?"

"Beats me, it just seems like things happen when I do. Personally, I think my friend, Annette, has bumped me up to the top of her prayer list. She leaves me daily scriptures on my phone. I also believe she's responsible for the ridiculous gospel tracts showing up at my door."

Nodding, Cheney bit into her turkey sandwich. "This Annette is probably hitting my house too. I wondered if Grandma BB has gotten any." Caught up with her own thoughts, she swallowed gulps of root beer as if she was dehydrated.

"Probably. Good thing you were home or I'd have camped out on your porch and ate the whole basket."

She held back a smile. "No you wouldn't have, you greedy thing. Grandma BB would've called the police."

They both laughed as a cool breeze danced around them. Minutes later, the food was gone.

"Actually, I had planned to learn how to play Spanish checkers with Brian, but it was canceled at the last minute. To stay busy, I'm going to sign up for a cooking class since I'm done with the major house renovations for now."

"What happened with your boyfriend?"

Cheney frowned. "What? Why would you want to know about Larry?"

Parke bent his knee and rested his arm as he stroked his chin. "Mmm, so I'm dealing with the ghost of Larry. Actually, I was referring to Brian."

"How embarrassing, I feel like I'm in one of those 'Want to Get-a-Way' commercials."

"I wasn't going to say anything—"

She punched him in the arm. "Shut up, Parkay." They laughed before Cheney cleared her throat. "Back to Brian. He says he borrowed his younger sister's allowance money to buy a video game, but he forgot to tell her. His memory loss is costing him two weeks without the computer, phone, or playing outside."

He gagged on his sandwich. "Yikes." Cheney's life seemed so simplistic to him, but satisfying to her. "How did you find out?"

"His mother e-mailed me with the details."

Parke soaked in the cool breeze. He wanted to change the mood. "I'm going to test the waters. You, Miss Reynolds, mesmerize me. There's a cooking school called The Chef's Kitchen not far from here that offers monthly cooking classes. I would be honored to be your partner."

"What am I going to do with you? You've got so many facets to your personality—sometimes you're sweet, conceited most of the time, and confusing all the time."

Taking a gulp from his can of iced tea, Parke reflected on her words before responding, "I'm only act like that with you."

"Mmm-hmm. I'm glad I bring out your best. I truly hope you find a very special woman."

"Stop dogging yourself out, Cheney. You're special. If this Larry character had treated the relationship right, you wouldn't keep second-guessing yourself."

"That was years ago. Believe when I say I have nothing to offer."

"Cheney, you're wrong . . ."

"You won't win this argument, Parke."

"Okay, I won't even try. How about a night of fun, games, food, and plenty of loud and crazy people?"

"Parke, I'm not getting on a gambling boat."

"I'm talking about my family, not a casino."

"I'd rather gamble."

The Chef's Kitchen was a large classroom located behind the kitchen of the Neighborhood Grill, a busy corner establishment that had to turn away customers to lock its doors at night. It was also the place where local culinary graduates practiced their skills. It was no surprise that all ten workstations with connecting kitchenettes, consisting of a sink, cabinet, microwave, and stove were occupied. Parke's client, Andre' Valroy, owed him a favor for turning a once worthless portfolio into a lucrative investment package. He let Parke bump a student to get in this month's class.

"Parke, did you notice we were the only ones coupled off?" Cheney whispered.

"The only thing I noticed was you. You look pretty tonight with your hair piled on top of your head. It's sexy."

Cheney was about to remove the hairpins when Parke stayed her hands. "Don't."

"Okay, let's get started," Andre' interrupted. "As you know, this is a three week course. Every week you'll try dishes from around the world. Tonight, it's Asian cuisine. Some will make a Vietnamese dish of peanut sticky rice, roast chicken balti, and fish korma from India. The rest of you will cook Cambodian eggplant with pork and shrimp, and Japanese new potatoes with sesame sauce."

"Cheney, let's do the eggplant. I like pork and shrimp."

"I was hoping to cook the fish korma."

"Pretty lady, I'm cooking the fish korma. I don't mind letting you have a taste," a dark-skinned, clean-shaven, bald-head brother turned around and commented. His smile gleamed.

"Thank you." Cheney smiled back.

"No, thank you. She doesn't need to taste yours because we're cooking the fish korma," Parke was quick to say.

The man looked boldly at Cheney's hand for rings and shrugged. "My name's Tyrone in case you change your mind."

"She won't," Parke snapped.

"I'll let you know, Ty," Cheney thanked him.

As Cheney concentrated on following the recipes, Parke kept an evil eye on Tyrone and three other men who approached their table, offering Cheney a taste. *What was it with the male species?* They insisted it was best to get Cheney's opinion since the other two women in the class were tipping the scales and would probably like anything, including the mixing spoon.

A dude named Shabazz made himself too comfortable at their work station. To keep from asking him to step outside to break his bones, Parke did the next best thing when Shabazz wouldn't take any more hints. He kissed Cheney on the forehead and whispered loud enough for two work stations to hear.

"Sweetheart, I'll cook any dish you want after we get home. I'll give you your back rub tonight, but we need to learn these recipes. You know how the triplets don't like to eat the same thing twice."

Cheney's mouth dropped open as the predators

scattered. Later that night, before Cheney slammed the door in his face, she chewed him out.

"What was wrong with you tonight? Those guys didn't want me," Cheney scolded.

"Well, I do."

"I suggest you tone down the testosterone. I'm not interested in them or any man."

Standing on Cheney's porch after they left the cooking class, she had slapped Parke silly. Parke retaliated by kissing her silly. A truce was finally called when Mrs. Beacon, who was eavesdropping, got tired of them bickering. Cheney agreed to help him prepare a dish for his upcoming family game night, but she wouldn't stay. With fingers crossed behind his back, Parke promised not to kiss her again.

CHAPTER 17

Spooked, Hallison had attempted to read her Bible every night since her mother's long, drowned out prayer. A verse was all she could tolerate. Of all the nights, why did she read the entire first chapter of Psalm?

"I don't care about the man being blessed because he didn't walk in the counsel of the ungodly." She didn't want to meditate on God's laws day and night, "And I don't want to hear about the ungodly perishing. I haven't seen it yet."

Tossing the Bible on a chair, Hallison rubbed her eyes, craving the taste of nicotine. "Why did I stop smoking?" She started the rebellious habit as soon as she left the church years ago. She quit after her mother's last long prayer.

Shaky fingers fumbled to turn off her lamp as her mind blocked out the scriptures. "I don't want to save myself from Malcolm." He would be her second major step of independence and rebellion. She did thank God that Malcolm never discussed church. Sighing, Hallison's lids drifted as her phone rang.

Please don't let it be Mama. "Hello?"

"Hi, sweetheart," Malcolm's rich, deep voice tickled her ears, calming the storm building inside of her.

Smiling, she whispered his name, "Malcolm, I didn't expect you to call. Didn't you have to work late?"

"I couldn't miss hearing you say my name with those gorgeous lips of yours. How did your day go? Anybody messin' with my baby?"

Yeah, God is nagging me, but you can't do anything about it. "I had a good day, but it gets better when I talk to you."

"Do you want to get kidnapped?"

"Yes, I'd be your willing captive." She smiled, thinking of all sorts of naughty thoughts."

"Then I'll sweep you away for a romantic weekend getaway at the Ritz Carlton. We'll go after Parke's get-together tomorrow night. Pack light."

Hallison's heart slammed against her chest as words stuck in her tightening throat. She needed a cigarette, patch, or pill. Oh yes, she was ready.

When she hesitated, Malcolm softly called her name, "Hali, talk to me, baby. We can wait." Tenderness and understanding saturated his words. There was no hint of disappointment.

Hallison's voice broke with emotion. "I'm so ready."

"Me too."

"Thank you."

"Why are you thanking me? I should be thanking you for being my woman."

"Thank you for being the man I'm crazy about."

"I'll pick you up around six-thirty tomorrow."

"Okay, good night."

"Good night, beautiful."

When Hallison hung up, she beat the bed with her heels in a blissful mood. "Hope Mama doesn't pray for me between now and Saturday!"

Friday morning, Hallison hummed as she danced across her bedroom floor. That night, she'd meet Parke's mystery neighbor, and then onto her rendezvous with Malcolm. Opening her window, Hallison could feel the lingering summer heat in the fall air. "A change is comin'."

Hallison was applying lip liner when her phone rang. Despite her three-inch heels, she leaped from the bathroom like a ballerina. *Malcolm.* "Good morning," Hallison answered almost singing.

"Good morning to you, sweetie."

"Oh." Her body slumped into a nearby chair. "Hi, Mama."

"What's the matter, baby?"

"Oh, nothing." Hallison gritted her teeth, lying and hoping her mother wouldn't pray for her, not today. Things always happened when her mother prayed.

"Well, I'll pray that you have a better day."

"No!" Panic spread through Hallison's body. "I mean, I'm fine, but I'm on my way out the door to work."

"I'm calling to let you know a package for you came yesterday. You want me to drop it off?"

Hallison would've cursed, but her mother was on the other end. She'd ordered shoes from a catalog to wear that night. She didn't know why she mistakenly gave her mother's address.

"No, I'll swing by after work. I have to go, Mama. Love you. Bye."

Late in the afternoon, Hallison realized she had spent most of her workday gazing at the clock instead of reviewing résumés and double-checking files. She dreaded the idea of stopping by her mother's house, but she knew Malcolm was going to love those shoes with her hip-hugging jeans.

The phone interrupted her musing. She answered, "Hallison Dinkins, director of personnel."

"Malcolm Jamieson, the man who is planning to love you senseless this weekend," he cooed into the receiver.

Hallison smiled. "Promise?"

"Yes, and I'd never break a promise to you, baby."

"Good to know."

"I'm calling to see how your day is going and throw some kisses your way."

Ridiculously happy, she giggled. "You're silly."

"One of my many qualities."

"I'll see you later?"

"Nothing can keep me away."

I sure hope not. "I'm stopping by Mama's on my way home."

"The lovely Mrs. Dinkins, tell her I said hi."

Wrinkling her brow, Hallison held her breath. *Not on your life.* "Okay."

Three hours later, Hallison parked outside her mother's white brick colonial house. Emerald-green shutters graced four large windows.

"In and out, go in, grab the package, and dash

out," Hallison coaxed herself as she followed the winding brick path to the emerald green front door.

"Hi, Mama," Hallison managed to choke out as her mother squeezed her in a bear hug at the door. "I can't stay long."

Patting her daughter's cheek, Addison smiled. "I know, baby."

Relaxing, Hallison enjoyed the touch. "Good. So you know I don't have time for a prayer right now?"

Her mother shrugged and waved her hand in the air. "Honey, I've already prayed for you this morning."

Hallison cringed as she walked to the sofa table and scooped up the package.

Kissing her mother's cheek, Hallison was ready to bolt. "I'll talk to you later, Mama, Okay?"

Addison studied Hallison as she reached for her daughter's hand. "Sure, baby. Remember, I love you."

"I know, and I love you too," Hallison said hastily as she tried to get out the door in record time, but her mother's grip stopped her.

"Hali, I know you're in love with that young man."

Uh-oh. Here it comes. Nodding, Hallison held her breath.

"You know, we've had many talks throughout the years. Not once have I ever suggested you use any form of birth control because you've always cherished God's Word for what it was, and His instruction on how to live holy. Something happened with you and you never told me what it was, but saints don't leave God overnight, it's gradual."

"I know, Mama, but—"

"Just a reminder, sex outside of marriage is fornication. The Bible doesn't treat it as a light topic. To indulge in it has consequences. I've got too much conviction to say if you engage in sex, take the pill, use a condom, or another form of protection. God would hold me responsible for bad counsel."

Addison stared into her daughter's eyes. "Sin is sin. I didn't make up the rules, but we have to strive to follow them. Here's an example. You tell me you want to rob a store and I say, 'I prefer you don't, but if you do, use a knife instead of a gun.' Either way, it's wrong."

"Mama, I'm not going to rob—"

Addison tightened her grip. "The point is, whatever you use so that you won't be caught doesn't mean you got away with it. God knows."

Beads of sweat lined Hallison's upper lip, but she remained quiet.

"All, I'm saying sweetie is if you sin, be prepared for the fallout—pregnancy, HIV/AIDS, venereal diseases, and spiritual death."

"Yes, ma'am, I'll remember." Hallison opened the door and hurried to her car. *A prayer would've definitely been better than her words of wisdom.*

In her apartment, Hallison fought to block out her mother's words by dressing to entice Malcolm. "It's not that I don't believe the Bible, I just don't believe everything in it."

Her friend, Tavia, didn't let the Bible, pastor, or anybody keep her from loving and marrying David, the man of her dreams. She couldn't believe her former pastor advised Tavia not to marry David because he wasn't ready spiritually. "That minister had a lot of nerve! We have no control over who we fall in love with." That day was the catalyst of her walking out of church and never returning, and no one ever knew why, including her mother. She didn't want the pastor dipping into her business all in the name of God.

Checking herself out in the mirror, she admired her tight fitted jeans, scooped neck short-sleeve jersey, and new shoes as her doorbell rang. All she knew was, to date, Tavia and David were happily married. A second chime made Hallison hurry to the door and open it.

Discharging a slow whistle, Malcolm perused Hallison from head to toe. He fingered her cheeks on his way to her soft shoulder-length curls. Eventually, his thumb nudged her face closer to his lips.

Hallison enjoyed Malcolm's appraisal before he indulged her in a slow, drugging kiss. "This evening, I'll share you with my family. Tonight and tomorrow, you're mine, woman."

It was a miracle that Cheney was speaking to him again. The woman stood in Parke's kitchen like she lived there. *Cheney acts like it was her kitchen*, Parke thought with a smirk.

"I can't believe I'm inside your house."

"I can't believe you know how to cook," Parke teased Cheney.

"Whose fault is it if I don't, Mr. Macho Man? I was looking forward to sampling the African dishes this week, but no. I can't go anywhere with you."

"You told your instructor friend to let someone else have my spot. Don't let me keep talking about it, or I'll dump this tetrazzini on your conceited head." Cheney lifted the six-quart baking pan overhead.

"You're serious, aren't you?"

"Yes, you suggested that place and then you acted like a fool."

"I apologize again, but it was your hairdo that drove me to it and those pack of wolves acting crazy that night. You're irresistible."

"Whatever."

"I felt it was safer to cook with you alone than in class. Grandma BB said your background check came back clean."

"Your neighbor is crazy."

"Yes, she is, so be careful. How often do the Jamiesons have a party, anyway?"

"We used to have family night every week, but now we only have it once a month since everybody's busy. You're still invited to stay."

Admiring Cheney's mint-green T-shirt and faded jeans, he smiled at her polka-dot socks. Pretending to sniff the dish, Parke leaned forward, inhaling Cheney's subtle scent. "Man, you smell good."

"You sure it's not the food you smell?"

"Yep, you always smell like sweet fruits. What's in that stuff anyway?" Parke lifted his eyebrow, eying the mess. "Please tell me you know what you're doing."

A mischievous grin spread across Cheney's face. "Maybe, I don't. Maybe I'm experimenting."

They both enjoyed a laugh before Cheney glanced around her surroundings.

"This is a fantastic kitchen by the way. Your entire house is nice."

Parke's phone rang just as Cheney sprinkled Parmesan cheese on top of the dish. "You better get that, Parkay, it could be a client needing a hot tip."

Picking up the phone, Parke watched Cheney move naturally around his kitchen. "Hello," Parke mumbled into the phone as she ignored him. "Mom, she doesn't know she's meeting any of you, so come at seven instead of eight o'clock. I told Malcolm yesterday."

"PJ, doesn't that poor girl know she's invited? If she's like any other woman, she'll want to look her best and—"

"Mom, I guarantee she won't want to impose. She's lonely, but she'll never admit to it. Her family is more hostile than al-Qaida, and her next-door neighbor is tougher than a pit bull on steroids," he whispered into the phone before they said their good-byes.

Parke smiled, proud to be part of a close-knit family. He snuck up behind Cheney, tempted to hug her and relish in their closeness. She continued to prepare dishes. Stupefied, Parke scrutinized the contents in the pan. "I thought you said you knew how to bake a cake?"

Nonchalantly, Cheney glanced over her shoulder, laughing at his grief-stricken expression. "It's dump cake, Parke. I don't need milk, water, or eggs. Then empty the cake mix in a pan. Pour a layer of sliced peaches, then add apple-pie filing." She demonstrated by leveling off the mound. "Cover with one stick of butter slices and *viola*, a masterpiece."

Parke scratched his head. "It looks more like a master mess."

Nostrils flaring, Cheney lifted one soft, sexy eyebrow. "Never challenge a new millennium woman who's six feet. You're likely to get slam dunked."

Swiftly, Parke moved within inches of her mouth, invading her space as he tried to intimidate her, but Cheney's intoxicating scent whipped around his head, and her long lashes held power over him. He was the one who felt weak in his knees. Cheney didn't back away or blink.

"On second thought, I'll give you your space." Grabbing a dishtowel, Parke rubbed at imaginary dirt on his counter, eyeing the clock, and praying he could keep Cheney there until his family arrived.

"Good idea, strong black warrior chief of the Diomande tribe."

His mouth dropped open like an unlocked gate. "You remember that?"

Walking to the sink, she bumped Parke out the way. "Of course."

"Ouch!" Parke rubbed his thigh, pretending he was injured. "Using your secret weapon again, I see, brickhouse."

Ignoring him, Cheney rinsed her cooking utensils before placing them in his dishwasher. "Your story is fascinating. How could anyone not remember?"

Offended, Parke jammed a fist in his side. "So you're not fascinated with me, huh?"

She tilted her head, thinking. "Nope, just your family heritage."

"Seriously, Cheney, don't you want all this?" Parke swept his hand in the air, showcasing material wealth.

"I already have a house and a kitchen."

"I'm not talking about your kitchen or home. What about a family, children to continue your heritage? What do you want for the future?"

"Sometimes, it's not good to dream the impossible dream. At one time, I wanted a family." She paused, staring past Parke, sighing. "Well, I've been domesticated enough today. I better head home before your family arrives."

Wanted a family, what changed? What happened to you, Cheney? Parke stole a peek at his watch. *Just hold her here for thirty more minutes.* He racked his brain, scheming. "Yeah, leave when you know a brother needs you. You know I can't remember how to make this fancy drink you suggested. I guess I'll serve Kool-Aid with your dish."

Cheney rolled her eyes. "Parfait, Parke. Three simple ingredients: soda, punch, and raspberry sherbet." Shaking her head, Cheney popped him with a wet hand towel. "You're sad, pitiful, and slow. Give me your punch bowl."

They were straightening the kitchen when the doorbell chimed, Cheney jumped. "Your family is early." Panic filled her voice. "I better go." She moved quickly, washing her hands and untying his checkered apron. Parke strolled out of the kitchen. He opened his front door to greet his parents. Their chatty and cheerful voices grew louder as footsteps echoed across Parke's hardwood floor. Parke imagined Cheney scurrying around the kitchen, stuffing her feet into her shoes as she grabbed her keys, purse, and cookbooks.

Hallison searched the room, balancing a fruit, cheese and cracker platter before Malcolm took it.

At that moment, jingling keys announced Cheney's

presence. "Hello, everyone, I'm Cheney Reynolds. I live in the neighborhood."

While Cheney captured his family's attention, Parke eyed his dad who was smiling. He had never seen the senior Jamieson grin appreciatively or approvingly at any of his dates. His father, hands down, liked Cheney. To impede Cheney's hasty retreat, Parke made introductions. Cheney was embraced like a regular member of the family.

"Hmm, something smells good. Parke, I know you didn't cook," Hallison teased.

"It's Cheney's tetrazzini."

Parke's dad rubbed his hands together. "Then, why are we standing around? Let's get this party started."

Cheney glanced at her watch. "Parke, give it about ten more minutes. Don't forget to toast the almonds and sprinkle them on top before you serve it."

Charlotte looked disappointedly at her son and his neighbor. "Aren't you staying, dear?"

"No, Mrs. Jamieson. This is your family night. I don't want to intrude."

"Intrude, please intrude," Hallison begged as everyone chuckled.

"You're very kind to offer, but I really must go. Have a good time. Good night." She continued to the door. Parke didn't follow.

When the lock clicked, Parke's dad whistled. "Your taste is improving, son. She's beautiful without trying."

Charlotte grinned. "She can cook. That means my eldest boy won't starve."

"What's that dessert I smell?" Charlotte's eyes widened.

"Cheney's dump cake."

Rubbing his belly, Malcolm linked his fingers with Hallison's, gently tugging her to Parke's dining room.

His dad twisted his lips, wiggling his bushy salt-and-pepper mustache. "Is something finally developing between the stalker and your prey?"

Laughter exploded. Even Parke chuckled before answering, "I'm trying, Dad."

"Try harder. Lose the cockiness, and you might have a chance." Mr. Jamieson reached over and patted Parke's back. "I don't know what is going on—only you can determine that—but remember the woman you fall in love with will determine your destiny. Don't mess up our name. C'mon. My stomach's growling."

Minutes later, with a punch bowl on the counter, Parke mixed the parfait according to Cheney's instruction.

Malcolm threaded his fingers through his curly hair. "Maybe we should go to Cheney's house and bring her back," he joked.

"I like her. I get good vibes from her," Hallison said, touching Malcolm's arm. "Plus, I think your brother's smitten."

Leaning close, Malcolm outlined her lips with his finger. "I know I am."

Charlotte's smile reached her eyes before she turned to Parke. "I think Malcolm has an excellent idea. Let's go."

"What? Wait a minute, you plottin' Jamiesons."

Parke stuffed his hands in his pockets. "Cheney's a private person who isn't accustomed to all these warm and fuzzy feelings, even from her own family."

Parke's father held up board games. "All the more reason to go."

Charlotte whispered to Hallison and they both laughed before packing up trays, paper plates and napkins like their party was over. "If Cheney won't stay for our party, then we'll take the party to her."

"Oh boy." Nodding, a grin spread between Parke's lips. "Let's go."

Cheney had enjoyed the harmless flirtation with Parke in his kitchen, but as soon as she stepped into her haven, her mood changed. Even a refreshing shower couldn't cleanse Cheney's melancholy. Her mind flashed back to the smiles, laughter, and love she witnessed at Parke's.

His brother held a striking resemblance to him except Malcolm was thicker. Mrs. Jamieson oozed with charm, classic elegance, and a warm spirit. She definitely fit an Elaine persona—beautiful and the mother of handsome sons.

Squatting by her bed, Cheney thrust her hand into a basket, grabbing a bottle of lotion. She thought about the major disconnect with her parents and siblings. She'd hurt them. Cheney's father drilled into her head the importance of life, regardless of the quality. Exhausted from thinking, Cheney closed her eyes, rubbing Hawaiian Ginger body cream between her toes, working her way up.

As if a lightning bolt zapped her, tears sprouted

and streamed down. Cheney covered her face, sobbing uncontrollably. After a while, she sniffed. "This is silly. I don't even know why I'm crying." Standing, Cheney put on her Mickey Mouse two-piece pajamas like a programmed robot. Still dazed, she walked to the bathroom mirror and systematically applied layers of cold cream to her face and neck.

While braiding her hair, she heard a faint ringing in the distance. She wasn't expecting anyone, so she ignored it. The doorbell ceased but was replaced by heavy knocking. Cheney panicked. "Oh, please. Don't let anything be wrong with Grandma BB." Cheney barely grabbed her robe as she raced out of her room, down the hall, and jumped two stairs at a time. Her heart pounded against her chest with anticipation of a pending disaster.

Checking the peephole, Cheney flung open her door, annoyed. "Parke, why are you beating on my door?" she growled before noticing his entourage. Cheney collapsed against her doorframe. She folded her arms and waited for an explanation. "Okay, somebody, anybody, tell me what's going on? The party's not here."

Parke leaned forward, close to her ear. "Ah, Cheney, if you're trying to scare the neighborhood with that stuff on your face, you succeeded. Trick or treat."

The man's attractiveness always seemed to contradict his natural humor, or maybe she had too much doom and gloom in her life, but Parke always seemed to lighten her mood. She would never admit it to Parke, but she craved him. Plus, the short kiss they shared was nice. Being away from him had caused her sour mood. She ignored the mischief in his eyes and poked her finger in his chest. "See, you don't have good sense." She dismissed him and turned to his mother.

"Mrs. Jamieson, pardon my rudeness. I usually reserve that for Parkay."

They cackled at the nickname, and Cheney ushered them inside before they disturbed Mrs. Beacon who might open her door with a loaded shotgun. "Why are you here?"

Mrs. Jamieson, the shortest of them, lifted her bags. "Dear, we wanted to include you in our games. I hope you don't mind, we even brought food, dessert, and PJ's parfait."

Cheney's face was starting to feel oily from the cold cream. She couldn't believe she was standing in her livingroom dressed in her favorite pajamas talking to Parke and his clan. She glanced at Parke's brother and his girlfriend. "This isn't making any sense."

Swiping his finger against her cold cream, Parke whispered, "Cheney, you might think clearer if you get that stuff off your face."

She smacked his hand away. "Believe me, I can look worse,"

Chuckling, Parke agreed. "Don't I know it!"

Hallison smiled. "Cheney, indulge us. You seem to be the only one able to keep PJ in line, so we basically invited ourselves."

Cheney lifted an eyebrow. *These people are truly crazy, like that explanation justifies them barging into my house.* "You seem harmless. Have a seat," Cheney conceded. "Make yourselves comfortable while I put on some clothes."

She zoomed up the stairs, appreciating their oohs

and ahs she overheard about her house, but ignored Parke's silly-looking pleased expression. Cheney quickly changed into her jeans and a black sweater. When she returned, food platters and a game board overtook her dining room table. As Cheney approached the only vacant chair, which happened to be next to Parke, the men stood. Parke's eyes were fixed as if he was memorizing or cataloging her movements. Once he seated her, the men retook their seats.

Hallison passed Cheney a plate already filled with her own tetrazzini, breadsticks, and salad. The pampering made Cheney wonder if she was dreaming. She sipped her parfait. "Parke, this is delicious."

He inched close to her face like he was going to kiss her. *What is his problem? Try it at your own risk*, her expression warned.

"I learned from a very talented, tall, and attractive twin," Parke complimented.

The room burst into laughter as Cheney nudged Parke in the ribs. "Stop playing around." She placed her glass on the table and took a deep breath. "Now, tell me about the game."

"Black Americans of Achievement, one of PJ's favorites," Charlotte offered.

Lifting her brow, Cheney faced Parke and smirked. "PJ, huh?"

Mr. Jamieson chuckled. "Yeah, that's what we call him when we're all together."

Cheney's eyes kept straying to Malcolm and Hallison. They were an attractive happy couple. She was drawn in by their magnetism. She detested romance books, movies, or plays, but what she was witnessing created a yearning. With others paired,

Cheney felt awkward. She and Parke were neighbors. Although she admitted they were gradually becoming a little more than friends.

"It does take some getting use to. The eldest Parke is given his honor. After that it's PJ1, PJ2, etc.," Hallison explained.

Charlotte asked Cheney, "Did PJ tell you about the Jamieson love story?"

"Yes, he did. I think it is beautiful for a love to last for so many years when you can't find commitment pass one week today."

Parke stretched his arm over the back of Cheney's chair. "The Jamiesons pride themselves on fidelity and loving their wives. There are no divorces reported in the direct descendants of Paki because we carefully chose to love our women for life."

"Okay, so tell me about this game," Cheney said, changing the subject, *enough about love and happiness.* Al Green wasn't joking when he sang it could make you do right or wrong. Larry was all wrong.

Parke shrugged. "Let's just say it's hours of good company and more than two thousand questions about blacks, spanning four hundred years in America."

Throughout the night, the Jamiesons challenged one another, joked, and teased Parke. Cheney tried to concentrate. Mr. Jamieson didn't spare any attention, especially when his wife answered correctly. They snuggled, winked, or kissed each other like they had won points on *The Newlywed Game.*

"Cheney, to redeem yourself and bring you and PJ to the next level with the rest of us, name the first black woman to open a bank," Hallison asked, reciting from a game card.

Biting her bottom lip, Cheney gave Parke a sad, pleading look. "Tell me," she whispered. "I know you know."

"Make me."

You're definitely playing with the wrong woman. Lifting a brow, Cheney lowered her voice to a husky tone. "Come closer."

Grinning, Parke cooed, "Yeah, baby."

Cheney pinched his cheek so fast he didn't know what hit him.

"Ouch!" he yelled, frowning as he rubbed his flesh.

Laughter erupted as his parents slapped the table and Malcolm clapped.

Cheney held back her laugh, scolding Parke, "We're on the same team."

"Okay," Parke said reluctantly. "Maggie Walker."

Hallison nodded. "Correct. For two extra bonus points, name the bank and the year it opened."

Despite her game face, Cheney winked at Parke who sat sulking. "The St. Luke's Penny Savings Bank, founded in 1903. Renamed Consolidated Bank and Trust, it's headquartered in Richmond. I believe it currently operates several branches in Virginia with close to $113 million in assets," she said with a slight bow. The women beamed with pride, clapping and high-fiving one another as if they were on the same team.

"Girl, we've got to hang out," Hallison insisted, beaming.

"Include me in your girls' day out," Charlotte added.

Cheney was drowning in the easy camaraderie. The game was indeed fun. Cheney moved closer to

Parke, but his quick reflexes allowed him to cover his face, evidently fearing she would pinch him again. She released a haughty laugh and taunted him, "Business major, Duke University. I just needed a hint, lover boy."

Her comment ignited laughter except for Parke who challenged, "I've got your lover boy."

"I thought the night would never end," Malcolm complained to Hallison later as he them drove away from Cheney's house. "Now on to our romantic weekend getaway."

Hallison nodded as her eye's eyes twinkled with excitement.

Arriving at the hotel, the doorman, dressed in royal-looking attire, greeted them. "Welcome to the Ritz Carlton. Enjoy your stay."

Malcolm smiled. "Thanks. We plan to."

CHAPTER 18

October, two weeks later . . .

He was sneaky, underhanded, and heartless. His craftiness underlined his ability to play fairly. Cheney was convinced he had backup as she smirked at her opponent. "I refuse to let you back me into the corner." Concentrating, she back-tracked Brian's last strategic move. "Okay, I know your mother is the mastermind. Can't even trust an eight-year-old."

She sipped an empty glass absentmindedly, for-getting she had drained her Kool-Aid after Brian beat her the first time. "Aha! I see an opening."

Cheney was about to click on the mouse and jump Brian's black checker when the phone rang, causing her to move the wrong piece. "No! That's the third straight win."

Happy faces popped on the screen, jeering her. Laughing, she glanced at the caller ID. Picking up the cordless, Cheney whined into the phone. "What Parke?"

"I have a proposition for you."

"This is not a nine hundred, talk-dirty line."
Click. Cheney snickered.

The phone rang again as Cheney watched Brian
set up a new board game on the screen. "You're interrupting a serious game of checkers, Parke," she
said into the phone receiver.

"Brian?"

"Yep, who else, but I think his mother or the
computer is helping him beat me," Cheney admitted.

"How about replacing your virtual checkers partner for a magical night with a flesh-and-blood, muscular black man who'll make stars twinkle above
your head, musicians serenade your soul, and charm
your troubles away."

She half-listened as Parke rambled before she
enthusiastically double-jumped Brian's checkers.
"Hmm, so that's your proposition. Well, I don't need
a man. Thanks."

Parke sighed heavily. "Woman, you could be an
insecure man's nightmare."

"Yeah, well, I'm living my own."

"You don't have to be. How about going with me
to Wabash Park's last outdoor concert? Malcolm
and Hali will be there, and Hali insists I bring you."

"Oh no, you didn't, you cheater!"

"I've never cheated on any woman. I've never
committed and every woman I've dated understood
that. Somehow those rules don't seem to apply with
you."

"Whatever, Parke, I'm talking about Brian."

"C'mon, you had a great time with us a few
weeks ago."

"You know, I'm working overtime to find something I don't like about you, but your family is wonderful."

His playful tone became serious. "I'm hard to get rid of, Cheney, especially when I choose to be here for you. I'd love to include you in all our family game nights."

Warmed on the inside, Cheney remembered the night of uninhibited laughter and pleasure. "If I don't, will everyone follow me home again, tonight?" Cheney hoped she disguised her desperation with irritation.

"That was a bold move, but don't deny you enjoyed it."

I enjoyed everything, including you. To admit that would only inflate Parke's ego. Distracted, Cheney's eyes bucked when she realized she had set herself up for Brian to jump three spaces to be crowned king. "Parke, I'm losing badly to a juvenile. I've really got to go."

"I refuse to hang up until you say you'll go."

"I can always hang up on you."

"Yeah, but I know where you live. I can pound on your door until you say yes."

"Or until Grandma BB loads her shotgun. Give her a reason and brother, you're target practice. Yeah, yeah, okay I'll go. Your brother and Hallison are great company. Good-bye."

Undeniably, Cheney enjoyed Parke's company. He was knowledgeable, entertaining, and somewhat stuck on himself. She better be careful though. Parke was starting to present a threat to her emotions and being around his brother and girlfriend made her heart wish for things that she didn't think were possible again.

* * *

As dusk set, Parke and Cheney idyllically saun-tered down Benton Street, crossing Powell Avenue to Wabash Park. Each carried a fluffy blanket. Parke didn't have a care in the world and he hoped Cheney didn't either.

Admiring the night sky littered with stars, Parke restrained himself from irritating Cheney, although he liked when she was fired up because she smiled. She was pretty and intelligent, but bitter or broken. He couldn't determine which, but at times he could see her mending from whatever that man had put her through.

Wearing body-fitting jeans, showcasing bulging muscles, Parke sported a fresh haircut revealing fine waves, and even changed his cologne, aftershave, and deodorant in hopes a night breeze would drive her wild. So far, she seemed oblivious to his changes. Or was she?

"I love walking through our neighborhood after dark. It's so peaceful and beautiful. Houses seem to come alive as indoor lights offer peeks of the fami-lies living inside," Parke sparked a conversation.

Nodding, Cheney greeted fellow concertgoers strolling past them. "Yes, I guess it is. Thanks for inviting me."

The park was jammed with lawn chairs and blan-kets. People were everywhere for the last outdoor event, signaling the beginning of fall. Strings of clear Christmas lights hung from trees, adding to the magic floating in the air.

It didn't take long for Parke to spot his brother and Hallison who were dressed alike in denim shirts and jeans. "It's amazing how Malcolm and his girlfriend outshine everybody in the crowd. They're practically glowing."

"They really do look good together, as if they're totally in sync," Cheney added with a sigh.

Parke watched as Malcolm incessantly seemed to have a possessive arm, hand, or his eyes on Hallison like she was worth billions and someone might snatch her away. *I could love Cheney. Have I lost my mind? Whoa, hold it. Could I? She is nothing like what I want, but seems to be everything I need.*

"Cheney, it's really good to see you again," Hallison greeted as the women exchanged hugs.

"It's good seeing you both again too. I only came because Parke told me you were coming." Forgetting about the men, they chatted amicably. After minutes of idle recipe swapping, the brothers separated them.

"You'll love tonight, Cheney," Hallison said, talking with frantic hand movements, then Hallison turned into Malcolm, wrapping her arm around his waist. She stared into his eyes, not caring they had an audience. Stroking his beard, Hallison caused Malcolm to inhale sharply.

Parke stole a glance at Cheney who wore an unreadable expression, neither longing nor disdain, just a blank look. Parke cleared his throat.

Malcolm bowed his head. "Sorry."

"You two don't need any music," Parke joked.

Guiding Cheney toward a free spot, Parke insisted they share a blanket. Although sitting next to each other, Cheney ignored Parke as she bobbed her head to Breezin', the band performing the soundtracks from the summer's blockbuster movies.

Using his peripheral vision, Parke beheld everything about Cheney as she leaned back on her hands. Cheney's lemon coloring was flawless, no moles or blemishes. Parke watched the wind twirl loose curls against her face, annoyed that her hair was in that blasted ponytail again. He would've thanked the wind if it could tousle every strand of her shiny black hair.

An hour later when the music stopped, one of the musicians tapped the microphone. "Before we end tonight, I want you to look at the person sitting next to you and see if you'll find "The Look of Love." The band began to play the tune made popular by Isaac Hayes."

Parke beheld Cheney's cautious look. She was scared. Winking, she smiled. Then Parke's eyes searched out Malcolm and Hallison. They were whispering in each other's ear and stealing kisses.

Lamenting inwardly, Parke turned back and tapped Cheney. "Malcolm and Hallison not only have the look, they're also wearing it quite well."

Tilting her head to the right, Cheney stole a glance in their direction. After a few seconds, she moved toward Parke and placed her hand on top of his, in a comforting gesture. "Your day is coming. You'll find that love you've been searching for. I can feel it." She grinned as she laid a hand over her heart. "I'm sure you'll charm some unsuspecting sister soon."

"You think so?"

She nodded.

I'm counting on it. He smiled smugly, wiggling his mustache. Whatever ice was around Cheney's heart, he was determined to chisel it away until Cheney was thawed out. He needed a prayer to do it.

CHAPTER 19

November

Snow—it was beautiful, soft, and treacherous. Five-inches deep and still falling, the white stuff could transform the most blighted neighborhood into a peaceful picturesque wonderland. The steady accumulation would also turn Cheney's Friday evening commute home into a nightmare.

Staring out her office window, Cheney daydreamed as the season's first snowfall threatened to immobilize the city. Known for panicking at the threat of an inch, St. Louisans would storm into grocery stores, leaving their shelves empty enough to starve a mouse.

She wanted to ignore the paperwork on her desk and go sled riding down Art Hill in Forest Park. She closed her eyes, embracing the snow's magical effect.

Cheyenne's childish giggles echoed through the yard as she formed an odd-shaped snowball, ready to aim.

"Ha, ha. I got you, Mommy. You're suppose to duck."

Cheney chuckled as mother and daughter frolicked in the snow before tumbling.

"Weee, you caught me, Mommy."

"Sure did. C'mon, let's make our snowman."

Cheney's eyes blurred as a teardrop splashed on the report on her desk. Would she always cry at the memories of what could've been? The guilt had to be exorcized. She closed her eyes and prayed, "God, how can I be set free? If you've been talking to me, I can't hear You, please show me a sign like you did to Gideon in the Book of Judges. Yeah, I need a sign, Amen," Cheney's voice faded as she nervously shuffled papers, hoping her fleet of twenty-one company cars wouldn't collide with other vehicles. Despite snowplows clearing paths, streets were covered again.

Two hours later, Cheney locked her office door, knowing she would be sequestered in her house the entire weekend. The ten minute drive home turned into a thirty minute trip. When Cheney steered her car into the driveway, Mrs. Beacon's house was dark. Her phone was ringing as she opened her front door. She raced across the room to the kitchen. "Hello?"

"It's about time I got ya. You had me worried."

"Oh, Grandma BB, I just got in. I was about to come over and check on you."

Mrs. Beacon's high-pitched laugh pierced Cheney's ear drum. "Chile, I'm stuck in Kirkwood."

"Kirkwood! What are you doing way out there?" The west St. Louis suburb was easily forty-five minutes on the other side of town.

"Yeah, my Red Hat Purple Ladies Club scheduled a day of movies, shopping, and the spa without checking the forecast. You need to come to this Westfield Mall. It's kickin' as you young people say.

Nordstrom's had a sale and I shopped until I was ready to drop, and you know at my age it's easier going down than it is to get back up."

Chuckling, Cheney envied her neighbor's care-free spirit—a teenager locked in a senior citizen's body.

"Anyway, about six of us are spending the night at my friend Gina's house. We're going to turn it into a slumber party, order some real scary movies, and make bowls of buttery popcorn."

"I hope no Chippendales dancers show up," Cheney joked.

"Hmm. Now wouldn't that be somethin'? But I'm worried about you, Heney. You going to be all right over there all by yourself?"

"Yeah." Cheney glanced around her quiet house. "Don't worry about me. I'll build a fire, relax, and watch some movies, but nothing scary for me. I'll find some reruns like *The Cosby Show*."

"Okay, make sure the fire is out in your fireplace before you go to bed and the doors are locked."

"Yes, Fairy Grandmother, good night."

Opening her refrigerator, she moaned at the near-empty shelves. Soup would have to do. Walking into her pantry, she sighed. A sparse number of cans were visible, but no soup. Throwing her hands up, she yelled, "Do I live here, or what?"

Lifting a Ritz crackers carton, the lightness told her it was empty. Smashing the box, she aimed for the trash just as the phone rung. "Hello?"

"I'm glad you made it home. I thought it was going to be a blizzard out there," Parke said on the other end.

"I just got here, but I should've braved the streets and headed for the store to fight over the last loaf of bread."

"Can I tempt you with homemade chili, made with my secret ingredients? I'm simmering it."

"Parke, how am I going to get it? I'm not driving in this stuff, at least not until tomorrow after the streets are cleared."

"I wouldn't want you driving anyway. I could bring over my big pot of chili, some funny videos, and you can build a fire."

Not wanting to get her hopes high, Cheney licked her lips, starving. "I don't think I've got enough logs to hold a fire for more than an hour, but the food sounds good."

"Okay, you supply the bread, then."

"Can't do that either," Cheney said, sighing.

"Okay, how about some crackers?"

"Nope."

"What do you have over there?" Parke chuckled.

"Plenty of snow and a can of French loaf dough."

"Excellent. I'll see you real soon."

"Parke?"

"Yes?"

"Thank you."

Parke grabbed bags and an empty crate when his phone halted his movements. "The woman said she was hungry. She better not be calling back to cancel," he threatened under his breath, reaching for the cordless.

"Hello?"

"Hey, Parke."

Holding his breath, Parke glanced at the clock. He loved Annette, but he didn't have time for her version of a Jesus conversation. "Hey, Annette, how you doing, babe?"

"I'm fine. I thought I'd call you since we're both snowed in with nowhere to go."

Parke tried unsuccessfully to hide his annoyance. "I do have somewhere to go, and I'm on my way out."

"You're drivin' in this stuff? Parke, the woman's bed isn't worth it."

"It's worth it, but I'm not going for her bed. I'm going for the woman."

"Hallelujah," Annette shouted. "Praise the Lord."

"I know you're not going to have church right here on the phone. I'll talk with you later."

"Okay, sweetie, but don't forget what I said before, Jesus is calling you."

Parke bent down and manipulated his six-quart pot in the crate. "I've already told you, Jesus and me, we're cool, but if you have to have a certain quota on your prayer list, then you can use my name."

Her voice softened, "Okay, make fun if you want, but, Parke, the Bible says, *'Search the scriptures; for in them ye think ye have eternal life: and they are they which testify of me.'* Jesus is the only answer. Love you. Bye."

"Hmm, I'm glad you love me, because you could do some damage if you hated me." He laughed, disconnecting.

Parke put on an extra pair of socks before cramming his feet into snow boots. He also added another sweater before donning his double-lined wool coat. He riffled through boxes in his basement storage room, searching for a metal laundry cart from his college days.

Dressed like the abominable snowman, he opened his front door and a gush of strong wind slapped him across his face. "I've lost my mind."

After three attempts, Parke was able to get out his front door and lock it behind him. Snatching an armful of wood logs off his porch, he haphazardly stacked them on top of the pot. When he jumped into his SUV and turned the ignition, his low fuel light flashed. Then he remembered it had been flashing on his way home. He had been so intent on getting home, Parke ignored the vehicle's warning. Now, he had less than five miles worth of gas. He got out and slammed the door. He didn't want to chance it.

"Yes, I have lost my mind," he said to no one as he started the ten minute, half-mile trek through snow that had drifted, forming small hills.

The ten minute journey took forty minutes before Parke stood at Cheney's door, shivering and sucking in the frigid air. Despite his fur-lined leather gloves, his hands were too numb to knock, so he slumped against the door, hoping Cheney would hear a thump.

"It's about time you—" She swung her door wide opened, greeting him with hardy laughs. "You look like a thug."

"Excuse me. Ice is stuck to my thermal underwear." His teeth chattered. "Can I come in?"

"Sorry," Cheney apologized, sounding anything but. "Take off your coat and leave those Herman Munster boots there." Cheney pointed to a towel-covered spot on the floor. "I've got a pretty good fire going in the living room. Don't know how long it will last."

With little effort, Parke slid to the floor, landing on his padded rump. He forced the airtight boots off his feet and stood. Gliding across the room, he added more logs. Ignoring his antics, Cheney carried the pot into the kitchen.

Using the mantel for support, Parke leaned in to thaw out. He scanned the neat stack of unopened mail and spied an envelope that had been ripped opened. Parke did a double take after reading the open letter's contents. He had one question, "Why?" he whispered before gazing into the fire.

"French loaf should be ready in a few minutes," Cheney yelled.

"Whenever you're ready," he answered, re-reading the letter.

Lugging dishes, glasses, and flatware to the dinning table, Cheney plopped down in her chair. "You're a lifesaver."

Parke gave nothing away of what had he saw. "How about being my lifesaver and eating on the floor closer to the fireplace? I'm still freezing."

"O-kay, I've got all this nice furniture and you want to sit on the floor."

They scooted the coffee table closer to the fire. Within minutes, they sat Indian-style across from each other, buttering warm bread. "Oops, we almost forgot to pray," Parke reminded her.

"Yeah, you're right. Let me." They bowed their heads and held hands. "God thank you for the food and bless it, Parke, and me. And please show me a sign. Thank you, Jesus. Amen."

Parke lifted a brow. "What kind of sign?"

Releasing hands, Cheney shrugged as she bit into her bread and swallowed a spoonful of chili. "I don't know. I guess God will show me. Mmm, this is really good."

"Impressed, aren't you? Admit you've never tasted homemade chili so good. My secret weapon: a touch of cayenne pepper," Parke boasted then something happened before his eyes.

Cheney's cheerful guise faded to a frightful, downcast look. "What happened? What did I say?" The following moments seemed rigid as an imaginary guest named Strained Silence invited himself to dinner. Parke scrutinized Cheney's closed lids as she ate her chili in a slow, mechanical manner.

Parke lost his appetite as dinner was abruptly finished minutes after it began. He reached over and laid his hand on Cheney's, hoping to pull her back from whatever place she had drifted. "Let's talk."

No response.

He lifted her six-foot lifeless frame and cuddled her close. Parke wanted to whisper consoling words, but what was he consoling? From all appearances, she looked comatose.

"Cheney, are you feeling okay? Why are you zoning out on me? Did you have some kind of allergic reaction? Is this the sign you asked God for?"

Shrugging, she stared into the flames and spoke in a trancelike monotone voice. "Sometimes it just hits me." Twisting her lip, tears trickled down her flushed cheeks. "Lately, the visions have been good, but the good ones gnaw at you."

"Baby, talk to me. What's haunting you?"

"Cheyenne."

"Who?"

"Cayenne sounds so close to Cheyenne."

The stressed-out, defeated creature he was staring at didn't resemble the tall, beautiful woman he had been spending time with over the past few months. His heart ached as Cheney closed her eyes, crying silently.

Her words became choppy. "When you mentioned cayenne pepper, it was like a bright flash, a deafening blast, and a sudden slow, burning pang snaked down my throat, igniting a fire that spread to the pit of my belly."

"I'm sorry. I forget everybody doesn't like spicy chili. I kinda go overboard with the seasoning—" Parke frowned. He couldn't recall anyone getting sick before.

She dropped her head in defeat, whispering her confession, "I aborted my baby, Parke. Everything within me tells me it was a little girl. A sweet, beautiful, adorable daughter I would've named Cheyenne.

"That burning sensation and the mention of cayenne triggered my memory. It took me back to the recovery room almost six years ago. My entire body was racked with constant vibrations of pain. My nerve endings were raw as a tiny viable part of me was ripped away. Imani is the only person who knows. My family might, judging from my imaginary leprosy that is keeping them away."

Parke exhaled a breath he didn't realize he was holding. "I'm honored that you've chosen me to be your confidant." Closing his eyes, he massaged his temples, thinking. Abortion was legal. He was sure he dated women who had one, but it wasn't a subject that a couple discussed over drinks.

Personally, he wouldn't tolerate any woman who

killed his offspring, a Diomande generation. It was his responsibility to Paki. He assessed Cheney. She was a ball of mysteries and a basket case, unraveling before him. He cleared his throat, contemplating the right words. "We all make mistakes. That's how we live, learn, and mature—"

Cheney's nostrils flared. "I was an educated fool." She pounded her fists on the floor. Her growl reminded Parke of a vicious dog waiting for the attack command.

"I still get so angry with myself for being so stupid!" Cheney attempted to close her red swollen eyes as she slumped back against Parke's chest in defeat. "Larry was all that to me—perfect, tall, handsome, and a very popular college football player who was studying to become an attorney."

"And the idiot who let you go."

Cheney's eyes pleaded with him for understanding. "I loved him. I believed in him, supported him, and all I was to him was a bed feast to satisfy his insatiable male appetite."

He gripped her hands and began slowly massaging her fingers. "You'll have other babies." *Maybe this is a good time to tell Cheney I'm falling in love with her.* It had to be love that kept him coming back for her insults, love that missed being in her presence, and love would sacrifice anything to see Cheney happy.

Glazed eyes flashed hate as Cheney pointed an accusatory thumb at her chest. "He whispered all the tender words that held my heart captive. He was the master romantic with his quick phone calls, short and sweet love notes, and thirsty kisses. I loved that man with everything I had only to find out he shared his love and kisses with at least two other women," she snapped with bitterness.

Things were starting to become clearer to Parke. No wonder Cheney avoided his advances. To her, he was another Larry although there was a big difference between him and this other character. Parke had never professed his love to a woman or forced his way into any woman's bed. Cheney began withdrawing from him again. He could feel she had more to say. He waited.

"I thought Larry didn't want a baby because we were too young or maybe because of our studies. I learned later that he found time for other types of studies and exams. He already had two children—no, let me correct that, one toddler and another baby on the way," she whispered between hiccups.

"What?"

"Can you believe that?" Cheney scanned the room like she was ready to throw something, and judging from the pent-up anger Parke was witnessing, she might choose him. "Larry practically dragged me to that abortion clinic, convincing me that we didn't have a choice, while he had another baby in the making and one already made—two years old. I never knew. I never suspected the dog!"

Hunching over, she mixed heart-wrenching moans with her sobs. "I wonder if those women fought with Larry for the life of their child, refusing to abort his seed, and accepted the unselfish life of a single mother. Was Larry excited about becoming a father? Who was he cheating on, Parke, them or me?"

"He cheated himself," he answered, sniffing.

Sluggishly, Cheney looked up and met Parke's eyes. "Why are you crying?"

Patting his face, Parke didn't realize tears soaked his cheeks. He couldn't recall the last time he had cried. "Because Larry didn't love you, nor did he deserve you or your love. Cheney, my soul is crying out as your anguish touches my very essence."

"I wish," she paused, "I wish someone had told me sooner about Larry."

"You wouldn't have listened. I'm told love has a power of its own, and in your situation, your love was strong enough to cover his lies."

"I'll never love like that again. I can't. Larry took too much from me." Cheney's voice was barely audible. "The procedure not only killed my baby and destroyed my mind, but butchered my body so that I can never bear children."

CHAPTER 20

Two days before Thanksgiving . . .

"**Y**ou are not staying home alone for the holidays! I can't have you getting in trouble like Macaulay Culkin."

Mrs. Beacon's humor didn't penetrate Cheney's sullen mood. "Don't worry about me. I'll be okay."

Positioning her hands on her hips and jerking her neck, Mrs. Beacon resembled a cowboy getting ready to draw a gun in an old-time western shootout. "I don't think so, not when your family is going to a South Carolina bed-and-breakfast. Humph! How convenient they forgot to invite you, huh?"

"They did invite me the night before as they packed.

The widow studied Cheney before fire danced in her. "Well, what better way to spend the holidays than alpine skiing with me off steep snow-covered mountains, dodging trees, and making flying objects out of other skiers?" Mrs. Beacon struck a ski pose, causing Cheney to release her gloomy thoughts and chuckle.

Scanning the room, Cheney admired the cream scalloped lace Priscilla curtains and thick rose-colored satin drapes. Cheney bit into one of her neighbor's homemade peanut butter cookies. Several were stacked on a silver tray on a coffee table in Mrs. Beacon's Victorian decorated bedroom. Crumbs spilled from Cheney's mouth as she tried to contain a chuckle. "Resting in a warm bed with no broken bones will cure any holiday blues," Cheney told her.

Mrs. Beacon gnawed on her bottom lip, mulling over a new strategy when her phone interrupted their friendly debate. She glanced at her bedside clock and shot daggers at the phone.

"Hello?" she answered, annoyed. Barely listening to the caller, Mrs. Beacon hung up without responding. "That child needs to go play in traffic."

The phone call seemed to irritate her more than frighten her. *What is that all about?* Cheney wondered as she watched Mrs. Beacon who didn't offer an explanation. Cheney didn't ask—this time.

She returned from her "commercial break" and picked up the conversation where she had left off. "I guess it's settled." Mrs. Beacon's voice became whiny. "I'm an old woman, climbing near one hundred, so close to death, I could go any second, and all I want to do is enjoy one last pleasure in life before my cold, lifeless body is lowered into the grave. All I ask is for a traveling companion so—"

Cheney fought back laughing at her neighbor's mischievous antics. The woman could lie. "What happened to the others kissing the wind on the slopes with you?"

Mrs. Beacon's near-death performance fizzled as she tapped into a renewed burst of energy. "There will be hundreds—no thousands, possibly millions—of glorious black men and women skillfully maneuvering obstacle after obstacle on the slopes. You'll witness the beauty of them in flight. My Midwestern African-American Skiing Club boasts at least three hundred members."

"Now Grandma BB, you know that many black folks don't ski. None of your medications cause hallucinating side effects, do they?"

Mrs. Beacon jutted her chin, taking offense. "This is a new time for colored people. We figure if Tiger can take over the greens, and the Williams sisters can dominate the tennis court, why can't blacks stroke the mountain slopes? Girl, you don't want to miss this."

"I do want to miss it." Cheney uncrossed her legs, stood, and affectionately hugged the woman who had become like a grandmother. "Close to death, my foot. You're a tough little granny with an imagination worst than Stephen King. If you're alone, it's because you scared everybody off, wearing Grandpa Henry's Stacy Adams."

"Hush, chile. That's my secret crazy old lady getup." Mrs. Beacon jammed a fuchsia and gray turtleneck in her suitcase, then strutted across the room, winking.

Cheney almost spewed hot chocolate on the woman's thick mauve thick carpet, trying to contain her laughter. Her neighbor was funnier than a cartoon character.

"Okay, I'll go to keep an eye on you." Cheney held up one finger. "If I break any bones, I'll make your life miserable."

"I say break a leg. There's nothing more romantic

than a volunteer ski patroller rescuing an amateur skier—them brothers could make a woman play dead for hours. Resuscitate me."

"You're truly a naughty grandma."

A wide grin spread across the seventy-two-year-old's face. "You better know it. We might pick up some fine-looking young men at Kissing Bridge, Niagara Falls."

"What? You can't be serious?" Cheney rolled her eyes and grunted. "Count me out. I am not looking for any romance."

Mrs. Beacon patted her curls, fresh from a recent salon visit. "Everybody smooches a little on the air-lifts, plus Kissing Bridge boasts thirty-something snow-covered slopes."

"Romance is like an instruction manual filled with too much drama. I've starred in a major role and didn't win an award."

"Nonsense, romance is exciting, mind-boggling, and contagious. Whew, honey, I can tell you about some sensuous drama that will heat up this room."

"On that note, I guess I better escort my over-active, Geritol-addicted neighbor. You're way out of control." Cheney stood and planted a big, juicy kiss on Mrs. Beacon's cheek before heading home.

An hour later, Cheney was packed, grateful she wouldn't be alone for Thanksgiving. Her thoughts fast-forwarded to Parke, and a slight ache stirred in her stomach. It had been three weeks and counting since her confession to Parke. She missed his warm, caring presence. He was the type of man she could love, if Larry hadn't ruined her.

"Me and my big mouth, some things are better

left buried. It probably cost me Parke's respect. I shocked him, shook him, and sent him packin'."

Despite the mess she had made of their evening together during the snowstorm, Parke had returned the next day to clear snow from her car, then stack plenty of wood logs against her house. She missed Parke.

One teardrop fell as Cheney imagined his probable disdain for her for destroying her lineage whereas he cherished his. "Sorry, Parke, but that's my guilt to carry, isn't it? I'm sorry, God, for doing it," she said to the wind.

Cheney hated talking to herself. As if telepathy, her phone rung. "Hello."

"What's the matter? I called to wish you Happy Holidays, but you don't sound happy."

"I told Parke, Imani." There was a moment of silence.

"All of it?"

"Yes," Cheney admitted.

"Hold on. Let me take a deep breath and sit down. Okay, what happened?"

"He cried with me, held me tight, and I haven't seen him since."

"Hmm, it was going good until you got to the last part. Cheney, I'm sorry. I was hoping, no, pulling for Parke to be the one. You want to fly to Paris for Thanksgiving? My treat. Maybe you can get you a White guy."

"There's nothing wrong with Black men, just Larry."

"So what are you doing for the holiday? I'm sure you aren't breaking bread with your family."

Cheney glanced at her open suitcase. "You're right. I'm going on an African-American ski trip with Grandma BB."

"Whoa. I'm going."

"Imani?"

"What?"

"Didn't you hear me? It's a Black ski trip."

"Try to stop me from coming. I'm on the next flight out." *Click.*

Cheney chuckled. One day, she was going to have to break the news to Imani that she wasn't Black.

In a better mood, Cheney walked to her closet and pulled three thick sweaters off the hangers. Her thoughts soon returned to Parke. "It wasn't like he suffered from my loss. I mean, the law says a woman has the right to chose."

Suddenly, it seemed as if the wind carried a faint voice whispering truths in her ear. *The law is not made for a righteous man, but for the lawless and disobedient, for the ungodly and for sinners. Read My Word in 1 Timothy.*

Trembling, Cheney stopped moving. Now God wanted to talk to her. She threw up her arms in defeat. *Why should she read His Word? Didn't He just call her lawless and disobedient?* she thought. No, shaking her head. Refusing to give in to another sullen mood, Cheney ran her bathwater to relax. As she soaked in a hot pineapple and strawberry foam bath, she dreamt.

The church's garden was expertly landscaped, flaunting a lush lawn. Large lilies, healthy ferns, and rows of bright red impatiens stood at attention while white roses chased a narrow path to a white gazebo. A warm sun il-

luminating a cloudless sky blinked its pleasure at the picturesque day, perfect for a noon wedding.

The groom was regal in his black tuxedo tails and deep polished black shoes. Layers of tulle hid the bride's face while a bright smile stretched across the groom's handsome mocha features. Jet-black, very wavy hair and a sculptured beard hinted of his recent sprucing from a barber. A stout, fair-skinned minister cleared his throat as he peered over tiny reading glasses watching the groom gently massage the bride's hand.

"Dearly beloved, we are gathered here today," the baritone voice boomed loud enough for a crowded cathedral.

Family and friends whispered as they sat watching two flower girls attempting to pull petals off nearby flowers and place them in their baskets. Some snickered.

"Do you, Parke Jamieson VII, take Cheyenne Reynolds to be your lawful wedded wife, to have and to hold—"

Cheney fought the water until her eyes popped open; her breathing was labored. With unsteady hands, she added hot water to the tub, but the chilly sensation kept seeping into her soul. There was no Cheyenne Reynolds. Cheney had killed her. "I cheated a man out of his wife?" Without needing an answer, Cheney knew her decision had a trickle-down effect.

Malcolm's one-line messages he left on Hallison's voice mail was bitter sweet—*I miss you, please call me, thinking about you, hugs and kisses.* Replaying his last message, she closed her eyes. *Hali, I would be honored if you would celebrate our first Thanksgiving together at my parents' house. I'm thankful I've found a woman who makes me so happy. Please call me, sweetheart.*

Malcolm's intensity scared her—no, drove her crazy since their weekend getaway. She thought she was ready, but she wasn't ready for what Malcolm had to offer. Hallison even had the nerve to tell God He would just have to understand the way she and Malcolm felt about each other. If she didn't sleep with Malcolm, another woman would.

So God fixed her so that when the time came, she freaked out as if Malcolm had turned into Satan himself. In the end, Malcolm suggested separate rooms. Days later, Hallison suggested he give her some space, which she got, until he coaxed her to attend the concert at Wabash Park with him. On the outside, they appeared just as cozy, and Malcolm assured her he was okay with them waiting again. Hallison wasn't. The incident made her feel like a fool, a tease, and a backslider. Hallison's intercom buzzed, interrupting her nagging thoughts.

"Miss Dinkins, your two o'clock appointment is here."

Refocusing, Hallison answered the receptionist who manned the front entrance, "Thanks, Sherri. Send her in."

Standing, she extended her hand to welcome a stunning plus-sized African-American woman who gracefully walked into her office, exuding self-confidence and an uncommon friendliness. After a six-week extensive job search, interviewing, and testing, Hallison was relieved to fill a job vacancy with a qualified sistah.

"Paula Silas, I'm Hallison Dinkins, director of personnel." They shook hands. "Please be seated."

Hallison had already reviewed Paula's file. A Washington University MBA graduate, Paula was bilingual, speaking fluent Chinese. She had been instrumental in her previous employer's merger with Asian entrepreneurs, wanting to invest in the American consumer lending market. Paula had also worked as a consumer loans assistant manager since her second year in college—another plus.

Bright eyes and a made-for-camera smile graced a honey-colored, oval face that hinted of sophistication. Paula had the prettiest features—even actress Mo'nique would have to agree. Within minutes, Hallison felt like she was chatting with an old girlfriend over lunch instead of hiring an applicant.

"I like your purple suit, and that gold scarf really brings out the highlights in your hair," Hallison complimented.

Blushing, Paula fingered her layered cut. "Thank you. Funny, I was just admiring your blue pinstripe suit. You're workin' it with your height."

Hallison chuckled. "I guess we better get down to business. Paula, this meeting is just a formality because Benton Duncan, the bank's vice president, highly recommended you. From the looks of your experience, business acumen, and the glowing comments from several professional references, you should be able to handle the chief credit manager position here with ease. Welcome aboard."

The woman closed her eyes and clutched her fists before pumping one hand in the air. "Praise the Lord. Thank you, Jesus, and Miss Dinkins," Paula's eyes twinkled as she gave praise. "I knew this was my job. I knew it. God told me so this morning."

Not the "J" word. He didn't have anything to do with this. *Well, there goes my invitation to lunch, shopping, or girlfriend chats.* Hallison sat frozen with a plastic smile without responding to Paula's outburst. Inwardly, she was rolling her eyes. *God just won't leave me alone.* "I'm happy for you. My secretary has your paperwork to sign, if we agree on the starting salary of one hundred twenty thousand dollars."

If she didn't see Paula again, it would be okay. Hallison avoided church people like shoplifters dodged security. A red flag should've gone up the moment Hallison read the woman's name and recalled its biblical significance. Silas was Apostle Paul's preaching companion. Hallison wasn't up for any sermonettes at work.

"God is so good," Paula whispered, her voice shaking. "That's the amount the Lord gave me last night."

People who spent time in prayer made Hallison uncomfortable, and shaking Paula's outstretched hand was unthinkable. Paula might try some type of 'touch and appoint handshake.' When Paula stood to leave, Hallison unbuttoned her knee-length pin-stripe coat jacket to keep her hands busy.

"Thank you, Miss Dinkins. May God richly bless you."

I surely hope not! That seems to be when my troubles begin. Hallison nodded. She collapsed in her chair after Paula floated out of her office, humming an old-time church praise and worship song. "That's my problem. Way too many people are praying for me."

Jeremiah chapter three, "*Turn, O backsliding children. For I am married unto you,*" seemed to crawl across Hallison's mind. It was a well recited verse in sanctified churches. Hallison sulked, folding her arms. "Then divorce me, God," Hallison growled through clenched teeth. Why couldn't God understand that she didn't want to be saved?

"*My thoughts are not your thoughts, neither are your ways My ways. Isaiah 5:5.*"

"I'm going crazy," Hallison said out loud.

"*My sheep know My voice.*"

CHAPTER 21

Cheney had asked God for a sign, but it was Parke who got the sign. He could deal with her abortion as long as it wasn't his kid, but the barren part slapped him. She was no longer a serious contender in his 'possible workable relationship' book.

Parke considered calling other female acquaintances, but guilt punched him, causing him to question what options Cheney had. *I had nothing to do with that.* Parke was determined to win this mind game.

It was Thanksgiving Day, and the holiday went handed in hand with the three Jamieson brothers. Hallison would be latched to Malcolm's arm. His mother, no doubt, would be cuddled next to his dad with her feet tucked under her, dozing. His dad would alternate between watching her as she slept and the football game.

And then there was Cameron. Parke hadn't seen his youngest brother in months, since the college sophomore opted to stay in Boston and work during the summer.

Soft Christmas jazz filtered throughout Parke's house. Humming, "Jingle Bells", he slipped into a blue corduroy shirt as powerful images of Cheney's vulnerability drowned out the music.

So what if he'd been avoiding her? "She can't advance my cause. I want a family." Shame stabbed his heart. "There's nothing I can do!" he shouted to an imaginary opponent.

"I'm Parke Kokumuo Jamieson VI. My destiny is to continue the African legacy." He had to erase Cheney from his memory, but what about his heart? Pursuing Cheney would be senseless. If only he could stop the battle of wills within his heart.

Unfortunately, Cheney had determined her destiny. Despite witnessing her misery, Parke's seventh great-grandfather had chosen the path for all first-born Jamieson men. Suddenly, before him, a misty black smoke covered his eyes. Glimpses of his past bed partners faded in and out.

Faintly, Parke heard a whimper. Children walked in front of him, but as Parke reach out to touch them, they evaporated. Then Parke recognized himself slumping to the ground, bawling pitifully. Jabs of severe pain pierced his stomach, nausea crawled up his throat.

Whimpers increased to moans as unbearable physical pain and unforgettable mental anguish attacked him from all directions. An infant appeared. In his heart, he knew it was his son, the next generation. Parke ached to hold him, but the child vanished as an older version zoomed passed on a tricycle. The Parke in the vision yelled out, "Don't leave," but the boy faded.

Parke's frustration continued. The child had grown to a young man; tall and magnificently handsome, accepting his high school diploma. Instead of bright eyes with hope for the future, they scolded Parke for what could've been. It all had been selfishly and brutally snatched away all in the name of love.

Emotionally exhausted and tormented, Parke saw himself old, bitter, lonely, and unforgiving. There were no sons or grandkids or great-grandkids—the void widened. He wanted out of the nightmare, now! As requested, the scenes vanished as fast as they had appeared.

Parke blinked and looked around, panting. Yes, he was still in his home. Everything seemed normal, but nobody would believe what he just saw. He didn't believe it or fully understand it. "What kind of torment was that?" Dazed, his heart raced, his pulse pounded, and his hands shook as he attempted to grip his car keys. When his phone rang, Parke checked his caller ID, it was Annette Barber.

"I feel like I've just been to abortion hell and back. I can't deal with Annette's witnessing right now," Parke mumbled, racing out of his house as if the dream was chasing him.

A while later and feeling almost sane again, Parke arrived at his parents' home. *It was only my mind playing tricks on me*, he tried to convince himself. Parke scanned the block as the scent of smoke from wood-burning fireplaces drifted past his nostrils.

He was about to put his key into the lock when an unprovoked image of Cheney flashed before his eyes. Parke repositioned it to the back of his mind and heart, proceeding inside. The aroma of turkey, dressing, and baked goods assaulted Parke's senses.

He rubbed his stomach before he was tackled from behind and rammed into a wall.

"Gotcha, man."

Laughing, Parke reacted swiftly and managed to get his brother in a bear hold. "Cameron, you'll never get the upper hand on me."

"PJ, I know you and Cameron aren't wrestling in my house! Take that horse play outside," Charlotte scolded from the dining room.

Embracing, the brothers exchanged mischievous looks. Parke stepped back and examined his baby brother who was his height, but thinner.

Cameron Daniel Jamieson was the quiet intellect of the family, winning more than two-hundred and fifty-thousand dollars in college scholarships. Cameron chose Massachusetts Institute of Technology in Boston where he said the city seemed to have more college students than residents and cabdrivers than police cars.

His wavy black hair was cut in a stylish fade, emphasizing his boyish look. He wore a large gray and red MIT sweatshirt with baggy jeans.

"Man, every time you come home, you're trouble," Parke teased, hugging his brother, then patting his shoulder.

"What else are baby brothers good for?" Cameron replied in a deep baritone that contradicted his childish statement.

The front door opened again, and a gush of wind swept Malcolm inside. Malcolm's designer coffee-colored leather boots stepped soundly on the hardwood floor.

Impressed, Parke admired Malcolm's ensemble.

He looked dangerous, dressed in a stylish camel-brown Indiana Jones hat, matching suede jacket, and worn jeans. Malcolm's dark sunglasses and beard added to his mysterious look.

Losing interest in Parke, Cameron strolled over to Malcolm and lifted him inches in a bear hug.

Grinning, Parke nodded to Malcolm. "Hey, lookin' good. I can't wait to see how Hallison is dressed. Where is she?"

Malcolm stiffened and looked away. His nostril flared, indicating he was determined not to say anything during the standoff.

Cameron mimicked Parke's stance with his own strange expression. "I've heard about Hallison all the way in Boston, and you didn't bring her? Go get her now," he taunted, pointing an accusing finger at Malcolm.

Removing his shades, Malcolm's scowl deepened, conveying any discussion about his woman was forbidden. "Not now, PJ, Cam."

What was going on with the Jamieson men? Parke had a bad dream while wide awake, and now Malcolm was tightlipped about his inseparable woman. Before he could interrogate, his parents interrupted.

Charlotte, arms opened wide and wearing a bright smile, glided into the foyer. The elder Parke eagerly followed, beaming proudly at his sons.

The brothers stopped their silent communication, gracing their mother with soft kisses on her cheek, and their dad with loud pats on the backs and hearty handshakes.

"It's good to see my boys together again. Mal-

colm, where's Hali? Is she meeting you here?"
Charlotte asked.

Parke wanted to know the answer to that too. It
was a known fact among the Jamiesons that Malcolm and Hallison were not only attached at the
hip, but in their hearts.

"She couldn't make it," Malcolm answered, but
didn't explain.

"Oh." Charlotte looked surprised as she looped
her arm through Malcolm's and led her family to
the dinning room table, saying nothing else, but
wearing that I'll-get-the-scoop-later expression.

Holding hands, they blessed the food before Cameron dominated the dinner conversation. "Mmm, I
still miss your cooking, Mama," he said as he bit
into one of his mother's homemade rolls, licking his
lips.

"We hadn't noticed," their father mumbled,
cramming a forkful of dressing in his mouth. "How
are your studies?"

"Good. Cameron turned to Parke. "I thought
Mama said you were stalking a neighbor. Cheney,
isn't it?"

The mere mention of Cheney's name was making
him a bit uncomfortable. Images of what she suffered kept sneaking into the corners of his mind.
"Stalking is not my style. We've clashed on several
issues. It was over before anything really started."

Parke's father didn't hide his disappointment.
"Oh? I concluded something different when I witnessed the battle of the sexes. I saw strength among
other things in that young lady."

"We were just playing a game, Dad," Parke
stated.

His dad had the nerve to sulk. "That's too bad, PJ. She seemed to pull your strings, and I loved her wit that one time I met her. What a shame."

Parke could no longer taste the cranberry sauce and turkey. He was dumbfounded to think he could dismiss Cheney from his family's inquiries so easily.

"Malcolm, where is Hali? I was hoping Cam would have a chance to meet her," Charlotte asked, changing the subject.

Malcolm lay down his fork. "I don't know what's going on. I think Hallison is trying to back away from me. She won't talk to me, so who knows what's on her mind."

"What?" everybody around the table shouted at Malcolm.

Charlotte stood. "Honey, talk to your sons. They're losing more than good women. They are losing their minds. Cameron, c'mon in the kitchen and talk to me."

Malcolm and Parke watched as their father pushed away from his half-empty plate, stood, and motioned with his head for them to meet him in the game room.

The elder Parke relaxed in his favorite steel-gray recliner and pointed a remote to the fifty-inch projection television monitor. Snarling, he clicked off the beginning of the Detroit Lions and Tennessee Titans football game.

Not a good sign. Dad never lets anything or anyone interrupt a Lions game, Parke thought, jamming his hands inside his pants pockets. He moseyed to the sofa. Malcolm stood at the other end. Both brothers exchanged looks before slumping into their seats.

In a quiet, controlled voice, Mr. Jamieson looked

sternly at his sons. "I want to know what is going on with you two. Malcolm, I'm shocked—no, make that disappointed about this news. What happened? I know you're in love with Hali."

Malcolm lowered his head in dejection. "Yeah, I guess I am," he admitted.

"Malcolm, if you have to guess, then I guess you're not," Mr. Jamieson snapped, before turning his attention to Parke. "PJ, if Cheney isn't the one, then who is? There's something about her. She's the closest woman to your equal that I've seen. What are you searching for, son?"

Parke wanted to watch the game, take out the trash, or go home. Not discuss Cheney. He leaned back on the sofa and released a deep sigh. "I'm looking for a woman who is beautiful, intelligent, and can have kids, which Cheney can't."

His father leaned forward, resting his elbows on his knees, his eyes wide with surprise. "What?"

Parke threw his arms up in the air in surrender. "Yeah, Dad, I know. Can you believe that?"

"What have you done, PJ?" His father's voice was laced with a reprimand.

"Nothing, I mean, I still care, but she can't give me what I want."

"For some reason, I believe Cheney gives you more than what you deserve. Do you have any idea what it means to have the right person walking with you through life's joys, dreams, and pains?"

Pain. Why did you have to mention that word? Parke thought, leaping up. He scurried to the fireplace. Staring into the flames, he remembered the last time he gazed into a fire. "Dad, haven't you been listening? Cheney can't give me a child."

His father stood, almost height for height, but eye to eye. He spoke in a low, steady tone. "I'm not feelin' you. I've watched as you jumped from woman to woman, but you seemed rooted with Cheney." Touching his chest, his dad continued, "There's a connection between you two. I sensed that before I laid eyes on her. You spoke with pride and adoration, your eyes twinkled when you mentioned her name, plus, you became addicted to wanting to do everything with and for her, so help me to understand why she's not the one."

Great, a Cheney fan club moment. Parke could feel his temper flaring. Hadn't he felt the special connection between them, too? He doubted Cheney did. Parke had witnessed the raw guilt eating away at Cheney when she divulged her secret. The bottom line was that he needed children, at least a son. What had *he* done in the past to sabotage that? "Dad," he said more forcefully than respectful, "you of all people know my responsibility to this family."

Nodding, the elder Parke lifted his brow. "Your first responsibility is to yourself. Paki endowed you with the knowledge, strength, and determination to achieve anything, son, anything. Elaine's love filled him with so much hope. They created a harmony many couples can't achieve today."

Parke wondered if his father was going deaf. He didn't want the Diomande tribe leadership in America to end because of him. As much as Cheney fascinated him, she wasn't worth it.

"PJ, Malcolm, haven't you two learned anything from your heritage? Paki and Elaine endured uncertainties to be together. Uncertainty always precedes the future. Elaine was determined to make Paki happy despite the ugliness surrounding them. Paki considered her a beautiful jewel given to him by the gods. She was worth more than his royal position in Africa."

The room became silent except for the wood crackling. Parke dropped his head back and looked up at the thick wood beams across the ceiling. There was no battle to win. "How come you're not in Malcolm's business?"

"You're my firstborn. He's next. PJ, I don't know why you or Cheney would believe she can't have kids." He held up his hand before Parke could speak. "I don't want to know, but I believe Paki would have been happy if Elaine didn't have one child. She was his strength and inspiration to live."

The grandfather clock chimed. His father squinted at the time, hinting of the game his sons were keeping him from watching. "Now, what's going on with you and my girl, Hallison? Please tell me it's not over some foolishness."

Malcolm glanced between his father and Parke. "Well, it's kinda personal, Dad."

"Talking about a woman a man cares about is always personal, but I need you and PJ to understand me. If you love a woman, never let her get away. Fight for her. Our conversation stays in this room."

Malcolm licked his bottom lip, debating. "We haven't been the same since our planned weekend getaway last month." Malcolm squeezed his lips together in hesitation, "Maybe, I was pushing her. I mean, Hali is the epitome of a sexy woman—the way she dresses, walks, and smells. I can't keep my hands off my woman."

Looking every bit the family patriarch, his father

pointed his finger at Malcolm with a tired expression. "I refuse to degrade Hallison by talking about your sex life with you."

"No need to worry about that. She was fine until we got to the Ritz. She freaked out. I suggested separate rooms on a different floor. She took it. That was our first argument. The next thing I know, she's crying, screaming we need a break from each other, and storms out. We went to a park concert after that, but it wasn't the same. Our affections seemed forced. We haven't been together since."

"Women are emotional creatures. If you love Hallison, try listening to her instead of talking, son. Maybe something's going on with her."

"You don't know how many messages I left trying to convince her there's no rush. She dumped me, throwing our feelings away."

The room was still as the elder Parke focused on Malcolm. "Keeping your hands to yourself might help. Women need to know you're operating on more than your sex drive." Malcolm nodded. "Do you love her?"

"Yes."

"Show her." The elder Parke grabbed his remote and aimed. "Now, go get my wife so I can enjoy the game."

CHAPTER 22

Cheney thought the ski trip was uneventful. Mrs. Beacon thought otherwise. Two weeks later, she was still bugging Cheney.

"Grandma BB, if you dangle one more Christmas light on this house, you'll blow the city's transformer. Then the neighborhood will be in the black, thanks to you."

"Chile, it ain't Christmas unless ya show off. Aren't you going to decorate?" Mrs. Beacon fussed, intertwining a rope of red Christmas lights with six feet of garland.

Cheney laughed as she stacked plates and bowls in Mrs. Beacon's dishwasher. "And deprive my neighbor of showing off? Nah, I wouldn't think of it. Besides, your house will be so bright, the wise men will be able to find us."

"You haven't told me if you called any of those doctors who were fighting over who would ride beside you on that airlift at the resort."

"One doctor in the family is enough. Remember,

my loving dad is a doctor." Cheney was almost one-hundred percent certain her father had gotten her medical files. There was no other explanation for her family's chill.

"Doctor Byron Bates was sexy, with his deep chocolate skin and sparkling white teeth. He made me want to take my dentures out and bite him."

Stunned, Cheney's jaw dropped. "You wear false teeth?"

"Of course not, but that's about the only thing I'm willing to take off to impress him."

"Not interested."

"Hmm-mmm, okay, forget the doctor. How about that engineer fella—Jeff, Jeffery, or Jeremy, something like that? He seemed interested and very handsome." She patted her hair. "In my day, a woman would be crazy to let the handsome, healthy, and wealthy ones slip away."

"You can have him."

Leaning on her knees, Mrs. Beacon pointed her arthritic finger like she was gearing up for a scolding, but her voice was soft and filled with compassion. "What's the matter, dear? Don't you want to get married and have children?"

Cheney was determined not to cry. "At one time I wanted both." She turned away and focused on the boxes half-filled with decorations. "Now, neither is possible." *I'm waiting on a sign, God*, she silently prayed.

"Why? Never mind, that's none of my business, but for a while I thought Parke was sweet on you."

"Parke Jamieson is interested in any woman."

"He never gave me a second look, and you know I'm adorable. At least call Eric, that computer programmer. He had the cutest little rump." Her neighbor winked.

The old woman's bluntness ceased to shock Cheney anymore. She provided humor in Cheney's life, especially during her darkest moments. "I bet you were something else in your day."

"It's still my day." Mrs. Beacon beamed.

They shared laughs until a phone call interrupted them. When Mrs. Beacon eyed the wall clock and made no attempt to answer the phone, Cheney offered to get it.

"Hello?"

"Jesus loves you." *Click*.

"What an odd call." Cheney looked at the receiver. "Wrong number, I think it was a child playing on the phone."

"It's a prank call. I don't know her name, but for the past year, she's been nagging me with the same thing. I've been close to cursing her out, but she hangs up too quick."

Clearing her throat, Cheney regained her neighbor's attention. "Since we're on the subject of kids, I got a letter a few weeks ago before Thanksgiving, stating if I was still interested in becoming a foster parent, they're ready to begin processing my application. I've been thinking about becoming one for a while. Would you be a reference and vouch for me?"

Sparkling eyes and a widening smile answered Cheney's question. "I love kids. Do you think you can have 'em by Christmas? As long as they aren't Bebe's kids . . ." Mrs. Beacon started plotting. "That will give me a reason for last-minute Christmas shopping, fighting over the last PlayStation 3 on the shelf—if we can get little girls, chile, we could dress them awfully fancy."

For the next thirty minutes, Mrs. Beacon filled Cheney's head with all the fun they were going to have with small kids, not once probing for more information. Maybe Mrs. Beacon's enthusiasm was a *sign*.

When Cheney returned home, she walked upstairs to her bedroom. It was too early to go to sleep. Restless, she sat at her desk and signed onto the computer. She hoped Brian was surfing the net so they could play a game of checkers, because she wasn't in a frame of mind to sit and read scriptures.

Cheney found herself entertaining ideas Mrs. Beacon had planted. "This is scary. Grandma BB is rubbing off on me."

Raking the bottom of her travel purse, Cheney scrounged up all the numbers forced on her during the ski trip. Feeling naughty, she dropped the business cards and scraps of paper into a shoe box, stirred them, and withdrew a name. Cheney took a deep breath and hoped this was not a bad idea as she dialed the number.

"Raymond? Hi, this is Cheney. We met in Niagara Falls."

His voice seemed to rumble with pleasure. "Ah, the beautiful Miss Reynolds, how are you? I'm glad you called," he replied, sounding sincere.

"Are you?"

"I am. How was your trip home?"

"Wonderful. Remember my senior citizen neighbor? The one who was the speed demon down the slopes during the day and the life of the party at night? Well, she was my lively traveling companion."

Raymond chuckled. "Miss B? Who could forget her?"

"That's Grandma BB's trademark. Show up and show off."

"No harm. She was having a good time. So, did you enjoy yourself?"

"Yes. Surprisingly, I did."

"I hope I contributed."

What arrogance. Cheney wanted to laugh. She loved his deep baritone voice, but his features were jumbled. Even without a face, the game was the same. Flirt, conquer, and move on. "Was that your goal, Raymond?"

"No it wasn't. As a matter of fact, my cousin needed another body to get the group rate, so I was coerced into going at the last minute. Now, I'm glad I did, because I met you, and you thought enough to call."

Yeah, right. Cheney closed her eyes. "So how many numbers did you get?" she queried, eyeing her own collection.

"I'm wounded," he said, lowering his voice. "None, you must have me confused with my buddies. They compared numbers like they were checking lottery tickets. If I met someone who was special and beautiful, then the trip was worth it. If not, it served as a diversion from work."

Cheney's suspicious nature kicked in. "Mmm. C'mon, Ray, not even one or two? You know honesty is the best ingredient to beginning a relationship."

"None," he repeated. "I didn't go to Niagara Falls to amass women's numbers like my friends, Fred Hanes, Larry Thimes, and—"

"Did you say Larry, Larry Thimes?"

"Yeah, I don't know him very well. He's a friend of my cousin's. Both are attorneys. Fred mentioned Larry was looking for Miss Right. Now that brotha was on a mission." Raymond chuckled. "The way he was scrutinizing the babes, I thought he was interviewing for a corporate position. Plus, I heard he had a track record. He boasted of breaking two engage—"

How about adding a broken heart to his list? Cheney was fuming. She slammed the phone down in Raymond's ear. She didn't care if he wasn't responsible for her pain. He was the messenger, and she had heard enough. "More than five long years have passed, I'm thousands of miles away, and I still can't escape Larry's name, memory, or his betrayal."

Cheney thought she saw a man resembling Larry on the slopes. She shrugged it off as her imagination. Then on the dance floor, a guy looked like Larry, only he was thicker and wore a beard. Again she convinced herself the probability of them being at the same place and same time after five years was close to none.

Did he know I was there and avoided me? What a missed opportunity. I could've slapped him, kicked him, and cursed him out—just one time and repent like Imani would. She grinned. A hypocritical Christian wasn't a bad thing.

Grabbing her cordless phone, she couldn't punch in Imani's cell number fast enough. She didn't care if her friend was in the air or just landed, she had to talk to her.

"Hey, girl," Imani answered, giggling. "Can I call you back? Captain Rogers and I were just goin—"

"Cancel it," Cheney snapped.

"What?"

"Cancel it, Imani. I need to talk to you now."

"Okay, hold on." Imani covered up the phone.

Cheney could hear a muffled male's terse voice because he had to reschedule their dinner date.

Imani came back on the line irritated. "Girl, you caused me to miss a free meal with a handsome captain. This better be a medical emergency, or that you're in jail and need bond money."

Cheney released her floodgate and became hysterical with hate, revenge, and anger. "Did you know Larry Thimes was at the ski resort when we were there? I could've eaten him alive."

"Yeah, I knew," Imani answered calmly.

"What! You saw him?"

"Yep."

"Imani! Why didn't you tell me? How could you not?"

"No need. I took care of him."

Cheney, who had been pacing the room, halted her steps. "If you didn't strangle him, then you couldn't have done the job."

"I can't believe I missed a seafood feast at an outdoor Moroccan restaurant overlooking the Mediterranean Sea to talk about that loser."

"Spill it, sister. What aren't you telling me?"

Imani sighed. "I hadn't planned to say anything, but yes I saw the pompous attorney. Remember, you

showed me his picture when I came to North Carolina to help take care of you while you were conva-
lescing. Of course, he didn't know who I was, but he
tried to woo me. He looked familiar, but as soon as
he introduced himself, bingo."

"And?"

"We met in the bar for drinks and a night I'm
sure he thought would be most pleasurable."

"But?"

"When we were outside the door to his hotel
room, I told him I had something for him. He was
stupid enough to tell me he wanted it too."

"Well, get to the end."

"Okay. I slapped him, twice. The second time I
had your name written on my hand. Not the chaste
tap, but the sucker-slap-the-butthead hit."

"What!"

"Yeah, he was about to retaliate, but I told him,
quote, 'Touch me and I'll scream assault. Who do
you think police are going to believe, a white
woman or a black man?' End quote."

Cheney fell back laughing. "No you didn't play
the race card."

"I did. Now, if you don't mind, I would like to
make that date tonight. We'll talk later." *Click.*

Cheney sat with mixed emotions. She wanted to
cry tears of happiness for what Larry got, but the
missed opportunity flared her hatred again. The
phone interrupted a tantrum brewing. She grabbed
it and barked into the receiver. "Hello."

"Whoa, I was calling to get my girl back, but it
sounds like you're having a bad attitude day?"

"I was never your girl."

"Sorry, how about my friend?"

"Not now, Parke. It's the wrong time, and I'm the wrong person to joke with."

"Cheney," his voice filled with concern, "please, don't be angry with me. I'm sorry for acting like a coward."

"It's not about you, Parke."

"Then, what's wrong?"

"Larry—"

Click. Cheney looked at the phone. *Is everybody crazy tonight, or is it just me?*

She was so mad, she felt like getting in the boxing ring with a worthy opponent like Laila Ali. "I probably could hold her to the ninth round too, pretending Laila was Attorney Larry Thimes."

Instead, she balled her fists and swiped the air at Larry's nose, his luscious mouth, his prized sex machine. Working up a sweat, Cheney concluded she needed to be more constructive, so she began cleaning imaginary dirt from her sparkling house. "After so many years, of all the places I could go, why there? Why now?" Cheney pounded a fist against the wall. "Larry has a lot of nerve, looking for Miss Right, when he's the Master of Wrong."

The doorbell suspended her rampage. She approached the living room, mocking a martial arts stance, yelling, "Unless you're Larry Thimes, now is not a good time for company." The chime stopped and pounding started.

Marching to the door, she flung it open to see Parke. Cheney sighed. Her patience and all pleasantries lay dormant as insanity reigned. "What are you doing here?"

Parke cleared the doorway, uninvited. "You're here and upset, so now, I'm upset, and I'm here." He reached for her hand. "I'm sorry how I reacted to your news. I freaked out. Believe me, I care about you. The hiatus I invoked on both of us proved that. What's going on? Let me fight your battles."

Perplexed, Cheney stared at the scowl on Parke's face. "You're an idiot. There is no apology necessary. Although I missed your absence, I expected it. Grandma BB is a good replacement. Believe me I don't need any help to fight Larr—"

"Where is he? What did he do this time? I couldn't stop Larry from hurting you the first time, but it ain't happening again. If he's here, then I'll personally put him out."

I've got a one-man militia in the house, Cheney thought. Parke's behavior was comical. She had a right to be mad, but he came storming in her home like her personal secret service detail ready to protect. Her battle was with bad memories.

Despite her anger, she wanted to laugh, but she was still too mad to crack a smile, but her heart warmed because of his concerns. "The jerk's not here. Ooh, I wish he was. I was on the phone—"

"Hold it. Get your coat. Let's walk and talk."

Without questioning Parke, Cheney submitted to his request. Once the chilly air hit her face, she could feel her anger subsiding. Bright, colorful lights and elaborate Christmas decorations greeted them as they walked. Parke waited for her to speak.

One block turned to several as Cheney rambled her frustration. Parke remained silent.

He pointed to a historic three story house. "You know, I like how the owner outlined the house using white lights."

"Hmm, I don't know. I like to see a lot of different colors flashing on and off."

He stopped and faced Cheney. "Feel better? You had enough steam to blow up your house."

Bowing her head in embarrassment, she nodded. "Yeah, I do. Thank you for coming over."

Thick snowflakes started to blanket them as if someone had pushed the on button. Parke put his arm around her shoulder like they were old buddies. "Didn't you know I'm a strong, fierce warrior who will fight all your battles if you let me?"

"If I'm not happy, I don't want him to be happy."

"It's time you let go of your past and build a future. Larry should only be a memory, not a stronghold on your life."

Cheney absorbed Parke's wisdom. Without realizing what she was doing, Cheney snuggled closer. "I'm trying, but Raymond—"

"Raymond who?"

"Never mind." Cheney looked up at the night sky. "Parke, I need a change in my life, a real change."

"Okay."

"I've decided to become a foster parent."

Parke halted his steps. He smiled as if something really wasn't funny. "I can't believe I'm going to say this, but I think you need to pray long and hard on this. It's a noble endeavor and a major responsibility. Cheney, I hope it's all for the right reasons. This is not the only answer to your situation."

"I really think this is a sign from God. I want kids so bad, I can see them. Actually, I don't really see them, but if everything goes well with my request to become a foster parent, then I'll adopt. This is a test case. I believe I've got a lot of love to give. Plus, I have the cutest rooms decorated for a boy and girl. I have to do this," she said trying to convince him. "Only one thing is holding me back. I need references."

"This is a sign too." Parke kissed her before Cheney could ask what. "You don't have to do this alone." He squeezed her shoulder and uttered words meant to soothe. "I'm here for you. Let's do this together."

"Forget it." She tried to break away, but Parke's grip was firm.

"Foster kids are victims like you. Their abuse could be physical, sexual, neglect, or even drug addiction."

"I know," Cheney whispered, blinking rapidly to fight the snowflakes landing on her lashes.

Wiping her lids, Parke softened his look. "I believe your abortion was a form of sexual and mental abuse."

"Parke, I've been living in hell. No one around me knew except Imani. I have a strong suspicion my family does, of course Larry, and God."

He took a deep breath. "Don't think I'm crazy, but I experienced something that kinda freaked me out. I can't explain. It was so real that I had to surf the 'Net to find answers. The letters I read on this Website confirmed that what I felt was real."

"What are you talking about?"

"Where do I begin?" He paused for a moment. "Shortly after you told me about the abortion, I had the strangest dream. I experienced the physical pain of an abortion as well as the mental anguish. It wasn't funny either. My body was possessed."

"Parke, this isn't story time."

"Truth is stranger than fiction. This isn't entertainment. I'm telling you I was transported to a place where I could see myself, the choices I made in life, and the consequences. Since experiencing that dream, revelation, or whatever you want to call it, I started researching abortions online. There were so many letters from young and middle-aged women who had them."

"Women Who had Abortions website," Cheney whispered.

"Yeah, Gargaro.com, right?"

"That's it."

"I've never posted a letter, but when I feel like no one understands what I'm going through or what I've experienced, I read the ones posted. Every time I do, the guilt resurrects itself."

"That's understandable because I cried, Cheney—for them, you, and our system that allows us to discard precious cargo like trash. That experience—real or imaginary—did something to me. I'm sorry I've stayed away for these past weeks when you really needed me."

It seemed like the snowfall wept uncontrollably as Parke told his story. Cheney's eyes misted. "Parke, you don't have to apologize." For some unknown reason, Parke's apology gave Cheney hope that everything would work out in her life.

As a dusting of snow covered the ground, being silly Parke playfully steered them around a tree to track their footprints in the snow. "C'mon, Miss

Reynolds, let's turn back and get you home. You were so hot you could've melted the snow."

"Was I that bad?"

"Yeah," Parke answered without making eye contact. "I see a change comin'."

Back on Cheney's porch, the old Parke was back as they stomped the snow from their shoes. Parke kneeled down and scooped up a handful of snow, shaping it just as Cheney unlocked and opened her door.

"Close your eyes," he commanded in a non-threatening whisper.

"Parke," she whined, "I'm not in the mood for having a snowball fight with you right now."

"This is not a brawl. Our fighting days are over. Trust me. Close your eyes and give me your hand."

She did as he asked, feeling the snow gently placed in her palm. Instead of a ball, Cheney opened her eyes to see a heart in her hand. "No pranks," she whispered.

"It's time for me to melt your heart." Parke leaned forward, within inches of her lips, and brushed the softest kiss against her cheek. His mustache tickled her skin. "Good night." He backed away.

Cheney wanted to resist his tenderness and hold on to her anger at Larry. Parke had performed a therapy foreign to her. His patience, concern, and gentleness soothed the tension from her mind and body. He was such a lovable guy; what woman wouldn't want to be his fantasy? She hugged him tight and he held her tighter.

"Now, you close your eyes," Cheney ordered, presenting Parke with her best seductive smile.

When he did, Cheney watched as he puckered his lips. Cheney's mischievous nature kicked in.

"Parke," she said in a low and husky voice, "open your eyes real slow. I want you to see this coming."

His lids fluttered open just as a wet snowball kissed his lips. He yelled. Cheney laughed, narrowly escaping his clutches before racing inside and clicking the lock.

Coughing and laughing, Parke gladly spat out the wet snow. He pounded on Cheney's door. "Okay, you got me this time." He loved Cheney's playful, unpredictable nature. He continued to bang on her door, more forceful. "C'mon out and play, you chicken."

His heart warmed to the muffled sound of Cheney's hardy laughter.

"Go home," she screamed, protected by the door.

Parke wanted to beat his chest like Tarzan. He didn't feel like going home, so he rolled a pile of snowballs and started throwing them against her front door and windows. Cheney opened her shutters, and teased him from the safety of her living room.

"Let her think I'm crazy," Parke mumbled, having the time of his life until a snowball whacked him on the side of his head.

Turning to his left, another ball met Parke's neck. He used his arms to shield his face as two more snowballs landed against his chest and leg. Parke almost slipped on the wet grass a few times as he dodged more snowballs as he hurried to his SUV for safe cover.

"Take that," Cheney's neighbor shouted, cackling.

Disengaging his vehicle alarm, Parke jumped behind the wheel as Mrs. Beacon's snowballs almost hit his Envoy. Wet, cold, and happy, Parke drove the few blocks home grinning from ear to ear.

CHAPTER 23

"This phone interview will take about ten or fifteen minutes. Do you have time?" Wilma Applewhite, the foster home licensing recruiter, asked Cheney in a friendly tone.

"Certainly." Although Cheney was behind her desk at work, she would make time. Rarely did she take her allotted breaks.

"Okay, first, Miss Reynolds, are you married, single, divorced, or widowed? Do you have any children of your own?"

"I'm single and no, I don't have any children."

"Do you have any experience with children, perhaps through your profession, family, or church?" Wilma continued.

"No. My degree is in business. I'm a manager at the local phone company."

"I see. Well, why do you want to become a foster parent?"

Think of a noble answer. Cheney began twirling

her hair. "I believe I have so much love to give, and I can't have kids." *And I have injustices to correct.*

"Oh," Wilma responded. "If you've never been married, how do you know that?"

Afraid to divulge her past with a stranger, especially over the phone, Cheney hesitated. She knew she had to be truthful since any discrepancies could disqualify her. "I had an abortion years ago." Cheney took a deep breath. "The procedure ruined my chances of ever giving birth," she rushed out.

"Hmm," Wilma murmured. "Did you undergo counseling after that, and how long ago was your last session?"

Whoa! What do my previous choices have to do with this? Don't you want my help? I thought your agency was begging for foster parents. "Excuse me, Wilma, what does my past have to do with helping children who need homes?"

"Everything, Miss Reynolds. I understand that you may be uncomfortable disclosing such personal information, but your file will remain strictly confidential. Every prospective foster parent must submit to a criminal, medical, and financial background check. A psychological evaluation is included in the medical check."

Maybe this wasn't a good idea. Cheney sighed, wondering if foster kids were worth it. "Why?"

"These children have been exposed to repeated abuse or neglect, sometimes both. The job of our agency is to make sure we aren't taking them from one bad situation to another."

Absently chewing on her bottom lip, Cheney understood. "I guess you're right. I've heard horror stories involving terrible foster parents."

"So, Miss Reynolds, in addition to your doctor's report and recommendation, we'll also need five referrals."

"Five!"

"Yes, professional, family, and friends."

Cheney felt as if a door that had an opening just slammed in her face. "Well, I'm estranged from my family."

"Hmm, can any church members vouch for you?"

Closing her eyes, Cheney confessed, "I don't go to church." She could hear the woman taking a deep breath. This was not going as she had hoped.

Wilma spoke in a slow, even tone. "Miss Reynolds, the law requires you to give us five references. I suggest you discuss your plans with at least one of your family members and find yourself a church home. All the children we place don't come from bad families, just bad situations. Plus, the poor things are often frightened, confused, or angry. They need a stable, loving environment."

On a Saturday morning at home, tears trickled down Cheney's cheeks as she mulled over what Wilma had said. It was days before Christmas, and she felt as if the Grinch, Scrooge, and King Herod had joined forces to destroy what little joy of having a foster child would bring during the holidays.

Grabbing her mail from the box, she scanned it. Despite her sullen mood, Cheney opened the Christmas card from her neighbor and laughed at Mrs. Beacon, sitting on the laps of two Santa Clauses. Her phone distracted her. "Hello?"

"Cheney, hey, this is Hali. I can't believe you used Parke as a go-between to ask me for a reference for adoption. Girl, you could've asked me instead of Parke begging and bribing me for a favor."

Hallison and Cheney had exchanged telephone numbers weeks ago. Within minutes, they had built a comfortable rapport, chatting about movies, clothes, and favorite foods. They hardly mentioned the men who introduced them. "Parke beat me to the punch. Actually, I'm applying for foster parenting."

"That's great. I read in the *St. Louis American* the other day about three young black boys up for adoption. They were so adorable. I felt like picking up the phone and bringing them home."

"They must've been real cute to make a single woman want to adopt three block-headed boys," Cheney said, chuckling. "I want to start with just one."

"Their story was so touching. They're brothers through adoption, not birth. They'd grown up together since infancy and their adoptive mother died."

Cheney felt foolish for indulging in her pity party earlier. Those three little boys needed a mother. "How old were they?"

"Three, four, and five."

"Wow. I don't know if I'm ready for adoption and three boys too?"

"I hear you. You'd be able to put a small dent into up to nine thousand children needing foster care."

"That many?" Cheney knew, without a doubt, she would subject herself to her family's ridicule if it meant she could help one or two children. She owed her baby that much.

"So, will you have any little ones by Christmas?"

"Once there check me out, I'll be eligible in about four months."

"Four months!" Hallison gasped. "They'll be almost grown by then."

"Yeah, tell me about it." They chatted a few minutes longer before wishing each other happy holidays and made plans to get together soon.

Around one in the afternoon, Cheney opened her door to check the mailbox and blinked. Mrs. Beacon's head popped in the doorway, Cheney saw a block of ice planted on her own porch.

"Chile, if you don't want that man, I'll take him. Henry was romantic, but this shows passion, imagination, and determination. Which young man from the ski trip sent this?"

Shivering, Cheney shrugged and turned around to grab her wool jacket. It was twenty-five degrees, too cold for her to be outside, but not cold enough to preserve the image before their eyes. Cheney reached out and fingered the ice sculpture as Mrs. Beacon nudged her.

"I saw the truck deliver it, so I had to come over to see for myself."

"It's beautiful. Look how each rose petal is delicately carved."

Both women hovered over the ice masterpiece, inspecting the ice replica of a long vase filled with a dozen long-stemmed roses.

Mrs. Beacon pointed to a sealed envelope. "Open it so I can go back inside."

"As you watch this melt, know that I'm also melting your heart. Parke K. Jamieson VI," Cheney read aloud. She gasped in shock. Since the night they walked in the snow, she hadn't heard from Parke.

"Humph, humph, humph. He's got me warming up," Mrs. Beacon admitted, pulling the scarf tighter around her neck and batting her lashes. "Now that's a man worth having around on a cold wintry day." Winking, she wobbled on her cane back across the snow-covered grass.

Cheney couldn't take her eyes off the sculpture. "Parke," she whispered, "you've picked the wrong woman." Throughout the day, Cheney would open her front door and stare at the beauty of the ice roses.

On Christmas Eve morning, Cheney helped Mrs. Beacon bake cookies, pies, and cakes to the sound of "Joy to the World."

"What are you going to do about Parke?" Mrs. Beacon asked, rolling dough.

"Nothing," Cheney answered, cracking nuts.

"You may be tall, but you ain't stupid." Mrs. Beacon pointed her rolling pin at Cheney. "I hope he doesn't go away. If that man hand-carved that ice, you better marry him, or I'll make your life miserable, reminding you daily that a good man is hard to find and keep."

Cheney repeated her reasons. It was the same story she had been telling herself for years—relationships were not for her. The argument was losing its strength. It was after dark when Cheney trudged across the snow back to her house.

Mrs. Beacon's home illuminated the Benton Street neighborhood like a scene from *Christmas Vacation*. She would've laughed, but she kept thinking about Mrs. Beacon's advice, "Marry the man." There was only one problem. Parke hadn't asked, and she didn't know what to say if he ever did.

CHAPTER 24

"Hello?" Parke mumbled, grabbing the phone as he snuggled under the warm covers on his bed.

"Happy Jesus' birthday, Parke!" Annette exclaimed over the phone.

Parke shook his head. The woman had too much energy at seven in the morning. She acted like she had stayed up all night, waiting for Santa. "Merry Christmas to you, too, babe."

"Finally, after twenty-eight years, Parke, I understand the true meaning of Christmas. I've invited some of our old classmates from college to worship service today. Nate and Kevin agreed. I was hoping you'd tag along. It's only for a few hours."

He wasn't sitting inside anybody's church on Christmas Day or any other holiday. Annette had truly lost her mind. "Ah, I've got other plans."

"Did you know that according to a recent survey, most black women say they desire a man with strong Christian ties?"

"Mmm-hmm."

" *'The day you hear God's voice, harden not your heart,'* my brother. That is what's keeping so many from getting saved. They don't want to hear from God. Parke, make sure you're not one of them."

Irritated, Parke began twisting the hairs on his mustache. "Annette, I've already told you, I'm a Christian, just not practicing."

Softening her voice, Annette didn't back down. "Never said you weren't. So was I before God really saved me, I mean really sanctified me. I was a watered-down version of what the Bible described as a true walking, talking, believing, living Christian. I only professed when I was challenged, but my lifestyle was everything, but godly. Did you know there was a list of things I was doing that was ensuring my spot in hell?"

Of all the fine, sexy, and intelligent women in the world that he had known, why did Annette want to question her faith now? She had plenty of time for that. "Whoa, babe, wait. You weren't that bad."

"Did you know that when I was expressing my feelings passionately during lovemaking, it wasn't love at all, but lust and fornication? Hell is filled with fornicators. That blew my mind. Once I stopped skipping over passages in the Bible and earnestly took a long look and studied what was written, I had to admit my life didn't reflect Christ. I had been foolin' myself."

Annoyed, Parke grimaced. Why was she discussing what happened in her bedroom? That abortion dream or whatever he had was spooky enough. This conversation was becoming exhausting and making him nauseated. "I can see you've been studying. Don't worry about me."

"I disagree. Is it wrong to worry about people you care about, to keep my friends from the pit of hell?"

Parke's thoughts drifted to Cheney. He had to get rid of Annette and her church talk. Parke gave an excuse and hung up.

Two hours later, he stood erect in a military stance outside Cheney's front door. He smiled at the remnants of his ice roses in the corner of her porch. He was dressed in a black full-length leather coat, gloves, a turtleneck, pleated pants, and leather boots. Parke felt like he was on a mission impossible.

Determined to turn the impossibilities into possibilities, for good luck, Parke had splashed on some Black Suede cologne his mother had given him for Christmas. The decision to intimidate, impress, and melt Cheney's heart had been made. Today was her day. *Look out, Cheney Reynolds, you're now under attack.*

Knocking loudly, Parke watched as Cheney's eyes sparkled when she opened the door. She tried to disguise her delight at seeing him by twisting her lips in annoyance. Leaning against the doorframe, she lifted a brow. "Mr. Jamieson, what are you doing here?"

He nodded. "Merry Christmas, I came to deliver your gifts." If Cheney liked his new look, she didn't comment as she continued her scrutiny.

"I didn't know I was on your list."

He moved forward, locking eyes with hers in a showdown stare. "You *are* on my list, and you're everything I want for Christmas," he confessed in a husky voice.

"Umm-hmm. What's with the new *Matrix* look?" She stroked her chin. "I like the new goatee. You're living dangerously now, or are you trying to look it?"

"I've been thinking dangerously, and it involves you and me." He held up his hand. "And don't say there is no you and me."

"I won't."

He grinned triumphantly. "Good, because beginning today I'm that man who can build you up, support your goals, and who will love you despite your past mistakes." His voice softened. "And fulfill the dreams you thought were lost."

"You can't replace what I've lost."

"I'll die trying, Cheney."

She intrigued him when she resisted. Her strength complemented his male might. With a sly grin, he removed his leather gloves. He reached inside his coat pocket and withdrew two small gold foil-wrapped boxes. "Merry Christmas."

Her expression was priceless. She looked truly surprised, hesitating before reaching for them. Cheney's defenses were starting to break down. She began to fumble with one box.

"I don't know what to say."

He took the liberty of putting his arm around her shoulder, nudging her back, and inviting himself in. "Say thank you." He paused. "Say your heart is melting."

Cheney didn't respond, but her eyes watered. Parke commanded his hands not to reach out to caress the worry lines above her eyebrows as she bowed her head, fingering the gold ribbons.

"I didn't get you anything, Parke."

"Then give me you," he whispered.

"Stop flirting with me," she said, warning him as she stomped her foot to show she wasn't affected, but she couldn't contain the bright smile that peeped through.

"See, that's where I'm having this problem. I can't." Parke removed his coat and plopped down on the sofa. He stretched his arm across the back like he lived there. "I'm not going anywhere until you open the box, even if it's next Christmas."

"Hmm, that might give Grandma BB a reason to load her shotgun." They both laughed.

Eagerly, Cheney opened one gift that contained a dazzling tennis bracelet. She thanked him. It was the other box that fascinated her as she pulled out a lotion-sized bottle, void of any rich, creamy, or sweet-smelling lotion. Instead, tiny rolls of colorful paper were stuffed inside. She gave him an odd look suggesting he had a reason for this. Knitting her brows together, she puckered her full lips. "A bottle. Thank you?" she stuttered.

"It's part Christmas, part Kwanzaa, and part commitment gift." He gently shook the bottle. "Here, take one out."

Cheney fingered a lavender scroll. "Do you stay awake all night and concoct these ideas, or is this sample from years of on-the-job training with other women?"

"These concoctions, as you call them, are not stale or leftovers. No woman could've prepared me for you. My motives are as original as you are unique." Parke massaged his goatee, holding her stare.

Nodding, Cheney untied a satin ribbon holding

the paper like a diploma. It was no bigger than half the size of a business card. She unrolled the paper. *Happiness is yours.*

"That's one of fifty love notes that represent all the wonderful emotions locked away inside you. I've got your key, baby." He memorized and cherished her surprised look of surrender. "You don't have to go looking for whatever is in that bottle. I'll bring it to you. I love you, Cheney."

"When did you fall in love with me, Parke? Last night?"

"The evening at the library, the makeshift picnic on your porch, the walk in the snow, the—"

Cheney jumped up with the bottle in one hand, balling her other hand in a tight fist. "I get the point. Are you crazy? What part of I am not the one do you not understand?" she yelled. "I can't have children," she said, emphasizing the last word. "I don't mind being friends or more than friends, but in love with me? My peace, dreams, and world died the day I allowed my baby to be ripped from me."

With measured slowness, Parke also stood, using his inches to tower over her.

Slapping a hand against her hip, Cheney released a haughty laugh meant to intimidate. She was mad. "Did you put a baby in that jar, Parke? That's about the only way you'll get one from me."

Grinning, Parke stepped closer. "Yes, as a matter of fact, I did, more than one."

"I've lost my baby, but you've lost your mind."

"No, Cheney, I've found the only woman who can fill me."

"What about your bloodline? I can't believe you're willing to give that up."

Tenderly, Parke pulled Cheney into a non-threatening embrace. "I've already made reservations for you in my life. I'm relinquishing my birth right to Malcolm. You don't need the foster kids. You've got me."

Cheney held his stare. "I think you're a sensitive, foolish, and handsome man with a fascinating family history, but I can't mess up your life because I messed up mine."

Parke tightened his hold. "You aren't going to push me away." Cheney jerked out of his arms.

"Who and what tribe is going to stop me?"

"Me," he growled. "If you're looking for a fight, then you've met your match, baby."

Stepping back, Parke reached for his leather coat and marched to the door before turning back. "I'll be back in ten minutes. Dress for battle, very warmly. The fight is on."

Perplexed and amused, Cheney watched Parke storm out her door before she stomped upstairs to change. *Why do I put up with him?* she thought as she got dressed. *Because he puts up with you,* a small voiced whispered. "Who does he think he is?" she mumbled, not knowing what he had planned. Inwardly, she enjoyed his challenges.

True to his word, Parke returned minutes later, dressed in snow gear. After locking her door, Cheney climbed into his Envoy, wearing so many clothes that the seat belt barely accommodated her. She observed Parke as he steered his SUV. No music was playing or words spoken. Parke's focused and stern expression was comical.

"Where are we going?" Cheney finally asked.

"Forest Park," he said without looking at her.

Twenty minutes later, Parke stopped in front of Art Hill across from the art museum. The large hill was home to snowboarders, sledders, and anyone who enjoyed tumbling in the snow.

Parke was silent as he turned off the ignition, opened his door, and walked around to Cheney's side. When he released her seat belt, he gripped the sides of her coat and lifted her out.

Cheney was slightly apprehensive. She didn't know what Parke had planned. "Let me down. Now!"

He ignored her outrage as he stomped hard, carrying her to a tree. "This is your side, mine is over there." He pointed a few yards away. Parke planted his hands on his waist. "Whoever wins the fight, wins the other's heart, totally."

Were Paki and Elaine this focused, headstrong, and crazy romantic? she wondered as she watched Parke march away.

"You've got exactly ten minutes to stockpile your weapons. Remember, winner takes all."

Cheney watched as Parke rolled snowballs. When Cheney saw he was serious, she hurriedly made her own pile. She didn't realize she had run out of time until the first snowball whizzed by her head.

Laughter echoed through the air. "That was just a warning. C'mon, sweetheart, give me all what ya got."

Armed with two snowballs in each hand, Cheney shot daggers. *No he didn't almost hit her then call her sweetheart?* It was on. Cheney began launching snowballs like a cannons.

Soon she understood why Parke positioned her

near a large tree. So far, he had hit her everywhere, but her face. Still, she wasn't ducking fast enough. Cheney's competitive spirit kicked in, she wasn't granting any mercy, aiming to wipe off the silly grin from Parke's face. Despite the cold temperature, the snow, and standing outside in a park on Christmas Day, Cheney was having a ball.

Out of nowhere, several preteens approached and offered Cheney some reinforcement, laying down what Cheney assumed were their new Christmas gifts. She grinned. "Sure, why not?"

Within minutes, Parke began running and ducking as one snowball after another clobbered him until another group of kids came to his rescue, attempting to even the score. As the crowd grew to a mob-like proportion, Parke tried to signal a time-out. It didn't work.

Failing to call a ceasefire, Parke and Cheney met halfway, making themselves a target.

Grabbing Cheney's gloved hand, Parke tugged her out of harm's way. "We better get out of here before they make us a pair of snowmen."

Hand in hand, they dashed to the Envoy torpedoed by snowballs. As Parke disarmed the alarm, Cheney assumed they would jump in their seats and take off. Instead, Parke shielded her from more blows. He took his time opening her door and lifted her onto the seat.

"The battle is over, Cheney. It's time to let it go. You're no match for the warrior. What I conquer, I keep."

"You didn't conquer me."

"Didn't I?"

Parke closed his cold lips over hers. It wasn't the

same tender kisses he bestowed the night she went ballistic after hearing Larry's name. Cheney should've taken the issue up with him then, but the gesture was so comforting. She welcomed it. She heard the snowballs hitting the door and Parke's back, but that didn't stop him from branding her. When he pulled away, he whispered, "That should convince you."

Stunned and dazed, she didn't respond. On the ride home, Parke blasted the heat and filled the air with musical instruments that tested the depths of love and passion through high-pitched notes. Every moment with Parke was becoming addictive. He had more strategies than Brian with checkers. She could never predict his next move.

As he slowed in front of Cheney's house, he turned down the music, silently assessing Cheney. "Merry Christmas. You're going to have to accept my love."

Determined to stare him down, she turned and met his eyes. His playfulness was gone, replaced with serious brown eyes that were soft and inviting.

She had lost the battle. Cheney could feel herself retreating. Her heart was settling into a comfort zone. Expecting Parke's comical antics, he showed her his tenderness and gentleness, which were incredibly soothing. Yes, he was beginning to melt the ice that covered her heart. She smiled. "Merry Christmas, Parke."

"Cheney, if I walk you to your door, I promise you, you'll be kissed again."

Giddy with anticipation, she raced out of the vehicle. She heard Parke's laugh fade as she jumped onto her porch. Once inside, she tugged out of her snow gear and changed clothes. She was in good spirits when she picked up the phone to call her parents and realized they had left her a message. *Cheney, I called to invite you over for Christmas brunch, but I see you aren't there. Maybe next year.* Cheney replayed the message three times, knowing she didn't hear right, but she did. Punching in her parents' number, her mother answered. "Mom, I just got in, I can be there in about an hour," Cheney said hopeful. This would be their first Christmas together since she returned home.

"Oh, don't worry about it. We all have eaten, and we're on our way to the theater, but we did get you presents, so I'll drop by tomorrow. I've got to run. The movie starts in thirty minutes," Gayle said, disconnecting.

"Whew, I must've been a witch five years ago." Cheney wiped away a lone tear. She was so removed from her family circle, with all the power God supposedly had, even He couldn't fix that. Cheney showered, dressed, and went next door to have Christmas dinner with Mrs. Beacon.

CHAPTER 25

Hallison sorted through the sale items at Bath & Body Works, overfilling her basket with mix-and-match scents as Cheney observed, laughing. From the store's checkout line, Hallison grabbed Cheney's arm and scurried to the after-Christmas sale at Victoria's Secret before zigzagging across the mall to Sam Goody.

"Hallison!" Cheney shouted.

"What?"

Panting, Cheney gripped Hallison's arm. Cheney really did appreciate the newfound friendship with Hallison when Imani wasn't near, but enough was enough. "Thanks for inviting me to go bargain shopping with you, but so far I haven't been able to keep up on your safari hunt."

"Sorry," Hallison apologized, chuckling. "I'm trying to keep my mind off Malcolm. I've been avoiding him, yet I crave him like a hot bath."

"Considering every other word is Malcolm, I'd say you're torturing yourself."

"I know. He's been calling, but I haven't answered. I thought I could handle Malcolm Jamieson, but his skills are no match for me."

"Really, I didn't get that impression when I first met you. Hallison, if you want to talk about it, I'm here. Can't say I'll give sound advice. Sometimes, I feel like my head isn't screwed on tight."

"Thanks."

As the women entered an "oldies but goodies" music store, beautiful lyrics serenaded customers while they browsed. Cheney had a finger on a Boyz II Men CD to give Mrs. Beacon when she stopped. "Is that Patti?"

Tilting her head, Hallison listened. "Yeah, it must be Patti LaBelle's *Love Songs* CD."

"I like that song."

"Yeah, I'm pretty sure that's "You are My Friend." After so many years, that woman has held on to her diva status," Hallison said.

"The words remind me of Parke. The man has been there for me, whether I wanted him to or not."

"Ah, the royal Jamieson prince. Since meeting you, the brother has done an about face. Whoa, here's Freddie Jackson's new CD. I'm getting it," Hallison stated, taking the CD from a stack. "Malcolm seems more determined now than before our big argument. I suggested we cool off."

"They're hard to get rid of. It was Parke's playfulness that pulled me out of my slump. Now, his seriousness is scaring me."

"Believe me, I know." Hallison paused. "Let's pay for these and grab a bite to eat. Bargains make me hungry."

"It's nothing like the strong fireworks you and Malcolm set off. I experienced joy mixed with jealousy when I saw how much you two adored each other. I thought I had that once. I was wrong. I don't know if I can survive another risk like that again."

"Demons," Hallison stated. "It doesn't seem like we can live without them. I wanted that man so much." She sighed. "Now . . . demons."

"Demons," Cheney whispered.

Minutes later, they entered the madhouse of the food court. Once finding a seat, and both offering quick prayers, Hallison feasted on McDonald's while Cheney had Chinese bourbon chicken.

"Hallison, I'm so glad we got together. We've been playing phone tag a while. This was perfect timing since I'm on vacation this week with nowhere to go and nothing to do. My best friend is somewhere in China. I do have family, yet I'm alone. I have a twin and we talk sometimes. Maybe it's my imagination that he's just tolerating me because we're connected."

"Don't let Parke hear you say that. He's very resourceful in finding activities."

"Yeah, don't I know it? I've already experienced one. The other day, Parke branded me, and I've been a basket case ever since."

"What do you mean branded you? Tattoos?"

"No, the man kissed me senseless. For Christmas Parke gave me one gift that was this stupid little bottle filled with notes, but the thought behind it was kinda cute. Christmas night alone at home, that bottle tempted me so I took the bottle and turned it upside down thinking 'Do I really want to know what else Mr. Jamieson has in store for me?' When I untied a scroll, the message read *Seductive smiles and drugging kisses.* Let me just say Mr. Jamieson delivered."

Hallison wore a knowing smile before draining the last of her soda. "I know Malcolm's lips are pure seduction. That's what started my internal battle."

"Honestly, Parke overwhelms me. Girl, I thought I was deep-frozen, numb, and practically heart-dead to experience any emotions because of a crushing breakup years ago. Parke says his kiss was a Diomande courting tradition."

"Don't let me have to fall out of this chair waiting. What did Parke Cuckoo Jamieson VI do?"

Cheney couldn't help but laugh along with Hallison before she gave some details, "First, we had this big snowball fight on Christmas Day, a sort of battle for our relationship." Cheney blushed. "It was fun. I was cold, but after he kissed me while I was sitting in his SUV, the meltdown began."

"Maybe Malcolm gave him some pointers," Hallison teased, winking.

"I watched as Parke's lips descended on mine with so much gentleness, I wanted to cry. After all that horseplay, he was delicate."

Cheney leaned across the table. Hallison eagerly met her halfway.

"I don't remember his lips leaving mine, but the next thing I knew, he was placing soft kisses against my ears, he said so I can recognize his voice. He confessed my brows had hypnotized him long ago. He branded them so I'd see and desire only him."

"Stop," Hallison interrupted. "I've been holding my breath. I need to swallow this food caught in my throat so I can breathe." Hallison turned her head, and noticed a young woman at the next table, reading a Bible while eating lunch. Feeling uncomfortable, Hallison refocused her attention on Cheney. "Wow. For the record, Parke didn't get that from Malcolm. Were you still conscious during this branding?"

"I must've been in a trance because I couldn't move to slap him, but there's more."

"I'm listening and learning." Hallison nodded.

Cheney picked at her food. "He called it tribal worship, kissing my nose so I could inhale his closeness, then his lips lingered on my forehead so my mind would understand him."

Making a time-out signal, Hallison eyed her eating companion. "Whew! That's romantic."

"Wait. I lost it when he kissed my fingers so I can touch his soul."

Hallison fanned her flushed face. "So why the sad face?"

"Because he wants and deserves so much more. Those demons you mentioned earlier, well, mine won't let me give him what he wants."

Demons and angels. Hallison stole a peek at the woman who was reading the passages like they were an action-packed adventure. "Yeah, I'm fighting my own demons from the past, too."

"Do you really think Parke branded me?"

"African or African-American, yes, tag you're it."

Cheney was still playing hard to get. The thought made Parke grin. He had left his office with an extra pep after meeting with three clients and reviewing their portfolios. He was free the rest of the day. For three days, he called Cheney, leaving sweet messages and encouraging her to keep shaking the bottle for her dreams to come true, but not once had she returned his calls. Parke hoped Cheney believed that Diomande tribe stuff he made up. Chuckling, Parke decided to cruise by Cheney's house.

Bitter wind chills wreaked havoc on the city. Temperatures plummeted so fast, residents were caught off guard. As Parke turned the corner, he could see Cheney down the street, walking a circle around her car. He pulled into her driveway behind her car and got out. Cheney's panicked expression alarmed him. "What's wrong, honey?"

Tears filled her eyes. "My locks and doors are frozen. I've got my first orientation meeting with the foster care people in forty-five minutes. It won't look good if I'm late or miss it."

Reaching for her hand, Parke pulled her closer. "Hop in. I'll drive you. You should've called my cell. Where are we going?"

He could tell she was about to protest. Opening the passenger door, Parke ushered her inside before brushing a soft reminder of his kisses on her lips. Cheney relaxed. "The Divison of Family Services in Clayton. Thank you."

Tracing her eyebrows, Parke couldn't believe how silky they were. He smiled as he backed away, grinning. "For the kiss, or giving you a lift?" He shut the door and walked around to the driver's side.

"The lift is definitely more valuable to me, right now."

"I'll make you pay for that comment later."

Parke concentrated on the road as strong winds rocked his SUV. He snuck glances at Cheney while she fidgeted in her seat. Grasping Cheney's hand,

Parke linked his fingers through hers, before kissing each finger. "Are you going to be okay? So, you're really going through with this?"

"Yes. I think it is a sign from God for me to be a mother even if I'm on loan."

"I wish I could convince you otherwise. Foster children may not give you the happy ending that you're looking for."

"Can you?" she whispered as she ignored him. Opening her misty eyes, Cheney faced him, but she didn't take his bait. He loved her and he would do everything in his power to make her whole again.

"I've already had an unhappy ending that I wrote with my own sins."

Parke's heart sunk. His mind screamed, *Annette.* Parke groaned, the things he was doing for love.

Without a good-bye or thank you, Cheney hastily exited Parke's SUV before it came to a complete stop at the curb. Gusty winds propelled her toward the revolving doors of the Missouri Division of Family Services building. She inhaled the cold air. "I can do this despite you, Rainey." Cheney couldn't believe her twin wouldn't vouch for her as a reference. She knew not to depend on her sister or parents, but Rainey?

"You sure can," Parke whispered close to her ear as she neared the elevator. "What does your brother have to do with this?"

Cheney whirled around. "Parke, what are you doing?" Her heart pounded against her chest. She didn't know if it was from her nervousness about the program or the fact Parke had been her rescuer ever since she had moved to Old Ferguson. She recalled one of his notes she read the other day: *Let me rescue you*. "And how did you get in here so fast? What did you do, park on the sidewalk?"

"Nope, across the street, a guy was just pulling out. I made a u-turn and—"

"Never mind."

"Okay, now tell me what's going on with your brother." His intense stare said Parke would patiently listen. She hadn't really looked at him when he picked her up. Scanning his attire, she hinted a smile. He was dressed in a cream turtle-neck and his chocolate-colored pants matched the color of his snake-skin shoes and cashmere coat. It was the hat he removed that she liked. "You look nice."

Parke lifted a brow. "So do you. Now, stop stalling."

"Okay." She paused, struggling to repeat what she wanted to forget. "When I confided in Rainey that I needed a reference to become a foster parent, he said sure. He should've kept it! Wilma, my foster care recruiter, called this morning. Rainey's exact words were 'Investigate her past thoroughly to make sure she's mentally stable to accept the responsibilities of caring for children.' Why would he say that?"

Parke's head fell back and he sighed heavily. "I don't know. I'm sorry you don't have your family's support, but you have mine. Did you try and call him?"

"I've left messages, but he hasn't called me back yet. Rainey's comments were a surprise."

The elevator opened and Parke ushered Cheney inside "Take a deep breath," Parke instructed, stroking the length of her nose. He disregarded the others in the elevator car with them. Leaning in close to her ear, Cheney inhaled and exhaled his cologne. He whispered, "I told you I'm a warrior, and I'll fight your family or everybody else to make you happy."

Cheney's emotions were too jumbled to protest, so she complied and leaned into his chest. Off the elevator and inside the large classroom, Parke asked questions, talking to other prospective parents as if he initiated the process. Every so often, he would stop and look her way, giving her a reassuring nod, and communicating his support and his love. He left her side only to get them refreshments.

"You're serious, aren't you?" she whispered when he approached with a cup of coffee and sat down.

Folding his arms, Parke didn't blink. "Yep."

"I think that woman is Wilma." Cheney grabbed his hand and stood. "C'mon, let's go introduce ourselves."

"Miss Applewhite?" Cheney queried as she walked up behind her.

The short, plump woman turned around. "Yes?"

"Hi, I'm Cheney Reynolds. We've talked on the phone."

"Oh, yes." Wilma smiled, extending her hand.

"And this is one of my references, Parke Jamieson."

Wilma tapped her pink-polished nails against her unpainted lips. "Parke Jamieson sounds familiar. Are there others? I mean do you have numbers behind your name?"

Parke frowned. "Yes, I'm the sixth, why?"

She shrugged. "That name seemed familiar."

"I'm one of her references. Remember?" Parke pointed out.

"Of course, oh well, I'm sure if we'd met, I would've remembered such a good-looking man as yourself."

Cheney shot daggers at the gray-haired woman as Parke shrugged innocently. She stabbed him in the side with her elbow.

A tall black woman about sixty years-old cleared her voice at the podium. "Let's get started. I'm Eva Moore. I've been a foster parent for more than twenty years. We have a lot of information to cover in the next three hours."

Everyone took their seats. Cheney hoped Parke wouldn't change his mind. He turned to her, lifted his brows, and mouthed "Three hours?" She nodded, and refocused on the speaker, releasing a breath of gratitude when he remained seated.

"One of your responsibilities as a foster parent is to support the rebuilding of a nurturing relationship between the children and their families," Eva instructed the audience of about twenty-five. "Children often feel angry or upset, and want to lash out because of their bad experiences. Their pain won't allow them to trust overnight, so be patient. It's a gradual process as kids learn to regain faith in adults and build confidence. It will take place one day at a time."

A heavy-set white woman leaned forward, raising her hand. "Do all the children who come through children services have these problems?"

Eva clasped her hands. "Unfortunately, most of them do, so expect it. In some cases, they're fright-

ened and confused about being separated from their
parents. Kids will have questions you honestly won't
be able to answer. In turn, their parents are angry
and feel threatened by outside intervention, which
makes their kids rebellious and depressed. Even
young babies can become irritable and fretful."

Parke touched Cheney's hand. "This isn't going
to be easy. Are you sure you want to do this?" he
asked again, whispering.

"Yes, I'm sure. All the children can't be that bad.
I'm sure they're telling us about the worst possible
scenarios."

"I hope you're right. In any case, I'm with you."

"Please remember," Eva continued, "As a foster
parent candidate, you are required to attend eight
more three-hour sessions."

The seminar turned into a question-and-answer
period before the moderator quoted statistics of
children who had endured the system and later became successful in life. Cheney's mind drifted. Who
would have thought attending college would've
changed her life so drastically. Bad choices had ruined her future.

She glanced at Parke. What would she do without him? Cheney didn't tell him she had called her
father when she couldn't reach Rainey. Roland didn't
conceal his hatred. She had counted five phone calls
he made to her father to engage in a meaningful dialogue. All Cheney got was pleasantries. Her family's alienation only intensified her guilt, so Cheney
figured why bother. This particular time she was
desperate.

"Hi Daddy," Cheney greeted over the phone.

"Hello, daughter, your mother's not here."

"I called to speak with you. I know the Division of Family Services contacted you about background information on me—"

"Look, Cheney, you wouldn't be in this situation if it weren't for your medical condition six years ago."

Cheney gasped. "You do know."

"Yes, I know and it was wrong. Is taking other people's children into your home some form of asking for forgiveness for your sins? Well, I can't forgive you, never, and I hope God doesn't either."

She didn't need to ask why, how, or when. Dr. Roland Reynolds had privileges with other medical professionals. What Cheney didn't know was if her doctor sought her father out, or her father requested a breach in patient confidentiality.

Eva's voice cracked Cheney's musings. "Before we dismiss tonight, I would like for you to see a short video about what to expect once a child comes into your home."

Cheney witnessed a six-year-old scratching a sleeping infant's face, a toddler drawing on the wall, a twelve-year-old smashing drinking glasses, and a little boy sitting in the center of the bed urinating. She hadn't realized she was pinching Parke's hand until he massaged her fingers.

A young man, sitting a few seats down from her, waved his hand in the air. "Please tell me that foster parents don't have to endure those nightmarish experiences without recourse."

Speaking in a controlled voice, Eva replied, "If you are uncomfortable with any child in your care, admit defeat. You do them a disservice not to have them removed from your home. Personality clashes do happen, but fostering is only effective when you and the child can bond."

"I don't know about you two, but I've seen enough. The two-hundred-and-something-dollars a month Missouri pays ain't worth the gray hairs them youngsters would give me," a woman behind them mumbled.

Cheney exchanged looks with Parke. At that moment Cheney didn't know which was harder, agreeing to an abortion, or agreeing to take on the responsibility of a foster parent. Her expression either revealed too much or Parke knew what she was thinking.

"You'll be a wonderful foster mother," he assured Cheney.

"Thank you, Parke."

When it was over, Parke pulled out his electronic organizer and began punching in information.

"What are you doing?" Cheney asked, peeking.

"Clearing my schedule," Parke answered like it was a given. "I want to attend every session." He crossed a leg over his knee and kept tapping away.

She looked at him incredulously. Although dressed in business casual, his demeanor spoke business. "This process could take up to four months."

Fingering his mustache, Parke shrugged. "Four months with the woman I love. Where do I sign up?"

Cheney couldn't explain why she blushed, but when she did, Parke winked.

As they stood to leave, Parke helped Cheney with her coat, buttoning each button and wrapping the scarf securely around her neck. Then, grabbing her coat collar, he tugged her forward. "Did you pull out one of my love notes today?"

"Yes."

"And Miss Reynolds?" Parke emphasized the Miss.

Their stare wasn't challenging, but soft. *"Like milk, I need hugs to make me strong."*

"I'll brand you with a hug before the day is over."

Cheney smiled, craving anything positive he was willing to give. She could feel the tears stinging her eyes. "Your faith in me makes me want to love you."

Parke froze. "Hold up. Did you just tell me indirectly you loved me?"

CHAPTER 26

Malcolm pleaded into Hallison's answering machine again, fingering a five-by-seven silver picture frame that captured him and Hallison smiling. Hallison looked elegant, sleek, and sensuous in a stunning black form-fitting dress. She was perfect for him. Physically, mentally, and spiritually, the woman held him captive with her tempting smiles and alluring perfume. The once organized desk was cluttered as Malcolm used his elbow, anchored on his desk, to hold the phone to his ear.

Malcolm sighed into the phone. "Know this. I'm a man serious about his woman. I've accepted your time away from me on Thanksgiving to spend time with your mother. I would've been glad to go if you would've asked."

He definitely had misread Hallison's signals. The perfect night planned at the Ritz backfired. Of all nights, they experienced their first argument. He thought they were back on track at the park concert, then all of a sudden Hallison wouldn't return his phone calls. "Christmas was hard for me. All I wanted was you. You're making your man suffer. Here's a love warning, sweetheart. It ain't no way I'm going to bring in the New Year without you." Knowing the recorder would beep any minute, Malcolm rushed his words, "and I'll be at your house tomorrow night, New Year's Eve, to celebrate the one year anniversary of our first date. I still have your Christmas present. I—"

Frustrated, Malcolm squeezed the receiver as her recorder disconnected. He pushed redial and waited impatiently until after her greeting. "I suggest you're ready at seven o'clock, or I'll camp out at your front door. Hali, whatever is bothering you is our problem. I miss you, sweetheart."

It was after nine when he arrived home and walked straight to his recorder. *One message.* Loosening his tie, Malcolm pushed play. "Hi, Malcolm." He smiled, hearing Hallison's voice. "I miss you, too. I'm sorry I've been shutting you out. We do need to talk. I need to unload my problems and there are some issues I can't resolve. I'll be ready, Mr. Jamieson. I can't have you waiting outside my door. Smooches." Relieved, Malcolm fell back into his recliner. His lady had the most drugging, husky voice he had ever heard. As he prepared for bed, he kept smiling.

New Year's Eve night, Malcolm dressed in a rust lightweight suede suit, color-coordinated perfectly with his leather Stacy Adams. He picked up a green gift box, a long-stemmed red rose, and his wool coat then headed for his car. Twenty minutes later, he arrived at Hallison's. After he knocked, she hesitantly opened her door, wearing a stunning bronze satin dress with alternating layers of bronze organza.

"Wow, I see what I've missed." Malcolm entered her apartment and right away subjected her to his kiss. It was time to touch and taste. "Hali, you make a man hungry. Don't ever shut me out again," he whispered against her baby-soft cheek.

"I'm sorry, but we need to talk—"

"Shh." Malcolm silenced her with his finger. "We'll talk tonight—all night if you want, until we're both satisfied, okay? Get your cape, baby, so we can go. Tonight, I'll talk first, you listen, then you say whatever you have to and you'll have my undivided attention."

"Aren't women supposed to go first?"

Handing her a single rose, Malcolm chuckled. "Not when her man has something very important to say." Malcolm wrapped a fox-trimmed black cape around Hallison's shoulders and escorted her to the front door.

The drive downtown was serene. He didn't want any music interrupting his thoughts. His sole purpose was to focus on his woman. He admired how she had swept up her hair with soft spiral curls dangling from the top of her head. *Gorgeous.* Soft blush sparkled on Hallison's cheekbones. *Sweet.* Full, perfectly shaped lips glistened with matching lipstick. *Irresistible.*

His fingers danced with Hallison's hand as he brought it to his face, rubbing her soft palm against his beard. "I've missed you, baby."

Hallison tightened her lips, displaying her dimples. "I've craved you like water and air." Her voice shook with emotion. "But—"

"It's okay." Malcolm squeezed her hand. "Hali,

whatever your fears, I'll crush them with all the strength within my bare hands. I promise."

She smiled when she realized they were in front of the Hilton. Malcolm smirked. "You remembered?" Her eyes bright with unshed tears.

"I haven't forgotten anything about us. Tonight, I want you to remember what we have is so special."

He escorted Hallison to the top-floor ballroom. Partygoers spilled into the halls chatting, laughing, and mingling. Entering the large festive room, the couple was on the dance floor within minutes, swaying to the enchanting, magical voice of Freddie Jackson crooning from a large room-sized video screen.

With Hallison's scent tickling his nostrils, Malcolm held her close, but still inches away so he could memorize how intently she watched him.

Snaking her arms around Malcolm's neck, Hallison appeared blissful. "Why are you staring at me?"

"Because I love you."

She froze and held his gaze as her eyes glazed over. "Are you sure? Malcolm, I have to be sure."

"Yes, very sure, I should've confessed a long time ago that I was falling in love with you before I took the liberty of suggesting a romantic weekend. Maybe that's why you questioned my motives, but I loved you then and even more now. This past year we've shared very special moments together. I know what it means to be completely satisfied, happy, and in love with only one woman."

Sniffing, Hallison blinked and allowed one tear to escape. "Thank God, thank God," she whispered, resting her head on his chest.

"I love you," Malcolm repeated closer to her ear. As the music changed to a faster beat, they continued swaying to their own rhythm. "Hali, I need to know if you love me." Holding his breath, Malcolm watched as she bowed her head, sobbing before meeting his worried stare.

"Yes. I wasn't sure how you felt or if I was special."

Exhaling, Malcolm hugged Hallison with relief and happiness. He loosened his embrace and stroked both of her cheeks, chuckling. "How could you not know? Our kisses, hugs, and talks are so intense. What we have is so hot."

Glancing at his watch, Malcolm noted the time. It was almost midnight, and they had danced at the same slow pace most of the night. "Baby, I felt you slipping away from me. I couldn't let that happen. You're my happiness."

"I desperately wanted to be branded as yours, but I needed something more. I've got to start going back to church. I can't ignore it anymore, Malcolm."

"Honey, I don't mind visiting a church."

When confetti drifted around them and cheers, horns, and clapping confirmed it was the New Year, Malcolm dropped to one knee and proposed. "Hallison Dinkins, I love you. You are my destiny, my world, my joy, and my peace. I promise to stand by you always to love you and support your dreams. Hali, will you marry me?"

She nodded. "I can't believe I've got you."

"Believe it." Malcolm stood and cradled her in his arms. He couldn't tell who was hugging the tightest. Malcolm smothered her with kisses as she smeared tears against his face. Displaying a green box, he teased, "Will you be still, woman, so I can claim my prize?" He slipped a three-carat diamond ring on Hallison's shaky finger.

"I'm engaged!" Hallison blurted out as soon as her mother opened the front door.

Fingering the diamonds on her daughter's ring, Addison whispered, "Congratulations, baby. Malcolm?"

"Yes." Hallison answered, hugging her mother with blurred vision.

Clutching Hallison's shoulders, Addison held her back, scrutinizing her face. "I want you to be happy with a good husband. I assume he loves you as much as you love him?"

"Yes, Mama."

"Good." Addison stared.

"What, Mama?"

"I was hoping you would come back to the Lord first. An unsaved husband makes it hard on a wife who wants to return to God. Remember, you'll both become one flesh."

"I love him so much. I can't see my life without him."

Patting Hallison's hand, Addison's eyes danced. "I like him, too. As long as the wedding isn't tomorrow, we've got time for him to repent, you to be reclaimed, and for me to start planning to make your day memorable. Hali, if you fast and pray, I believe God will save Malcolm."

"Why would I do that? I don't want Malcolm saved, Mama."

Addison wiped away a tear. "A saved man today could mean happiness later. Hold out, baby. You've got a fiancée who is living outside of the church and God's Will."

Plummeting from bliss to doom, Hallison left her mother's house and headed to work. Mid-morning, the conversation with her mother was still fresh in Hallison's mind as were the memories from the last visit with her praying mother. Closing her eyes, she tried to shake her mother's words.

"Why can't you just be happy for me, Mama? At least I won't be a fornicator," she mumbled as her phone rung. It could've been worst, Hallison shrugged. *Mama could've said God told her Malcolm wasn't the one*.

"Good morning, Hallison Dinkins, director of personnel," she answered.

"Good morning, soon-to-be Mrs. Hallison Dinkins Jamieson, my personal diva, who is going to direct her man on how to make her happy," Malcolm's baritone voice resounded through the receiver.

"It'll be just Mrs. Jamieson," she cooed back.

"Before this conversation goes any farther, I love you."

The corner of Hallison's mouth curved upward. *Can it get any better than this?* she wondered "And, I love you, too, for the third time this morning."

"Can I help it if I'm obsessed with you?"

"I'm addicted to you too," Hallison affirmed.

"Good. Now that we've admitted to our addiction, why don't we have a counseling session at lunch say, twelve-thirty?"

Hallison was ecstatic. She didn't care what her mother said. No sanctified man could give her this much joy.

"Twelve-thirty is fine. What do you have a taste for?" she agreed after checking her desk calendar.

"You," Malcolm growled into the phone like a wild animal about to attack its prey.

"Malcolm," Hallison scolded, jokingly.

"Don't ask me that when I'm craving you."

"You're too much."

"Yeah, but my woman can handle me."

Wonderfully distracted, she scribbled Hallison Jamieson several times on a pad. "We better hang up before we start something on this phone."

"Ooh, let's start something, baby."

"Behave, Mr. Jamieson. Good-bye." She giggled as she heard Malcolm smacking kisses on the other end of the phone before she disconnected.

Grasping the edges of her desk to stand, Hallison froze, admiring the stones on her engagement ring as they reflected the hues of sunlight. "Malcolm, this is gorgeous, just like you," she mumbled.

Cheney was on Hallison's list of people to call and share her exciting news, but it would have to wait. With the receptionist on vacation, Hallison had to deliver the new employee benefit handbooks to another department upstairs herself. Blissfully happy, she strolled out of her office on her way to the tenth floor.

Her two-inch heels clicked against the lobby's marble floor as she approached a set of triple elevators. Hallison squeezed the booklets while humming Luther Vandross's "Here and Now." Of all the songs she and Malcolm had danced to on New Year's Eve, that one seemed to rotate in her head. "It's scary being this happy."

Suddenly, Paula Silas, the new credit manager,

bounced off the elevator headed her way. A smile lit Paula's face when she saw Hallison. All Hallison could do was groan inwardly.

"I'm glad I ran into you," Paula greeted with a genuine smile.

I'm not. Hallison forced her lips into a fake smile. "How are you? I've heard wonderful things about how you're running your department."

Paula beamed. "I don't want to let anybody down—my staff, you, and definitely not God who blessed me with the position in the first place."

Hallison wanted to roll her eyes and throw up. Instead, she fingered her hair in annoyance, keeping her lips glued together.

As the woman's eyes widened, Paula's mouth dropped open as her manicured hands went up in the air. "Wow. That's some rock. You're engaged?"

Although Hallison wanted the world to know, Paula was not one of them. Guarded, Hallison nodded.

"Well, congratulations, Miss Dinkins."

Glowing, Hallison glanced down at her ring. "Thank you. My honey proposed to me New Year's Eve."

Paula touched Hallison's ring hand. "May God bless both of you."

Uh-oh, there she goes with putting God in this again. Hallison quickly interrupted, "Thanks, but I need to catch this elevator. I'll talk—"

As if it were natural, Paula looped her arm through Hallison's. "I'll ride with you. I was just taking a break anyway, on my way to the cafeteria."

One thing Hallison didn't dare do was to be rude to God's people, although she was on the verge.

Shrugging, she said, "Okay." She hoped they wouldn't stop on every floor.

After Hallison pushed the tenth-floor button, Paula talked nonstop. "You know, I was engaged last year to a wonderful and successful black man, but I had to let the brother go. After God saved me, I realized it wouldn't work."

Why did Hallison have the strangest feeling she didn't want to hear the rest of Paula's story?

"Humph, and the brother was fine too. Good job, nice house, and great parents. I gave him up for Christ. Now," Paula added, grinning, "I'm waiting for Jesus to send me my mate—a real soul mate. Someone who can love me, pray for me, and take care of all my needs, including helping my spiritual walk with God. I can't wait. God has promised to give me something better. I plan to prove God's Word."

Just Hallison's luck they stopped on almost every floor. Hopefully, Paula's testimony would end soon. They had three more floors to go.

Pausing, Paula gave Hallison an intense look. "You and your fiancé are in the church, aren't you?" She looked worried.

"Not at the present time, but we're working on it," she stated firmly, plastering a pleasant smile on her face.

"Thank the Lord. There ain't nothing like a God-fearing, on-his-knees-praying, Holy Ghost-filled man." She winked. "When I catch one of them, I'll have me something."

When the elevator stopped on the tenth floor, Hallison raced out.

CHAPTER 27

"These are lovely children's rooms you've decorated, Miss Reynolds. Your home is simply lovely. " Wilma smiled as she wrote a check mark in boxes on the Missouri licensing form. "I feel compelled to ask, how long have you thought about becoming a foster parent?"

Cheney walked to the dollhouse-shaped bookshelf and fingered a native Indian doll. She shrugged. "I don't know. A few years after I accepted I wouldn't be able to bear any kids."

Wilma pushed her small wire-rimmed glasses up on her nose. "Have you decided how many children you want to take in, their ages, or if you want to be an emergency, specialized, traditional, or long-term foster parent?"

Twisting her fingers, Cheney hoped, wished, and even prayed that she would be accepted. Hallison's year started off with good news of her engagement, so maybe, just maybe, it was Cheney's turn for good news. Plus, she had Parke's love and support without asking for it, and this was her sign from God.

"Right now," Cheney explained, "I can't do the specialized training for children with behavioral and medical problems. I don't know why, but somehow I feel a kinship for being an emergency parent for on-call crisis situations. I think the thirty-day limit would work for me starting off."

Nodding, Wilma added, "We might ask you to take a child in the middle of the night with just the clothes on his back. Sometimes, you may have a child just for the weekend until regular placement is found. Not every child you take in will be with you for a month."

Cheney's mind was made up. "I want to do it. I read through the information you sent. I know it requires additional skills and extra training. I'm committed."

"I'll note your preference on your application. That's a plus in your favor. Most people prefer the traditional foster parents—no surprise wakeup calls, just ordinary kids not living in the best situations."

"Later, I may take in babies or toddlers under long-term care for possible adoption. That way, they wouldn't have been exposed to so much pain."

Wilma folded her arms with her clipboard against her chest. "Everybody has a history, including the children at the division. There's a record somewhere—family, prenatal, birth, and hospital—regardless of their ages."

"Hmm, I know, but the younger they are, hopefully the less they will remember of their bad circumstances and grow to appreciate the nice things."

"It's not about nice things, Miss Reynolds. Many people make the assumption that abused children will feel grateful to be with another family. On the contrary, most kids truly care about their parents, siblings, and other relatives. Most would return to their 'crisis' environment in a minute just to be around the ones they love."

Cheney ingested Wilma's reprimand in silence.

The recruiter turned and strolled out of the bedroom. "That's why I requested records from your psychologist. In addition to good physical health, mental and emotional stability, you'll have to be able help the child understand the position of foster and natural families. Children should never be made to feel they have to choose between families because one is better than the other."

The woman took her job seriously. Too bad all workers didn't, otherwise kids wouldn't suffer abuse at the hands of their foster or adoptive parents, or get lost in the system like five-year-old Rilya Wilson from Miami, who wasn't reported missing for fifteen months because the caseworker lied about conducting monthly visits. To Cheney's knowledge, little Rilya had not been found. Wilma continued to tour the house. She inspected smoke detectors, searched for possible health hazards, and looked for structural violations that could keep her from becoming a licensed foster care provider.

An hour later, Wilma and Cheney sat at her kitchen table, sipping tea and discussing her application. "Miss Reynolds, another concern of mine is your relationship with your immediate family. Without question, you'll need a support system." She chuckled. "Mrs. Beatrice Beacon convinced me of her surrogate relationship with you. Parke Jamicson—there's something about that name that still sticks out—his background and references checked out as well as his parents' statements about you, Wilma paused and shuffled through papers in her file, "Miss Hallison Dinkins spoke highly of you."

Cheney beamed. Parke's family and friends had come through for her and made the difference. Rainey never returned her calls, so Cheney made a mental note to pay him a visit. She was almost as happy as Hallison when she spoke of her engagement then mumbled something about demons from her past not wanting her to be happy.

Demons, Cheney could identify with them. As if Cheney had some power over demons, she threatened them that they were not invited to her foster care house inspection. Cheney had spent the morning reading scripture after scripture, and it was paying off. She was home free until Wilma twisted her lips downward. *Here comes the bad news.*

"Unfortunately, the responses from your family are mixed. Let's see." She scanned two sheets of paper. "Besides your twin—I informed you of his comments—your mother says she can't provide a support system for you because you've distanced yourself from them. This information is not glowing and will have to remain a permanent part of your files."

Cheney's distance was five years ago. What was her family's excuse? Demons from her past had indeed reared their ugly heads.

*   *   *

The next few months, Parke faithfully accompanied Cheney to the remaining training classes, without any complaints, while Mrs. Beacon stockpiled Disney home videos, computer games, and books. By the end of March, Cheney received the phone call she had been hoping for and dreading.

"Congratulations, Miss Reynolds. Your criminal and financial background checks are complete, and the results are superb. Your home has passed inspection. You're now a licensed emergency foster parent," Wilma congratulated.

Dropping the phone, Cheney screamed hysterically. Within minutes, Mrs. Beacon was banging on her door with a distressed-looking Parke close behind, walking up her porch steps.

"I passed! I passed!" Cheney shouted.

Parke swept her into his arms in a tight hug, lifting her off the ground and kissing her hard on the lips. Mrs. Beacon sauntered into Cheney's living room, mumbling, "About time. You're making enough noise to raise the dead."

Cheney detangled herself from Parke's embrace. "Oh no, I left Wilma on the phone." She raced back into the kitchen, her support-team trailing. She lifted the phone to her ear. "Wilma, I'm so sorry. Yes, yes, I'll be here to sign the contract. Thank you." Cheney felt Parke's hand around her waist, slightly squeezing her side in a show of support. His eyes were misty.

Wilma smothered her amusement. "Congratulations, foster mom. See you in an hour."

After hanging up, all three stood in Cheney's kitchen sniffing, drying teary eyes, and hugging.

"You're going to need a swing set in the backyard," Mrs. Beacon commented.

"Do you have enough toys?" Parke asked.

Cheney folded her arms. "Wait a minute. Whose kids do you think they are anyway?"

Mrs. Beacon and Parke answered without hesitation. "Ours."

A distant ringing bounced off Cheney's bedroom walls. She scooted farther under the covers, burying her head into a fluffy pillow. When realization hit, Cheney rummaged for the phone. "Hello," her voice forced out, drugged with sleep.

Wilma's voice was on the other end rapidly explaining a child's needs. Cheney pushed herself up in bed, shaking her head. Clumsily, she searched and switched on the night lamp.

"Okay, okay." Cheney took a deep breath. "I'm awake, I think. Now, repeat everything."

"I have a two-year-old girl who was just removed from a home after a drug bust and eight family members were arrested. She's being checked out at Children's Hospital. Can you meet me there and take custody of her?"

Rubbing her eyes, Cheney looked cross-eyed at the clock, frowning. It was 3:42 in the morning. She groaned. *Why can't people do illegal drug activity during normal business hours?* "Sure," Cheney mumbled as she pushed back the covers, debating if she should call Parke.

Forty-minutes later, Cheney sat in the emergency room, drinking four cups of coffee, and trying to recall all her emergency foster care procedures. Three hours later, she chided herself for not waking Parke. "Isn't it like a man to sleep through the night while the woman stays awake with the child? There's no way I'm going to work today." Mrs. Beacon had already agreed to care for any little ones during the day if Cheney couldn't take off work, and Parke volunteered for the nights and weekends if needed.

Cheney stood when Wilma approached, carrying a beautiful little girl with two forgotten braids. She wore a dingy once-white T-shirt and pink corduroy overalls, looking frightened and tuckered out.

Wilma motioned for Cheney to remain seated. "This is Kami Fields, a biracial child of a fifteen-year-old white teenage mother, who's pregnant with another child. Her father is a seventeen-year-old African-American whose income comes from selling drugs—coke, crack, and heroine. This is his second parole violation. It doesn't look good for him."

What a bad environment to rear a baby, Cheney thought, reaching for the toddler, but Kami pulled back, clinging to Wilma.

"I'm sorry it took so long. Since she was around drugs, we had to conduct developmental tests and give her a physical."

Cheney swallowed hard. "Is she okay?"

"Luckily, she is. Otherwise, I would have to place her with specialized foster parents instead of with you. I hope you can take a few days off work."

"Not a problem. I haven't taken any time off; yet, this year, and my immediate boss knows I've trained to become a foster parent."

The women talked as Kami dozed. Cheney took

the sleeping child, wrapped her inside her trench coat, and left.

She laid Kami in the car seat the hospital lent her, fumbling with the straps. *I'm going to have to get my own car seat and clothes for her.* Sitting behind the wheel of her Altima with cell phone in hand, Cheney called the executive office and left a message for her boss that she was taking off. Next, Cheney speed dialed Parke. Dread threatened to fill Cheney, but glee won out. It had happened. Cheney Reynolds was a foster parent.

"Hello."

"Parke—"

"Hey, sweet lady," he interrupted. "I was dreaming about you last night. Want me to tell you about it?"

"While you were dreaming, I was at the hospital."

"What!" Panic filled Parke's voice. Cheney heard his razor shut off. She would've roared with laughter if her precious foster child wasn't resting behind her.

"Yeah, I've got a little girl. She was removed from a drug house with only the clothes on her back."

"What's her name?" Parke sounded in awe.

"Kami," Cheney hushed, smiling. "She's a cutie."

"I bet she is," Parke said, chuckling. "I'll go shopping and get her some clothes."

"Oh no, you don't. Little girls are supposed to wear matching socks, smell like flowers, and have straight parts in their hair with colorful barrettes and ribbons. What do you know about that?"

"Are you saying I can't do my job as a foster dad?

Watch me, Miss Reynolds. See you later. I'll call my secretary and take off work so all three of us can spend the day together, bonding. Next time, wake me up, sweetheart. I don't want my new millennium woman to handle everything by herself." *Click*.

She smirked. Parke Jamieson was perfect. Had she created this African prince from her own imagination? He was truly genuine, very caring, and a determined black man. Cheney's opinion of him had come full circle. They weren't in an intimate relationship, yet he was so committed to her cause. She was falling hard for him. His branding kiss and his endurance of the foster care classes did her in.

Cheney checked on Kami before pulling into traffic. She called her neighbor. "I hope you're working on breakfast because I've been up most of the morning with my first child."

Mrs. Beacon huffed while music from Janet Jackson's video blasted in the background. "Yippee. We got ourselves a baby."

"We've got a scared little thing who isn't going to be happy to see you or me when she wakes up," Cheney mumbled tightly, glimpsing another look at Kami for the thousandth time. The little girl slept through the car ride and a couple of hours more when Cheney got her home. Finally, she had a little girl to tuck in at night. She scanned her handiwork in the bedroom and nodded. "Yeah, everything's going to be just fine," she whispered to the toddler, backing out the room and leaving the door cracked.

It was almost eleven in the morning and despite the aroma of Mrs. Beacon's hot biscuits, strawberry jam, and sausage links she brought to Cheney's kitchen, Kami whimpered, refusing a taste. When Parke arrived with a large teddy bear, three bright colorful balloons, and two large shopping bags over-stuffed with sundresses, pants, lightweight jackets, pajamas, and cartoon underwear, Kami stopped crying as she held out her arms for Parke to pick her up. Cheney and Mrs. Beacon exchanged dumbfounded looks as Parke winked, cradling the child like he had been a dad all his life.

"Ya just gotta know what the little lady wants," Parke instructed.

"Shut up, Parke," Cheney and her neighbor barked in unison.

Cheney's house was the meeting place for a family affair. Malcolm and Hallison arrived loaded with books and clothes for Kami. Parke's parents weren't much better, dropping off educational games, food, and offering free baby sitting, calling Kami their foster granddaughter. The Reynolds were no-shows.

Less than a week later, Wilma phoned to inform Cheney that Kami might go into traditional care because the child's maternal grandmother didn't want to have anything to do with a mixed child, and Kami's teenage mother had yet to contact the Division of Family Services to schedule any weekly visits.

"The dad's family is so dysfunctional," Wilma commented, "I doubt any of them would survive the three-week kinship training classes. Most of them are substance abuse offenders themselves."

"It's amazing people live like that," Cheney said out loud.

Wilma sighed. "It's more amazing that Kami isn't

a drug baby. God must've been watching over her." Cheney immediately offered to keep her longer. "Since you requested emergency cases, she can't stay more than a few extra weeks at the most."

After Wilma answered more of Cheney's questions, they disconnected. Cheney observed Kami cuddled in Parke's arms, enjoying *Snow White*, a video Mrs. Beacon had purchased. They were so natural as father and daughter. Parke turned, met her stare, and smiled contentedly before giving Kami a tight hug.

Happiness cocooned Cheney, too. Foster care was the answer to all her problems. She reflected on the conversation with Wilma. "I can't believe nobody would want to fight for that beautiful little girl."

Kami remained subdued and alienated for a toddler, but she had begun following Cheney around the house and eagerly expected her arrival at the day care the agency suggested when Mrs. Beacon was unavailable. Parke stopped by every morning to eat breakfast with them. In the evening, he returned, sometimes bringing dinner, or to help prepare meals.

In no time, Cheney understood how foster parents became attached. After Kami, the cycle would begin again. Cheney hesitantly walked to where Parke and Kami sat. Looking up, Parke stretched out an arm to welcome her in his embrace. Cheney's heart sank. She scooted close to them and buried her head into Parke's shoulder.

"What's the matter, sweetheart, good or bad news?" he asked her.

Lifting her head, Cheney's breath caught at the tenderness in his face. "For me, bad news."

Immediately on alert, Parke stiffened. "Why?"

"The more I spend time with you, the deeper I fall for you."

"And that's a bad thing?"

"Parke, this is as close to having a baby." She pointed to Kami. "Parke the seventh won't come through me."

Loosening his arm around Kami, Parke guided Cheney's chin closer to his mouth, whispering, "If you're in deep, then I've got you right where I want you. I'm not going to let you dig out." Parke gave Cheney a thorough kiss, commanding her to surrender.

Cheney felt herself drifting away into a blissful existence until a sharp pain forced her to break away. Her tormenting scream caused Parke's lids to flutter open, and his eyes bulge. Kami's small fingers had gripped Cheney's check. Blood and red streaks marred Cheney's once flawless skin.

Kami's usual blank expression transformed into a game face—frown, hateful stare, and a pout—designed to instill fear into the fiercest beast. "Mine," she spat out, hugging Parke.

Parke jumped up with Kami clinging to his arms. "Cheney," he cried. He was furious as Cheney's face welt and bled. How could this little baby lash out like a wild animal? Bonding with Kami was important, but Parke would protect Cheney at all costs. She had suffered enough emotional abuse at the hands of a man. No one, not even a small child, would hurt Cheney again. Fuming, he reached out and touched Cheney's face. "Let me see, baby."

His nostrils flared as he grimaced. Turning to the toddler in his arms, Parke gave her his own game face. "Kami, don't you ever touch Cheney again. She's mine." He pointed to his chest. Parke recalled his pre-service training emphasizing no corporal punishment, but Cheney was his. He raised his hand and tapped Kami three times on her tiny hand.

There was no reaction. She was accustomed to abuse. Kami expected it, emotionally and physically. Evidently, she built a resistance against it. The child's response reinforced what Parke already knew. Cheney wandered into the kitchen and returned with a towel pressed against her face. He couldn't decipher Cheney's mood. Since her scream of agony, she hadn't said a word.

Cheney reached for the toddler. "Let me have her, Parke." Her voice was soft, gentle, and non-threatening.

Kami resisted. Cheney cooed the child's name over and over. Parke disengaged Kami from him, watching Cheney work her magic. She sat down, gently cuddling Kami on her lap. She rocked back and forth, whispering in Kami's ear. "I'm yours, too, Kami. Cheney loves you, and I'm yours too."

Parke wanted to embrace them, but he knew Cheney would have to handle Kami when he wasn't around, so he let her deal with it in her own way. Despite what Cheney thought of herself, the woman had strong maternal qualities. Cheney would be his wife. She was a fighter, and every strong Jamieson woman had to know how to fight for what she wanted and believed in. Parke hated Larry for cheating Cheney out of bearing her own children.

CHAPTER 28

Hallison and Malcolm met with their wedding planner, perusing honeymoon destinations. "What about Aruba, or another island for our honeymoon?" Hallison asked, flipping through pages of a thick bridal magazine. For the past few minutes, Malcolm had become touchy, twirling her curls around his finger or gently squeezing her hand.

Wedding planner Sara Duffy's eyes sparkled as she watched them. "Ah, true love. I can spot it anywhere. Aruba is known for island magic."

Malcolm stroked his beard, listening. "I believe in Hali magic."

Hallison exchanged looks with the planner, blushing.

"Is your young man always so focused?" The older plump woman with a slight gap between her front teeth asked, winking.

Hallison turned to Malcolm, looking at him under the hood of her lashes. "Always." She brought two fingers to her lips then touched Malcolm's. Malcolm's large hands held Hallison's fingers in place. "Keep that up woman, and we'll elope."

"That's where you're wrong, Mr. Jamieson," Sara interjected, chuckling. "I'm focused on your spending your money and giving you two a fairy tale wedding."

"By all means, Mrs. Duffy, do whatever it takes to make my baby happy," Malcolm said, nodding.

Later, they met with Addison for lunch. Before Addison left for an appointment, she prayed for them. "You two still have time to come to Jesus," she had said, hugging Hallison and Malcolm good-bye.

Inwardly, Hallison cringed while Malcolm hugged Addison back, whispering, "I'm not against prayer so please continue to pray for us."

"Don't think I'm not, young man." Addison said. "When I pray, I believe God listens."

Cheney and Kami had settled into a nightly routine and understanding. Kami would splash around in her bubble bath, then Cheney would wrap the slippery child in an oversized bath towel and read her funny bedtime stories, compliments of Mrs. Beacon.

When Kami became frustrated, she would pinch Cheney on her arms or legs. Learning was a slow process. If Parke didn't stop by, he would call nightly and speak to Kami, assuring her he was still around. Everything was all right in Cheney and Kami's world.

Monday night around midnight, Cheney's phone startled her out of a restful sleep. She answered before the ringing woke Kami. "Hello?"

"Cheney, this is Beverly Thom, on-call placement coordinator in the licensing unit. I've got an emergency situation with a brother and sister. Police have them in their patrol car. Can you accept them?"

Cheney's head started spinning. "What can you tell me about them?"

"Sasha is an eleven-year-old girl. She told police her stepfather fondled and attempted to rape her. When her thirteen-year-old brother, Dre, found out, he went ballistic, severely beating the step dad with a brick. Can you handle them?"

"I don't know, but I'll try."

Climbing out of bed, Cheney quickly dressed and washed her face. Walking downstairs, she peeked through her shutters every five minutes. She hated the waiting.

At twelve-fifty, a police cruiser parked in front of her home. Two officers got out and coaxed the brother and sister to her door.

As one officer introduced them, the honey-colored girl looked frightened and wouldn't meet Cheney's eyes. Her brother appeared to be older than thirteen. His eyes held an angry, cold stare; his mouth stretched into a line of defiance and his arms were folded in a challenging position.

Cheney ushered the officers and the children inside, thinking this was going to be a long night. She hoped Kami would sleep straight through. Less than an hour later, Parke barged through the door. On cue, Kami scooted down the stairs, rubbing her eyes before racing toward Parke.

Scooping up the child, Parke marched to Cheney. "What's going on? You okay?" he asked, almost breathless. Cheney nodded as he embraced her tightly, feeling his heart pound wildly against her face. "I was doing my usual nightly drive-bys before heading home when I saw the police car and the lights on and—"

The tall, gray-haired officer who looked days away from retiring, stepped forward and cleared his throat. "You are?" authority implied in two words.

Parke placed Kami on her feet despite her protest, but kept his arm wrapped around Cheney. "I'm Parke Jamieson. I'm the foster care parent assisting Miss Reynolds."

The rookie officer's eyes hinted there was more to Parke's story. "That name sounds familiar. Do you have any outstanding warrants?"

"Of course not, but I'm sure you'll check. You've probably seen my name listed somewhere as a storyteller or as a broker."

The young officer rocked on his heels and tilted his head, squinting. "Maybe."

When the phone rang, Cheney didn't have to guess who was on the other end. After explaining to Mrs. Beacon about the new arrivals and Parke's presence, her neighbor agreed not to change out of her skimpy night attire into something more appropriate and come over. Cheney said good-bye, hung up, and returned to her unexpected guests.

Sasha hid behind her brother. Dre kept his arms folded in a protective stance, daring anybody to touch them. Cheney wondered how many more emergency cases she would get.

Cheney fought to keep her eyes open. She knew Sasha and Dre had to be exhausted. She made a mental note to stock up on different size pajamas for these emergency cases.

"If you have everything under control, we're leaving, but remember we're a 9-1-1 call away," the older cop advised, casting a warning glance at Dre before turning and walking out the door. His young cadet followed, but not before lifting a brow to confirm what his partner had said.

After the police left, Parke reached out to touch the brother and sister, but Sasha jumped back. Dre snarled like an attack dog, allowing Chency a glimpse of his aggressive behavior.

When they didn't respond, Parke didn't blink. "It's okay. I can handle it, honey. Are you two hungry?"

"I'll go make coffee and hot chocolate," Cheney offered, dragging her bare feet across the living room floor to the kitchen, Cheney knew it was going to be a very long night.

Kami was sound asleep in Parke's arms when she returned with four mugs on a tray. Dre and Sasha were huddled together in the corner on the edge of her sofa. She offered both of them hot chocolate. They accepted only after their stomachs growled.

"Dre and Sasha, I know it's been a very long evening. If you want to talk, then we can stay up all night," Cheney said, sipping her black coffee. "If you're sleepy, I have warm beds upstairs for you to try and get some rest. If you want to cry, I'll cry with you." At least this time, her company came on a Friday night.

Parke sat back observing Cheney while she tried to reach out to the siblings. The training sessions they attended were right. These two didn't look like they were on the verge of trusting anybody. Cheney was patient and Parke was so proud of her. She had taken her role as a foster parent seriously and was accepting some unpredictable emergency cases. *She needs to rethink this though. At least traditional cases would knock at your door between nine and five*, Parke thought.

He was convinced Cheney didn't miss out by not having children of her own. Kids seeking temporary shelter would benefit. After a long rebellious time, Sasha evidently accepted Cheney's embrace as they cried together. Cheney wiped at both their tears.

Parke stood and went into Cheney's kitchen to prepare everyone a snack. He returned to the living room with a platter of food to feed about ten people. Since taking in Kami, he kept Cheney's shelves stocked for emergencies like tonight.

Dre wasn't shy as he alternated between eating two ham-and-cheese sandwiches and pacing Cheney's hardwood floor. "I'll never go back there. My mother can have that nasty old man. Mama should've listened when Sasha told her the first time," he fussed, ripping meat from his sandwich. Getting seasick from Dre's movement, Parke joined Dre's pacing and let him talk until the boy ran out of steam.

"If you or any other man tries to touch my sister again, I'll kill you." Dre's expression and body language suggested he wasn't bluffing.

"What your stepfather did is not the norm. You have a right to be angry. You did the right thing to protect your sister, man," Parke reassured the teenager.

Dre looked shock. "That's not what my mother said."

Finally, Dre agreed to engage in a man-to-man talk with Parke. His demand was his sister would remain in his sight. After four hours of discussion and sniffing, Cheney carried a sleepy Kami upstairs to bed with Dre and Sasha dragging behind.

Parke knew he would have to go purchase jeans, sweats, and other clothing for their new arrivals. "I hate to go," Parke uttered when Cheney returned. "You know, I can sleep here on the couch in case you need me. I'm a little worried about leaving you alone with Dre agitated."

"Didn't you know I'm a new millennium woman and I can handle anything?" Cheney attempted a smirk.

"Really?" Parke lifted his brow. "Good, then you can handle me and all the love I have. You're my woman now, and I'm not letting you do this alone."

Cheney relaxed her head against his chest. He didn't know if she was content with him being there or too tired to stand. His fingers combed through her wavy hair with gentle strokes.

"I shook from the bottle today," Cheney admitted, shyly looking up through hooded lashes.

"And?"

"It said you would prove your love for me."

"I will."

"It's not a question of me handling your love. Do I deserve it?"

Parke placed soft kisses on Cheney's face. "Baby, I'm only going to say Larry's name one last time. He didn't deserve you, your love, or your heart. "

"I wish I could forget about Larry."

"Trust me, you will," Parke advised before leaving.

* * *

During the night, Parke couldn't sleep. He would love to have five minutes alone with Larry. "I could do damage in three." Parke frowned at his thoughts. He wasn't a violent person, but he wanted Cheney happy.

He was also worried about her with the late-night arrivals. He dialed her number. "How are you and your house guests?"

"Everybody's sleeping," she whispered in a husky voice. "And, I was dreaming about this warm, very good-looking, and good-smelling man, but you woke me up." *Click.*

Laughing, Parke rolled over, not believing Cheney hung up on him. At peace, Parke drifted into sleep, smiling.

CHAPTER 29

After three morning phone calls, Cheney warned Parke not to call her house one more time. If he wanted to know how everybody was doing, come and find out. At one in the afternoon, Parke did just that when her doorbell rung. Mrs. Beacon had already come and introduced herself before leaving for her Salsa class.

"We had a setback last night," Cheney revealed as she greeted Parke at the door.

"Uh-oh. Who?" Parke asked, moaning.

"Kami. I think it was too much excitement."

"What did she do?" Parke didn't wait for an answer as he walked through Cheney's front door, juggling three large pizzas, cinnamon sticks, and two liters of soda. He paused and planted a hard kiss on Cheney's lips. "Do I want to know, sweetheart?"

Kami bolted out of the kitchen, heading straight for Parke's long legs. "Whoa." Parke steadied himself. "That girl is getting stronger every day," he said, continuing toward her kitchen.

Cheney bent down and scooped up the little terror. "You can give him a hug once he puts the food down, Okay?" Cheney nodded yes for Kami to mimic, and the child did.

In the kitchen, Parke spoke to the teenagers before strolling out with his arms stretched out for a hug. Kami began her trot, but Parke's eyes were steady on Cheney. "Wait a minute, Kami. I need to hug Cheney first, remember?" He stepped in front of Cheney, waiting for her to fill his arms. His hug was tight, but brief. "You look pretty."

Cheney closed her eyes. "Thank you."

"I love it when you wear your hair down. It softens your already beautiful features."

"Thank you, again," she said, blushing. Something she hadn't done as much since the first few months with Larry.

"I love you," he added before kneeling so Kami could plant a juicy kiss on his cheek.

"So dee." Kami clapped her hands.

"Go back in the kitchen and Dre will pour you a cup. Like a wound-up toy, Kami took off.

Parke looked at Cheney. "Okay, now tell me what happened last night."

Cheney rested her forehead against Parke's. "This morning, I went into their room to check on Sasha. Poor thing was crying in her sleep, so I laid down and gathered her to me, holding and rocking her. Basically, I was just trying to comfort her. We dozed off."

Nodding, Parke listened without interrupting as they walked back into her living room, ignoring Kami's cries, Dre's yelling, and Sasha's whining as they argued in the kitchen about which bottle of soda to open.

"Next thing we know, Kami's biting Sasha's leg, yelling, 'Cheney mine.' Sasha screamed, and Dre barged through the door ready for battle."

"We're going to have to talk to the counselor about her aggressive outbursts." Relaxing his frown, Parke smiled, massaging Cheney's cheek. "On a lighter note, if I had known Dre was a one-man army, I would've gotten a good night's sleep instead of worrying."

"You leave protecting your woman to a thirteen-year-old?"

"A new millennium woman can handle anything," Parke reminded her.

Cheney playfully latched on to Parke's lips, subjecting him to a stirring kiss before Kami ran out the kitchen. She patted Cheney's leg and tugged onto Parke's pants. They opened their eyes confused by the interruption, and looked down. "At least she didn't scratch or bite me," Cheney whispered against Parke's lips.

Parke and Cheney joined the kids in the kitchen after Parke had retrieved bags of clothes for the siblings from his SUV. Soon everyone was stuffed with pizza.

"Dre, Sasha, you can call home, only if it won't upset you," Cheney offered, waiting for their reaction. It didn't take long.

Anger flashed across Dre's once content face. "Nah. Do I have to?"

Sasha's eyes were riveted on her brother. She remained silent.

"No," Parke answered for Cheney, gathering trash.

Collecting plates, Cheney loaded the dishwasher. "Hey, why don't you go next door? Remember Grandma BB from earlier? She should be back by now. Don't tell her I let you two know that she was almost arrested, wrestling over the last PlayStation 3 at Target." Cheney's mouth stretched into a slow grin. "I think she's been practicing."

Dre tried his best to act unfazed, toying with the invitation.

"It's okay, Dre. You two are safe there. Go on, you're not in a prison," Parke encouraged. "When is the last time you played?"

Again, Dre mulled over the invitation. A frown held back a smile. When Sasha nudged him, Dre practically knocked over his chair pushing back from the table. "I guess we can go and check it out. C'mon."

"First, try on your new clothes," Parke ordered.

"Nah, that's all right," Dre said, shrugging as he grabbed his sister. When Kami protested, he took her hand. Hesitantly, the trio headed for the door as Cheney and Parke exchanged cautious looks.

Sunday night, when the siblings were still at Cheney's house, she called Wilma to find out what she should do about them for school. Wilma informed her if it wasn't a burden, she could take them back to their old school, and Cheney agreed. She would have to leave earlier in the mornings.

By the next weekend morning, Cheney had fallen into another routine with Sasha and Dre. They dressed after cleaning their rooms. The counselor returned for a second evaluation within a week because of the severity of Sasha and Dre's problems. "They're adjusting well," she informed Cheney.

After lunch, they were preparing to bake cookies until Parke showed up. Kami raced to the door with Dre tagging along. Sasha was still uncomfortable around Parke, so she stayed behind with Cheney in the kitchen. Kami's giggles and loud talk, mixed with Dre's excitement, filtered throughout the house.

Parke stepped into the kitchen with a bright smile and mischief written all over his face as he brushed his lips against the top of Cheney's hair. "Hey, baby."

"Hey." Tilting her head, Cheney smiled. "Why are you so happy? What are you up to?"

He whipped out five tickets. "The Cards vs. Cubs baseball game begins in two hours."

Cheney's mouth dropped open. She looked around at her audience. Dre was standing behind Parke with praying hands, pleading. Kami was holding on to Parke's free hand, sucking her thumb. Sasha wouldn't meet Cheney's eyes.

"We just took everything out to bake cookies, and the kids —"

"Unless you want the children to see how a man kisses the woman he loves, I suggest you agree," he leaned closer, murmuring against her lips.

She hated when Parke got the upper-hand so she bit his bottom lip.

"Ouch!" Parke yelled, rubbing his lip. He looked around and all the children were laughing, even Sasha. He turned back to Cheney and mouthed, "I'll get you for that."

Teasingly, Cheney lifted her brow and threw him

a kiss. *He makes me happy. God, thank you for Parke and the children.*

Dre tapped Parke on his shoulder. "Ah, can you and Cheney get each other another time, so we can get to the game, man?"

Parke and Cheney shared a laugh before Cheney breathed a sign of relief. She didn't know what Dre was like before, but she believed the game would allow him to be a kid again. Less than an hour later, everybody was settled in Parke's Envoy. Parke reached across the seat and engulfed Cheney's hand in his. Cheney glanced in the backseat, noticing Kami had reached on both sides to hold hands with Dre and Sasha. Cheney smirked.

Outside Busch Stadium, Parke purchased Cardinal red baseball caps and jerseys for everybody. Kami giggled as Parke swung her above his head, anchoring her legs on his shoulders. Dre's eyes lit brightly as he idolized Parke's playful nature. Sasha seemed less heavyhearted as she admired the new purchases, but she still remained latched on to Cheney's hand.

They were several feet away from the entrance gate when a petite medium-brown-skinned woman wearing a white baseball cap, a red Cardinal T-shirt, white shorts, and bright red lipstick yelled Parke's name. He spun around and smiled at the gorgeous woman coming their way.

"Kelsi, it's good seeing you." His smile didn't reach his eyes. Clearly, he was lying.

She stopped in front of Parke with folded arms, scanning his companions. Cheney could see the woman was gearing up her black sistah attitude—

rolling her neck, hands on hips, and spitting daggers.

"I can't say the same." She rolled her eyes. "No wonder you haven't returned my calls. So this is the little family," she said, snarling before balling her hands into fists and slapping them on her hips. "Funny," she paused, rolling her head. "You never mentioned them before we—"

Kami bent down swinging her arms and screaming, "Mine. Mine."

Horrified, Kelsi stepped back. "You can have him, honey." She twitched her nose and sauntered away into the crowd.

Sasha gripped Cheney's hand tighter after the confrontation. Kami, who was now in Parke's arms, smothered him with kisses, and Dre was rubbing the make-believe hair on his chin, grinning.

"Man, Parke. She sure was fine," Dre said with his eyes on a retreating Kelsi.

Parke patted Dre on the back before squeezing his neck. "Not as fine as Cheney." He focused on her and mouthed, "Past trash and you know I love you."

Cheney shivered. She realized Kelsi's drama didn't faze her. She mouthed back, "I know."

Inside the stadium, and sitting behind third base, Parke stuffed the kids with hot dogs, peanuts, and popcorn.

"We just ate at home," Cheney scolded Parke.

"I like hot dogs, Miss Cheney," Sasha confessed with mustard smeared on her chin. Cheney knew the girl didn't participate in their conversation frequently, so Cheney shut her mouth and smiled.

At the beginning of the seventh-inning stretch, Parke and Cheney escorted the kids to the bathroom. When Cheney and the girls stepped out of the ladies' room, Dre and Parke were waiting for them by a concession stand. As Cheney approached them, a honey-colored sister cut off her path.

"Parke!" The woman waved, rotating her hips with each step.

Sasha whispered, "Oh no, not again."

Cheney was thinking the same thing when Kami broke free from Cheney's hand and charged toward Parke yelling, "Daddy, Daddy's mine."

The woman stopped in mid-strut with shock written all over her face. "You've been busy, Parke," she said accusingly.

Scooping Kami up in his arms, Parke grinned. "Hey, Nyla, it's good seeing you, too. Yeah, I have."

"Well, she looks just like you, you two-timing, unfaithful, slimy dog." She stormed off.

Parke planted a big kiss on Kami's cheek, mumbling, "You make a great bodyguard, girl."

Whew. Cheney's head was spinning as she wondered about Parke's past, but two women within hours? That's a bit much. Cheney and Sasha moved cautiously through the crowd toward Parke, Dre, and Kami.

Parke's eyes held hers in a trance. "We can't change our past, Cheney."

She nodded, agreeing. "Yeah, I know."

"Did you hear her call me daddy?" he grinned like he had just given birth to her.

Ignoring him, Cheney rolled her eyes upward and walked ahead.

* * *

Parke knew it didn't look good, but he loved beautiful women. He still did, which was why he had fallen in love with Cheney. A shocker, considering he fought the losing battle. The others were flings, so he didn't owe them an explanation. Parke grabbed Cheney around her waist and tugged her back to their seats. They needed to talk.

Once they were reseated and the game was underway, Parke turned to Cheney and started to work his magic. "Those ladies were my past. Please don't hold it against me."

"How can I hold anything against you? You're not holding my past against me, but they're gorgeous, Parke."

"So are you Cheney," he whispered with a sly grin. "When we're alone, I'll point out all your beauty spots." He forced her to bite off a piece of his hot dog before sealing her lips with a kiss.

Dre nudged Parke in the side. "You two sure do kiss a lot."

Parke pulled the baseball cap over Dre's eyes. "Ah, eat your peanuts."

At the ninth inning, the Cubs threatened a win, but the Cards came back in the bottom of the ninth with a three-run homer to win, seven to six.

Standing to leave, Parke gathered his crew. He hoped he wouldn't run into any more of his lady friends. He needed to keep Kami close to his side for protection. They filed in line with other fans as they streamed down the ramp and out the ballpark.

Parke was preoccupied, thinking how Cheney's dream of being a foster parent—even if it was limited to thirty days under her emergency care status—had become a reality, although it was cramping their dating time. Now, what could he do about her guilt?

Fans scattered to nearby parking lots. While waiting for a light to change at the corner of Broadway and Market Streets, Parke heard a familiar voice scream his name. He cringed. Dre clapped his hands and mumbled, "All right."

Annoyed, Parke could've recognized that voice anywhere, even in his sleep. She was the one woman he didn't want to see. As usual, she was expertly dressed, wearing a red and white short sleeve sweater, a long white skirt, and red scandals.

The heels made her almost as tall as Cheney. Her shoulder-length brown hair matched her healthy caramel skin, which gave her an exquisite look. She wore a bright smile and spoke in the softest, sweetest voice. She fell into his arms, hugging him for dear life.

When Cheney noticed the woman's male companion tagging along and smiling, she seemed to relax. Even Kami didn't appear hostile. With little choice, Parke welcomed the embrace as he kissed her cheek. "Annette, believe it or not, I'm really glad to see you."

Annette laughed and punched him in the arm. "Sure you are, liar." Observing Parke's audience, Annette smiled at Kami as she reached out and rubbed the child's arm. "What a beautiful little girl. Parke, I know you don't have any kids, but she could pass as yours."

Instead of Kami snarling, she leaned her head back against Parke's shoulder like she was shy. Parke tickled the toddler's stomach. "This little monster is

Kami, Cheney's foster child, and I guess you can say mine too."

Kami stuck her tiny finger in Parke's neck. "Mine." She showed a toothy grin.

"She's adorable," Annette cooed before spinning around and coming face-to-face with Cheney.

The women eyed each other. Parke couldn't tell what was going on in their minds, but it appeared Annette was gathering strength. He needed a diversion. No telling what was about to come out her mouth. Parke made the introductions.

"Cheney," Annette paused like she was meeting a world-famous celebrity. "I'm sure you're behind the change in this knucklehead." Annette flung herself at Cheney and hugged her like she had known her for sixty-years instead of sixty-seconds.

The shock on Cheney's face was priceless. Parke held in his laughter. She had no choice, but to absorb Annette's hearty embrace.

Dre leaned over and whispered. "She's fine, too. I'm going to have to hook up with you when I'm older."

Embarrassed, Parke elbowed Dre into silence.

Annette glanced over her shoulder at Parke, wrinkling her nose. "You're a very special woman who has entered Parke's life. I can feel it." She leaned closer to Cheney's ear. "Tie him down, honey. Parke is a good man. He just needs Jesus in his life." Annette turned, giving Parke an award-winning smile.

"I don't have Him in mine so I can't help Parke," Cheney explained.

"God has always been there. Sometimes we find Him at different stages in our lives, but the most important thing is we find Him. You will," Annette said convincingly before she moved onto Dre. "You sure are a handsome young man. Jesus loves you and so do I." Dre didn't look convinced. She gently held Sasha's shoulders as Parke looked on. "What's your name, sweetie?"

"Sasha," the girl uttered under her breath.

Parke was certain Annette didn't hear it.

"That's such a beautiful and classy name for a sweet and beautiful young lady. Jesus loves you too."

Making eye contact with Annette's companion, Parke offered a handshake. "Parke Jamieson. Annette's not only nosy, busy, and talkative, but she has taken on a rude quality."

"I'm Dyson Kidd. Nice to meet you man. Annette said I had to meet you outside church since you wouldn't step foot insides ours."

Oh no, not two church folks at one time on a street corner. Parke's smile faded, his body stilled.

"Sorry guys, I'm just happy to see Parke. He's cut ties with me ever since I decided to follow Jesus," Annette explained as sadness filled her eyes.

"That's not true. Cheney and the kids have been keepin' me busy," Parke reasoned.

"Not that busy, Parke," Cheney instigated, displaying an innocent smile that triggered her dimples.

"Cheney, you're supposed to be on my side."

She gave him an indifferent shrug as Dyson pulled Annette closer. He recognized the look they exchanged. They were in love. Parke was amused.

"Well, if a certain person hadn't been avoiding me, maybe you would've met Minister Dyson Kidd," Annette turned and faced her companion. "I've been inviting Parke to church, Cheney, but he won't come. I hope you can convince him, and please bring these lovely children with you. They're such cutie pies."

"Sorry, I'm not the one to convince anybody to attend church," Cheney said.

Dyson interjected, "Please, be both our guests this Sunday."

"Annette, we have plans with the kids, but thanks anyway. Well, we better get these rugrats home," Parke replied, checking his watch. He sighed. It was one thing to end a conversation with Annette over the phone, but how could he get rid of her now?

"Do you mind if we pray for you before you leave?" Dyson asked.

Parke gritted his teeth. He knew it! He would rather face more of his ex's than pray with Annette. Looking around, Parke knew Dyson's offer was serious. No one was paying attention to them, but Parke didn't want to start a revival on the street corner. He was about to decline when Cheney softly answered, "Please." He lifted his brow. What was going on here? Parke held his tongue.

"Let's join hands. Whatever you need, God's got it." Dyson said, bowing his head and closing his eyes. "Father, in the name of Jesus, we stand before you, thanking you for today."

Making sure he had a strong grip on Kami's small hands, Parke kept one eye opened. Even Dre's head was bowed as every hand was linked together. *We're standing on a street corner!*

Dyson continued, "God, You know our needs before we ask, and you're able to grant them. Please bless us, and draw us closer to your great salvation and give us peace. In Jesus' name. Amen."

"Amen," Annette repeated.

The kids and Cheney echoed their amen's while Parke mumbled his.

After releasing hands, Annette gave Cheney a bear hug. "The Holy Ghost is telling me you need something from God. Whatever it is, it's yours for the asking."

Cheney didn't answer as a single tear slid to her chin. He wanted to strangle Annette for upsetting his woman. After four tries, Parke was finally able to pull Annette and Cheney apart for them to go their separate way.

Within minutes of getting in Parke's SUV, the children dozed as Cheney stared out the window. Parke reached for her hand and placed a soft kiss inside her palm. "Tired?"

Leaning her head against the headrest, Cheney faced him, smiling. "Exhausted, but I had a great time. There's a certain peace about Annette. I like her."

"You would. Let's get these rascals back to your house and in bed. I want us to talk for a few minutes."

"Tonight?" Cheney's voice slurred.

"Yeah, tonight. I need to explain about those women earlier."

"No need. I knew you were a certified player."

"See, that's why we need to talk. I'm simply a good man who has been looking for a good woman who fit the profile."

"Mmm-hmm."

Cheney's eyelids drooped. She had taken in three kids and had a reason to be worn out. "Okay, another night, but I want you to go straight to bed, Miss Reynolds."

Mouthing *okay*, Cheney slowly closed her eyes. Parke rubbed his thumb against her soft hand. She was beautiful. He turned his attention back to the highway and drove his sleeping cargo to Benton Street.

Around ten-thirty, Parke entered his quiet house, showered, and prepared for bed. He was knocked out as soon as his head hit the pillow. When the phone startled him out of his sleep, Parke hunted for his cordless and pushed talk, "Yeah."

"Sorry to wake you," Cheney's drowsy voice apologized.

Alarmed, Parke shot up in bed. "Are you all right? Please tell me nothing's the matter."

"Well, the on-call placement coordinator called. She's bringing me a seven-year-old girl who's the victim of neglect."

"What?" Parke jumped out of bed, searching for his clothes. "I forbid it. You have enough responsibility." He was furious. The system was taking advantage of his baby. He buttoned his shirt, missing holes. "I'm on my—"

Softly sobbing into the phone, Cheney mumbled, "I thought I was doing the right thing. I can't turn any child away, but this is too much. Maybe this wasn't God."

"Don't cry, sweetheart. I'm on my way." He disconnected, stressed. "This is not the answer and it's going to stop, now, tonight."

When Parke turned the corner, he realized he

was only wearing one sock. Too bad, he wasn't turning around. He walked in Cheney's house moments before the social worker knocked on Cheney's door. The lady was toting a little girl, named Tina, who looked like she hadn't eaten a meal in weeks. "I'll handle this."

Parke stepped outside with the woman and child, closing the door behind him. "I'm sorry for the confusion, but Cheney is about to break. She's an excellent foster mother. However, she can't handle any more emergency cases right now. Please find another home for this child tonight. I'm sorry."

The social worker nodded. "I understand, but Miss Reynolds agreed. I was hoping I could place this little one with foster parents instead of putting her in our residential home," she explained, walking away with Tina.

Taking a deep, satisfying breath, Parke opened the door to find Cheney curled up on her sofa, dozing. He didn't disturb her at first. Lifting her head, Parke sat down, and replaced her head on his lap.

"Where is she?" Cheney asked, yawning.

"She's going somewhere else tonight," he paused, "Cheney?"

"Hmm?"

"I love you, and I think you're a special lady, but after three foster kids, I don't think I'll mind if it's just you and me."

Her lids fluttered opened. "What are you saying?"

"I'm saying, let me spoil you, pamper you, and love you. Make you my priority."

"You have to give up too much for me."

Bending down, he brushed a kiss against her

cheek. "Not more than what you've given up. You're worth it, baby."

"I guess it's time I have to admit defeat. I thought the foster kids would help ease the guilt clinging to my insides, but it's still there." Cheney whimpered. "I don't know what else to do. I'm at my wits' end, and I'm becoming too attached. It's been a temporary happiness. Maybe this wasn't a sign from God."

His eyes also watered. After weeks with Kami, Parke was attached too. They only had one more week together. He hoped Annette was really praying for them because Cheney was searching for something he didn't know how to give her.

Cheney sat up and looked him over. "Parke?"

"Yeah, baby?" he snuggled her closer.

"You only have on one sock."

"I know." *One sock and a half of a brain for letting her do this foster parenting thing.*

CHAPTER 30

The call came unexpectedly. Wilma Applewhite normally communicated with Cheney. So why was she calling Parke?

"Parke, sorry to bother you on a Sunday morning, but it just hit me," Wilma announced with just enough of frantic in her voice to cause panic.

"What just hit you, Wilma?" Parke stopped dressing. He had the strangest feeling this wasn't good news concerning Kami.

"Were you aware that there was a child by the same name as yours in our foster care system?"

"No," his voice faded as if his last breath escaped. He lowered to the bed, but barely missed it. Confused, he wondered if someone had moved his bed. "Are you sure?"

Wilma was quiet, thinking. "I'm pretty sure, but I'll check the records once I get into my office tomorrow. I don't know where the child is now if he's been adopted, or still in our system."

Closing his eyes, Parke didn't know how to respond. Did he have a son out there somewhere, or did an old girlfriend give a baby Parke's name as a joke? Uncertainty battled with joy and fear. In the end, confusion reared its head.

Maybe the vision Parke saw wasn't about enduring an abortion. Maybe it was about a child he didn't know existed. He held tears of joy in check until he knew for sure if this child was his first born son, his only son. "You'll let me know for certain?"

"Of course," Wilma assured him before they said their good-byes.

Wow. Parke sucked in his breath an hour later when Cheney opened her door, dressed for church. There stood a stunning replica of a *Vogue* magazine model. Funny, he had never seen Cheney look more beautiful and dainty in a dress. Forget the call from Wilma. The moment was all about Cheney Reynolds.

"Wow," he repeated aloud, exhaling. He leaned against the step up to her foyer, placing his right hand over his heart. "You slay me."

Ignoring Parke's dramatics, Cheney pouted for a kiss. She wiggled her silky eyebrows, signaling her impatience. Parke obliged, taking his time to absorb her taste.

"Thanks, I needed that." Cheney took a deep breath.

"Nervous?"

"Hopeful."

His woman. Parke's eyes danced as he stroked his goatee. "Forget what they say about the woman in red. You are sizzlin' in black." He jammed two fingers in his mouth and a whistle escaped. Cheney glowed as spiral curls flowed down her back. His eyes were glued to her sling back pumps and black sheer stockings hugging sculptured legs.

"Where have you been hiding that dress?"

"It's new. I wanted to look nice."

"You look more than nice."

Parke perused her attire. Even though the dress was inches below her knees—modest for church—it hinted of her shapely places. Parke closed his eyes and inhaled an unfamiliar scent. "Hmm, you smell very, very good."

"You're making me blush with all this attention." Cheney mouthed "thank you." She seemed to float to his face. "You look very handsome," she whispered as she wrapped her arms around his waist. "Thank you."

"For what?"

"For always caring about the part of me I've buried so deep inside that only you've been able to reach." She sighed with the saddest expression. "Because of you, I met your friend Annette. She seemed to possess a comfort level I so desperately want. I'm glad she invited us to church."

He disengaged himself from Cheney and began to pace her living room, rubbing the back of his neck. "Listen, Cheney, I got the strangest call from Wilma this morning."

"Wilma? Why did she call you? What did she want?" Cheney frowned.

"She asked me if I knew that there was a boy in foster care with a similar name as mine."

"Oh." Cheney searched for the nearest chair and dropped down.

Parke couldn't read her expression. He couldn't even decipher his thoughts. "I *may* have a son somewhere. Or some woman gave her son my name as a joke. Even that sounds absurd. Or some rejected lover decided to have a baby who could be mine and gave him away as a punishment. Whatever scenario I conjure up would only be speculation. I don't know who the mother is, or what the circumstances are, but if this boy proves to be my son, I plan to take possession immediately."

"Despite these tears," she paused, sniffing. "I'm happy." She closed her eyes and leaned back into the chair. After a few silent minutes, she perked back to life. "Parke, this is all so strange. I mean, I had an abortion which resulted in me not having children. I become a foster parent to right my wrong. I meet this neighborhood stalker—"

"I'm a lover baby, not a stalker. You are my princess." Parke smiled, sitting in the twin chair close to her.

She smiled back and continued on her second hand, counting out the facts. "Anyway, for no reason, but to make me happy, you've become some type of foster-parent-in-waiting. Parke, I've never been absolutely positive about anything in my life except for knowing that if my child had been born it would've been a girl. I know it. I'm feeling the same way with this boy. I don't think you need me to tell you. I think you know this child is yours. I can't explain it, Parke, but I know it."

Parke nodded, without saying it, he did feel there was a kinship. He just needed to find this boy, the mother, or have a paternity test to prove it.

"You'll make a wonderful father."

"You humble me. My desire will always be to fulfill your needs, Cheney."

Her words had touched his soul. Checking his watch, Parke returned to reality. "Let's go praise the Lord. Annette may already have sent the church van to pick us up. When I told her we were coming, she dropped the phone and started shouting hallelujah." Parke kept to himself that Annette sensed Cheney's looking for some deliverance. What had Annette become, a prophetess or something? Save her from what?

"Let me run upstairs and grab my purse. I'll be right back." Cheney stood and hurried upstairs.

As Parke waited, he thought this was supposed to be an ordinary Sunday. Taking an exceptional woman to an ordinary church, the day was proving to be interesting. Last night, he called and asked Mrs. Beacon to babysit. He didn't know how long church service would last and Parke didn't want the children to become restless, especially if he did. "Church!" Mrs. Beacon had shrieked into the phone. "If no one's dead, what ya going for? Take those kids to the park for a picnic or to a movie."

After convincing Mrs. Beacon that Cheney might enjoy it, she relented. Cheney returned with her purse and Parke chanced another glimpse of the captivating creature. For a second, Parke was tempted to take Mrs. Beacon's advice to skip service, kidnap Cheney, and get lost in her sweet kisses. *Not a bad idea*, he thought as Cheney's phone rang.

Cheney's heels clicked against the hardwood floor as she walked across the room to answer it. "Hello?" she answered with her back to Parke. She laughed before turning to Parke with a smile. "It's Grandma BB. She says Kami's tearing up her house, trying to get over here to you. She was looking out the window when you came."

Parke stretched out his hand. "I guess we better stop next door."

"We're on our way out," Cheney said into the phone.

"You know, baby, we could skip church and enjoy the day, just you and me."

Cheney paused from locking her door. "You don't want to go?" She tried to hide it, but Parke heard the disappointment in her voice.

Not really. I'd rather spend the day alone with you. Stuffing his hands in his pants pockets, Parke smiled. He promised himself and Cheney that he would make her dreams come true, so it was off to church. "Just kid—"

As they turned around, Cheney and Parke stopped in mid-step. Dre, Sasha, and her neighbor, holding a squirming Kami, posed picture-perfect on Mrs. Beacon's porch.

"You look pretty, Miss Cheney," Sasha yelled, waving.

"Yeah," Dre agreed, grinning. "You clean up real good. You look better than the chicks at the baseball game."

"Remind me to have a man-to-man talk with you later, Dre," Parke warned, wanting to forget about the day at the ball park.

"If you stay here any longer, you can play poker with us," Mrs. Beacon offered with a mischievous grin. Kami moved hysterically in her arms, screaming Parke's name. Her possessiveness always gave Parke an undeserved sense of pride. "That's my girl." He crossed the lawn to receive her loving hug and mushy kisses. Cheney followed. Kami gave Parke her sixty seconds of love then waved good-bye.

Parke smiled as he assisted Cheney inside his Envoy. "How much longer do we have with Kami?"

"Not long, ten days maybe," Cheney answered.

"I'm going to miss her."

Cheney blew kisses to the group as Parke pulled away. "Yeah, Wilma says the family isn't being very cooperative in trying to get Kami back. She may have to leave me and go into long-term traditional foster care."

Parke turned into Faith Miracle Church's over-crowded parking lot. "Whoa, how many people attend this church?"

"Hmm, I was thinking the same thing," Cheney said absently. "The preacher must be doing something right."

Maybe. He didn't comment. Parke didn't know what to believe at that moment. When had he become so cynical? Parke maneuvered his SUV into a narrow space. He got out, walked around to the passenger side, and helped Cheney get out. "I hope I'm not making a mistake," she mumbled under her breath.

Parke intertwined his hand with Cheney's as they walked toward a majestic one-story white brick building with gray stone accents.

Annette paced behind a double-glassed door. When she saw Parke and Cheney coming, she grinned. When they were within a foot of the entrance, Annette flung open the door and playfully yanked

Cheney inside, engulfing her with a bear hug, ignoring Parke.

"Ooh, I'm so glad you could come," Annette rattled. "When Parke called me this morning, I just thanked Jesus." She looped her arm through Cheney's and escorted them to their seats. As an afterthought, Annette turned her head. "Oh. Hi, Parke, I'm glad to see you too. Did you play the CD I gave you for Christmas?"

"How nice of you to notice me, dear friend, yes, I did," Parke mumbled as he followed them down a mint-green ceramic tile floor, recalling the song's effect on Cheney.

Annette had insisted at the end of their phone call that Parke play Donnie McClurkin's *Stand* CD on the way to church. When the singer first asked a simple question, Cheney became immersed. As the music filled his vehicle's interior, Parke heard Cheney's sniffing as the singer encouraged his listeners to hold on. At one point, Cheney faced the window, wiping away a tear. The song mentioned guilt, shame, and past mistakes, active ingredients in anyone's life.

Parke's ears zoomed into the song that called out problem areas in Cheney's life. "We'll stand together against our past decisions, just like Paki and Elaine, who couldn't undo the past, but boldly shaped a future," he had told Cheney.

Annette opened the sanctuary door, exposing Parke and Cheney to thousands of worshippers who packed the auditorium. Some sang and clapped, others sat rocking from side to side with their eyes closed. Parke guessed they were meditating. The organ's pipes caused the sanctuary walls to vibrate.

Numerous sounds from wind and percussion instruments exploded, harmonizing with a choir too large to number.

Seating arrangements were divided into six sections with a balcony stretching from one end of the sanctuary to the other. Annette had saved them seats on the main floor. Annette sat next to Parke, and he next to Cheney whose face was unreadable. Parke scooted closer and wrapped his arm around her shoulder. "Are you all right, honey?"

Forcing a weak smile, Cheney nodded. "I can't remember going to a church with my family. Besides a wedding or funeral, there was never time left after studies, extracurricular activities, and social events."

As if privy to Cheney's remarks, Annette nudged Parke's left shoulder, wearing a pleased expression. Mission accomplished. She had gotten Parke inside her church walls, using his woman as bait. Dressed in a two-piece coffee-brown suit, Annette clapped to the drummer's beat. Standing, she swayed with choir members.

When Cheney whispered his name, he refocused on his woman. "Yeah, baby?"

"Thanks for bringing me. I don't think I would've ever come by myself."

He nodded, frustrated, despising the memories that continue to torment her. Parke wasn't sure if church was exorcising her pent-up fears or recycling them to another level. Unlike Cheney, the Jamiesons did attend church, not regularly, but as a routine, copying other families. Church had been a socializing opportunity to be seen and make business connections. At his parents' house, an old-family Bible laid on a table in the foyer. Parke didn't know what book was opened or the page number. He did know it contained the names, births, and deaths of his ancestors.

As the music died down, a middle-aged, pecan-shaded man dressed in a beige-and-black preacher's robe came to the podium. "Praise the Lord, everybody. Let's give God a hand praise. Whether you're sitting, standing, or sick in your body, put your hands together for Jesus. Even a small child can clap. Luke 19:40 warns us if we withhold our praise, the stones will immediately cry out with praise. You showed up today. Now, let's show off for Jesus."

A thunderous roar erupted throughout the auditorium. Folks all around Parke had their eyes shut, clapping vigorously, except for Annette whose hands shook wildly in the air as she yelled, "Thank you, Jesus."

Cheney remained seated, slumped over, barely participating. Parke was about to touch her when her head drifted back, revealing a trail of tears glistening down her cheeks. He didn't know what to expect when they came to church, but Cheney's crying wasn't it.

As the noise settled down, the minister shouted, "Don't you feel better?"

Some in the crowd yelled, "Yeah." Others waved their hands. Parke exhaled when Cheney nodded, dabbing her face with a Kleenex Annette had handed her.

"Then, let's have church," the minister responded.

Annette leaned across Parke and informed Cheney the pastor's name was Elder Baylor Scott.

"Despite the praise a few minutes ago, somebody

didn't praise Him. Some of you may ask, 'How do you know, Pastor? It sure sounded like it.' Just like the woman with an issue of blood who pressed the crowd to touch the hem of Jesus's garment, Jesus knew the moment power left Him. It's the same thing now. In the midst of shouts, God knows who that someone was who didn't praise Him."

Focused on the task at hand, Pastor Scott turned the pages in his Bible. Cheney touched Parke's thigh. Parke leaned forward.

"That was me," Cheney confessed.

What is she talking about? He looked perplexed.

"Although I clapped, I felt like such a hypocrite."

Parke was dumbfounded. Even in church, Cheney's trespasses were weighing her down. He racked his brain to offer some soothing words, but the pastor interrupted him.

"Everybody turn your Bible to 1 Peter, 5:7. If you don't have your Bible, share with the person next to you."

Parke wasn't surprised when Annette whipped out a huge Bible, thrusting it in Parke's hand for him and Cheney to use. "When God starts working, I always come prepared," she said with compassion.

The minister cleared his throat. "Let's read together. *'Casting all your care upon Him; for He careth for you.'* Regardless of what problems you walked through the door with this morning, God is commanding you to throw them away with a great force—to fling, to drop, to shed, to rid yourself of all that is weighing you down, keeping you up at night, or eating you up inside. Give it to God, today. Why? Because God cares for you without any prejudices. You can't hide your sins from God. He already knew about them before you committed them."

"Thank you, Jesus," someone shouted behind Parke's head.

"Amen," an older woman sitting two rows in front of them yelled. Others clapped, encouraging the pastor to preach the Word.

Cheney sat in a trance, concentrating on the minister. Parke knitted his brows and twisted his lips in confusion. *The man only read one scripture. Why is everybody getting so worked up?* he wondered.

"When God takes our burdens, we can wave them good-bye, so long. They won't be back. They won't be back."

Parke loss track of the time as the minister preached about a carefree life, tossing away the bad and grabbing the good. Cheney listened attentively while Parke wondered if he fathered a discarded son because of his carefree lifestyle.

The preacher finished his sermon with a resounding, "Hallelujah." Some members around Parke jumped up, waved their arms or danced to a secret.

"Let us stand and pray. Jesus, you know our needs. You see the souls that are marred with sins, and the cries that are pleading for deliverance. Lord, we know we can't make a change without you," the minister prayed.

Parke couldn't explain it, but the atmosphere was changing. He listened as the choir hummed the melody to "Jesus is Love," a song he connected with Lionel Richie. Without lifting a bowed head, he noticed Cheney's grip on the back of the seat in front of them. Her knuckles had reddened.

Pastor Scott warned, "Listen to me. This moment is not about churches or religions, it's about your soul and where you will spend eternity," his voice pierced the air. "I don't have to tell you whether you're saved or not. You are the ones living in sin or sanctification. You know and God knows. Make your choice today. Don't walk out of this building and back into sin. Repent."

Subliminal spirits agitated the crowd. He chanced a glance around. He could count the number of faces where the message seemed to hit home. The frowns and heavy breathing revealed an unspoken guilty plea.

"Friends, I'm not preaching just because it's Sunday. I'm concerned about your soul! Tomorrow's breath is not promised today. Don't leave this place with your soul in the same condition it came in here with. From where you are, repent of your sins."

Parke didn't know if anyone else's heart dropped like an elevator and then zoomed to the top floor. Cheney leaned into him at the same time as someone clapped in a fast rhythm that wasn't to the beat of the choir's humming that had transformed into words. If they were standing in the middle of a cornfield, they could see a tornado coming. Instead, he heard a quick rush of wind, it's origin uncertain.

"If you say that you've accepted Christ, yet still have problems living holy, leave from where you're standing. C'mon down and let God wash your sins away and give you power to live right. We have baptismal clothes for you now. We're ready to serve you now. Are you ready? No need to make an appointment or put it off. You can leave here today a new creature filled with the Holy Ghost and have the evidence of speaking in unknown tongues," he begged the crowd until one by one, many left their seats.

"That's right. Come on. The Bible says in the book of Acts chapter nineteen, *'Then said Paul, John verily baptized with the baptism of repentance, saying unto the people, that they should believe on him which should come after him, that is, on Christ Jesus. When they heard this, they were baptized in the name of the Lord Jesus. And when Paul had laid his hands upon them, the Holy Ghost came on them; and they spoke with tongues, and prophesied.'* That's right. Let God give you some power to live right," Pastor Scott encouraged then paused, folding his arms. As he bowed his head as in prayer, moans, cries, and some screams of deliverance permeated the air.

The pastor looked up and scanned the sanctuary. Many people reacted to his message either in prayer, wailing, or walking down the aisle. He adjusted the microphone. "Know that God is big enough to take away your burdens. Make your way to the front altar, repent, and give God your life." He turned to the choir. "All right, let's close with a little of Walter Hawkins' "Thank You." God bless you," the minister took his Bible and went back to his seat where he knelt, prayed, and then sat down.

Cheney faced Parke. "I want to go, will you walk with me?" Her face displayed a childish innocence he had never seen before.

Parke felt like someone was twisting him up inside as he stared into Cheney's watery eyes. *Yes* was on the tip of his tongue, but *no* was shouting from his heart. He wanted no part of this. The sad thing about his resistance was he had no legitimate reason for it.

He couldn't blame it on Annette. She had always been a good friend and steered him in the right direction. Parke had nothing against God or His blessings. Where were the ill feelings coming from? Cheney's eyes pleaded with him before she turned away and bowed her head.

Annette reached across Parke and stroked Cheney's arm. "I'll walk with you." She led Cheney down a long aisle that quickly swelled with others—young, old, and a few in wheelchairs. Parke couldn't believe his eyes. In front of the pulpit, Cheney whispered into Minister Dyson Kidd's ear, Annette's friend from the baseball game.

Nodding, he uttered something to Cheney before laying his hand on her head. He closed his eyes and prayed fervently while Annette stood behind Cheney with her head bowed. Parke didn't like it— Dyson touching his woman or praying for her.

Within minutes, Cheney stretched out her arms as if she was submitting to something. Two women approached her, dressed in white suits, and wrapped their arms around Cheney's waist. Then they steered her through a side door.

Annette gave Parke an accusatory glance when she returned to her seat. She was about to say something when the pastor returned to the podium.

"Many have come today, but somebody's still holding out. Perhaps you feel you aren't carrying any burdens, but are you guilty of works of the flesh?"

The choir's distinctive words to a song had subsided into soft humming. Parke turned to Annette, whispering, "Where is my baby? What is that man talking about, 'works of the flesh'?"

"Evidently, Cheney has decided to get her sins washed away, so she's on her way to get baptized." She curved her mouth into a mischievous grin. "And, knowing Pastor Scott, he'll explain—"

"Let me break it down for you, friends," the minister continued, "Are you guilty? Are you mixed up in adultery, are you a fornicator—sex outside marriage—what about lasciviousness? Galatians, chapter five, beginning at verse nineteen lists idolatry, witchcraft, hatred, wrath, strife, sedition, heresies, envying, murder, drunkenness, and such will not inherit the Kingdom of God, which means you will not get to heaven. Are you guilty? My advice is let it go."

Elbowing Parke, Annette twisted her mouth. "See your name linked to any of that?"

He thought about this Parke boy again. Could the child be Parke VII? "Okay, okay. I'm guilty." Parke dropped his head in his hands as he leaned forward. Although noise and people surrounded him, he sensed it was just him and his Creator. *God, please forgive me if I've wronged my own child. Forgive me of sins that I didn't realize I committed. God, show me what it means to live for You because I have no idea,* he said silently.

Annette almost choked Parke with a bear hug, squealing. Parke began his walk down the same path as Cheney had. Parke felt like he was being summoned to the king for a beheading. After Minister Kidd prayed for him, the next thing Parke remembered was being dressed in all white like Cheney, standing at the edge of a pool facing her.

Oh man, this is all Annette's fault, he thought as he was submerged under the water.

CHAPTER 31

Cheney was heartbroken after Parke's hesitation. He had her spoiled, saying yes to many of her requests, but not this time. The urge to walk down the aisle was so strong Cheney had to go alone.

The pastor directed that sermon to me. Cheney needed not only to forget and forgive herself about the abortion, but she wanted God's forgiveness too. The Bible had helped, but it wasn't enough. She had done all that she could do to shake the guilt. Taking in foster kids hadn't worked. Renovating a forgotten house hadn't worked. Nothing had. She believed the preacher when he said she wouldn't leave out the door the same way she came in, swollen by guilt, bitterness, and self-pity.

" *'And God will subdue our iniquities and cast all our sins into the depths of the sea.'* Rest assured my brothers and sisters, the sea is too deep for your sins to rise again, so you're walking away fresh today, and God will remember your sins no more," a short, bald man said to the dozens gathered for their baptism. He quoted an Old Testament scripture from a big white Bible.

Nervously, climbing three steps to a large water tank, Cheney's heart pounded against her chest. When she steadied herself on the platform and looked up, Parke stood on the other side. When he mouthed, *I love you*, tears blurred Cheney's vision.

Two ministers stood waist-deep in the pool, beckoning for Cheney and Parke to begin their descent into the water. Cheney faced Parke. Curving his lips into a bright smile, Parke whispered, "I realized I had to get myself cleaned up, too."

A minister instructed Cheney to turn around with her back facing Parke. "Cross your arms against your chest, Sister." Cheney heard the other minister repeat the same instructions to Parke.

Gripping the back of her garment, the man lifted one arm in the air. "My dear brother and sister, upon the confession of your faith and the confidence that we have in the blessed Word of life, concerning the death, burial, and grand resurrection of our Lord and Savior Jesus Christ, we now baptize you in the name of Jesus for the remission of your sins. You shall receive the gift of the Holy Ghost. Amen." Despite his firm hold, he gently dipped Cheney back, submerging her under water.

"Your sins are now buried, Sister," were the first words out the minister's mouth when Cheney rose. "Praise the Lord. Don't let the devil convince you to dig them up again. Let God fill you with His precious Holy Ghost."

Spitting profusely, Cheney wiped water from her eyes, nose, and mouth to see if Parke was okay. Before she could turn around, Parke screamed, "Hallelujah," from the top of his lungs as the two ministers encouraged him to worship God. Something was happening to Parke. Cheney didn't know what it was, but she wanted to be a part of it.

A woman motioned Cheney toward the steps to assist her out of the pool just as another female baptismal candidate walked down.

"Now, don't you feel better, sugar?" the woman asked as she draped a warm white towel over Cheney's shoulders.

"Surprisingly, yes, I feel like I dumped a heavy load," Cheney confessed with her mind on Parke. She had never seen him so emotional, besides the night he shed tears with her.

Inside a large ladies' dressing room, two older women assisted Cheney in drying off before she changed back into her black dress, which somehow seemed so inappropriate.

"You're a new creature, sweetie." A short, grandmother-looking woman patted Cheney's cheek with a white towel. "Thanks to Jesus' death on Calvary, you've got a clean slate."

"Sho does," the other women agreed, rolling wet socks off Cheney's feet. "You feel up to tarrying for the Holy Ghost? It looks like that man in the pool with you may already have received it."

Cheney's head shot up. "What? What do you mean tarrying and Parke's got it?"

Neither woman stopped working with Cheney's clothes as they talked.

"Usually when someone starts shouting like that in the water, if they don't have the Holy Ghost, they've got the anointing," said the shorter woman.

"Sho 'nuff," the taller woman added, smiling. "Baby,

you want God to fill you with his power, because you're clean, sanctified, and before the devil tries to come back with more demons to tempt ya."

"You mentioned tarry. What does that mean?" Cheney asked.

"Sister Ethel, you're using terman'l'gy the girl don't understand," the shorter woman scolded.

"Tarry simply means waiting for God to give you His gift with the evidence of speaking in unknown tongues. That's just the beginning, the break-through," Ethel explained.

"Well, whatever God has for me, I want it all," Cheney said with finality. This was the first time in six years she was at peace. Somehow, she believed her life would turn around.

"You can read all about the Holy Ghost and speaking in tongues in the book of Acts," Ethel in-structed.

"Will I know what I'm saying?"

"Only if God has a message for you, otherwise, it's God's way to edify you," Ethel answered.

"Oh." Minutes later they arrived at a small chapel filled sparsely with other baptized converts, some were crying, but mostly they all were shouting, "Thank you, Jesus" or 'Hallelujah," except for Parke who dominated a far corner with his hands in the air talking a mile a minute in a language she didn't recog-nize.

"Yeah, he's got it," the shorter woman stated matter-of-factly. The other woman agreed.

All three of them sat on a back row. The women instructed Cheney to just thank God, and praise Him for being God. Cheney shrugged as she closed her eyes. She didn't know how to pray other than

"Our Father," so thanking Jesus for a second chance seemed simple enough. Funny, baptism was such an effortless task to rectify a serious act. Cheney didn't know how Parke "got it," but she wanted this Holy Ghost too.

A while later, words unrehearsed, unlearned, and indistinguishable exploded from Chency's mouth. The sensation along with the words began in her belly and spread throughout her body. It was as if she was experiencing an out-of-body episode, but was fully aware of her involuntary praise and worship.

Cheney heard herself speaking, and felt her lips moving, but she couldn't control the words, speed, or volume. She didn't understand what she was saying, but the spiritual, supernatural connection was undeniable. Rejoicing roared through the room.

"Sho 'nuff, she's got it!" a woman yelled.

Unbelievable. Cheney didn't know what kind of high junkies experienced, but she was sure it couldn't compare to what just occurred. "It's real. It's real. The day of Pentecost isn't limited to the biblical time," Cheney said aloud to anyone who was willing to listen. The power was still very much alive in the new millennium. Her burdens, guilt, and hate were finally extinguished.

"My life is over," Hallison complained, stomping around in her bedroom. With Paula Silas at work, her mother's daily salvation reminder calls, and now Cheney and Parke receiving the Holy Ghost, church was becoming more than Hallison could tolerate. "It's unbelievable, unthinkable, and unfortunately indisputable." The handwriting was on the wall. God was closing in on her.

Hallison wanted to curse to relieve her frustration. God would probably strike her dead for blasphemy. She had faked sickness, lied, and turned down her mother's last three offers to attend church. Now, Malcolm wholeheartedly agreed to attend church with the newly converted, happy, and rejoicing Pentecostals.

"Baby, we're not making any commitments, they are," he had said.

Whatever demons Cheney had, they had been exorcized. All Hallison wanted was the peace to live in sin, out of sin, or with sin. She was a contented backslider. She was becoming agitated that God kept sending His servants to keep reminding her of how she was living. Unfortunately, her so-called demons were angels from God, and they had more warfare than any devil could conjure up.

Tugging at a plum-colored suit off the rack in her closet with too much force, she snagged several other outfits down with it. *Great.* "Who am I kidding? If I step foot in church, I may turn to a pillar of salt like Lot's wife." She clenched her teeth. "Malcolm, why do you have to be so accepting? Ever hear of just saying no?" she shouted.

Possessing a foul mood, Hallison blamed God. "I don't want to be saved anymore. Accept it." Her mild irritation was escalating into a major temper tantrum as the phone rang, interrupting her ranting and raving. "Hello," she answered with too much attitude.

"Hey," Malcolm hushed into the receiver. "This

can't be my woman. You aren't starting your day off like that. Close your eyes and sit down."

Hallison rolled her eyes. Her mood wasn't condusive to romance. What was going on around her was big, real big. "Mal—"

"Sweetheart, I phone you every morning to love you with soft words and sweet thoughts. What is ruining it today?"

Flopping down on her bed, Hallison debated if she should discuss her fears with Malcolm. Without warning, tears spilled from her eyes. Her steady, angry voice became weak and shaky. "I'm so scared, Malcolm."

Malcolm cooed into her ear. "Hali, I've got time. I suggest you make time to talk to me now, or I'm calling your office all day. Now, sweetheart, I love you, so tell me what's scaring you."

She grunted. "The thought of going to church." She sighed. "Then, there's Parke and Cheney receiving the Holy Ghost and the pressure to share their jubilation."

His laugh held a touch of relief. "Oh, don't let them scare you. They've been excitable every time they recount their experience. They've been finishing each other's sentences, giddy like school kids, and praying for folks on the spot. I'm kinda interested to see for myself what happened to them."

"They spoke in other tongues, Malcolm. That's called receiving the Holy Ghost. That's what happened to them. I was once like that."

"Then what's the problem?" Malcolm asked, confused.

"I don't want to be like that anymore. I mean, I'm

all for going to church, but I want to do what I want to do and not be reminded that I'm sinning against God."

Malcolm became quiet. She thought he might've fallen asleep.

"Sweetheart, you know I'm not one for pressure, especially when it comes to religion," Malcolm finally spoke. "I've already accepted their invitation for church. I thought you and Cheney were becoming good friends. Hali, if you're uncomfortable, I can tell Parke we can't make it. I don't understand why you're stressed."

She loved her man deeply, but at the moment, Hallison could've shook Malcolm like a rag doll. He should've checked with her before agreeing. Malcolm didn't know how she felt. "You're right. I guess I'm just freaking out. I'm sorry."

"It sounds like I need to spend more time with my woman. Like I told you before our hiatus, you'll get no more pressure from me. Feel up to dinner and dancing later?"

"All right," she agreed, sighing.

"Oh," Malcolm said, chuckling. "Don't think this conversation is over."

Shutting out bad vibes, Hallison closed her eyes and smiled. "I just love you so much. I don't want anything to come between us, not even church. I keep getting these strange feelings that something is trying to steal my happiness."

"If that's what's worrying you, then you don't know how strong my love is. You're mine and I'm yours. We'll do everything together, including church. Now, Miss Dinkins, say, *"I love you, Malcolm."*

The man was irreplaceable. "I love you, Malcolm, my strong, handsome and fearless warrior."

Hallison was content the remainder of the day, but when she stopped by the Galleria on her way home, the strange feeling came back to her. She was about to dismiss it when she heard her name. She turned to that direction, squinting. "Tavia, is that you?"

"Yeah, girl, it's me. How have you been?" Tavia answered as they embraced.

Hallison didn't recognize her old friend from her church days. Tavia was heavier, hair shorter, and she didn't look like she had been taking care of herself. "How's David?"

"Girl, don't say that man's name." Tavia's eyes bucked. "I should've never married him."

"What? You two were so in love."

"Yeah, and pastor told me not to marry him."

Hallison waved her hand, dismissing that advisement. "Well, he was wrong. You're happily—"

Tavia shook her head. "No, Hali, pastor was right. He wasn't saved. He was on drugs, he beat me, and tried to kill me."

"No!" Hallison slapped her cheeks. How could the pastor have known, or did he know? "Are you okay?"

"Only by the grace of God, David was stabbed to death while buying drugs. I repented big time and called the pastor and apologized. I've learned my lesson. When the man of God tells me something, I'm going to listen for now on."

For years, Hallison had misjudged God concerning Tavia and David. Maybe God was talking to her now, but she didn't want to listen. The women hugged. Hallison headed home; her shopping spirit was crushed.

"I can't believe what you're asking of me. Please tell me you're not on a religious crusade. Go to church? It ain't going to happen, unless it has bingo tables."

Parke folded his arms as he glanced around Mrs. Beacon's living room. "Cheney, you said she would be difficult."

"Yeah, I know. We could use force."

"I just wanna know who is bad enough to tie me up and carry me out of here?" Mrs. Beacon challenged.

"Please," Cheney pleaded, "come one time. The experience is unexplainable. Finally, after so many years I have peace after I made a bad decision. God can get rid of your bitterness."

"I'd rather hold on to it." Mrs. Beacon squinted. "He's the cause of it. God's responsible for all my lonely nights, cloudy days, and something else. I'll remember it in a minute. I'll bargain with God if He hands over the hit-and-run driver who took Henry away and I might believe in Him again."

Kneeling in front of Mrs. Beacon, Cheney rested praying hands on her lap. "Grandma BB, I don't have all the answers. He has already proven Himself to me in a way that's indescribable. A woman at church came up to me and said God's mercies are new every morning. I wake up every morning trying to find out. Look, I need to get next door with those three kids at my house. Will you please come to church with us, just one time?" Cheney stuck one finger in the air. "I want to share this incredible experience."

Mrs. Beacon folded her arms. "One time, Heney, and I'm going late and leaving early."

"That's better than nothing. I guess God will have to work quickly on you."

As Parke and Cheney walked next door, Parke asked, "She's serious isn't she, about going late?"

"Yep, but it's hard to convince her when I'm still learning and don't know the right words or scriptures to say."

"It may take us a lifetime to learn, Sister Cheney Reynolds."

Laughing, they stepped onto Cheney's porch. "I wish God had saved me sooner. I'm almost positive I would've never gotten involved with Larry."

"Hush, woman. That name is now on our bad word list."

"You're right. Hey, has Wilma said anything else about the little Parke boy?"

Parke frowned, shaking his head. "Nope, if that child proves to be mine, nothing is going to stop me from getting to my boy. Wilma did say the little fella in question has bounced from one foster home to another."

As the couple walked through the front door, Kami dropped her sandwich on the hardwood floor. She made a mad dash to Parke, leaving peanut butter on his cheek.

He examined the jelly stain on his shirt and Kami whimpered, "Sorree."

"Miss Cheney," Sasha's voice yelled from upstairs, "I need help packing."

"Coming," Cheney shouted back, snickering at Parke. Strolling to Dre, she teasingly rubbed his peach fuzz-covered chin. "I'm going to miss you and Sasha. You two are really good kids. Don't let anybody say otherwise."

Their maternal grandmother was whopping mad when she learned what happened to Sasha and Dre. The woman had stormed into family court, demanding custody of her grandchildren. Cheney would miss them, but was glad a bad situation had a certain degree of a happy ending.

Dre flew into Cheney's arms, hugging her tightly. "Thank you for taking care of us. I'll miss you, Parke, and Kami." He looked up with tears in his eyes. "Could we come back and visit?"

Cheney kissed the top of Dre's cornrows. "Of course." She sniffed and exhaled. "Now, I better check on Sasha."

Upstairs in the girls' bedroom, Sasha sat solemn in the rocking chair, hugging one of the international dolls. Cheney walked quietly into the room and settled on the bed.

The young girl didn't make eye contact with her. "You know, I'm glad my Grandma cares about me, even if my Mama don't."

Stretching out on the bedspread, Cheney patted the space beside her. "I'm glad too."

Sasha climbed on the bed and cuddled in Cheney's arms for a long time without speaking. "Why doesn't she love me?"

Instead of lying, Cheney said what was in her heart. Didn't she read in her Bible what Jesus had said about truth? It was in the book of John, *Ye shall know the truth, and the truth shall make you free.* It was only one of three scripture that had settled in her heart. With sixty-six books in the Bible, Cheney had a long way to go.

She wanted Sasha to be free—body, soul, and heart. "Sasha, people, including your mother and me, make mistakes. Sometimes, we're scared and do stupid things."

"But, I'm her daughter, Miss Cheney."

"I know." Cheney sighed. The child she aborted came to mind, but this time, without experiencing any lingering guilt, she felt redemption. Cheney couldn't think of another scripture. "I'll pray that one day she realizes how important you are to her before it's too late." Sasha's blank expression showed her lack of understanding.

Later that night, Cheney, Parke, and Kami said a tearful good-bye to Sasha and Dre. Even Parke's parents stopped by to say their good-byes, give hugs, and bring gifts. Parting wasn't a sweet sorrow, it was an aching *pain*. Eventually, Cheney fell asleep in Sasha's bed trying to console Kami who had grown accustomed to the older girl's brief presence. Kami's departure could be any day, so Cheney had her on borrowed time.

Kami drifted off after chanting Sasha's name for minutes. The Blue's Clues wall clock chimed at 10:30. Cheney yawned and decided to close her eyes again for a few minutes before getting up and going to her own bedroom.

"Cheney," a voice called, sounding like a loud whisper.

"Hmm?" Cheney moaned without opening an eye.

"*Cheyenne is fine. I knew her soul before she was con-*

ceived. I returned her to Me when her life no longer existed. She's resting. Now let your soul rest," the deep voice rumbled thunderously with so much power the bedroom shook.

Cheney sprang up; her eyes popped opened. She scanned the softly lit room. Kami was sound asleep in the kiddie bed Parke had purchased, arguing that the twin beds were too big. She knew her burglar alarm was activated so no one could break in.

If what she thought she heard had really happened, Kami would've wakened. Wouldn't she? Glancing at the wall clock, it chimed 10:30 again. Disoriented, Cheney padded across the hall to her bedroom in search of her Bible. Flipping the pages, she had no idea what she was looking for. Going back and forth, Cheney kept returning to Jeremiah, chapter one. As she read, she looked for a possible connection of what she thought she just heard. Then she saw it in verse four. Her fingers began shaking. *Then the Word of the Lord came unto me, saying, Before I formed thee in the belly I knew thee; and before thou camest forth out of the womb I sanctified thee.*

CHAPTER 32

"Whoa, baby." Malcolm's eyes twinkled as he glanced at Hallison from head to toe. "I like the church look."

It had taken Hallison more than an hour to dress. Her coral straw hat matched her two-piece suit. The long, narrow skirt was void of the thigh-high splits Malcolm enjoyed. She grabbed her old Bible, which she tried reading since running into Tavia, but nothing stayed in her head. *Did God give ministers advance warning that she was coming?*

Her fiancé looked shamefully handsome dressed in a navy blue pin-striped suit accessorized with a blue and orange paisley tie. He winked when he caught Hallison's roaming eye. His long and curly lashes were his most appealing assets.

His silky beard and mustache hinted of a recent shape-up and trim. Hallison inhaled his sweet musk-scented cologne. She felt a battle stirring within, a strange sensation she couldn't shake. *Will I return home the same person? Of course, He's a free will God.*

Closing the space between them, Hallison thrust her Bible in Malcolm's hand. She reached up and massaged his beard before luring his lips in the most possessive kiss they had ever shared.

Ending the kiss, Malcolm frowned, searching Hallison's face. "That wasn't a kiss of love, but sadness." He reached for her cheek, teasing her tiny earring stud on the way. "Sweetheart, it's going to be okay. No pressure."

Hallison desperately wanted to surrender to the power of Malcolm's brown eyes. His look showed his determination to move mountains for her, fueled by the love he possessed. The only problem was God had the power, and Malcolm wouldn't be able to move God's mountains.

On the drive to the church, Malcolm kept his voice low, sultry, and husky, describing what he had planned for their honeymoon. He turned into Faith Miracle Church's parking lot. In no time, he spotted Parke's Envoy, so they parked next to him and they got out. Parke and Cheney were outside the vehicle, struggling with something in the backseat.

"What are Cheney and Parke trying to get out of his SUV?" Hallison asked.

Shrugging, Malcolm helped Hallison out of his car, kissing the inside of her hand. "Just remember, I love you." His eyes lingered on her lips before turning to Parke. "What's wrong? You two need some help?"

"Only if you've got a straight jacket," Cheney solicited with a lifted brow.

"Huh?" Hallison and Malcolm exchanged looks.

Cheney positioned a fist on her hip, tapping her

shoe on the concrete. "It's my neighbor. She refuses to come out after she agreed to come to church."

"Not the fearless Grandma BB you told me about?" Hallison chuckled, her mood improving.

"Oh, yeah. The one and only, who says it's her prerogative to be fashionably late, but Cheney and I don't want to miss anything. Plus, I don't want Kami to get restless. If I yank her, I might hurt her. I can always throw her over my shoulder and make a grand entrance," Parke added, winking.

"Humph! This body is conditioned like Janet Jackson," Mrs. Beacon defiantly shouted from the backseat.

While everybody roared with laughter, in one smooth motion, Parke unbuckled and scooped up the woman so fast she didn't know what happened. He then planted her feet on the ground. "Malcolm, Hallison, let me introduce Mrs. Beacon. Believe it or not, she did want to come."

The sharply dressed woman ignored Parke's sly remark as she squinted over her rimmed glasses and pointed a manicured red fingernail at Malcolm and Hallison. "I'll let you know when you can call me Grandma BB."

"C'mon, y'all, let's shake this joint up," Mrs. Beacon said, adjusting her clothes before looping her arm through Cheney's.

Hallison chuckled, mumbling, "She's worse than me."

Malcolm doubled over in laughter as he tried to nod his agreement, snickering all the way as they strolled to the front door. Once inside, Hallison was prepared to dislike the church, the people, the pastor, even the floor tile, but too much Holy Ghost power surrounded her.

Once settled in the sanctuary, Mrs. Beacon gripped the bottom of her seat. The choir's fast-paced song coerced her feet to tap, then her shoulder lifted to the beat before her hands met in one clap after another. The next thing Hallison knew, the woman was swaying in her seat. Focusing on the woman's antics had actually allowed Hallison to unwind.

After Parke took Kami to the church nursery first, Hallison's stomach began churning as she watched people flock, young and old, to greet Cheney and Parke with hearty handshakes and hugs like they had known them for years. Some encouraged Parke and Cheney to keep walking with God. Malcolm stood to meet them. Hallison only offered a courteous smile.

She warned her mind to ignore the bass guitar's rhythm as Cheney and Parke got up and clapped in sync with the music. Something deep down inside of her wanted to bust out, and Hallison didn't know if she could stop it. Malcolm sat relaxed, swaying in his seat. Parke and Cheney glowed, not only with the Holy Ghost. It was easy to see the love growing between them.

A minister stepped to the podium, also swaying with the choir. His feet started moving faster than his body. Restraining himself, he introduced the pastor, Elder Baylor Scott.

"Praise the Lord, everybody," the pastor shouted with as much enthusiasm as the entire choir before softening his voice. "I want to talk about choices for this morning's sermon," he stated as voices hushed throughout the auditorium.

Malcolm squeezed and massaged Hallison's fingers as she cringed inside, sighing.

Mrs. Beacon, who was sandwiched between the two couples, leaned toward Hallison. "What kind of message is that? I know he ain't talkin' to me," she stated matter-of-factly, wrinkling her nose.

"Turn your Bibles with me to St. Luke, 16:11. Jesus spoke in many parables, so those listening would have an understanding, but some things don't need an explanation because their message is clear. Verse thirteen says, '*No servant can serve two masters: for either he will hate the one, and love the other; or else he will hold to the one, and despise the other. Ye cannot serve God and mammon.*' Mammon means material wealth or gain."

Parke and Cheney listened attentively while Malcolm relaxed his arm around Hallison, squeezing her shoulders as he crossed his ankle over a knee. Mrs. Beacon nudged Hallison in the side. "I ain't giving up nothing for God. He's already got my Henry, He might as well forget it. I could've taken Kami to the park instead of sitting here."

"I know many of you enjoy your life and the things you've accumulated and feel you don't need God, but rest assured one day your soul will be required of you, according to Hebrews 9:27, '*And as it is appointed unto men once to die, but after this the judgment*.' "

After thirty minutes, Hallison tuned out the sermon by listening to Mrs. Beacon doze.

Pastor Scott lifted one finger. "I'm warning you today. You don't want to be lukewarm with God," he admonished before rapidly turning pages in his Bible. "Revelation chapter three says, '*Because thou sayest, I am rich, and increased with goods, and have need of nothing and knowest not that thou art wretched, and miserable, and poor, and blind, and naked.'* God help each and every one of us today not to fool ourselves."

"Yes, Lord!" a woman shouted loud behind Mrs. Beacon. Balling up a fist, Mrs. Beacon lifted an eyebrow and was slowly turning around.

"It's okay. You'll get use to it," Cheney whispered, patting Mrs. Beacon's hand.

"I doubt it," Mrs. Beacon spat out before pinching her lips together and flaring her nostrils like a charging bull. "That man sure does talk too much."

Cheney hushed the woman. "He's hasn't preached an hour yet."

"That's thirty minutes too long."

A while later the minister closed his Bible. "You've heard the voice of God today, harden not your hearts."

Hallison released an audible sigh. Even after so many years, she had the service memorized. This was the part she had to stay strong against, the altar call. As the congregation was about to stand, the spirit of God started moving sporadically throughout the sanctuary. The hairs tingled on Hallison's body as her heart slammed against her chest. She felt no longer felt steady on her feet.

Like a child's game, people popped up, shouting across the church as if lightning zapped them. The Spirit's movement was slow and deliberate as it stirred closer to Hallison. She trembled as her arms flew in the air involuntarily. She barely escaped Mrs. Beacon's cane when the woman bolted from her seat and spun around without provocation. Hallison could explain what was going on even if her eyes were closed.

With the haste like a dollar sale, worshippers rushed into the aisle heading toward the altar. Before Hallison could blink, she was one of them. Tears washed the makeup from her face. The hat she wore was missing and her neat clothes were twisted. Her spiritually deprived soul took control. Playtime was over. When a minister laid his hands on her head and prayed for Hallison, unclean spirits seemed to leap from her. Afterwards, two women led her to a room off the sanctuary, which Hallison knew for the tarry or prayer room where she remained for a while worshipping God in tongues.

In the distance, Hallison recognized the rapid speech of unfamiliar tongues. Fluttering her eyes open, she was shocked to see Mrs. Beacon with her arms lifted in the air and her mouth moving non-stop. It had to be for more than twenty minutes. When Hallison was able to return to some semblance of control, she couldn't believe the two most likely church militants were in the prayer room and filled with the Holy Ghost. *Where was Malcolm?* Hallison wondered.

Some time later, Hallison and Mrs. Beacon were back in the sanctuary. "That was exhilarating and unbelievable. It's real. The Holy Ghost is real, chile. It got a hold of me. I never heard myself speak in another language. Well, I guess I might have to come back. God and I will have to do some negotiations about revealing my husband's killer," Mrs. Beacon said, fanning her face with a Kleenex. "I told God I was sorry, but I'm sure God and I will work out our differences."

CHAPTER 33

After three weeks, Parke could honestly say his outlook on life was changing. Both he and Cheney had a noticeable peace, and Parke couldn't take the credit. He understood what it meant to be at church every time the doors opened. He was hungry to have a new understanding of God and His power through the Holy Ghost. Fascinated with the Bible studies they had attended, Parke could add Bible history to his interests although each class generated more questions than he had answers.

Humming, Parke slid across his kitchen floor, preparing dinner for Cheney. His mother had given him a recipe for stuffed Cornish hens. He seasoned the roasted vegetables, drained the pineapple chunks, and mandarin orange slices for the Ambrosia salad, then poured two tablespoons of melted butter over simmering brown wild rice.

After shoving a dozen rolls into the oven, Parke hurried upstairs to shower. Dressing in a dark salmon-colored long-sleeve silk shirt with matching double pleated pants and his butterscotch Kenneth Cole wingtips, Parke was ready for his guest. He phoned Cheney for the third time. "Hi, baby, just reminding you dinner will be served in twenty minutes. Grandma BB is watching Kami, right?"

"Parke Jamieson VI, if you stop calling me, maybe I can get ready. Yes, Grandma is watching her. Who else would the little terror let keep her?"

Parke agreed and they said good-bye. Since receiving the Holy Ghost, Parke had sincerely tried to change his lifestyle, including stockpiling Christian and inspirational music for meditation and encouragement. He still struggled with temptation, but God's Word said He was able to deliver him. He bridled his tongue only to have pride escape in some situations. He requested strength for sanctification when he wanted to rip Cheney's clothes off and make love to her.

The pastor continually instructed that the road wasn't smooth, but to stay the course and spiritually pack for the journey with prayer, meditation, and fasting. Family services still hadn't located the boy named Parke, but he had faith in God the child would be found. For some unexplainable reason, he knew that the boy was his child, but he still needed proof. Kami remained with Cheney only because of administration bureaucracy.

Ben Tankard's saxophone filled the downstairs just as the doorbell rung. A single red rose tickled his nose when he opened the door. Parke took the flower, reached for Cheney's hand, and tugged her inside. "Praise the Lord. Thank you, honey," he whispered.

Parke perused Cheney's appearance—a dainty

lilac-colored dress that flowed when she walked. "I like it when you dress up for me." His voice filled with emotion. They indulged themselves in a strong embrace and a weak brush of their lips. "And I can't do a thing about it. This modesty is killing me." Throwing caution to the wind, Parke pulled Cheney back into his arms and enjoyed a passionate kiss. "Ah, that's better."

She lovingly stroked his cheek. "I don't know. I kinda like holding back. At least I know you're not after my body."

"Who says?"

"Stop it."

Cheney sucked in her breath when he guided her to his dining room where candles burned in all four of his brass wall sconces. His extra-long dining table was intimately set for two at the far end with china, silverware, and sparkling crystal stemware. He cracked his French doors to enjoy a cool night breeze. "Everything is so beautiful."

Placing his hand on her waist, Parke led her to the chair. "I hope you say the same thing about dinner."

"It doesn't matter. It's the thought that counts."

"Thanks, but it matters to my growling stomach." After walking into the kitchen, Parke returned carrying one entrée at a time to the table. He played a game of placing soft kisses on Cheney's lips before going back for another dish.

Sitting down, Parke reached across the table, joined hands with Cheney, and prayed, "Lord, I have so much to be thankful for, besides not burning dinner. I didn't deserve your salvation or this wonderful woman, but you found her for me. Now, I ask that you sanctify and bless our food and help us to grow stronger in you. In Jesus' Holy name, Amen."

"Amen," Cheney repeated before laughing.

"What's so funny?" Parke asked, forking off a piece of meat.

"Me, you, us, Grandma BB, Hallison, but not Malcolm. It's like God is cleaning up the neighborhood."

Parke nodded. "The biggest difference is praying. Don't get me wrong. I like the quick, quiet prayers, but hearing me—or rather, God—speaking through me in tongues is confirmation that there is a God and He's having this private dialogue with me."

Cheney frowned, thinking. "I can't find it, but I remember seeing a scripture that says, '*He that speaketh in an unknown tongue edifieth himself, but he that prophesieth edifieth the church*'."

Parke piled a hungry-man portion of roasted vegetables onto his plate. "I think it's somewhere in first Corinthians courtesy of those weekly new saints meetings and Bible studies."

She bit into her Cornish hen and moaned. "You've been holding out on me. If I had known you could throw down like this, the kids and I would've been sitting on your steps every day waiting for dinner."

"I've been holding out *for* you, sweetheart."

"You knew how to cook when you enrolled in that cooking class with me, and when you pleaded for my help in preparing dishes for your family game night, didn't you? You crook."

"I'm guilty, baby. Guilty of love," he confessed, reaching for her hand.

"You're amazing, Parke Kokumuo Jamieson VI, just amazing."

Harold Rayford's Christian instrumental melodies serenaded them as they ate and engaged in loving smiles, harmless flirts, and teasing winks. After sampling marbled cheesecake, compliments of Charlotte Jamieson, Parke cleared his throat. "Our plates are empty, the music has stopped, and the sunset is waiting for us."

Bending on one knee, Parke pulled a black velvet box out of his pants pocket. Parke brought Cheney's hand to his lips, inhaling her scented lotion and exhaling his nervousness. "Cheney Denise Reynolds, you're the profile I've been searching for and I didn't know it. Only you can fill my life with happiness."

Sniffing, Cheney's eyes watered as her lips slightly trembled.

"I didn't realize my journey began the day you moved onto Benton Street. You'll never know how you rescued me from settling for less. The women I wasted—and I do mean wasted— my time with made me realize that my soul was restless, searching for you and God, and maybe this little boy with my name."

Speechless, Cheney reached out and touched Parke's cheek with her free hand, mouthing *I love you*. "Have you figured out who the mother of little Parke could've been?"

"No, and I don't want to talk about another woman right now. This is all about you. Will you take me for all I have and don't have, and be my wife?" Parke broke contact with her as he opened the box, displaying a cluster of shining diamonds.

Cheney's mouth opened as tears spilled. "I haven't seen the rich and famous wear that many diamonds on one ring."

"Yeah, I know I went a little overboard." He dabbed at her tears. "When Elaine gave Paki a son, it was recorded he carved a three-dimensional face from wood, blending his face and hers into a face of their child as a gift. Of course, it has never been found."

She bowed her head. "You kno—"

"Shh, baby, you talk too much. The answer is a three letter word." He brushed a finger against her lips. "The diamonds represent the stars dangling in the sky." Parke smirked. "The jeweler warned me if I add any more diamonds, although small, they wouldn't insure the ring. Will you marry me?"

"I can't bear your seed."

"But it's many things you can do for me," Parke whispered, repeating, "Marry me?"

"Are you sure?"

"Cheney?"

"Yes, I'd be honored to be your wife." She wrapped her arms around his shoulders, squeezing him so tight that she almost cut off Parke's air supply.

"Whew! You made me beg for that," he said, chuckling as he slid the ring on her finger.

The time had come. *I'm losing another baby*, Cheney thought. No excuses, no sickness, or family crisis would detain Kami another day. The disturbing truth made Cheney restless. She crossed the hall to the familiar room. Cheney sniffed as she folded and packed the clothes she and Parke had purchased for Kami, stuffing them into three large suitcases and a kiddie-sized one that Kami could handle.

Despite her melancholy, peace was finally seeping into Cheney's mind, knowing her own baby was safe with Jesus. "What about Kami? Will she be safe, Lord?"

The day before, Cheney along with Mrs. Beacon and Parke, indulged Kami in a little going away party. All the Jamiesons were in attendance as well Hallison. They were making so much fuss over the child that Cheney barely heard someone knocking.

Opening her door, Cheney blinked, stunned, and on guard. She was almost happy to see her mother. She had contacted her family after she turned her life over to God, but they all offered her pity.

Conversations with her mother had consisted of nothing more than polite talks. Rainey and her dad seemed to have the same schedule when she called, unavailable so she stopped calling weeks ago. Janae was always too busy with her kids to talk. So Cheney prayed and asked God what to do.

Gayle, dressed elegantly in a soft rose coatdress, offered a faint smile. Her hair, as usual, was styled without a strand out of place. Gayle's face was void of the high-and-mighty sneer Cheney saw the day of her housewarming—their last encounter. "Mother?" In a flash, Parke and Mrs. Beacon were at her side like summoned bodyguards.

Her mother anxiously looked away before facing Cheney again. "May I come in? I won't be long."

They all moved backwards as Kami scrambled to the door, peeping at the visitor. Latching onto Parke's leg, Kami whispered, "Mine," instead of screaming and attacking. Cheney smiled, hoping the next family would appreciate the toddler's possessiveness.

After the pleasantries were exchanged and tea served, Gayle got down to the business at hand. "I'm sorry, Cheney, truly."

"For what, Mom?"

"Because I despised you for carelessly getting pregnant, and then having the abortion. God has been dealing with me of late, and believe me it's not because I sought Him. The past months I kept bumping into the same woman at the grocery store, bank, and while shopping. She was always dressed in black with a clergyman's white collar, but it was her expressionless face that scolded me without uttering a word until our last encounter."

"What did she say?" Cheney asked curious.

Mrs. Reynolds bowed her head, toying with the rings on her fingers. "She warned me that hatred stirs up strife, but love covers all sins." Her tear-filled eyes met Cheney's. "She also told me to get my house in order because my soul would be required of me sooner than I was prepared for."

Cheney gasped. She engulfed her mother in a bear hug before sobbing. The division, bitterness, and finger-pointing evaporated. "No." She dropped to her knees. When Parke and Mrs. Beacon saw Cheney's distress, they knelt also. Even Kami mimicked them. "Jesus, help us all," Cheney pleaded in prayer. "Lord, I learned last night that Hezekiah petitioned for death not to come, and you added fifteen more years. Speak the Word, Lord, and reverse the curse."

Gayle, also crying, dropped on her knees. "God, please forgive me."

Charlotte seemed as if she wanted to participate, but was uncertain. Charlotte and the elder Parke watched the prayer with interest and curiosity before leaving. Afterwards, Mrs. Beacon and Hallison took Kami next door, giving mother and daughter some privacy.

Before leaving, Parke whispered in Cheney's ear, "Forgive, so we can be forgiven." Cheney nodded before turning back to Gayle. "Mother, I love you, and I made a series of personal mistakes. Although I'm sorry, I only have to answer to God," Cheney murmured tearfully.

Gayle clasped her hands and dropped her head. "I'm sorry, too, but that's to God and you."

The women alternated between sobs, hugs, hiccups, and "I love you." Finally, Cheney pulled away and smiled. "Mom, Parke and I are engaged."

"Are you happy?" Gayle smiled back.

"I have no right to be as happy as I am."

"Cheney, I owe you an explanation." She sighed. "We had a family crisis that ripped our family apart when you were in your second year at Duke."

"I didn't know. How come no one told me?"

"We didn't want to upset you. Plus, it was personal."

"I thought my situation was too personal for family too," Cheney stated with an accusatory edge.

Gayle pinched her lips together in embarrassment, showcasing the dimples Cheney inherited. "Rainey's

girlfriend, Shanice, became pregnant. We were disappointed, of course, but excited about our first
grandbaby." She paused. "Shanice was four months
pregnant when she and Rainey had a big argument
and broke up. Your father and I tried to encourage
Rainey to work it out, but Rainey wouldn't budge,
saying he wouldn't allow Shanice to use their baby
to threaten him. Well, to make a long story short,
when Shanice saw Rainey on a date with another
girl, she aborted their child, just like that." Gayle
snapped her fingers.

"Two abortions in one family," Cheney whispered.

Her mother nodded. "Rainey went from devas-
tated to ballistic. We barely survived when two years
later—"

"I got pregnant."

"Yes. Your father became suspicious when you
wouldn't come home or allow us to visit. Fearing
drug use or worse, Roland contacted a fellow physician who snooped around North Carolina's hospital
admissions and accessed your file. We couldn't say
anything to you because we had violated your privacy, but pure embarrassment triggered your father's anger. We had hoped you would tell us, but
you never did. I'm so sorry."

"Daddy discussed my condition with Rainey and
Janae?"

"He dropped hints, which your brother and sister
never got. When you moved back home, your father
told them as a way to hurt you for hiding it from
us."

"Mother, I did have a right to my privacy."

"True, but your dad was outraged, because, again,

we had been cheated. I'm sorry, Cheney. We should've been there for you, instead of alienating you. Why didn't you call us? Why?"

"At that time, I was caught in a place between heaven, having a baby, and hell, uncovering Larry's true intentions." Cheney's head was spinning. "I can't believe what my family did! My own family kept my twin's business from me, yet was privy to mine. Maybe, if I had known about Rainey's situation, my outcome would've been different."

"I guess we made you bear the guilt of what Shanice did to Rainey and our family. I'm so sorry."

Her mother stayed for hours until Mrs. Beacon brought Kami back, asleep. Drained, Gayle stood and hugged Cheney, asking for patience as the family healed. Cheney nodded her agreement.

An hour later, the memories of the conversation with Gayle still lingered when Cheney's phone rung. "Hello?"

"Hey, sweetheart, I'm on my way back. I saw a few lights still on. Is something wrong?" Parke's voice was on the edge of panic. "Is everything okay?"

"Not really, I just couldn't sleep with Kami leaving in the morning."

"I wish we could keep her." He sighed. "I called Wilma about letting Kami stay indefinitely as our foster child or even adopting her, but Wilma said the agency has to follow procedures, and other children are waiting to take her place."

"I know."

The line went silent as they collected their thoughts.

"Cheney, I know we'll both miss her, but if we stay faithful, God's Word says, *'No good thing will He withhold from them that walk uprightly'.*"

"Still reading Psalm, huh, Parke?"

"Yeah. David fascinates me. He was always getting into trouble, but the brother knew how to repent. I have a new perspective now on the stories in the Good Book. Instead of thinking of them as fables, I view them as testimonies from a man who struggled to obey God."

"I feel the same way. Hey, why are you coming home so late anyway, Mr. Jamieson?" she teased.

"Oh, that's right. I'm now engaged. I have to give an account of my whereabouts. I've been over at Malcolm's again. He put on a brave act at your house earlier, but in truth, he hasn't recovered from the day he came to church."

CHAPTER 34

The following morning at nine, Wilma rang Cheney's doorbell. Kami ran happily to the door and waited, expecting Parke. Cheney suggested Parke stay away because of Kami's attachment to him.

"Good morning, Cheney," Wilma greeted as Cheney opened the door and invited her in. Scooping up Kami in her arms, she offered a timid smile.

Cheney twiddled her fingers, holding back tears. "I know this is suppose to be a clean sweep, so I'll help carry her things to the car," she said in a shaky voice.

Wilma nodded, scanning her livingroom door.

"Parke and Grandma BB said their good-byes last night at a little party we gave Kami."

Wilma nodded again as she walked out the door with Kami. Waving good-bye to Kami, who was strapped in a car seat, Cheney returned to her house without looking back. Inside, she closed the door and cried until the tears dried up and her head ached.

* * *

"Hali, how could you just break my heart like that?" Malcolm questioned as he sat at his desk snapping pencil after pencil. Losing Hallison happened so fast, Malcolm didn't see it coming. It had been more than a week, and Malcolm still remained clueless. "If only I'd have known how unhappy you were, baby." Malcolm rubbed his face in frustration, remembering Hallison walking down the church aisle—not to the altar, but away from him.

Malcolm scanned his neat, small office then the chaos on his desk. "Why did I even bother coming to work today?" He couldn't focus. Malcolm closed his eyes, recalling that the worst day of his life had been in church. He remembered every detail.

"Congrats, Sister Dinkins," Cheney rocked Hallison in a hug. Parke also offered a hug, placing a kiss against her forehead.

"Praise the Lord, my future sister-in-law," Parke greeted, grinning with pride.

Cheney's neighbor, Mrs. Beacon, stepped forward. "I'm still trying to figure out how God did this thing, grabbing both of us today."

Clueless, Malcolm had stood back, letting Hallison soak in their love. She looked relieved, like a burden had been lifted. Malcolm made eye contact with Hali, watching her as he approached. He cupped her chin. "Hey, baby, why am I congratulating you, huh?" His eyes sparkled.

Hali treated him to a priceless smile as she gripped his hands. "Malcolm, God reclaimed me, despite how much I fought against what was right and turning my back on Jesus. I started repenting in my seat, and He forgave me." Her voice shook with disbelief. "My soul was saying yes, even as my mind screamed and kicked no."

Massaging her arms, Malcolm smiled again before hugging her. "If you're happy, then, baby, I'm happy."

"Oh, Malcolm, did you come down to the altar?" Hallison searched his face. "I got caught up in me, I forgot about you. I'm sorry."

Malcolm's hand lovingly stroked her cheek. "Don't worry about me, baby. I didn't leave my seat. I enjoyed the service and we can come back anytime, but nothing compelled me to jump up and shout or race down an aisle. God knows my heart and I'm satisfied as long as I have you."

"Malcolm, don't you want to be saved?"

"Never thought about it." He shrugged, stuffing hands in his pant pockets.

"Bible says to preach the gospel and he who receives it shall be saved, but to him that rejects it will be damned. Malcolm, please."

"Now, you sound like Parke. I'm happy for you and that's all that's important."

Hallison's sobbing was heart wrenching as he gathered her into his arms." What did I say? Shhh, don't worry about me."

Parke and Cheney exchanged worried looks that hinted they knew something Malcolm didn't. Composing herself, Hallison stepped slowly out of Malcolm's embrace. Staring at him with an unreadable expression, Hallison twisted off her engagement ring.

"What are you doing?" Malcolm asked, agitated by Hallison's gesture.

"As much as I love you, Malcolm, and I do love you, I can't accept this ring right now. I'm not an unbeliever

anymore. A house divided cannot stand. I've been living under grace, now it's time for me to stand."

"All of a sudden?" His heart had cracked as he fingered her ring. "Is this a joke? You can't be serious. One day in church and you're ready to walk away from me and the love we share?"

"I don't have a choice," she admitted, nodding shamefully as more tears threatened to spill. "I walked away from God once. So many people don't make it back, but this could've been my last chance."

"Baby, this isn't making sense." Malcolm stepped closer.

"It's simple. When I met you, I was living a lie. The more I pushed God away to be with you and what you wanted, the more tormented I became. Today, God spoke to me loud and clear. My last chance ran out. He will no longer wink at my sins. I've got to put Him first this time."

Malcolm was hot. "And where does that leave me? I can't believe this! I come to church and God steals my woman."

Parke tried to calm Malcolm down, but it didn't work. "We're in church, and that's your woman you're raising your voice at."

"She's no longer my woman, PJ, didn't you hear? I've just been dumped in church." Malcolm spat sarcastically.

It wasn't fear, but something flashed across Hallison's face and she turned away, "Parke, do you and Cheney mind giving me a lift home?"

"What!" Malcolm advanced toward Hallison as she stepped back and Mrs. Beacon maneuvered her walking cane, blocking his approach. "I brought you and I will take you home."

"No, Malcolm, you brought me, but left me spiritually stranded. I can't fight any longer. I've been at war internally too long."

Blurred vision jolted Malcolm back into the present. "I miss you, baby." His heart ached for her smile. His hands itched for her soft perfumed skin and silky hair. He took one woman into church and another one emerged. Grabbing the receiver, Malcolm punched in his ex-fiancée's work number. *Ex-fiancée.* He couldn't comprehend what that meant. "Hallison Dinkins, please."

"I'm sorry, she's doing payroll and can't be disturbed," the receptionist said, a little too patronizing for Malcolm. The woman had become Hallison's watchdog.

"Thanks." Malcolm slammed down the receiver and stood, scattering pencils. "Ten days is long enough." His fist pounded his desk. "You're going to see me, woman, with or without an audience. I won't be refused today." Patting Hallison's ring dangled on the gold chain around his neck, Malcolm stormed out. "Never mess with a black man in love, and I'm a Jamieson too. That's a hostile combination."

Thirty minutes later, Malcolm's heart was racing when Hallison's receptionist saw him and apparently hurried to alert her. Malcolm was quicker, entering Hallison's office a second sooner and almost bumping the woman back into the hall.

"I'm sorry, Miss Reynolds. I tried to warn you," the woman said, flustered.

Hallison remained seated behind her mahogany desk, looking radiant in her lilac suit. Her brown hair hung straight past her shoulders with her face glowing without any makeup, not even lipstick.

How can she sit there, look so beautiful and act calm? Malcolm was irritated, agitated, and dying inside. His peripheral vision closed in on Hallison's lips. Like a predator, he moved carefully toward her. Malcolm's eyes flashed and his chest heaved as he tried to control his sporadic breathing.

He leaned against her desk. "Hallison Dinkins, how can we work out our differences if you refuse to see and talk to me?" Malcolm inhaled her subtle sweet perfume he had bought her the month before. Malcolm's bold appraisal was meant to be threatening, but it weakened his knees. *Do you know how much I love you?*

"Because you're my weakness," she whispered, taking a deep breath.

Focusing on her mouth, Malcolm leaned closer. "And, you're my weakness."

"Please don't make me cry—"

Kissing her, Malcolm absorbed her words until she broke away, panting.

"If only you wanted to be saved."

"Sweetheart, I don't need holiness to be saved, but if that's the only way I can get you back, count me in."

"Baby—sorry that slipped. Your salvation has nothing to do with me. You've got to want it for yourself. Malcolm, you don't know enough about it to reject it. When God's power hit me, I did an about-face. I tried to forget the consequences, but God retrieved every memory that Sunday."

Why was she putting them through this? He hadn't

done a thing wrong except be honest with her. His temper broke. "Hali," he called through clenched teeth, "do you love me?"

When she hesitated, Malcolm hammered his fist on her desk, causing her to jump. "Hali, you know I love you, and I'd never hurt you."

Her eyes pleaded with Malcolm. "I know how special your love is, but it isn't enough anymore," her voice faded. "It's hard to explain, but before I walked to the altar, God showed me myself burning in flames. Malcolm, it was either I make a choice then, or never. I chose then."

"I can protect you. I'd never let anything happen to you, baby." Malcolm jammed his fists on his waist. "Hallison, I'm not feelin' I need God to direct what I say and do, but I sure do need you. Again, I'm asking you, do you love me?"

Hallison looked away, not answering. Malcolm knew he was a good person who truly loved her. The man upstairs could appreciate that. When Hallison remained quiet, Malcolm nodded. He had his answer. He turned toward her office door to leave when Hallison faintly answered, "Yes."

Malcolm swung around, not realizing he had been holding his breath. "Then this is not over." He believed Hallison was worth fighting for, even if the competition was God.

Sometimes Parke didn't know how to pray, and what to pray for, but the Reynolds were at the top of his list. The day after Cheney's tearful reunion with Gayle, Parke prayed the other family members would follow. In his office two days later, Parke was starting to get answers to his prayers when the phone rang.

"Parke Jamieson," a deep voice on the other end stated, not asking, when Parke said hello.

"Yes?" Parke lifted his brow. The voice wasn't familiar, but the tone alerted Parke to be on guard.

"I'm Dr. Roland Reynolds, my daughter's pitiful father. I understand you've asked my daughter to marry you."

Parke nodded to himself, but didn't respond. He decided to the let the man dig himself out of his hole.

"I want to repair the relationship with Cheney Denise. I'm hoping you can help me with that," the strong, confident voice dissolved to a humble plea.

Thirty minutes later, after listening to the man's unbelievable story, Parke ended the call saying, "Do you mind if I pray for you, Roland?"

"Please."

"In the Name of Jesus, I worship you for the power of your blood that can not only wash away our sins, but our guilt."

CHAPTER 35

Summer was a memory, but the second week in October was perfect for a fall outdoor wedding. Mrs. Beacon's backyard was the backdrop: professionally landscaped with a rock garden; a miniature waterfall cascading into a goldfish pond; and stone benches lining a brick walkway to a common ground.

"Cheney, Parke couldn't have gotten a better bride," Imani said, standing in her bridesmaid's dress. "Who knows, maybe Captain Rogers and I might be next. The first time, I was young and stupid. Now I'm mature and smart. Like you, I'm not going to let a good man—white or black—get away."

"Imani, all of us aren't engaged." Cheney tilted her head.

"Oops, sorry."

"That's all right. I'm so happy for both of you," Hallison said tearfully.

"I know this can't be easy for you," Cheney said, hugging her friend.

"No, it's not. Every day I try to fall out of love

with Malcolm. I'm praying that by walking away, God will send him back into my life a changed and spirit-filled man."

"Right now he's not only a thorn in your side, but everybody else's, too."

"It's funny. We're both complete opposites of what we were before going to church."

"He's mentioned several times that losing you is not his definition of being a Christian, and the world has gone crazy except for him."

While Imani styled Cheney's hair, Cheney reflected on what had been altered in her life. Her relationship with her mother was as on the road to recovery. They spoke every morning and prayed, lunched together, and set aside a church girl's night out with Addison Dinkius and Hallison, and Charlotte Jamieson attended from time to time, and of course, Mrs. Beacon told tales about her mystery caller who was part of a children's evangelistic ministry. Then, there was Parke, her Parke. *Her Parke.* At first, she was drawn to and irritated by him. Now, he was like a touch of spice to a bland dish.

"Imani, you promised to come to church with me after my honeymoon," Cheney reminded her.

"Of course, you'll be another person I can ride on the coattails for prayer."

"Imani, you're going to have to get it for yourself."

Parke stood regal, gazing at the emotions playing across Cheney's face as she stepped toward him. This afternoon, the Jamieson clan, Cheney's mother, Dre, and Sasha along with their maternal grandmother sat in attendance to witness the nuptials. "We're finally getting a daughter-in-law," had been his parents' words.

During the last months, Cheney smiled more with her eyes, enticing him with the lift of her brow. Their once charged combative encounters were replaced with quiet time, relaxing or studying scriptures. His heart did its thing again, fluttering at the sight of her. She was more than gorgeous. *How could he have thought differently?*

Cheney was magnificently dressed in a long-sleeve, pearl-white satin gown with a long, flowing court train, sprinkled with white pearls and translucent beads. Her headdress was Chantilly lace mixed with pearls.

"Who gives this woman away?" Pastor Scott asked.

Expecting Cheney's mother to respond, she was surprised to see Roland Reynolds walking into the garden, announcing his presence. "I do."

Parke winked at Cheney's shocked expression. Over the months, unbeknownst to Cheney, Roland was trying to draw closer to God. The big shock was learning that Roland had distanced himself from Cheney not because of her abortion, but because of his guilt twenty years earlier.

"Parke, I love my daughter, but I hate myself."

Parke lifted a brow. "Really."

"I was the hit-and-run driver who killed Henry Beacon. When I found out that Cheney moved next door, I went crazy and out of my way not to be invited. I couldn't face Mrs. Beacon, knowing what I did and got away with it."

Roland had been drinking. The following day

when he read in the newspaper about the accident and there were no witnesses, Roland assumed he got away with it until Cheney moved back to Missouri and next door to his past.

It wasn't easy for Parker to keep that information to himself, but Roland pleaded with him. They decided to wait until after the wedding to tell Cheney and Mrs. Beacon who was sure to lynch him before he would turn himself into theauthorities. Parke had come to accept that being saved didn't mean everything would fall in place just as Hallison was learning.

Hearing Pastor Scott's prompting, Parke recited his vows, understanding the importance of his heritage and responsibility to future generations, biologically or adopted.

"Cheney, I stand before you knowing we belonged to each other long before we knew it. I promise my faithfulness, undying love, and friendship. Baby, I will cherish you above all riches. You are my treasure. I will keep you safe and securely close to my heart. I love you and will honor your position beside me, always lifting you up as my best part, not counterpart, until death do us part."

Her misty eyes matched his, but it was the sniffing behind Parke that made him turn around. Malcolm was fighting back tears, tortured that Parke had beaten him to the altar. Parke ached for his brother's loss.

Cheney stepped into Parke's space. Her manicured nails touched his hand. She scanned his face as if memorizing his features. Closing her eyes, she inhaled his cologne, smiling. Cheney was branding him hers.

Bowing her head, he heard Cheney pray before

reciting her vows. "Parke Kokumuo Jamieson VI, it's so hard for words to describe what I'm feeling today. I will be forever grateful that you walked out of my dreams and into my life. You've given me unwavering love, friendship, and humor." They smiled, blinking back tears. "I want to give you abundant, overflowing, endless happiness, my love, and submission so that you will never regret asking me to be your wife. I promise to honor you and listen to you when you speak and when you don't. I promise to be faithful to your needs and desires, and love you until my last breath."

They ignored Malcolm as he cleared his throat, choking back his emotions.

As Pastor Scott pronounced them man and wife, a gentle breeze stirred the trees, sprinkling autumn leaves for showers of blessings.

Epilogue

Parke climbed out of bed without disturbing his wife of six months, two weeks, and twelve hours. He couldn't resist stroking her shiny curls. He whispered, "I love you." close to her ear. She didn't stir.

The house was quiet, his house that had become theirs. Imani purchased Cheney's because she was the only one Mrs. Beacon agreed not to harass. Imani felt her home would be safe when she was away, because Mrs. Beacon was better than a guard dog.

He looked out the bedroom's French doors. This was Parke's favorite time of the morning, when random spears of light from the sky hinted of the day's possibilities. Another day the Lord had made. What would God show him today?

Folding his arms, he glanced back at his bed. White netting hung loosely over eight-foot bedposts, creating an exotic ambience fit for his queen. The image of Cheney snuggled under their satin comforter completed Parke's mystic musing. Over the months, Parke watched as Cheney had transformed his bachelor bedroom into a cozy honeymoon suite where they played hide and seek, enjoyed sunsets, and indulged each other with breakfast in bed. Life couldn't be better.

An early riser, Parke used this time to pray, mediate, and thank God for the woman He sent into his life. He monitored Cheney's even breathing. She was fast asleep. He thought about their small garden wedding, which Cheney said she had dreamed about. Everything was perfect, except the tension between Malcolm and Hallison, which was thicker than their wedding cake, and the whereabouts of the boy who could be his son.

His weekly ritual included calling Wilma and his private investigator for anything new. Surely, he didn't just fall off the face of the earth.

He chuckled, thinking about Mrs. Beacon mumbling through the nuptials about having to break-in new neighbors. His parents embraced his new religion with skepticism, but ecstatic about Cheney becoming his wife. Malcolm was growing more rebellious about the whole idea of God and church, but Parke had to believe prayer changed things.

Cheney moaned. He was at her bedside in seconds. Then she smiled in her sleep. Good, she wasn't in pain like the previous nights. He returned to his spot at the window. Parke loved watching her. He had memorized her unique sounds, amusing expressions, and routine positions. "C'mon, baby, it's about time for you to scoot to my side of the bed and rub that expanding stomach of yours against me," he coaxed in a hushed voice.

Within seconds, Cheney did as Parke predicted. Grinning with satisfaction, he stretched, sat down in a chair next to the window, and folded his hands behind his head. He closed his eyes, remembering the doctor's diagnosis.

"Mrs. Jamieson, I have your files in front of me. I've examined you myself. You're infertile. The symptoms you're experiencing are possibly associated with fatigue and the stress of a new marriage."

Parke didn't care for Doctor Kufu's attitude or advice. Parke reached for Cheney's hand across the examining table. "Baby, we'll see what God says."

Doctor Kufu smirked. "Suit yourself," he mumbled as he left the room.

That night, they prayed until God spoke, instructing them to find another doctor. A day later, they met a childlike physician, fresh out of residency who confirmed Cheney's pregnancy, but warned there might be complications if she carried to full term. Doctor Cates had the nerve to suggest an abortion, saying the pregnancy would be too risky. Again, they prayed and God told them to believe.

Now, Cheney was beginning her second trimester with a Jamieson growing inside. They would keep their faith in God despite Cheney's spotting last week. Tears filled Parke's eyes. Would they have a boy or a girl? Who would the tiny creature look like?

"Daddy," a shrieking voice echoed from down the hall.

He stood and tiptoed out of their room, racing down the hall. Like clockwork, Kami woke at the same time every morning, even on the weekends. The child terror went ballistic with her new foster parents, tearing up their house, wetting the bed, and staying up all night. The parents admitted defeat after two weeks. That was the third set of foster parents since leaving Cheney's.

Without any hesitation, Cheney and Parke took her back. Soon, Kami Fields would become a Jamieson, before her baby brother or sister was born. Dre and Sasha were excited about the baby and had come to visit a few times. They were adjusting well with their grandmother.

Parke returned to his room just as Cheney's lids fluttered.

"Good morning," Cheney greeted in a dream-like state.

Parke kneeled on the floor, facing his wife. "Hi, sweetheart."

"You're watching me sleep again?" Cheney turned on her side, finger-combing Parke's thick, wavy hair.

"A man's got a right to watch over his greatest possession."

Cheney reached for Parke's large hand and placed it on her pouch of a stomach, closing her eyes as Parke prayed, "Lord, in the name of Jesus, I thank You for my life, my wife, and my soon-to-be tribe."

READERS GUIDE

1. What is the one thing in your past that you never got over?

2. Hallison knew what God expected of her, yet she tried to ignore everything she learned for a feel good moment. Are you guilty of this?

3. What is the most extreme thing you have done for love?

4. Do you think church can instantly change someone?

5. Paula Silas gave up her man because he wasn't saved. Later, Hallison did the same thing. Could you turn a man away you are truly in love with because of God?

6. How do you feel about men who judge women who can't bear them natural children?

7. The Reynolds judged Cheney without confronting her. If a family member or friend did something you don't agree with, would you embrace them or shun them?

8. Was Parke too excessive with his family history? How important is that to you? How flexible would you be?

9. How often have you let a man or situation stop you from moving forward?

10. What was the turning point in Cheney's life that she stopped fighting Parke?

11. When God saved you, did you have Annette's zeal to save your friends too?

12. Do you think Paula Silas and Annette Barber symbolized people God has put in your presence to help you with your salvation walk?

From the Author:

Thank you for supporting me by purchasing *Guilty of Love*. Remember when things get to hard to bear, give it to God.

I would like to introduce my great-great-grand mother who I brought back to life in one of my characters: Charlott Jamison (considered a mulatto) was born in 1842 in South Carolina. By 1850, she was believed to be in the household of slaveholder, Robert Jamison in Mississippi. On the 1860 census in Chickasaw, Mississippi, there was white John Wilkinson living in the household of Robert Jamison. John is listed as a "teacher in Academy." He was 23 years old and born in Alabama. Most likely he is my great-great-grand father.

Charlott was 18 years old. In 1865, two years after the Emancipation Proclamation, my great-grand-father, William Wilkinson (Wilkerson) was born. In 1867, the birth of Sam was recorded. By 1880, Charlott Wilkinson was a widow.

Her son, William, died in his 80s. Both sons were considered near-white. Family rumor has Sam Wilkinson going up north to pass. To date, no one knows of his or his descendants' final whereabouts. John Wilkinson married Artie Jameson and had five sons.

In 1880, Charlott Wilkinson was living with another widow, Martha Leopard. I have spoken with one of her descendants.

The world of family genealogy is fascinating, and in every novel, I bring one of my ancestors to life. If we share the same tree, or you enjoyed *Guilty of Love*, please let me know.

www.patsimmons.net
Pat@patsimmons.net

Coming Soon

Still Guilty

CHAPTER 1

How did my life become so complicated? Parke Koku-muo Jamieson VI wondered. He was the first-born son of the tenth generation descendant of Paki Kokumuo Jaja, the chief prince of the Diomande tribe of Côte d'Ivoire, Africa. Parke was destined to procreate the eleventh generation.

It was an honorable task that Parke had relished fulfilling until he met Cheney Reynolds. He had tossed caution, commonsense, and responsibility to hurricane-strength winds. Cheney was his destiny, and Parke was determined to have her even after being advised she was sterile. Addicted to her strength, determination, and beauty, Parke proposed anyway—more than once.

Six feet without heels, Cheney's height complemented his six-foot-five frame. Her long lashes and shapely brows were showstoppers, but it was Cheney's delicate feet that were his weakness, after her hips of course. Her feet were always manicured and soft, and they seemed to nurture a slight bounce to her catwalk.

Cheney's skin held a touch of lemon coloring, and her lips were a temptation for kisses. Within a year of their marriage, God performed a miracle against medical odds. Cheney became pregnant twice. Both times, they lost: first through a miscarriage, the second—a precious son—delivered stillborn.

Late one night, while studying his Bible, Parke petitioned God for a sign as to whether a son would ever come through his seed. He stumbled across Genesis 16—the story of Abram; his wife, Sarai; and Sarai's handmaiden, Hagar. Parke read the passage three times. "What are you telling me, God?"

With his sharp intellect, Parke interpreted that Cheney portrayed Sarai. Although, Parke had just turned thirty-six, he prayed his reproduction bank wasn't as dormant as Abram's in order for God to perform a miracle. He wasn't asking for anything major like the parting of the Red Sea; just something on a smaller scale. Maybe there was hope. Closing his Bible, he slid to his knees and prayed, then climbed into the bed and wrapped his arms around his wife. As he reached to turn off the lamp, he wondered, for argument's sake, if he was Abram and Cheney was Sarai, then who was cast as Hagar?

An answer from God came the next day when his private investigator called. "I hope you're sitting down."

Sipping his cup of coffee, Parke stood, leaning against the kitchen counter, when he was eating breakfast on the run. As a senior financial analyst, he was mentally contemplating his workload for the day.

Clients were clambering for his attention to review their personal portfolio and make recommendations concerning safe investments. Parke didn't answer him right away. "Nope. What's up?"

"If I'm lying, I'm dying, and God knows I'm not ready. What are the odds that I've found your son?" Ellington "The Duke" Brown stated then paused. "I think."

The hunt had actually started two years earlier. Parke had initiated a search after a social worker who was screening him and Cheney for the foster care program, questioned the name similarity to Park Jamie, a toddler somewhere in the system. The woman had risked disciplinary action or termination for breaching client confidentiality. "I feel God wants me to say something to you," she had explained.

Parke contacted his long-time friend and Lincoln University Kappa Alpha Psi frat brother Ellington, the CEO of Brown Investigations. The last time they had spoken, Ellington had basically told Parke the rumor was unfounded.

Now seven hundred and four days later, Parke froze—his hand, mouth, and breathing—as his heart collided against his chest. Once he was able to thaw, he spewed coffee across the counter like a wayward water sprinkler. Dumping his cup in the sink, Parke used all his strength to gulp pockets of air. Somewhat composed, he sniffed as his vision blurred.

He stretched his hands in praise, forgetting about the cordless phone in the mishap. It tumbled to the floor. "Yes! Thank you, Jesus. Praise God—"

"Wait, Parke. Parke!" Ellington screamed repeatedly until Parke picked up the phone.

"Whew. Sorry about that. That's good news, Ellington." Parke grinned. He couldn't help it. "Thank God for Hagar whoever she is," he whispered.

"Ah, there's a slight twist I should tell you. If he is your son, you're no longer his father." Ellington cleared his throat. "Your parental rights have been terminated. He's been adopted."

"What?" Parke shouted. As the words sunk in, visions of his life seemed to appear in slow motion before some internal fury raced to the surface. He glanced around the room, searching for any moveable object that Cheney wouldn't miss it if he were to throw it. "When? Why? Who?"

Ellington told Parke what he had learned, and Parke didn't like the answers as he began to clean up his mess.

Fast forward almost three weeks later, and Parke wasn't any closer to getting his son. "I'm tired of waiting. If I need to prick my finger, rub a swab in my mouth, pee in a cup, or pull out a hair sample, bring the DNA test on," Parke barked, anchoring his cell phone on his shoulder and thumb-steering his new Escalade Hybrid as he swerved around a pothole.

The vehicle's brakes suffered the abuse of Parke's frustration. He squinted at the clock on the dashboard and increased his speed to pick up his daughter. Racing through traffic on Chambers Road, Parke calculated the minutes to his destination— Mrs. Beatrice Tilley Beacon's house on Benton Street in Ferguson, Missouri, a suburb of St. Louis. She was his wife's former neighbor, surrogate grandmother who answered to Grandma BB only if she liked you, a reliable babysitter, and the only alleged suspect in the shooting of Cheney's father.

A traffic light snagged him. He huffed, venting, "Ellington, I'm capable of doing two things at one time, but arguing while driving isn't a preferable combination. A cop is right behind me, and I'm not up to hearing the wrath of my little diva if she's late for her marital arts lesson. That girl has a mean left kick."

"I'm not scared of your four-year-old. As a matter of fact, Kami loves me. Anyway, you're not paying me. The last time I checked, I quit after you fired me the second time."

That was true. Parke hadn't really meant to briefly lose control or sidestep the Holy Ghost. When it came to anything remotely Jamieson-related, his emotions often overrode his sensibility. "I was hoping you had forgotten about that—or at least, hadn't taken me seriously. You didn't, did you? I'll double my last offer."

"You can quadruple it, buddy, but four times zero is still nothing, so stop harassing me," Ellington retorted. "You asked me to check out a rumor that you had a son in the foster care system. Do you know how long that took?"

Too long in Parke's opinion, but he didn't voice it. He shrugged. It was a good thing Ellington couldn't see his nonchalant behavior.

"I located a Park Jamie. His mother was a petite Latina who died in a car crash . . ."

"I don't need a summary of your report. I remember Rachel Lopez. God help me if I could forget that woman's legs—yeah." Parke shook himself and re-focused. "I want Parke Kokumuo Jamieson VII." He scowled. "As his birth father, I have a right not only to see my son, but to take immediate custody."

"Parke, the child was adopted two months ago . . . and his name was changed. Even if a judge grants a paternity test, you'll have to prove you didn't voluntarily give up your rights as a parent," Ellington tried to console. "You can't bake a cake and have a clean pan, too."

"What? You know that didn't make any sense, right?" Parke frowned, irritated.

"It didn't, did it?" There was silence. "My point is you're an adoptive parent. You know the process. What if Kami's parents had challenged her adoption?"

That wasn't the same. Kami's natural family was so dysfunctional they probably didn't notice her missing when she was placed into the system. With a blink of an eye, the teenage mother and father had signed the papers, dissolving their parental rights.

"Listen, man, I'm just your friend/amateur shrink /professional investigator. You're at the end of the road with me. Call your attorney."

"I did. Can you believe he removed himself from the case, then hung up on me?" Parke snarled.

"Yup. I'm not surprised. What did you do or say?" When Parke told him, Ellington exploded with untamed laughter. "That makes how many attorneys—two? I'm telling you, you should've called my cousin, Twinkie, the first time. Don't let the name fool you. She's more than a sweet little snack. The girl squashes her competition. If there's a loophole in the law, she'll widen the gap. Until then, wait on the Lord as you always tell me. Quote a scripture or something and you'll be all right."

Parke grunted, then disconnected without saying good-bye. He was tired of waiting.